NUMB
FALL 2019

DERELICTS

M000218391

the sensation of depth is overwhelming. And the darkness is immortal."
—Carl Sagan

CONTENTS CONTINUED NEXT PAGE

Black Infinity is published semi-annually by Rocket Science Books, an imprint of Dead Letter Press.

www.DeadLetterPress.com   www.BlackInfinityMagazine.com   ISBN-13: 978-1732434448

COVER FEATURE: THE *JUPITER II* ENCOUNTERS AN ALIEN SHIP, IN THE SECOND EPISODE OF *LOST IN SPACE* (1965), "THE DERELICT" CBS STUDIOS AND 20TH CENTURY FOX TELEVISION

INTERIOR ILLUSTRATIONS: ALLEN KOSZOWSKI, FRANK R. PAUL, ED EMSHWILLER, AND H. W. WESSO

EDITOR AND PUBLISHER: TOM ENGLISH
COLUMNISTS: MATT COWAN; TODD TREICHEL
PRODUCTION STAFF: HAL-9000, ROBBY R. AND ROBOT B-9

PLEASE STAND BY

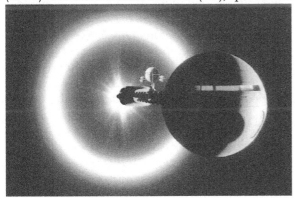

AMYSTERIOUS DERELICT SPACESHIP DRIFTING SILENTLY AMONG THE STARS—WHO CAN RE-SIST THE THOUGHT? Certainly not most readers, or for that matter, most writers. In fact, more than two dozen short stories and poems featuring derelicts were published, most of which are simply titled "Derelict" or, perhaps to be more creative, "*The* Derelict," by pulp writers such as Hugh B. Cave, Raymond Z. Gallun, Robert A. W. Lowndes, and Alan E. Nourse.

British author John Wyndham, best known for his creepy SF novels *The Day of the Triffids* (1951) and *The Midwich Cuckoos* ('57),[1] presented his readers with one, the aptly titled 1939 story "The Derelict of Space"; not to be confused with "The Derelict of Space" (1954) by Randall Garrett; or "The Derelict of Space" (1931) by Ray Cummings —reprinted in this issue, but mercifully retitled "Doom Ship." And in a span of less than two years, 1941 to '42, three different "Cosmic Derelict" tales appeared in the pages of SF magazines, one each by Neil R. Jones, John Broome, and John Russell Fearn.

Andre Norton featured or referenced derelicts in several of her novels, including *The Sargasso of Space* (1955), *Plague Ship* (1956), *The Time Traders* (1958), and, of course, *The Galactic Derelict* (1959). (One of her few short stories, "All Cats Are Gray," also features a derelict, and is reprinted in this issue.)

Arthur C. Clarke featured a derelict ship in two of his best-known novels, his Hugo- and Nebula Award-winning *Rendezvous with Rama* (1973), as well as his first sequel to *2001: A Space Odyssey* (1968), *2010: Odyssey Two* (published in 1982, and quickly adapted for film). And, in his 1987 novel *Sphere*, Michael Crichton hid one at the bottom of the ocean.

Sphere, also, like most of Crichton's fiction, was adapted for film, in 1998, further adding to the long list of movies and television segments involving encounters with strange derelict ships. Matt Cowan discusses a few of the cinematic examples in this issue's installment of Threat Watch, and later I list some of the more notable ones from vintage television; but together we only scratch the surface. We're limited by the space of 200 double-column pages, and derelict ships seem to pop up everywhere. After all, the derelict ship is the science fiction equivalent of a favorite Hollywood movie theme, "the old dark house"[2]— a reliable vehicle for mystery and suspense.

---

[1] *The Day of the Triffids* was first adapted for the screen in 1963. *The Midwich Cuckoos* was first filmed, as *Village of the Damned,* in 1960. Both novels inspired further adaptations.

[2] Old Dark House movies include *The Cat and the Canary* (1927 and '39), *The Bat Whispers* ('30), *The Secret of the Blue Room* ('33), *The Black Cat* ('34 and '41), *Night Monster* ('42),

(Incidentally, did you know that the first and final episodes of an iconic 1960s animated adventure series involved derelicts? Which show? Don't rush me, I'll get to it… eventually.)

Regarding the popularity of derelict ship stories, when did it all start?

Since the days when men first ventured from the shores and security of their homelands, "sailors" have related fantastic tales of sea serpents and spectral ships; unfathomable mysteries both above and below the often-tempestuous surface of the cold, dark deeps. No doubt these storytellers were inspired by such strange-but-true revelations as the fate of the *Jenny,* an English schooner that departed from Isle of Wight in 1822. Eighteen years later, the Jenny was found by a whaling ship in the Drake Passage, located between South America's Cape Horn and the South Shetland Islands of Antarctica. Both the Jenny and the perfectly preserved corpses of her crew had been frozen solid.

Or the HMS *Erebus* and the HMS *Terror,* which departed England in 1845, on a scientific expedition to the Canadian Arctic. Both ships became trapped in the ice off of King William Island, and were abandoned months later. While journeying overland to the south, the officers and crews of the two ships, numbering about 130 men, eventually died, either from starvation or hypothermia.

Or the *Mary Celeste,* found drifting in the mid-Atlantic off the Azores in 1872, less than a month after she departed New York City for Genoa, with not a soul onboard. And yet her cargo of denatured alcohol was untouched, and the possessions of her missing crew undisturbed.

Maritime history is filled with dozens of such eerie accounts, fueling the imaginations of superstitious seamen who tended to embellish the facts. But whether fact or fiction, the appeal of such stories transcends time and cuts across countries and cultures. For instance, in the "Letter of Saint Paulinus to Macarus" (1618), the French publisher and theologian Marguerin de La Bigne relates the tale of an old man who is the sole survivor of a derelict ship manned by angels and steered by the "Pilot of the World."[3]

Spoken accounts of the *Flying Dutchman,* a legendary haunted ship cursed to sail the seas for all eternity, began circulating in the 17th century, during the heydays of the shipping and trading conglomerate the Dutch East India Company. Recorded references to the legend, however, didn't appear until the late 18th century, with one of the earliest being in 1795:

I had often heard of the superstition of sailors respecting apparitions and doom, but had never given much credit to the report; it seems that some years since a Dutch man-of-war was lost off the Cape of Good Hope, and every soul on board perished; her consort weathered the gale, and arrived soon after at the Cape. Having refitted, and returning to Europe, they were assailed by a violent tempest nearly in the same latitude. In the night watch some of the people saw, or imagined they saw, a vessel standing for them under a press of sail, as though she would run them down: one in particular affirmed it was the ship that had foundered in the former gale, and that it must certainly be her, or the apparition of her; but on its clearing up, the object, a dark thick cloud, disappeared. Nothing could do away the idea of this phenomenon on the minds of the sailors; and, on their relating

---

The House of Fear ('45), *The House on Haunted Hill* ('59), *House of Usher* ('60) and—wait for it—James Whale's *The Old Dark House* (1932), to name just a few.

[3] From *Magna Bibliotheca Veterum Patrum*

the circumstances when they arrived in port, the story spread like wild-fire, and the supposed phantom was called the Flying Dutchman.

The notion of the ghostly *Flying Dutchman* continued to capture the public imagination for decades, and a host of writers eagerly elaborated and expanded the legend, including John Leyden (1803), Thomas Moore (1804), Sir Walter Scott (1812), Frederick Marryat (1839; with *The Phantom Ship*), Washington Irving (1855), and W. Clark Russell (1888; with *The Death Ship*). Samuel Taylor Coleridge may have been inspired by the legend as well.

In his weird lyrical ballad *The Rime of the Ancient Mariner,* published in 1798, Coleridge depicts the fate of a sailing ship and her crew after her "captain" needlessly kills an albatross that had brought the men good luck. Following this act of inhospitality, supernatural forces intervene and send the mariner's ship into uncharted equatorial waters where it is becalmed, "as idle as a painted ship upon a painted ocean." Following many days without drinkable water, the angry crew forces the mariner to hang the dead albatross around his neck.

Later, their ship encounters a ghostly derelict carrying the skeletal figure of Death and the lady "Night-mare Life-in-Death," who roll the dice for the souls of the mariner and his crew.[4]

Still more tales of spectral ships followed. In 1886 the German author Wilhelm Hauff thrilled his readers with "The Haunted Ship." And William Hope Hodgson repeatedly depicted derelict ships, sometimes trapped in Sargasso Sea-like waters, in several of his novels and stories. Hodgson's fascination with the subject is exemplified in his 1907 short story "The Mystery of the Derelict Ship," reprinted in this issue.

As science fiction developed and rose in popularity during the first half of the 20th century, reader interest slowly shifted from the mysteries of the sea to the wonders of "the final frontier," and the derelict ship soon found a place

---

[4] As to the ultimate fate of the mariner and his crew, there's more, much more; but *The Rime of the Ancient Mariner* is freely available on the Internet, and I encourage readers to find the ballad and enjoy it themselves.

among the stars, adrift on the oceans of space. And finally, like all things SF, these strange abandoned spaceships started popping up in film, television, and comics.

In television the earliest derelict ship stories unfold in Rod Serling's *The Twilight Zone* (1959-1964). In "The Arrival" (1961), a commercial plane lands at an airport—with no pilot, crew, or passengers onboard. In "The Thirty-Fathom Grave" (1963), a U.S. Navy destroyer investigates eerie

knocking sounds emanating from a sunken WWII submarine resting at the bottom of the Pacific. And in Richard Matheson's "Death Ship" (1963) three astronauts surveying an alien world find a crashed spaceship that looks exactly like the one in which they arrived. Inside the wreckage they discover their own corpses.

Derelict ships also figure prominently in an early Hanna-Barbera cartoon produced especially for prime-time viewing: *Jonny Quest*, a pioneering, cross-genre adventure series that set the

pattern for all future animated shows of its type. In the September 18, 1964 series premiere, "The Mystery of the Lizard Men," young Jonny accompanies his father, Dr. Quest, along with special agent Race Bannon, to the Sargasso Sea, where the trio soon learn the strange disappearances of ships in the area are linked to one of the many hulks trapped and rotting amidst the seaweed.

Jonny Quest also has the distinction of being the only TV series, animated or live action, to both begin *and* end with a derelict story. Its final episode, "The Sea Haunt" (March 11, 1965), features our heroes (now a quartet, following the introduction in episode 2 of the resourceful Indian youth Hadji) trapped on a derelict ship with a prowling sea monster. One might cite this tale as an inspiration for the 1979 film *Alien*, but actually the "snakes on a plane" formula was first used in 1958, in the effective B-movie *It! The Terror from Beyond Space*.

While on the subject of series premieres—

and cartoons—the Emmy Award-winning *Star Trek: The Animated Series* (1973-'75) also began with an episode featuring a derelict, "Beyond the Farthest Star," in which Captain Kirk and his crew encounter a damaged alien starship harboring a malignant intelligence bent on possessing the *Enterprise*. The script for this initial outing is by Samuel A. Peebles, who also wrote the screenplay for "Where No Man Has Gone Before," the second pilot for the original *Trek* series, but the *first* segment to feature Kirk).

"The Time Trap," the twelfth episode of the animated series, features an interdimensional sargasso sea littered with ancient, derelict starships. After both the *Enterprise* and a Klingon vessel become trapped in the area, the crews of the two ships must work together if they hope to escape. Unbeknown to Kirk, however, the Klingon commander is planning to sabotage the *Enterprise*.

Four episodes of the original *Star Trek* series (1966-'69) feature a derelict: "Space Seed" (1967), which introduced the genetically-engineered conqueror Khan, played by Ricardo Montalbán; "The Doomsday Machine" (1967), written by novelist Norman Spinrad; "The Omega Glory" (1968); and "The Tholian Web" (1968), discussed in our Strange Dimensions issue.

In creator and producer Irwin Allen's first science fiction television series, *Voyage to the Bottom of the Sea* (1964-'68), the highly-advanced submarine *Seaview* frequently encounters derelict ships: in the first season episode "The Mist of Silence" (1964); "The Graveyard of Fear" and the eerie "The Phantom Strikes" (both from 1966 and the second season); the third season episodes "The Haunted Submarine" (1966) and "Death from the Past" (1967); and, from the fourth and final season, "Cave of the Dead" (1967), which riffs on the Flying Dutchman legend.

Irwin Allen's second foray into SF, *Lost in Space,* also features a derelict in two of the show's most memorable episodes. The second episode of the first season, "The Derelict" (1965) chronicles an early interstellar adventure of the Space Family Robinson not long after leaving earth, in which the *Jupiter II* is drawn inside a mammoth starship, a veritable "old dark house" drifting in space, complete with a few monstrous residents. Despite some wonky science—and who watches *LiS* for scientific accuracy, anyway?—"The Derelict" is an excellent example of the abandoned alien vessel theme,

and is celebrated on this issue's cover.

The season three premiere of *LiS*, "Condemned of Space," contains some of the show's most exciting sequences, and features yet another derelict, this time a malfunctioning prison ship filled with frozen convicts. Gregory L. Norris fondly remembers *Lost in Space* in this issue's special feature.

I could go on, but I'm running out of pages in this already overstuffed issue. So I'll end this all-too-brief survey with one last capsule synopsis—of "Dragon's Domain":

Years ago the commander of a failed space mission was discredited after abandoning his probe ship and eventually returning to earth claiming his crew members were consumed by a ravenous creature lurking within a graveyard of derelict space vessels. Now, seeking both vindication and retribution, the man returns to the sector, and to his own darkened

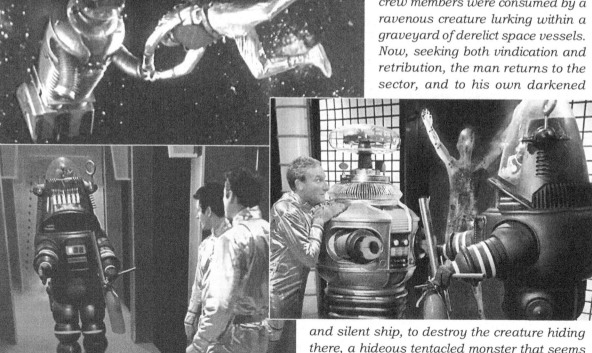

and silent ship, to destroy the creature hiding there, a hideous tentacled monster that seems unstoppable.

(CONTINUED ON PAGE 46)

SALVAGE IN SPACE

BY JACK WILLIAMSON

HIS "PLANET" WAS THE SMALLEST IN THE SOLAR SYSTEM, AND THE LONELIEST, THAD ALLEN WAS THINKING, AS HE STRAIGHTENED WEARILY IN THE HUGE, BULGING, INFLATED FABRIC OF HIS OSPREY SPACE ARMOR. Walking awkwardly in the magnetic boots that held him to the black mass of meteoric iron, he mounted a projection and stood motionless, staring moodily away through the vision panels of his bulky helmet into the dark mystery of the void.

His welding arc dangled at his belt, the electrode still glowing red. He had just finished securing to this slowly-accumulated mass of iron his most recent find, a meteorite the size of his head.

Five perilous weeks he had labored, to collect this rugged lump of metal—a jagged mass, some ten feet in diameter, composed of hundreds of fragments, that he had captured and welded together. His luck had not been good. His findings had been heartbreakingly small; the spectro-flash analysis had revealed that the content of the precious metals was disappointingly minute.[5]

On the other side of this tiny sphere of hard-won treasure, his Millen atomic rocket was sputtering, spurts of hot blue flame jetting from its exhaust. A simple mechanism, bolted to the first sizable fragment he had captured, it drove the iron ball through space like a ship.

Through the magnetic soles of his insulated boots, Thad could feel the vibration of the iron mass, beneath the rocket's regular thrust. The magazine of uranite fuel capsules was nearly empty, now, he reflected. He would soon have to turn back toward Mars.

Turn back. But how could he, with so slender a reward for his efforts? Meteor mining is expensive. There was his bill at Millen and Helion, Mars, for uranite and supplies. And the unpaid last installment on his Osprey suit. How could he outfit himself again, if he returned with no more metal than this? There were men who averaged a thousand tons of iron a month. Why couldn't fortune smile on him?

He knew men who had made fabulous strikes, who had captured whole planetoids of rich metal, and he knew weary, white-

---

[5] The meteor or asteroid belt, between the orbits of Mars and Jupiter, is "mined" by such adventurers as Thad Allen for the platinum, iridium and osmium that all meteoric irons contain in small quantities. The meteor swarms are supposed by some astronomers to be fragments of a disrupted planet, which, according to Bode's Law, should occupy this space.

in the dark gulf below it; Mars, nearer, smaller, a little ocher speck above the shrunken sun. Above him, below him, in all directions was vastness, blackness, emptiness. Ebon infinity, sprinkled with far, cold stars.

Thad was alone. Utterly alone. No man was visible, in all the supernal vastness of space. And no work of man—save the few tools of his daring trade, and the glittering little rocket bolted to the black iron behind him. It was terrible to think that the nearest human being must be tens of millions of miles away.

On his first trips, the loneliness had been terrible, unendurable. Now he was becoming accustomed to it. At least, he no longer feared that he was going mad. But sometimes....

Thad shook himself and spoke aloud, his voice ringing hollow in his huge metal helmet:

haired men who had braved the perils of vacuum and absolute cold and bullet-swift meteors for hard years, who still hoped.

But sometime fortune had to smile, and then....

The picture came to him. A tower of white metal, among the low red hills near Helion. A slim, graceful tower of argent, rising in a fragrant garden of flowering Martian shrubs, purple and saffron. And a girl waiting, at the silver door—a trim, slender girl in white, with blue eyes and hair richly brown.

Thad had seen the white tower many times, on his holiday tramps through the hills about Helion. He had even dared to ask if it could be bought, to find that its price was an amount that he might not amass in many years at his perilous profession. But the girl in white was yet only a glorious dream....

The strangeness of interplanetary space, and the somber mystery of it, pressed upon him like an illimitable and deserted ocean. The sun was a tiny white disk on his right, hanging between rosy coronal wings; his native Earth, a bright greenish point suspended

"Brace up, old top. In good company, when you're by yourself, as Dad used to say. Be back in Helion in a week or so, anyhow. Look up Dan and 'Chuck' and the rest of the crowd again, at Comet's place. What price a friendly boxing match with Mason, or an evening at the teleview theater?

"Fresh air instead of this stale synthetic stuff! Real food, in place of these tasteless concentrates! A hot bath, instead of greasing yourself!

"Too dull out here. Life—" He broke off, set his jaw.

No use thinking about such things. Only made it worse. Besides, how did he know that a whirring meteor wasn't going to flash him out before he got back?

He drew his right arm out of the bulging sleeve of the suit, into its ample interior, found a cigarette in an inside pocket, and lighted it. The smoke swirled about in the helmet, drawn swiftly into the air filters.

"Darn clever, these suits," he murmured. "Food, smokes, water generator, all where you can reach them. And darned expensive, too. I'd better be looking for pay metal!"

He clambered to a better position; stood peering out into space, searching for the tiny gleam of sunlight on a meteoric fragment that might be worth capturing for its content of precious metals. For an hour he scanned the black, star-strewn gulf, as the sputtering rocket continued to drive him forward.

"There she glows!" he cried suddenly, and grinned.

Before him was a tiny, glowing fleck, that moved among the unchanging stars. He stared at it intensely, breathing faster in the helmet.

Always he thrilled to see such a moving gleam. What treasure it promised! At first sight, it was impossible to determine size or distance or rate of motion. It might be ten thousand tons of rich metal. A fortune! It would more probably prove to be a tiny, stony mass, not worth capturing. It might even be large and valuable, but moving so rapidly that he could not overtake it with the power of the diminutive Millen rocket.

He studied the tiny speck intently, with practiced eye, as the minutes passed—an untrained eye would never have seen it at all, among the flaming hosts of stars. Skillfully he judged, from its apparent rate of motion and its slow increase in brilliance, its size and distance from him.

"Must be—must be fair size," he spoke aloud, at length. "A hundred tons, I'll bet my helmet! But scooting along pretty fast. Stretch the little old rocket to run it down."

He clambered back to the rocket, changed the angle of the flaming exhaust, to drive him directly across the path of the object ahead, filled the magazine again with the little pellets of uranite, which were fed automatically into the combustion chamber, and increased the firing rate.

The trailing blue flame reached farther backward from the incandescent orifice of the exhaust. The vibration of the metal sphere increased. Thad left the sputtering rocket and went back where he could see the object before him.

IT WAS NEARER NOW, rushing obliquely across his path. Would he be in time to capture it as it passed, or would it hurtle by ahead of him, and vanish in the limitless darkness of space before his feeble rocket could check the momentum of his ball of metal?

He peered at it, as it drew closer.

Its surface seemed oddly bright, silvery. Not the dull black of meteoric iron. And it was larger, more distant, than he had thought at first. In form, too, it seemed curiously regular, ellipsoid. It was no jagged mass of metal.

His hopes sank, rose again immediately. Even if it were not the mass of rich metal for which he had prayed, it might be something as valuable—and more interesting.

He returned to the rocket, adjusted the angle of the nozzle again, and advanced the firing time slightly, even at the risk of a ruinous explosion.

When he returned to where he could see the hurtling object before him, he saw that it was a ship. A tapering silver-green rocket-flier.

Once more his dreams were dashed. The officers of interplanetary liners lose no love upon the meteor miners, claiming that their collected masses of metal, almost helpless, always underpowered, are menaces to navigation. Thad could expect nothing from the ship save a heliographed warning to keep clear.

But how came a rocket-flier here, in the perilous swarms of the meteor belt? Many a vessel had been destroyed by collision with an asteroid, in the days before charted lanes were cleared of drifting metal.

The lanes more frequently used, between Earth, Mars, Venus and Mercury, were of course far inside the orbits of the asteroids. And the few ships running to Jupiter's moons avoided them by crossing millions of miles above their plane.

Could it be that legendary green ship, said

once to have mysteriously appeared, sliced up and drawn within her hull several of the primitive ships of that day, and then disappeared forever after in the remote wastes of space? Absurd, of course: he dismissed the idle fancy and examined the ship still more closely.

Then he saw that it was turning, end over end, very slowly. That meant that its gyros were stopped; that it was helpless, drifting, disabled, powerless to avoid hurtling meteoric stones. Had it blundered unawares into the belt of swarms—been struck before the danger was realized? Was it a derelict, with all dead upon it?

Either the ship's machinery was completely wrecked, Thad knew, or there was no one on watch. For the controls of a modern rocket-flier are so simple and so nearly automatic that a single man at the bridge can keep a vessel upon her course.

It might be, he thought, that a meteorite had ripped open the hull, allowing the air to escape so quickly that the entire crew had been asphyxiated before any repairs could be made. But that seemed unlikely, since the ship must have been divided into several compartments by air-tight bulkheads.

Could the vessel have been deserted for some reason? The crew might have mutinied, and left her in the life-tubes. She might have been robbed by pirates, and set adrift. But with the space lanes policed as they were, piracy and successful mutiny were rare.

Thad saw that the flier's navigation lights were out.

He found the heliograph signal mirror at his side, sighted it upon the ship, and worked the mirror rapidly. He waited, repeated the call. There was no response.

The vessel was plainly a derelict. Could he board her, and take her to Mars? By law, it was his duty to attempt to aid any helpless ship, or at least to try to save any endangered lives upon her. And the salvage award, if the ship should be deserted and he could bring her safe to port, would be half her value.

No mean prize, that. Half the value of ship and cargo! More than he was apt to earn in years of mining the meteor-belt.

With new anxiety, he measured the relative motion of the gleaming ship. It was going to pass ahead of him. And very soon. No more time for speculation. It was still uncertain whether it would come near enough so that he could get a line to it.

Rapidly he unslung from his belt the apparatus he used to capture meteors. A powerful electromagnet, with a thin, strong wire fastened to it, to be hurled from a helix-gun. He set the drum on which the wire was wound upon the metal at his feet, fastened it with its magnetic anchor, wondering if it would stand the terrific strain when the wire tightened.

Raising the helix to his shoulder, he trained it upon a point well ahead of the rushing flier, and stood waiting for the exact moment to press the lever. The slender spindle of the ship was only a mile away now, bright in the sunlight. He could see no break in her polished hull, save for the dark rows of circular ports. She was not, by any means, completely wrecked.

He read the black letters of her name.
Red Dragon.

The name of her home port, below, was in smaller letters. But in a moment he made them out. San Francisco. The ship then came from the Earth! From the very city where Thad was born!

The gleaming hull was near now. Only a few hundred yards away. Passing. Aiming well ahead of her, to allow for her motion, Thad pressed the key that hurled the magnet from the helix. It flung away from him, the wire screaming from the reel behind it.

Thad's mass of metal swung on past the ship, as he returned to the rocket and stopped its clattering explosions. He watched the tiny black speck of the magnet. It vanished from sight in the darkness of space, appeared again against the white, burnished hull of the rocket ship.

For a painful instant he thought he had missed. Then he saw that the magnet was fast to the side of the flier, near the stern. The line tightened. Soon the strain would come upon it, as it checked the momentum of the mass of iron. He set the friction brake.

Thad flung himself flat, grasped the wire above the reel. Even if the mass of iron tore itself free, he could hold to the wire, and himself reach the ship.

He flung past the deserted vessel, behind it, his lump of iron swung like a pebble in a sling. A cloud of smoke burst from the burned lining of the friction brake, in the reel. Then the wire was all out; there was a sudden jerk.

And the hard-gathered sphere of metal was gone—snapped off into space. Thad clung desperately to the wire, muscles cracking, tortured arms almost drawn from their sockets. Fear flashed over his mind; what if the wire broke, and left him floating helpless in space?

It held, though, to his relief. He was trailing behind the ship. Eagerly he seized the handle of the reel; began to wind up the mile of thin wire. Half an hour later, Thad's suited figure bumped gently against the shining hull of the rocket. He got to his feet, and gazed backward into the starry gulf, where his sphere of iron had long since vanished.

"Somebody is going to find himself a nice chunk of metal, all welded together and equipped for rocket navigation," he murmured. "As for me—well, I've simply *got* to run this tub to Mars!"

He walked over the smooth, refulgent hull, held to it by magnetic soles. Nowhere was it broken, though he found scars where small meteoric particles had scratched the brilliant polish. So no meteor had wrecked the ship. What, then, was the matter? Soon he would know.

THE *RED DRAGON* WAS NOT LARGE. A hundred and thirty feet long, Thad estimated, with a beam of twenty-five feet. But her trim lines bespoke design recent and good; the double ring of black projecting rockets at the stern told of unusual speed.

A pretty piece of salvage, he reflected, if he could land her on Mars. Half the value of such a ship, unharmed and safe in port, would be a larger sum than he dared put in figures. And he must take her in, now that he had lost his own rocket!

He found the life-tubes, six of them, slender, silvery cylinders, lying secure in their niches, three along each side of the flier. None was missing. So the crew had not willingly deserted the ship.

He approached the main airlock, at the center of the hull, behind the projecting dome of the bridge. It was closed. A glance at the dials told him there was full air pressure within it. It had, then, last been used to enter the rocket, not to leave it.

Thad opened the exhaust valve, let the air hiss from the chamber of the lock. The huge door swung open in response to his hand upon the wheel, and he entered the cylindrical chamber. In a moment the door was closed behind him, air was hissing into the lock again.

He started to open the face-plate of his helmet, longing for a breath of air that did not smell of sweat and stale tobacco smoke, as that in his suit always did, despite the best chemical purifiers. Then he hesitated. Perhaps some deadly gas, from the combustion chambers....

Thad opened the inner valve, and came upon the upper deck of the vessel. A floor ran the full length of the ship, broken with hatches and companionways that gave to the rocket rooms, cargo holds, and quarters for crew and passengers below. There was an enclosed ladder that led to bridge and navigation room in the dome above. The hull formed an arched roof over it.

The deck was deserted, lit only by three dim blue globes, hanging from the curved roof. All seemed in order—the fire-fighting equipment hanging on the walls, and the huge metal patches and welding equipment for repairing breaks in the hull. Everything was clean, bright with polish or new paint.

And all was very still. The silence held a vague, brooding threat that frightened Thad, made him wish for a moment that he was back upon his rugged ball of metal. But he banished his fear, and strode down the deck.

Midway of it he found a dark stain upon the clean metal. The black of long-dried blood. A few tattered scraps of cloth beside it. No more than bloody rags. And a heavy meat cleaver, half hidden beneath a bit of darkened fabric.

Mute record of tragedy! Thad strove to read it. Had a man fought here and been killed? It must have been a struggle of peculiar violence, to judge by the dark spattered stains, and the indescribable condition of the remnants of clothing. But what had he fought? Another man, or some thing? And what had become of victor and vanquished?

He walked on down the deck.

The torturing silence was broken by the abrupt patter of quick little footsteps behind him. He turned quickly, nervously, with a hand going instinctively to his welding arc, which, he knew, would make a fairly effective weapon.

It was merely a dog. A little dog, yellow, nondescript, pathetically delighted. With a sharp, eager bark, it leaped up at Thad, pawing at his armor and licking it, standing on its hind legs and reaching toward the visor of his helmet.

It was very thin, as if from long starvation. Both ears were ragged and bloody, and there was a long, unhealed scratch across the shoulder, somewhat inflamed, but not a serious wound.

The bright, eager eyes were alight with joy. But Thad thought he saw fear in them. And even through the stiff fabric of the Osprey suit, he felt that the dog was trembling.

Suddenly, with a low whine, it shrank close to his side. And another sound reached Thad's ears.

A cry, weird and harrowing beyond telling. A scream so thin and so high that it roughened his skin, so keenly shrill that it tortured his nerves; a sound of that peculiar frequency that is more agonizing than any bodily pain.

When silence came again, Thad was standing with his back against the wall, the welding arc in his hand. His face was cold with sweat, and a queer chill prickled up and down his spine. The yellow dog crouched whimpering against his legs.

Ominous, threatening stillness filled the ship again, disturbed only by the whimpers and frightened growls of the dog. Trying to calm his overwrought nerves, Thad listened—strained his ears. He could hear nothing. And he had no idea from which direction the terrifying sound had come.

A strange cry. Thad knew it had been born in no human throat. Nor in the throat of any animal he knew. It had carried an alien note that overcame him with instinctive fear and horror. What had voiced it? Was the ship haunted by some dread entity?

For many minutes Thad stood upon the deck, waiting, tensely grasping the welding tool. But the nerve-shattering scream did not come again. Nor any other sound. The yellow dog seemed half to forget its fear. It leaped up at his face again, with another short little bark.

The air must be good, he thought, if the dog could live in it.

He unscrewed the face-plate of his helmet, and lifted it. The air that struck his face was cool and clean. He breathed deeply, gratefully. And at first he did not notice the strange odor upon it: a curious, unpleasant scent, earthly, almost fetid, unfamiliar.

The dog kept leaping up, whining.

"Hungry, boy?" Thad whispered.

He fumbled in the bulky inside pockets of his suit, found a slab of concentrated food, and tossed it out through the opened panel. The dog sprang upon it, wolfed it eagerly, and came back to his side.

Thad set at once about exploring the ship.

First he ascended the ladder to the bridge. A metal dome covered it, studded with transparent ports. Charts and instruments were in order. And the room was vacant, heavy with the fatal silence of the ship.

Thad had no expert's knowledge of the flier's mechanism. But he had studied interplanetary navigation, to qualify for his license to carry masses of metal under rocket power through the space lanes and into planetary atmospheres. He was sure he could manage the ship if its mechanism were in good order, though he was uncertain of his ability to make any considerable repairs.

To his relief, a scrutiny of the dials revealed nothing wrong.

He started the gyro motors, got the great wheels to spinning, and thus stopped the slow, end-over-end turning of the flier. Then he went to the rocket controls, warmed three of the tubes, and set them to firing. The vessel answered readily to her helm. In a few minutes he had the red fleck of Mars over the bow.

"Yes, I can run her, all right," he announced to the dog, which had followed him up the steps, keeping close to his feet. "Don't worry, old boy. We'll be eating a juicy beefsteak together, in a week. At Comet's place in Helion, down by the canal. Not much style—but the eats!

"And now we're going to do a little detective work, and find out what made that disagreeable noise. And what happened to all your fellow-astronauts. Better find out, before it happens to us!"

He shut off the rockets, and climbed down from the bridge again.

When Thad started down the companionway to the officers' quarters, in the central one of the five main compartments of the ship, the dog kept close to his legs, growling, trembling, hackles lifted. Sensing the animal's terror, pitying it for the naked fear in its eyes, Thad wondered what dramas of horror it might have seen.

The cabins of the navigator, calculator, chief technician, and first officer were empty, and forbidding with the ominous silence of the ship. They were neatly in order, and the berths had been made since they were used. But there was a large bloodstain, black and circular, on the floor of the calculator's room.

The captain's cabin held evidence of a violent struggle. The door had been broken in. Its fragments, with pieces of broken furniture, books, covers from the berth, and three service pistols, were scattered about in indescribable confusion, all stained with blood. Among the frightful debris, Thad found several scraps of clothing, of dissimilar fabrics. The guns were empty.

Attempting to reconstruct the action of the tragedy from those grim clues, he imagined that the five officers, aware of some peril, had gathered here, fought, and died.

The dog refused to enter the room. It stood at the door, looking anxiously after him, trembling and whimpering pitifully. Several times it sniffed the air and drew back, snarling. Thad thought that the unpleasant earthy odor he had noticed upon opening the faceplate of his helmet was stronger here.

After a few minutes of searching through the wildly disordered room, he found the ship's log—or its remains. Many pages had been torn from the book, and the remainder, soaked with blood, formed a stiff black mass.

Only one legible entry did he find, that on a page torn from the book, which somehow had escaped destruction. Dated five months before, it gave the position of the vessel and her bearings—she was then just outside Jupiter's orbit, Earthward bound—and concluded with a remark of sinister implications:

"Another man gone this morning. Simms, assistant technician. A fine workman. O'Deen swears he heard something moving on the deck. Cook thinks some of the doctor's stuffed monstrosities have come to life. Ridiculous, of course. But what is one to think?"

Pondering the significance of those few lines, Thad climbed back to the deck. Was the ship haunted by some weird death, that had seized the crew man by man, mysteriously? That was the obvious implication. And if the flier had been still outside Jupiter's orbit when those words were written, it must have been weeks before the end. A lurking, invisible death! The scream he had heard....

HE DESCENDED INTO the forecastle, and came upon another such silent record of frightful carnage as he had found in the captain's cabin. Dried blood, scraps of cloth, knives and other weapons. A fearful question was beginning to obsess him. What had become of the bodies of those who must have died in these conflicts? He dared not think the answer.

Gripping the welding arc, Thad approached the after hatch, giving to the cargo hold. Trepidation almost overpowered him, but he was determined to find the sinister menace of the ship, before it found him. The dog whimpered, hung back, and finally deserted him, contributing nothing to his peace of mind.

The hold proved to be dark. An indefinite black space, oppressive with the terrible silence of the flier. The air within it bore still more strongly the unpleasant fetor.

Thad hesitated on the steps. The hold was not inviting. But at the thought that he must sleep, unguarded, while taking the flier to Mars, his resolution returned. The uncertainty, the constant fear, would be unendurable.

He climbed on down, feeling for the light button. He found it, as his feet touched the floor. Blue light flooded the hold.

It was filled with monstrous things, colossal creatures, such as nothing that ever lived upon the Earth; like nothing known in the jungles of Venus or the deserts of Mars, or anything that has been found upon Jupiter's moons.

They were monsters remotely resembling insects or crustaceans, but as large as horses or elephants; creatures upreared upon strange limbs, armed with hideously fanged jaws, cruel talons, frightful, saw-toothed snouts, and glittering scales, red and yellow and green. They leered at him with phosphorescent eyes, yellow and purple.

They cast grotesquely gigantic shadows in the blue light....

A cold shock of horror started along Thad's spine, at sight of those incredible nightmare things. Automatically he flung up the welding tool, flicking over the lever with his thumb, so that violet electric flame played about the electrode.

Then he saw that the crowding, hideous things were motionless, that they stood upon wooden pedestals, that many of them were supported upon metal bars. They were dead. Mounted. Collected specimens of some alien life.

Grinning wanly, and conscious of a weakness in the knees, he muttered: "They sure will fill the museum, if everybody gets the kick out of them that I did. A little too realistic, I'd say. Guess these are the 'stuffed monstrosities' mentioned in the page out of the log. No wonder the cook was afraid of them. Some of them do look hellishly alive!"

He started across the hold, shrinking involuntarily from the armored enormities that seemed crouched to spring at him, motionless eyes staring.

So, at the end of the long space, he found the treasure.

Glittering in the blue light, it looked unreal. Incredible. A dazzling dream. He stopped among the fearful things that seemed gathered as if to guard it, and stared with wide eyes through the opened face-plate of his helmet.

He saw neat stacks of gold ingots, new, freshly smelted; bars of silver-white iridium, of argent platinum, of blue-white osmium. Many of them. Thousands of pounds, Thad knew. He trembled at the thought of their value. Almost beyond calculation.

Then he saw the coffer, lying beyond the piled, gleaming ingots—a huge box, eight feet long; made of some crystal that glittered with snowy whiteness, filled with sparkling, iridescent gleams, and inlaid with strange designs, apparently in vermilion enamel.

With a little cry, he ran toward the chest, moving awkwardly in the loose, deflated fabric of the Osprey suit.

Beside the coffer, on the floor of the hold, was literally a mountain of flame—blazing gems, heaped as if they had been carelessly dumped from it; cut diamonds, incredibly gigantic; monster emeralds, sapphires, rubies; and strange stones, that Thad did not recognize.

And Thad gasped with horror, when he looked at the designs of the vermilion inlay, in the white, gleaming crystal. Weird forms. Shapes of creatures somewhat like gigantic spiders, and more unlike them. Demoniac things, wickedly fanged, jaws slavering. Executed with masterly skill, that made them seem living, menacing, secretly gloating!

Thad stared at them for long minutes, fascinated almost hypnotically. Three times he approached the chest, to lift the lid and find what it held. And three times the unutterable horror of those crimson images thrust him back, shuddering.

"Nothing but pictures," he muttered hoarsely.

A fourth time he advanced, trembling, and seized the lid of the coffer. Heavy, massive, it was fashioned also of glistening white crystal, and inlaid in crimson with weirdly hideous figures. Great hinges of white platinum held it on the farther side; it was fastened with a simple, heavy hasp of the precious metal.

Hands quivering, Thad snapped back the hasp, lifted the lid.

New treasure in the chest would not have surprised him. He was prepared to meet dazzling wonders of gems or priceless metal. Nor would he have been astonished at some weird creature such as one of those whose likenesses were inlaid in the crystal.

But what he saw made him drop the massive lid.

A woman lay in the chest—motionless, in white.

In a moment he raised the lid again; examined the still form more closely. The woman had been young. The features were regular, good to look upon. The eyes were closed; the white face appeared very peaceful.

Save for the extreme, cadaverous pallor, there was no mark of death. With a fancy that the body might be miraculously living, sleeping, Thad thrust an arm out through the opened panel of his suit, and touched a slender, bare white arm. It was stiff, very cold.

The still, pallid face was framed in fine brown hair. The fair, small hands were crossed upon the breast, over the simple white garment.

A queer ache came into his heart. Something made him think of a white tower in the red hills near Helion, and a girl waiting in its fragrant garden of saffron and purple—a girl like this.

The body lay upon a bed of blazing jewels.

It appeared, Thad thought, as if the pile of gems upon the floor had been hastily scraped from the coffer, to make room for the quiet form. He wondered how long it had lain there. It looked as if it might have been living but minutes before. Some preservative....

His thought was broken by a sound that rang from the open hatchway on the deck above—the furious barking and yelping of the dog. Abruptly that was silent, and in its place came the uncanny and terrifying scream that Thad had heard once before, on this flier of mystery. A shriek so keen and shrill that it seemed to tear out his nerves by their roots. The voice of the haunter of the ship.

WHEN THAD CAME BACK upon the deck, the dog was still barking nervously. He saw the animal forward, almost at the bow. Hackles raised, tail between its legs, it was slinking backward, barking sharply as if to call for aid.

Apparently it was retreating from something between Thad and itself. But Thad, searching the dimly-lit deck, could see no source of alarm. Nor could the structures upon it have shut any large object from his view.

"It's all right!" Thad called, intending to

reassure the frightened animal, but finding his voice queerly dry. "Coming on the double, old man. Don't worry."

The dog had reached the end of the deck. It stopped yelping, but snarled and whined as if in terror. It began darting back and forth, moving exactly as if something were slowly closing in upon it, trapping it in the corner. But Thad could see nothing.

Then it made a wild dash back toward Thad, darting along by the wall, as if trying to run past an unseen enemy.

Thad thought he heard quick, rasping footsteps then, that were not those of the dog. And something seemed to catch the dog in mid-air, as it leaped. It was hurled howling to the deck. For a moment it struggled furiously, as if an invisible claw had pinned it down. Then it escaped, and fled whimpering to Thad's side.

He saw a new wound across its hips. Three long, parallel scratches, from which fresh red blood was trickling.

Regular scraping sounds came from the end of the deck, where no moving thing was to be seen—sounds such as might be made by the walking of feet with unsheathed claws. Something was coming back toward Thad. Something that was *invisible!*

Terror seized him, with the knowledge. He had nerved himself to face desperate men, or a savage animal. But an invisible being, that could creep upon him and strike unseen! It was incredible ... yet he had seen the dog knocked down, and the bleeding wound it had received.

His heart paused, then beat very quickly. For the moment he thought only blindly, of escape. He knew only an overpowering desire to hide, to conceal himself from the invisible thing. Had it been possible, he might have tried to leave the flier.

Beside him was one of the companionways amidships, giving access to a compartment of the vessel that he had not explored. He turned, leaped down the steps, with the terrified dog at his heels.

Below, he found himself in a short hall, dimly lighted. Several metal doors opened from it. He tried one at random. It gave. He sprang through, let the dog follow, closed and locked it.

Trying to listen, he leaned weakly against the door. The rushing of his breath, swift and regular. The loud hammer of his thudding heart. The dog's low whines. Then—unmistakable scraping sounds, outside.

The scratching of claws, Thad knew. Invisible claws!

He stood there, bracing the door with the weight of his body, holding the welding arc ready in his hand. Several times the hinges creaked, and he felt a heavy pressure against the panels. But at last the scratching sounds ceased. He relaxed. The monster had withdrawn, at least for a time.

When he had time to think, the invisibility of the thing was not so incredible. The mounted creatures he had seen in the hold were evidence that the flier had visited some unknown planet, where weird life reigned. It was not beyond reason that such a planet should be inhabited by beings invisible to human sight.

Human vision, as he knew, utilizes only a tiny fraction of the spectrum. The creature must be largely transparent to visible light, as human flesh is radiolucent to hard X-rays. Quite possibly it could be seen by infra-red or ultra-violet light—evidently it was visible enough to the dog's eyes, with their different range of sensitivity.

Pushing the subject from his mind, he turned to survey the room into which he had burst. It had apparently been occupied by a woman. A frail blue silk dress and more intimate items of feminine apparel were hanging above the berth. Two pairs of delicate black slippers stood neatly below it.

Across from him was a dressing table, with a large mirror above it. Combs, pins, jars of cosmetic cluttered it. And Thad saw upon it a little leather-bound book, locked, stamped on the back "Diary."

He crossed the room and picked up the little book, which smelled faintly of jasmine. Momentary shame overcame him at thus stealing the secrets of an unknown girl. Necessity, however, left him no choice but to seize any chance of learning more of this ship of mystery and her invisible haunter. He broke the flimsy fastening.

Linda Cross was the name written on the fly-leaf, in a firm, clear feminine hand. On the next page was the photograph, in color, of a girl, the brown-haired girl whose body Thad had discovered in the crystal coffer in the hold. Her eyes, he saw, had been blue. He thought she looked very lovely—like the waiting girl in his old dream of the silver tower in the red hills by Helion.

The diary, it appeared, had not been kept very devotedly. Most of the pages were blank.

One of the first entries, dated a year and a half before, told of a party that Linda had attended in San Francisco, and of her refusal to dance with a certain man, referred to as "Benny," because he had been unpleasantly insistent about wanting to marry her. It ended:

Dad said tonight that we're going off in the *Dragon* again. All the way to Uranus, if the new fuel works as he expects. What a lark, to explore a few new worlds of our own! Dad says one of Uranus' moons is as large as Mercury. And Benny won't be proposing again soon!

Turning on, Thad found other scattered entries, some of them dealing with the preparation for the voyage, the start from San Francisco—and a huge bunch of flowers from "Benny," the long months of the trip through space, out past the orbit of Mars, above the meteor belt, across Jupiter's orbit, beyond the track of Saturn, which was the farthest point that rocket explorers had previously reached, and on to Uranus, where they could not land because of the unstable surface.

The remainder of the entries Thad found less frequent, shorter, bearing the mark of excitement: landing upon Titania, the third and largest satellite of Uranus; unearthly forests, sheltering strange and monstrous life; the hunting of weird creatures, and mounting them for museum specimens.

Then the discovery of a ruined city, whose remains indicated that it had been built by a lost race of intelligent, spider-like things; the finding of a temple whose walls were of precious metals, containing a crystal chest filled with wondrous gems; the smelting of the metal into convenient ingots, and the transfer of the treasure to the hold.

The first sinister note there entered the diary:

Some of the men say we shouldn't have disturbed the temple. Think it will bring us bad luck. Rubbish, of course. But one man did vanish while they were smelting the gold. Poor Mr. Tom James. I suppose he ventured away from the rest, and something caught him.

The few entries that followed were shorter, and showed increasing nervous tension. They recorded the departure from Titania, made almost as soon as the treasure was loaded. The last was made several weeks later. A dozen men had vanished from the crew, leaving only gouts of blood to hint the manner of their going. The last entry ran:

Dad says I'm to stay in here today. Old dear, he's afraid the thing will get me— whatever it is. It's really serious. Two men taken from their berths last night. And not a trace. Some of them think it's a curse on the treasure. One of them swears he saw Dad's stuffed specimens moving about in the hold.

Some terrible thing must have slipped aboard the flier, out of the jungle. That's what Dad and the captain think. Queer they can't find it. They've searched all over. Well....

Musing and regretful, Thad turned back for another look at the smiling girl in the photograph.

What a tragedy her death had been! Reading the diary had made him like her. Her balance and humor. Her quiet affection for "Dad." The calm courage with which she seemed to have faced the creeping, lurking death that darkened the ship with its unescapable shadow.

How had her body come to be in the coffer, he wondered, when all the others were— gone? It had shown no marks of violence. She must have died of fear. No, her face had seemed too calm and peaceful for that. Had she chosen easy death by some poison, rather than that other dreadful fate? Had her body been put in the chest to protect it, and the poison arrested decomposition?

Thad was still studying the picture, thoughtfully and sadly, when the dog, which had been silent, suddenly growled again, and retreated from the door, toward the corner of the room.

The invisible monster had returned. Thad heard its claws scratching across the door again. And he heard another dreadful sound—not the long, shrill scream that had so grated on his nerves before, but a short, sharp coughing or barking, a series of shrill, indescribable notes that could have been made by no beast he knew.

THE DECISION TO OPEN the door took a huge effort of Thad's will.

For hours he had waited, thinking desperately. And the thing outside the door had waited as patiently, scratching upon it from time to time, uttering those dreadful, shrill coughing cries.

Sooner or later, he would have to face the monster. Even if he could escape from the room and avoid it for a time, he would have to meet it in the end. And it might creep upon him while he slept.

To be sure, the issue of the combat was extremely doubtful. The monster, apparently, had succeeded in killing every man upon the flier, even though some of them had been armed. It must be large and very ferocious.

But Thad was not without hope. He still wore his Osprey-suit. The heavy fabric, made of metal wires impregnated with a tough, elastic composition, should afford considerable protection against the thing.

The welding arc, intended to fuse refractive meteoric iron, would be no mean weapon, at close quarters. And the quarters would be close.

If only he could find some way to make the thing visible!

Paint, or something of the kind, would stick to its skin.... His eyes, searching the room, caught the jar of face powder on the dressing table. *Dash that over it!* It ought to stick enough to make the outline visible.

So, at last, holding the powder ready in one hand, he waited until a time when the pressure upon the door had just relaxed, and he knew the monster was waiting outside. Swiftly, he opened the door....

Thad had partially overcome the instinctive horror that the unseen being had first aroused in him. But it returned in a sickening wave when he heard the short, shrill, coughing cries, hideously eager, that greeted the opening of the door. And the quick rasping of naked claws upon the floor. *Sounds from nothingness!*

He flung the powder at the sound.

A form of weird horror materialized before him, still half invisible, half outlined with the white film of adhering powder: gigantic and hideous claws, that seemed to reach out of empty air, the side of a huge, scaly body, a yawning, dripping jaw. For a moment Thad could see great, hooked fangs in that jaw. Then they vanished, as if an unseen tongue had licked the powder from them, dissolving it in fluids which made it invisible.

That unearthly, half-seen shape leaped at him.

He was carried backward into the room, hurled to the floor. Claws were rasping upon the tough fabric of his suit. His arm was seized crushingly in half-visible jaws.

Desperately he clung to the welding tool. The heated electrode was driven toward his body. He fought to keep it away; he knew that it would burn through even the insulated fabric of his suit.

A claw ripped savagely at his side. He heard the sharp, rending sound, as the tough fabric of his suit was torn, and felt a thin pencil of pain drawn along his body, where a claw cut his skin.

Suddenly the suit was full of the earthy fetor of the monster's body, nauseatingly intense. Thad gasped, tried to hold his breath, and thrust upward hard with the incandescent electrode. He felt warm blood trickling from the wound.

A numbing blow struck his arm. The welding tool was carried from his hand. Flung to the side of the room, it clattered to the floor; and then a heavy weight came upon his chest, forcing the breath from his lungs. The monster stood upon his body and clawed at him.

Thad squirmed furiously. He kicked out with his feet, encountering a great, hard body. Futilely he beat and thrust with his arms against the pillar-like limb.

His body was being mauled, bruised beneath the thick fabric. He heard it tear again, along his right thigh. But he felt no pain, and thought the claws had not reached the skin.

It was the yellow dog that gave him the chance to recover the weapon. The animal had been running back and forth in the opposite end of the room, fairly howling in excitement and terror. Now, with the mad courage of desperation, it leaped recklessly at the monster.

A mighty, dimly seen claw caught it, hurled it back across the room. It lay still, broken, whimpering.

For a moment the thing had lifted its weight from Thad's body. And Thad slipped quickly from beneath it, flung himself across the room, snatched up the welding tool.

In an instant the creature was upon him again. But he met it with the incandescent electrode. He was crouched in a corner, now, where it could come at him from only one direction. Its claws still slashed at him ferociously. But he was able to cling to the weapon, and meet each onslaught with hot metal.

Gradually its mad attacks weakened. Then one of his blind, thrusting blows seemed to burn into a vital organ. A terrible choking, strangling sound came from the air. And he heard the thrashing struggles of wild convulsions. At last all was quiet. He prodded the thing again and again with the hot electrode, and it did not move. It was dead.

The creature's body was so heavy that Thad had to return to the bridge, and shut off the current in the gravity plates along the keel, before he could move it. He dragged it to the lock through which he had entered the flier, and consigned it to space....

FIVE DAYS LATER Thad brought the *Red Dragon* into the atmosphere of Mars. A puzzled pilot came aboard, in response to his signals, and docked the flier safely at Helion. Thad went down into the hold again, with the astonished port authorities who had come aboard to inspect the vessel.

Again he passed among the grotesque and outrageous monsters in the hold, leading the gasping officers. While they marveled at the treasure, he lifted the weirdly embellished lid of the coffer of white crystal, and looked once more upon the still form of the girl within it.

Pity stirred him. An ache came in his throat.

Linda Cross, so quiet and cold and white, and yet so lovely. How terrible her last days of life must have been, with doom shadowing the vessel, and the men vanishing mysteriously, one by one! Terrible—until she had sought the security of death.

Strangely, Thad felt no great elation at

the thought that half the incalculable treasure about him was now safely his own, as the award of salvage. If only the girl were still living.... He felt a poignantly keen desire to hear her voice.

Thad found the note when they started to lift her from the chest. A hasty scrawl, it lay beneath her head, among glittering gems.

> This woman is not dead. Please have her given skilled medical attention as soon as possible. She lies in a state of suspended animation, induced by the injection of fifty minims of zeronel.
>
> She is my daughter, Linda Cross, and my sole heir.
>
> I entreat the finders of this to have care given her, and to keep in trust for her such part of the treasure on this ship as may remain after the payment of salvage or other claims.
>
> Sometime she will wake. Perhaps in a year, perhaps in a hundred. The purity of my drugs is uncertain, and the injection was made hastily, so I do not know the exact time that must elapse.
>
> If this is found, it will be because the lurking thing upon the ship has destroyed me and all my men.
>
> Please do not fail me.
> —Levington Cross

Thad bought the white tower of his dreams, slim and graceful in its Martian garden of saffron and purple, among the low ocher hills beside Helion. He carried the sleeping girl through the silver door where the girl of his dreams had waited, and set the coffer in a great, vaulted chamber. Many times each day he came into the room where she lay, to look into her pallid face, and feel her cold wrist. He kept a nurse in attendance, and had a physician call daily.

A long Martian year went by.

LOOKING IN HIS MIRROR one day, Thad saw little wrinkles about his eyes. He realized that the nervous strain and anxiety of waiting was aging him. And it might be a hundred years, he remembered, before Linda Cross came from beneath the drug's influence.

He wondered if he should grow old and infirm, while Linda lay still young and beautiful and unchanged in her sleep; if she might awake, after long years, and see in him only a feeble old man. And he knew that he would not be sorry he had waited, even if he should die before she revived.

On the next day, the nurse called him into the room where Linda lay. He was bending over her when she opened her eyes. They were blue, glorious.

A long time she looked up at him, first in fearful wonder, then with confidence, and dawning understanding. And at last she smiled.

"Salvage in Space" first appeared in the March 1933 issue of Astounding Stories. *(Stock illustration by Jack Coggins)*

In 1928, twenty-year-old John Stewart Williamson sold his first pulp tale to Amazing Stories, *the flagship magazine of science fiction publishing pioneer Hugo Gernsbach. Thus began the long and distinguished writing career of Jack Williamson, author of such landmark works as "With Folded Hands" (part of his The Humanoids series) and the novel* Darker Than You Think, *which deals with shapeshifters.*

Highly creative, extremely prolific, and always entertaining, Williamson wrote through-out the freewheeling days of the pulps, and well into the 21st century, publishing The Stonehenge Gate *in 2005. Earlier, in 2001, and at the age of 92, the author won a Hugo Award for his novella* The Ultimate Earth.

THE PILGRIMAGE

BY GREGORY L. NORRIS

THE PLANET LANGO ORBITED AN ORANGE DWARF STAR AND EXISTED FAR FROM WARP CORRIDORS AND THE WELL-TRAVELED SPACE LANES TO OTHER WORLDS IN ORION'S ARM. Ocean covered more than ninety-nine percent of the planet's surface. What land there was, mountain peaks masquerading as islands, fell under ownership of the Manifest Guild. The majority of Lango's population was relegated to the hardscrabble life of floating cities like the Mountain of Lost Hope, a collection of rusting hulks purchased at auction on the cheap and hauled to Lango in sections for reassembly to house the labor force that served the Guild on the island of Zamboanga. Every few seasons, another of the former cruise liners capsized or was scuttled by high seas during storm season. More wrecks for the shallows off Zamboanga's coast. Lango's oceans were littered with debris, most but not all from the brief war that took place in high orbit above the planet when numerous opposing sides laid claim to the water world.

Arthur Court's family came to Lango like most during the first and third waves of colonization: they simply had nowhere else to go. They'd run out of choices and warp jumps. Lango was the last and only option.

On the morning the Manifest Guild yacht drew up to Section 19, his parents were dead. All of the Courts were gone save for his cousin, Maggie. Their adjoining rooms were in the central corridors and lacked view ports.

"Come outside with me," Arthur again begged.

Maggie sat in the old recliner, as she did most days, avoiding direct eye contact. "Why?"

"To see the world."

At this, she offered a humorless chuckle. "To see a hundred kilometers of ocean? No thank you."

"Then you can watch me paint or forage for supplies to make paint."

She closed her eyes, the conversation ended. As he picked up the bag fashioned from fabric scraps, it struck him that she would soon follow the rest of the Courts to whatever afterlife awaited. She'd abandoned her dreams of marrying into island life or working for some Manifest Guild landowner. She was a child of Lost Hope, and like so many others had given up.

He kissed her pale forehead on his way out of the dark rooms that were their only home and tried to find hope on the march down the long corridors, through the dining hall where the usual meal would be served to Section 19 residents twice that day—sea grapes, lemon fish, and an assortment of aquatic vegetable dishes from the tangled gardens growing in abundance across the shallows.

The saline quality of the air thickened, replacing old cooking odors and older sweat. Light spilled down through the fracture that had once been a balcony until the storm season of his seventeenth year. Three years had passed, and the repairs looked ready to follow the part of the ship sheared off by the storm's fury into the deep.

"There goes the artist," said one of the workers he passed en route to the top deck, the man speaking just loud enough for Arthur to hear his tone of resentment.

Arthur stopped and turned, but the man was already lost in the small crowd of bodies moving back and forth, unaware that little if anything they did mattered, and that, like for his cousin, hope was dwindling.

"I am an artist," he said. "*Art* is in my name!"

Nobody listened, and if anyone heard him, they didn't appear to care.

THE TOP DECK, as on most bright days, was filled with bodies sunning themselves, exercising, or bartering for flesh. Arthur cut around to the aft of Section 19, which faced the coast of Zamboanga. Past 20, 21, and 22, Section 23 was still visible from its deserted upper decks. It had sunk during storm season but snagged on an outcrop of rock ledge. Farther out, 24 could barely be seen as a dark shadow under the surface of the turquoise water.

So many unfortunates hadn't made it free from 23. But, Arthur wondered, his eyes lingering on the hulled floating city, maybe Maggie was right. Maybe the dead were really the lucky ones to be done with life, done with Lango.

No, his inner voice interrupted, bringing him back.

Arthur blinked. He was low on pigments, even lower on the canvasses he made from the husks of discarded pale kelp he salvaged from the weekly harvests. He'd gather rust from the oxidizing sea liner's metals, shells and inks from the kitchen, those leftovers from the day's catch unwanted by all save him. He'd grind the shells, mix the inks, hydrate the rust. And from those meager resources he would create art, beauty from ugliness. Beauty in an ugly, mean world.

He remembered the workman's snide comment. Yes, Arthur was an artist, and he bartered the paintings he made on pale husk canvasses dried in Lango's sunshine to clothe and feed what was left of his family. Hope briefly rose up from his gut, filling him better than anything subsidized by the Manifest Guild in Section 19's dining hall. Its sparkle was brief, because this was the Mountain of Lost Hope.

Arthur drew in a deep sip of air and just as deeply expelled the cleansing breath. He resumed his search for supplies with which to paint but only got a few steps farther along the gangway when, from the cut of his eye, he noticed movement from the direction of the island. A vessel cut water. No surprise there—the shallows off the continental shelf buzzed with a flotilla of fishing trawlers, harvesters, and repair craft. Only the longer he looked, the clearer it became that this vessel wasn't one of the usual support boats.

It was bigger, sleeker, shinier than the ragtags normally operating off the floating city. A vessel belonging to the Manifest Guild, Arthur realized. And it was heading directly toward Section 19.

He watched it draw nearer, a symbol of some rich titleholder within the Guild's hierarchy. And Arthur could guess as to why it was there. *Flesh*, he thought. Whether for servitude or pleasure, the only time the Guild traveled from land to Lost Hope was for fresh bodies.

Disgusted, he turned away when the yacht maneuvered in to dock with Section 19's aft. He had supplies to gather, art to create, and hope to hold onto. The last part was like trying to paint with water-soluble colors in the rain at the best of times, which this wasn't.

Arthur moved down the liner's corroding exterior to an expanding patch of rust where he often harvested raw material. He hadn't been there long when the commotion reached his ears, and he looked back in the direction of the aft deck.

"You," an older man in a dark yellow toga called. Two armed Guild sentries flanked him. "You, *artist.*"

Arthur froze. For the second time that morning, a hostile figure had invoked the sobriquet. The trio of Guild visitors hastening toward him looked more hostile than any of 19's denizens. Their clothing was new, shiny like their yacht, their hair cut neat, their skin lacking the obvious cuts, scars, and lesions of life in Lost Hope. But they were Guild, and that made them dangerous, deadly.

He turned, instinct kicking in, and bolted. The port side of Section 19 seemed to stretch out in his building panic and fill with more obstacles. It was as if everyone who lived aboard the liner chose that exact moment to take a leisurely stroll.

"Wait," the man dressed in yellow called.

Arthur dodged the living obstacles in front of him. The Guild guards gave chase.

AIR BURNED IN HIS LUNGS. Why him? He'd done nothing wrong, nothing against the rules. Bartering art was as acceptable under living mandates as offering time to fish the shallows or repair external or internal damage. So Arthur ran, unable to recall that there was nowhere to run to in order to escape his pursuers.

He made it back to the ship's prow. A germ of a plan had formulated on the mad dash—remove shirt, slink up to some glistening sunbather, and blend in. Only he tripped over one of the bodies using that corner of the top deck and spilled down, dropping his bag of supplies. Angry voices roared around him. He started to rise, stepped over a limb, and tumbled a second time. When next he stood, it was with the help of the Guild guards.

"Are you the artist?" the man in yellow demanded, his expression harsh, sour.

Arthur didn't answer. One of the guards picked up his bag. The man in yellow examined the contents and then turned back to Arthur, a slippery grin forming on his thin lips, the gesture more snarl than smile.

"Excellent. Just whom I've come all this distance to meet. Your name?"

Arthur struggled out his answer. "Arthur Court."

"Why did you run?" the man asked, his predator's smirk persisting. "Oh, I understand."

He gestured with a tip of his chin and the two guards released Arthur. The man handed over the fabric bag and its precious contents.

"Would you do me the honor of hearing me out, Arthur Court? I have need of a skilled artist."

Arthur cleared his throat and nodded.

The man's eyes shifted around, taking in the growing press of spectators.

"Not here. On my boat."

"But—?" Arthur protested.

The man and his guards were already in motion and walking back in the direction of the shiny Guild yacht.

Left with no other choice, Arthur followed.

THE ROOM WAS PANELED in lustrous wood from actual trees, the furniture new and comfortable. They offered him wine, roasted meat from land animals, and small, colorful confections that melted upon contact with his mouth. Arthur had never tasted such delicacies and soon grew lightheaded.

"I've seen your work," said the man, who introduced himself as Harris Smith, Chief Administrator of Zamboanga.

Arthur set down the goblet, which was fashioned from a mother-of-pearl shell with a glass stem. "My art?"

"I put forth feelers into the community. Of all the so-called *artists*," Smith stressed the word with a hint of distaste. "Your work was the most suitable for my needs."

"What kind of needs? Portraiture? Landscape?"

Again, that snarl-smile appeared. "You could say that, yes. For your services, I'm willing to compensate you well. My offer is—"

"Housing for two on Zamboanga," Arthur interjected.

Smith blinked. "Pardon me?"

"You said it yourself—my artwork is the most suited for your needs. So you'll make room on the island for my cousin, Margaret Court, and me. It doesn't have to be anything special, just warm, dry, and with windows. Do this and I'll paint whatever you want, for as long as you want me to."

Smith's grin widened, exposing a length of teeth not much less yellow than his garb, and Arthur regretted the ease of his victory.

"We have a deal," Smith said.

THEY STEPPED OFF THE YACHT and onto solid footing. The private marina's planks led away from the pleasure craft and gunboats lined before the villa. Arthur helped Maggie along, aware of how weak she'd grown in her room on Section 19. He cast a look across the ocean. Far beyond shore, at the limit of the horizon, rose Lost Hope, the only home they'd known until that afternoon.

"I must be dreaming," Maggie said.

"It's no dream," said Arthur.

Smith moved past them. "Indeed, it is not. We need an artist like your cousin, and we need him quickly. You are lucky he cares so deeply for you."

From the marina, they passed onto actual land. The paved pathway led through rocky coastline, past beach plants, and through a stone arch, to the pavilion beyond. Within the small, walled city of the villa were a main house, guest cottages, and numerous out-buildings. All of it sat under the gathering gray of storm clouds—the sunny morning out at sea was over, as were their old lives in the floating ghetto.

"Arthur is good. The best," Maggie said.

"So we've seen—and so we're counting on," said Smith.

Their cottage was one of the chain sitting before the main house, designed for support staff. The space was clean and bright. Fruit trees heavy with ripening jewels wreathed the small house, which was twice the size of their old rooms aboard Section 19.

"You can bathe and change, and I'll send someone with food," said Smith.

"Thank you," Maggie said.

Arthur saw that his last living relative had woken from her surrender. She eyed the bright walls and clean space with hopeful glances. They now stood on land, as humans were meant to.

Smith nodded to her and faced him. "After you're refreshed and settled, we'll talk."

"About art?"

Smith narrowed one eye. "That, too."

HE EMERGED FROM the cascade of hot water, clean and rejuvenated. *Baptized*, Arthur thought while changing into luxurious, new clothes that caressed his flesh with the comfort and lightness of clouds.

Maggie drowsed in her room, which he appreciated. Life on Lost Hope had ended. She might sleep for days before waking to appreciate their new good fortune. But in the silence of the small house filled with abundance, Arthur realized what was missing: the gift that had brought them from the ocean to land.

No art supplies or dedicated art space existed in the cottage. Surely, his demand hadn't been a surprise to Smith. Those condemned to Lost Hope only ever dreamed of leaving there for destinations like Zamboanga or the Archipelagos. When they had something to barter with, it was always land life expected in the trade.

Unease crept over his skin. Outside, the storm had swallowed the sun and the first drops of rain pelted the windows. Arthur sat and waited, his consciousness drifting into a fugue state with the cadence of the rain and Maggie's snores in counterpoint playing in the background.

Untimed minutes later, a knock sounded on the cottage's front door. Arthur roused and answered. Smith stood outside beneath a yellow umbrella, his smile made even slipperier by the rain on his face.

"Young Mister Court, it's time we talked."

Here it was, proof of the wrongness Arthur had felt since the Guild yacht pulled up to Section 19.

SMITH SAT IN ONE OF THE CHAIRS. "Your cousin, how is she?"

"Asleep. She has a lot to be exhausted over."

"No doubt. Have you rested?"

"No," Arthur said.

Smith didn't flinch. His eyes, until then locked on a section of pristine white wall, shifted to Arthur. "About the business that brought you here..."

Arthur ceased pacing and sat opposite his new benefactor. "Yes?"

"We need you to paint."

"We?"

"I and other associates in the Manifest Guild," Smith said.

"But not portraits, not landscapes?"

Smith's mouth tightened, that slight frisson in body language impossible to misread. "Not exactly. You will be sent into a place on Lango not on any maps. One intentionally avoided by satellites, ships, and drones."

Arthur's pulse quickened. "Why?"

"To observe—with your artist's eye. Strictest attention to detail is absolutely paramount to your success. When you have gone there, seen all that you can, you will return and paint everything you've observed."

The temperature in the room plummeted. "This place—?"

Smith, still scrutinizing him, hesitated. "You will have the best paints and canvasses," he eventually said.

"Forget the supplies," Arthur said. "Tell me—what are you sending me to paint?"

Smith rose, stirring the scent of rain and the man's cologne, a too-sweet resin. "Come with me."

Steeling himself, Arthur followed Smith out of the cottage and into the rain.

THE STORM LASHED ZAMBOANGA. On his march to the main house sans umbrella, Arthur cast another glance out to sea. The Mountain of Lost Hope existed somewhere far from shore and couldn't be seen, the floating city obscured by banks of dense fog roiling over the ocean.

Smith led him up a colonnaded path, through double doors, and into a grand foyer. The walls were made of glass tanks that contained colorful fish, living seashells, and other aquatic creatures native to the shallows—the continental shelf's most beautiful life forms. Over their heads, suspended from the ceiling by cables, was a colossal skeleton, one of the deep ocean's formidable predators, picked clean. Its giant mouth was lined with massive, razored teeth.

From there, they passed through a polished stone arch to an officious looking room with chairs and a conference table. The space lacked windows. A holographic image projector sat before the largest of the chairs at the table—the one reserved for Smith, no doubt.

Smith glided over to a side table upon which a decanter filled with red liquid and several glass-stem goblets stood. "Drink?"

"No, thank you."

Smith poured, drank. At the table, he activated the projector. Light drifted up.

"Establish security protocols," Smith ordered.

Several musical notes answered before a male computer voice said, "Protocols in effect. No external threat detected. System registers two humans within the security zone. You are advised to—"

"Disengage warning and project image code named *Susurrus*."

The computer obeyed. An image formed in the space above the conference table, a static view looking down upon turquoise waters surrounding a barren outcrop of land. The island wasn't much, though on Lango every inch of dry ground was considered priceless, sacred.

Upon this lifeless crag was a dark platinum blur sprawled over the time-eroded rock and extending into the sea.

"At first, we thought it was one of ours," Smith said, bringing Arthur out of his thoughts. "The oceans of Lango are littered with a known fifty-seven frigates or support craft from the skirmishes over planetary ownership before the Guild made that point clear. What you're looking at is number fifty-eight."

Arthur's next breath came with difficulty. "Is it—?"

"Alien? It certainly isn't one of ours. We can't get close to it with any sea-worthy vessel, flying craft, or satellite."

"Why not?"

"There's an active power source somewhere inside. The ship disables anything that gets close enough for a look. What you're seeing was a split-second capture from high orbit before it shot down one of our eyes-in-the-skies."

Arthur blinked, turned. He sucked in a deep breath. "And you expect me to … *what*? Go there and get blasted off the face of Lango, too?"

Smith killed the image, drank some more, and smiled. "We're certain you'll be safe. Fish swim around that island and some creatures even go on land to lay their eggs. None of them are attacked. We believe the energy source on that wreck is a defensive system attuned to attack other powered objects. One man in a raft traveling under current and oars should be safe."

"Then send one of your guards," Arthur spat.

Smith's smile dropped. "None of them have your gift. We need an artist who will come back and depict what he observes, in starkest detail."

TWELVE HOURS LATER, while Maggie dined on fruit and morning meal delicacies and rain pounded the land, Arthur boarded the military gunboat parked beside Administrator Smith's yacht. The gray-skinned juggernaut showed plenty of metal teeth in the form of deck cannons and projectile launchers.

He passed from the open top deck and into the shelter of the vessel's inner armor. Smith gave orders to set sail and the juggernaut sped away from the private marina. Less than a full day after his arrival to land, Arthur once more was back at sea. The roiling surface sped past beyond the direct vision ports. Part of him wondered if this newest storm would claim any of the floating city's sections.

Hours passed, with offers of food and refreshments, most of which he refused. At one point, a hard-faced man with short silver hair dressed in the Guild's uniform entered the cabin.

"Ah, Robley, good," Smith said.

Arthur's heart resumed its gallop.

"Please tell young Mister Court about the next phase of his duties."

"Susurrus," the new arrival said. "We can't trust getting any closer than three kilometers. Normally, it would be five but we're coming in from a southeastern angle, which puts the bulk of the island between us and your objective. You'll be working with the tide, which will help. Are you conversant with the operation of raft and oar?"

Arthur shrugged. "I guess so."

"The raft is outfitted with a compass. You'll continue in that direction until you spot the contact by visual means. From there, you'll proceed to the island, complete your mission, and return exactly in the reverse. We'll be waiting here for you to join us."

Arthur nodded. "And then, I paint."

Smith stood. "Yes, and then you paint."

The vessel continued its charge forward. Arthur willed his racing pulse to calm. It did not.

THEY LOWERED THE RAFT. Darkness fell early, welcomed in by the storm. But the rain appeared to be letting up and warmth billowed with the fog.

"We can't risk even the barest battery powered device," Robley said. "The compass lights on phosphorescence. That's all, I'm afraid."

Spotlights lit his way down the metal ladder to the waiting raft. The ocean shifted beneath his weight, more menacing than he ever remembered, even during the worst of storm seasons on Section 19. It struck Arthur that had he known their true interest in his ability as a painter, he might have kept on running. Running until they gave up and found another artist to carry out their insane plan.

He settled and lifted the oars. Already, the current was spiriting him away from the gunboat, as predicted.

"Good luck," Smith called down from the rail. "We'll be waiting."

Arthur nodded, picked up the oars, and rowed.

HE WORKED with his back to the Guild gunboat, his eyes aimed ahead. Watching the military vessel fall out of sight would have unnerved him, he sensed, to the point of obliteration. It was a reminder that he was thousands of kilometers from Zamboanga, the floating city, or any landmass other than the island with its scuttled alien derelict spaceship. And that thought would lead to others, like what swam beneath him—schools of the fanged giants kin to the skeleton hanging in Smith's palatial seat of power? Worse?

And what of the alien spacecraft? What if Smith and the best brains in the Guild were wrong about how it worked? What if phosphorescence was enough to activate the ship's automatic weapons?

Panic built, helped along by the mist, the rocking of the waves, and the oppressive night. At any moment, teeth would tear through the raft, tear through *him*. Or the weapons of the derelict hulk would lash out, vaporizing him. He only wanted to paint. Paint images of the ocean and its creatures and portraits of the citizens of Lost Hope. Paint with the humble peasant colors he scrounged from the world around him and available for free. The lure of life on land and all the expensive art supplies Smith had promised meant nothing if he was dead.

Turn around, his inner voice urged, eroding the little sanity left to him. *Return to the boat, get out of this arrangement. You were mostly happy on Section 19—*

But it was too late for that. The deal had been struck, and he doubted a bureaucrat like Smith, a man who made business deals signed for in blood, would allow him to exit their agreement. And what of Maggie? On Zamboanga, she had a chance. On Lost Hope, she was doomed. There was no going back unless he first went forward.

Arthur ceased rowing. Fog billowed around him, making it impossible to glean his surroundings beyond ten or so meters. Neither of Lango's two moons broke the darkness imposed by the clouds. Three kilometers from land might as well have been three hundred or thousand. Three million.

The cadence of waves and ocean his mind had registered since leaving the Guild gunboat broke with an unfamiliar sound. Arthur waited, breath held, and listened. It came again, a furtive trickle of water being displaced. His heart attempted to jump out of his ribcage and into his throat. Once more, the sound reached him. He focused into the darkness, in the direction he believed it originated. Nothing.

Arthur tried to sell himself that it was an illusion, a phantasm. The noise sounded a fourth time, from a different location. He turned, and riding above the water was an outcrop of dark land perhaps twice the size of the raft. There one moment, it was gone the next, submerged beneath the waves. Fresh panic surged through his insides. A sea creature—and, judging from the differing locations, more than one. A whole school. A multitude of undersea giants!

He clamped his mouth shut to trap the scream and resumed rowing, faster and faster, no longer caring if he traveled in a southeasterly direction. It would only take one of the lurking predators, now aware that a tasty meal of human flesh was cutting the surface, to capsize the raft. Then they would feed in a bloody frenzy.

Arthur sensed them down there, swimming beneath the raft and oars. But he never spilled out of his only protection against the ocean, and the feeding frenzy never claimed him, and, at one point, he saw through wide eyes the shimmer of something metallic on the horizon.

LANGO'S DAWN BROKE overcast. The rain had stopped and the clouds thinned enough to show bands of blue among the gray.

The jagged island rose up from the waves directly ahead. Half mad with exhaustion and fear, his muscles aching almost to paralysis, Arthur rowed. The worry that, at any second, a particle beam might lash out and vaporize him fell into the background of his immediate thoughts as the day brightened and he drew nearer to the island. Smith and Robley were right. There was nothing on him or the raft to trigger the alien defensive grid.

He rowed, hungry but unable to consider the rations of food and fresh water sent along for the voyage. There'd be plenty of time for refreshments once he saw all and returned to the Guild gunboat to begin his documentation in paint on canvas. Now, a kind of sharpness washed over him. He grew focused. He was ready. It was time to observe and record without distraction.

On first glance, the island was a lifeless outcrop of time-smoothed rock. On closer examination from the shore, that judgment proved false. The boulders beneath the surface were coated in frilled green vegetation, and when he pulled up enough to vacate the raft, a dozen slender creatures that might or might not have had legs scurried away between the rocks.

Arthur dragged the raft out of the water, shook off, and straightened. Turning, he faced the direction of the curiosity that had brought him so far from all that was familiar and willed his legs into motion over the island's hardscrabble surface.

A low wind moaned in a spirit's voice. Arthur ambled over a rise, crossed through clefts in the rock, and emerged for his first clear look at the derelict. He knew instantly that it wasn't Guild or from any of their human rivals. The shape appeared asymmetrical, though it was difficult to be certain given that half of the spaceship was submerged. What he could glean was trapezoidal, with a rounded command module aimed into the ocean and numerous interlocked squares at the aft section deteriorating on land.

Engines, Arthur thought.

Of course, that was applying human design principles to a spaceship constructed by unknown, alien hands. Or limbs that lacked hands in the known definition. It was possible that the forward section was engine, the rear cockpit. Or that none of it matched his assumptions.

Arthur recorded the shape, the colors, and, when close enough, the textures, risking a touch of the external superstructure. None of those worst-case scenarios he'd imagined happened following contact. The hull felt more ceramic than metallic. He rounded the giant to starboard, where impact had opened up the interior to the elements.

A shiver teased the fine hairs on the nape of Arthur's neck. He fought its caresses, failed. The chill tumbled. The same level of fear he'd suffered throughout the long night spent on the ocean embraced him. The vast, dark interior loomed ahead, and though he didn't want to enter the derelict spaceship, he knew he must. Seconds dragged past with the weight of minutes, hours.

Arthur stared. The darkness inside the hulled spacecraft evaporated, his eyes adjusting to the rising of Lango's sun behind a thin filter of dissipating storm clouds. Ahead and above him, the ship's rib bones defined the cavernous interior, curiously empty of rooms, machinery, and the expected. The only other details were a pattern of grooves along the walls. These seemed purposeful, not a result of the elements. He committed their loops and dips to memory, along with the pallid metallic color of the wall's surface.

The wind gusted past him and into the exposed belly of the crashed giant, creating a haunting resonance. Far ahead, toward the area he assumed to be the fore, the section sitting in water, he detected a faint glow. Arthur entered the derelict and pressed forward. The breeze pursued, gossiping in its counterfeit human whisper. The hollow cadence of his footsteps across the detritus blown through the gap between rib bones waned, replaced by the steady clomp of new soles over ancient metal floors. Deeper, deeper still, he pressed.

The cavernous ceiling steadily narrowed toward his destination. Throughout, Arthur took mental snapshots, recording colors, textures, dimensions. At one point, he realized he was operating on automatic, his terror sitting icy over his flesh, his eyes sore from wideness and not blinking. On that final leg of his journey toward the glow in the distance, his mind played a little game to keep from snapping. *What color will I use for the walls? Platinum? Perhaps a dark gun metal for the grooves. Oh, yes, a jonquil-yellow for that light up ahead. Given his wardrobe choices, Smith will appreciate that.*

Art again saved him as he reached the doors.

They had to be doors, given their shape and location. The glow came from a fixture inset in the platinum wall beside the fenestration, one with three grooves. Arthur peered at the details until his eyes burned. Three grooves, each seemingly made for the insertion of a single finger. He willed the three middle digits of his right hand into the proper pattern and extended them into the grooves. A mechanical note blared around him, gonging and heavy at first. He attempted to pull out his fingers but the fixture held on. The gong sped up. The wall moved inward, releasing his flesh. The fenestration irised open, expelling a noxious cloud of bottled air.

Arthur turned away and covered his nose. Breathing through his fingers, he faced the interior of the cockpit. All of the mechanisms missing from the vast torso of the derelict spaceship were here, in pristine condition. The technology rose in trellises around the oval expanse that soared up to a ceiling where more systems were housed. Circular portholes showed the ocean outside—he had traveled into the submerged fore of the ship and now stood untold meters from the barren island, under the sea.

Here, the hum of an undercurrent tickled his sweaty skin and made the hair on his arms stand. One of these instrumentation trellises controlled the automated defenses responsible for shooting down Guild intruders. He wandered among the rises, eyes going to the portholes, the curves, the lights, taking in all for future depiction on paper and canvas. At first, he was so absorbed with the task that he didn't see the body, or recognize it as such, until the odor of decay alerted him to the truth.

Arthur froze.

The corpse, what was left of it, was a shrunken, desiccated mass attached to one of the instrumentation trellises. He couldn't tell what was organic from clothing. Both had blended together in the creature's decay. Its elongated face was skin stretched over bone, the sockets mostly empty, the skull longer, thinner than that of a human. It clutched at the trellis with a three-fingered hand, beside which another of those fixtures glowed.

Arthur reached shaking fingers toward the device. After inserting them, the trellises' system activated. Lights lit, and, standing before him, was an elegant, blue-skinned creature whose hands each bore three fingers.

HE ROWED.

And rowed.

Eventually, the Guild gunboat appeared ahead of him, gray on the horizon.

ROBLEY AND ANOTHER CREWMAN helped him up the last stretch of the metal ladder and onto the deck. Smith stood under his yellow umbrella, that snarl-smile displayed.

"Well, *well?*"

Arthur flashed a grin of his own. "I've been there and have returned. I'd like to begin while it's still fresh."

"Of course," Smith said.

They led him to a cabin aboard the gunboat outfitted with art supplies, more than he'd ever seen or dreamed of during his life on Section 19. Fine papers and canvasses were neatly arranged in abundance beside an easel and chair. A kaleidoscope of paints lined shelves, along with clean palettes and other supplies.

"What can you tell us?" Smith persisted.

"Give me some time and I can show you."

Reluctantly, Smith left him to work. Despite his exhaustion, Arthur selected his first canvas and colors and began to paint.

DRAWING FROM MEMORY, he recreated the view of the alien ship first glimpsed from the cleft in the rocks, then used pen and ink to detail the view from its gutted starboard side. He painted the interior with its whirls and cavernous darkness, and the door, first closed, then irised open following his connection to the mechanism.

He painted until they reached Zamboanga where, like Maggie, Arthur fell into the deepest sleep.

IN HIS DREAMS, Arthur returned to the alien ship. He stood beside the trellis, three fingers within the glowing detail. A sense of purpose rushed through him—desperation mixed with relief. He knew the emotion wasn't his but belonged to the dead alien.

Then the alien stood before him. Not the real alien pilot but its specter, captured in photons. The ship had remembered its captain as Arthur had been tasked to remember the ship, drawing the alien in holographic brushstrokes.

Why we came here, the alien said, not with his mouth but through words that registered in Arthur's mind.

Images passed between them in that blurry sum of seconds. A humanitarian crisis. A thirsty desert planet, desperate for water. An alien race that had gone to war over ownership rights, as had happened centuries later here, with the Manifest Guild and its rivals in the skies over Lango.

Arthur woke, unsure where he was at first. The late afternoon light spilling down through the leaves of the fruit trees outside the small house reestablished his location. Saying nothing, he got out of his new bed in Smith's villa and padded into the makeshift artist's studio that now contained the finest of art supplies.

He picked up the sketchpad and charcoal pencil. Arthur drew other details from the interior of the cockpit that came as clearly to him on Zamboanga as at the downed alien ship.

They came to quench the desert planet's thirst, Maggie, Arthur thought.

Whirls appeared on the blank page, some looping into figure eights.

That ship ... it would have completed a connection had it not been shot down. A connection between Lango and the desert world.

Opened a rift. Gave them the water so desperately needed. Only—

The tip of his pencil stilled, clutched between three fingers. He closed his hand. Arthur hesitated, aware of the sough of the wind around the little house and the up-tempo beat of his heart. He traveled back to the derelict and stood with his fingers on the device. The ship pulsed like his heart. He sensed the lingering relief from the dead alien's essence still contained within the ship's mechanism. Once inserted into the fixture, a clockwise turn at long last activated the system. The ship's other functions powered up.

The filters and pumping technology in the prow began to extract, the whirls to transport through space-folding generator tech. A thousand gallons every second. One tenth of Lango's water was headed for the desert planet through the derelict's pumps.

The operation would take years. Still...

Maggie, Arthur thought and resumed sketching, *before long, there will be plenty of dry land rising out of the sea for the citizens of Lost Hope and those other floating cities to claim as their own.*

👽 👽 👽

"The Pilgrimage" debuts in this issue of Black Infinity.

*Raised on a healthy diet of creature double features and classic SF television, Gregory L. Norris is a full-time professional writer, with work appearing in numerous short story anthologies, national magazines, novels, the occasional TV episode, and, so far, one produced feature film (*Brutal Colors, *which debuted on Amazon Prime, January 2016). A former feature writer and columnist at Sci Fi, the official magazine of the Sci Fi Channel (before all those ridiculous Ys invaded), he once worked as a screenwriter on two episodes of Paramount's modern classic,* Star Trek: Voyager. *Two of his paranormal novels (written under his nom-de-plume, Jo Atkinson) were published by Home Shopping Network as part of their "Escape with Romance" line—the first time HSN has offered novels to their global customer base. He judged the 2012 Lambda Awards in the SF/F/H category. Three times now, his stories have notched Honorable Mentions in Ellen Datlow's Best-of books. In May 2016, he traveled to Hollywood to accept HM in the Roswell Awards in Short SF Writing. Follow Norris' literary adventures at www.gregorylnorris.blogspot.com*

STILL AVAILABLE!

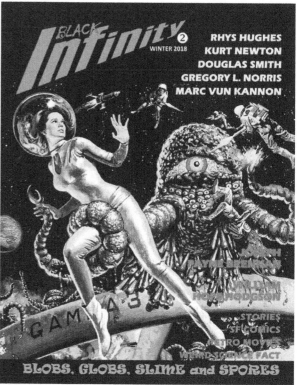

PURCHASE ONLINE AT AMAZON OR BN.COM
—OR ORDER THROUGH YOUR LOCAL BOOKSTORE.

Strange science, weird worlds, hostile aliens, renegade robots ... and the cold vacuum of space.

200 oversized pages packed with exciting stories and art by some of the best writers of yesterday, today and tomorrow. Each issue features fiction, science, comics and retro movie reviews, all focusing on a different fun topic familiar to fans of SF in both print and celluloid.

Black Infinity: Deadly Planets (#1): Fiction by award-winning authors Douglas Smith, Simon Strantzas, and others; a classic comic story by Jack Kirby; plus, science and retro movie reviews—all celebrating one of the darker sides of SF: the often-deadly exploration of alien and hostile worlds! • ISBN: 978-0996693677

Black Infinity: Blobs, Globs, Slime and Spores (#2): New fiction by Rhys Hughes, Gregory L. Norris, Marc Vun Kannon, and more; classic tales by William Hope Hodgson and Joseph Payne Brennan; an overview of blobs, slime and spores in the entertainment media; weird science, a creepy SF comic and more! • ISBN: 978-0996693684

DERELICT

by Alan Edward Nourse

JOHN SABO, SECOND IN COMMAND, SAT BOLT UPRIGHT IN HIS BUNK, BLINKING WIDE-EYED AT THE DARKNESS. The alarm was screaming through the Satellite Station, its harsh, nerve-jarring clang echoing and re-echoing down the metal corridors, penetrating every nook and crevice and cubicle of the lonely outpost, screaming incredibly through the dark sleeping period. Sabo shook the sleep from his eyes, and then a panic of fear burst into his mind. The alarm! Tumbling out of his bunk in the darkness, he crashed into the far bulkhead, staggering giddily in the impossible gravity as he pawed about for his magnaboots, his heart pounding fiercely in his ears. The *alarm!* Impossible, after so long, after these long months of bitter waiting— In the corridor he collided with Brownie, looking like a frightened gnome, and he growled profanity as he raced down the corridor for the Central Control.

Frightened eyes turned to him as he blinked at the bright lights of the room. The voices rose in a confused, anxious babble, and he shook his head and swore, and ploughed through them toward the screen. "Kill that damned alarm!" he roared, blinking as he counted faces. "Somebody get the Skipper out of his sack, pronto, and stop that clatter! What's the trouble?"

The radioman waved feebly at the view screen, shimmering on the great side panel. "We just picked it up—"

It was a ship, moving in from beyond Saturn's rings, a huge, gray-black blob in the silvery screen, moving in toward the Station with ponderous, clumsy grace, growing larger by the second as it sped toward them. Sabo felt the fear spill over in his mind, driving out all thought, and he sank into the control chair like a well-trained automaton. His gray eyes were wide, trained for long military years to miss nothing; his fingers moved over the panel with deft skill. "Get the men to stations," he growled, "and will somebody kindly get the Skipper down here, if he can manage

to take a minute."

"I'm right here." The little graying man was at his elbow, staring at the screen with angry red eyes. "Who told you to shut off the alarm?"

"Nobody told me. Everyone was here, and it was getting on my nerves."

"What a shame." Captain Loomis' voice was icy. "I give orders on this Station," he said smoothly, "and you'll remember it." He scowled at the great gray ship, looming closer and closer. "What's its course?"

"Going to miss us by several thousand kilos at least. Look at that thing! It's *traveling.*"

"Contact it! This is what we've been waiting for." The captain's voice was hoarse.

Sabo spun a dial, and cursed. "No luck. Can't get through. It's passing us—"

"Then *grapple* it, stupid! You want me to wipe your nose, too?"

Sabo's face darkened angrily. With slow precision he set the servo fixes on the huge gray hulk looming up in the viewer, and then snapped the switches sharply. Two small servos shoved their blunt noses from the landing port of the Station, and slipped silently into space alongside. Then, like a pair of trained dogs, they sped on their beams straight out from the Station toward the approaching ship. The intruder was dark, moving at tremendous velocity past the Station, as though unaware of its existence. The servos moved out, and suddenly diverged and reversed, twisting in long arcs to come alongside the strange ship, finally moving in at the same velocity on either side. There was a sharp flash of contact power; then, like a mammoth slow-motion monster, the ship jerked in mid-space and turned a graceful end-for-end arc as the servo-grapplers gripped it like leeches and whined, glowing ruddy with the jolting power flowing through them. Sabo watched, hardly breathing, until the great ship spun and slowed and stopped. Then it reversed direction, and the servos led it triumphantly back toward the landing port of the Station.

Sabo glanced at the radioman, a frown creasing his forehead. "Still nothing?"

"Not a peep."

He stared out at the great ship, feeling a chill of wonder and fear crawl up his spine. "So this is the mysterious puzzle of Saturn," he muttered. "This is what we've been waiting for."

There was a curious eager light in Captain Loomis' eyes as he looked up. "Oh, no. Not this."

"What?"

"Not this. The ships we've seen before were tiny, flat." His little eyes turned toward the ship, and back to Sabo's heavy face. "This is something else, something quite different." A smile curved his lips, and he rubbed his hands together. "We go out for trout and come back with a whale. This ship's from space, deep space. Not from Saturn. This one's from the stars."

THE STRANGE SHIP HUNG at the side of the Satellite Station, silent as a tomb, still gently rotating as the Station slowly spun in its orbit around Saturn.

In the captain's cabin the men shifted restlessly, uneasily facing the eager eyes of their captain. The old man paced the floor of the cabin, his white hair mussed, his face red with excitement. Even his carefully calm face couldn't conceal the eagerness burning in his eyes as he faced the crew. "Still no contact?" he asked Sparks.

The radioman shook his head anxiously. "Not a sign. I've tried every signal I know at every wave frequency that could possibly reach them. I've even tried a dozen frequencies that couldn't possibly reach them, and I haven't stirred them up a bit. They just aren't answering."

Captain Loomis swung on the group of men. "All right, now, I want you to get this straight. This is our catch. We don't know what's aboard it, and we don't know where it came from, but it's our prize. That means not a word goes back home about it until we've learned all there is to learn. We're going to get the honors on this one, not some eager Admiral back home—"

The men stirred uneasily, worried eyes seeking Sabo's face in alarm. "What about the law?" growled Sabo. "The law says everything must be reported within two hours."

"Then we'll break the law," Loomis snapped. "I'm captain of this Station, and those are your orders. You don't need to worry about the law—I'll see that you're protected, but this is too big to fumble. This ship is from the stars. That means it must have an Interstellar drive. You know what that means. The Government will fall all over itself to reward us—"

Sabo scowled, and the worry deepened in the men's faces. It was hard to imagine the Government falling all over itself for anybody. They knew too well how the Government worked. They had heard of the swift trials, the harsh imprisonments that awaited even the petty infringers. The Military Government had no time to waste on those who stepped out of line, they had no mercy to spare. And the men knew that their captain was not in favor in top Government circles. Crack patrol commanders were not shunted into remote, lifeless Satellite Stations if their stand in the Government was high. And deep in their minds, somehow, the men knew they couldn't trust this little, sharp-eyed, white-haired man. The credit for such a discovery as this might go to him, yes—but there would be little left for them.

"The law—" Sabo repeated stubbornly.

"Damn the law! We're stationed out here in this limbo to watch Saturn and report any activity we see coming from there. There's nothing in our orders about anything else. There have been ships from there, they think, but not this ship. The Government has spent billions trying to find an Interstellar, and never gotten to first base." The captain paused, his eyes narrowing. "We'll go aboard this ship," he said softly. "We'll find out what's aboard it, and where it's from, and we'll take its drive. There's been no resistance yet, but it could be dangerous. We can't assume anything. The boarding party will report everything they find to me. One of them will have to be a drive man. That's you, Brownie."

The little man with the sharp black eyes looked up eagerly. "I don't know if I could tell anything—"

"You can tell more than anyone else here. Nobody else knows space drive. I'll count on you. If you bring back a good report, perhaps we can cancel out certain—unfortunate items in your record. But one other should board with you—" His eyes turned toward John Sabo.

"Not me. This is your goat." The mate's eyes were sullen. "This is gross breach, and you know it. They'll have you in irons when we get back. I don't want anything to do with it."

"You're under orders, Sabo. You keep forgetting."

"They're illegal orders, sir!"

"I'll take responsibility for that."

Sabo looked the old man straight in the eye. "You mean you'd sell us down a rat hole to save your skin. That's what you mean."

Captain Loomis' eyes widened incredulously. Then his face darkened, and he stepped very close to the big man. "You'll watch your tongue, I think," he gritted. "Be careful what you say to me, Sabo. Be very careful. Because if you don't, *you'll* be in irons, and we'll see just how long you last when you get back home. Now you've got your orders. You'll board the ship with Brownie."

The big man's fists were clenched until the knuckles were white. "You don't know what's over there!" he burst out. "We could be slaughtered."

The captain's smile was unpleasant. "That would be such a pity," he murmured. "I'd really hate to see it happen—"

THE SHIP HUNG DARK and silent, like a shadowy ghost. No flicker of light could be seen aboard it; no sound nor faintest sign of life came from the tall, dark hull plates. It hung there, huge and imponderable, and swung around with the Station in its silent orbit.

The men huddled about Sabo and Brownie, helping them into their pressure suits, checking their equipment. They had watched the little scanning beetles crawl over the surface of the great ship, examining, probing every nook and crevice, reporting crystals, and metals, and irons, while the boarding party prepared. And still the radio-man waited alertly for a flicker of life from the solemn giant.

Frightened as they were of their part in the illegal secrecy, the arrival of the ship had brought a change in the crew, lighting fires of excitement in their eyes. They moved faster, their voices were lighter, more cheerful. Long months on the Station had worn on their nerves—out of contact with their homes, on a mission that was secretly jeered as utter Governmental folly. Ships *had* been seen, years before, disappearing into the sullen bright atmospheric crust of Saturn, but there had been no sign of anything since. And out there, on the lonely guard Station, nerves had run ragged, always waiting, always watching, wearing away even the iron discipline of their military background. They grew bitterly weary of the same faces, the same routine, the constant repetition of inactivity. And through the months they had watched with increasing anxiety the conflict growing between the captain and his sullen-eyed second-in-command, John Sabo.

And then the ship had come, incredibly, from the depths of space, and the tensions of loneliness were forgotten in the flurry of activity. The locks whined and opened as the two men moved out of the Station on the little propulsion sleds, linked to the Station with light silk guy ropes. Sabo settled himself on the sled, cursing himself for falling so foolishly into the captain's scheme, cursing his tongue for wandering. And deep within him he felt a new sensation, a vague uneasiness and insecurity that he had not felt in all his years of military life. The strange ship was a variant, an imponderable factor thrown suddenly into his small world of hatred and bitterness, forcing him into unknown territory, throwing his mind into a welter of doubts and fears. He glanced uneasily across at Brownie, vaguely wishing that someone else were with him. Brownie was a troublemaker, Brownie talked too much, Brownie philosophized in a world that ridiculed philosophy. He'd known men like Brownie before, and he knew that they couldn't be trusted.

The gray hull gleamed at them as they moved toward it, a monstrous wall of polished metal. There were no dents, no surface scars from its passage through space. They found the entrance lock without difficulty, near the top of the ship's great hull, and Brownie probed the rim of the lock with a dozen instruments, his dark eyes burning eagerly. And then, with a squeal that grated in Sabo's ears, the oval port of the ship quivered, and slowly opened.

Silently, the sleds moved into the opening.

They were in a small vault, quite dark, and the sleds settled slowly onto a metal deck. Sabo eased himself from the seat, tuning up his audios to their highest sensitivity, moving over to Brownie. Momentarily they touched helmets, and Brownie's excited voice came to him, muted, but breathless. "No trouble getting it open. It worked on the same principle as ours."

"Better get to work on the inner lock."

Brownie shot him a sharp glance. "But what about—inside? I mean, we can't just walk in on them—"

"Why not? We've tried to contact them."

Reluctantly, the little engineer began probing the inner lock with trembling fingers. Minutes later they were easing themselves through, moving slowly down the dark corridor, waiting with pounding hearts for a sound, a sign. The corridor joined another, and then still another, until they reached a great oval door. And then they were inside, in the heart of the ship, and their eyes widened as they stared at the thing in the center of the great vaulted chamber.

"My God!" Brownie's voice was a hoarse whisper in the stillness. "Look at them, Johnny!"

Sabo moved slowly across the room toward the frail, crushed form lying against the great, gleaming panel. Thin, almost boneless arms were pasted against the hard metal; an oval, humanoid skull was crushed like an eggshell into the knobs and levers of the control panel. Sudden horror shot through the big man as he looked around. At the far side of the room was another of the things, and still another, mashed, like lifeless jelly, into the floors and panels. Gently he peeled a bit of jelly away from the metal, then turned with a mixture of wonder and disgust. "All dead," he muttered.

Brownie looked up at him, his hands trembling. "No wonder there was no sign." He looked about helplessly. "It's a derelict, Johnny. A wanderer. How could it have happened? How long ago?"

Sabo shook his head, bewildered. "Then it was just chance that it came to us, that we saw it—"

"No pilot, no charts. It might have wandered for centuries." Brownie stared about the room, a frightened look on his face. And then he was leaning over the control panel, probing at the array of levers, his fingers working eagerly at the wiring. Sabo nodded approvingly. "We'll have to go over it with a comb," he said. "I'll see what I can find in the rest of the ship. You go ahead on the controls and drive." Without waiting for an answer he moved swiftly from the round chamber, out into the corridor again, his stomach almost sick.

It took them many hours. They moved silently, as if even a slight sound might disturb the sleeping alien forms, smashed against the dark metal panels. In another room were the charts, great, beautiful charts, totally unfamiliar, studded with star formations he had never seen, noted with curious, meaningless symbols. As Sabo worked he heard Brownie moving down into the depths of the ship, toward the giant engine rooms. And then, some silent alarm clicked into place in Sabo's mind, tightening his stomach, screaming to

be heard. Heart pounding, he dashed down the corridor like a cat, seeing again in his mind the bright, eager eyes of the engineer. Suddenly the meaning of that eagerness dawned on him. He scampered down a ladder, along a corridor, and down another ladder, down to the engine room, almost colliding with Brownie as he crossed from one of the engines to a battery of generators on the far side of the room.

"Brownie!"

"What's the trouble?"

Sabo trembled, then turned away. "Nothing," he muttered. "Just a thought." But he watched as the little man snaked into the labyrinth of dynamos and coils and wires, peering eagerly, probing, searching, making notes in the little pad in his hand.

Finally, hours later, they moved again toward the lock where they had left their sleds. Not a word passed between them. The uneasiness was strong in Sabo's mind now, growing deeper, mingling with fear and a premonition of impending evil. A dead ship, a derelict, come to them by merest chance from some unthinkably remote star. He cursed, without knowing why, and suddenly he felt he hated Brownie as much as he hated the captain waiting for them in the Station.

But as he stepped into the Station's lock, a new thought crossed his mind, almost dazzling him with its unexpectedness. He looked at the engineer's thin face, and his hands were trembling as he opened the pressure suit.

HE DELIBERATELY TOOK LONGER than was necessary to give his report to the captain, dwelling on unimportant details, watching with malicious amusement the captain's growing annoyance. Captain Loomis' eyes kept sliding to Brownie, as though trying to read the information he wanted from the engineer's face.

Sabo rolled up the charts slowly, stowing them in a pile on the desk. "That's the picture, sir. Perhaps a qualified astronomer could make something of it; I haven't the knowledge or the instruments. The ship came from outside the system, beyond doubt. Probably from a planet with lighter gravity than our own, judging from the frailty of the creatures. Oxygen breathers, from the looks of their gas storage. If you ask me, I'd say—"

"All right, all right," the captain breathed impatiently. "You can write it up and hand it to me. It isn't really important where they came from, or whether they breathe oxygen or fluorine." He turned his eyes to the engineer, and lit a cigar with trembling fingers. "The important thing is *how* they got here. The drive, Brownie. You went over the engines carefully? What did you find?"

Brownie twitched uneasily, and looked at the floor. "Oh, yes, I examined them carefully. Wasn't too hard. I examined every piece of drive machinery on the ship, from stem to stern."

Sabo nodded, slowly, watching the little man with a carefully blank face. "That's right. You gave it a good going over."

Brownie licked his lips. "It's a derelict, like Johnny told you. They were dead. All of them. Probably had been dead for a long time. I couldn't tell, of course. Probably nobody could tell. But they must have been dead for centuries—"

The captain's eyes blinked as the implication sank in. "Wait a minute," he said. "What do you mean, *centuries*?"

Brownie stared at his shoes. "The atomic piles were almost dead," he muttered in an apologetic whine. "The ship wasn't going any place, captain. It was just wandering. Maybe it's wandered for thousands of years." He took a deep breath, and his eyes met the captain's for a brief agonized moment. "They don't have Interstellar, sir. Just plain, simple, slow atomics. Nothing different. They've been traveling for centuries, and it would have taken them just as long to get back."

The captain's voice was thin, choked. "Are you trying to tell me that their drive is no different from our own? That a ship has actually wandered into Interstellar space *without a space drive*?"

Brownie spread his hands helplessly. "Something must have gone wrong. They must have started off for another planet in their own system, and something went wrong. They broke into space, and they all died. And the ship just went on moving. They never intended an Interstellar hop. They couldn't have. They didn't have the drive for it."

The captain sat back numbly, his face pasty gray. The light had faded in his eyes now; he sat as though he'd been struck. "You—you couldn't be wrong? You couldn't have missed anything?"

Brownie's eyes shifted unhappily, and his voice was very faint. "No, sir."

The captain stared at them for a long moment, like a stricken child. Slowly he picked up one of the charts, his mouth working. Then, with a bitter roar, he threw it in Sabo's face. "Get out of here! Take this garbage and get out! And get the men to their stations. We're here to watch Saturn, and by god, we'll watch Saturn!" He turned away, a hand over his eyes, and they heard his choking breath as they left the cabin.

Slowly, Brownie walked out into the corridor, started down toward his cabin, with Sabo silent at his heels. He looked up once at the mate's heavy face, a look of pleading in his dark brown eyes, and then opened the door to his quarters. Like a cat, Sabo was in the room before him, dragging him in, slamming the door. He caught the little man by the neck with one savage hand, and shoved him unceremoniously against the door, his voice a vicious whisper. "All right, *talk!* Let's have it *now!*"

Brownie choked, his eyes bulging, his face turning gray in the dim light of the cabin. "Johnny! Let me down! What's the matter? You're choking me, Johnny—"

The mate's eyes were red, with heavy lines of disgust and bitterness running from his eyes and the corners of his mouth. "You stinking little liar! *Talk*, damn it! You're not messing with the captain now, you're messing with me, and I'll have the truth if I have to cave in your skull—"

"I told you the truth! I don't know what you mean—"

Sabo's palm smashed into his face, jerking his head about like an apple on a string. "That's the wrong answer," he grated. "I warn you, don't lie! The captain is an ambitious ass, he couldn't think his way through a multiplication table. He's a little child. But I'm not quite so dull." He threw the little man down in a heap, his eyes blazing. "You silly fool, your story is so full of holes you could drive a tank through it. They just up and died, did they? I'm supposed to believe that? Smashed up against the panels the way they were? Only one thing could crush them like that. Any fool could see it. Acceleration. And I don't mean atomic acceleration. Something else." He glared down at the man quivering on the floor. "They had Interstellar drive, didn't they, Brownie?"

Brownie nodded his head, weakly, almost sobbing, trying to pull himself erect. "Don't tell the captain," he sobbed. "Oh, Johnny, for god's sake, listen to me, don't let him know I lied. I was going to tell you anyway, Johnny, really I was. I've got a plan, a good plan, can't you see it?" The gleam of excitement came back into the sharp little eyes. "They had it, all right. Their trip probably took just a few months. They had a drive I've never seen before, non-atomic. I couldn't tell the principle, with the look I had, but I think I could work it." He sat up, his whole body trembling. "Don't give me away, Johnny, listen a minute—"

Sabo sat back against the bunk, staring at the little man. "You're out of your mind," he said softly. "You don't know what you're doing. What are you going to do when His Nibs goes over for a look himself? He's stupid, but not that stupid."

Brownie's voice choked, his words tumbling over each other in his eagerness. "He won't get a chance to see it, Johnny. He's got to take our word until he sees it, and we can stall him—"

Sabo blinked. "A day or so—maybe. But what then? Oh, how could you be so stupid? He's on the skids, he's out of favor and fighting for his life. That drive is the break that could put him on top. Can't you see he's selfish? He has to be, in this world, to get anything. Anything or anyone who blocks him, he'll destroy, if he can. Can't you see that? When he spots this, your life won't be worth spitting at."

Brownie was trembling as he sat down opposite the big man. His voice was harsh in the little cubicle, heavy with pain and hopelessness. "That's right," he said. "My life isn't worth a nickel. Neither is yours. Neither is anybody's, here or back home. Nobody's life is worth a nickel. Something's happened to us in the past hundred years, Johnny— something horrible. I've seen it creeping and growing up around us all my life. People don't matter any more, it's the Government, what the Government thinks that matters. It's a web, a cancer that grows in its own pattern, until it goes so far it can't be stopped. Men like Loomis could see the pattern, and adapt to it, throw away all the worthwhile things, the love and beauty and peace that we once had in our lives. Those men can get somewhere, they can turn this life into a climbing game, waiting their chance to get a little farther toward the top, a little closer to some semblance of security—"

"Everybody adapts to it," Sabo snapped. "They have to. You don't see me moving for anyone else, do you? I'm for *me*, and believe me I know it. I don't give a hang for you, or Loomis, or anyone else alive—just me. I want to stay alive, that's all. You're a dreamer, Brownie. But until you pull something like this, you can learn to stop dreaming if you want to—"

"No, no, you're wrong—oh, you're horribly

wrong, Johnny. Some of us *can't* adapt, we haven't got what it takes, or else we have something else in us that won't let us go along. And right there we're beat before we start. There's no place for us now, and there never will be." He looked up at the mate's impassive face. "We're in a life where we don't belong, impounded into a senseless, never-ending series of fights and skirmishes and long, lonely waits, feeding this insane urge of the Government to expand, out to the planets, to the stars, farther and farther, bigger and bigger. We've got to go, seeking newer and greater worlds to conquer, with nothing to conquer them with, and nothing to conquer them for. There's life somewhere else in our solar system, so it must be sought out and conquered, no matter what or where it is. We live in a world of iron and fear, and there was no place for me, and others like me, *until this ship came—*"

Sabo looked at him strangely. "So I was right. I read it on your face when we were searching the ship. I knew what you were thinking...." His face darkened angrily. "You couldn't get away with it, Brownie. Where could you go, what could you expect to find? You're talking death, Brownie. Nothing else—"

"No, no. Listen, Johnny." Brownie leaned closer, his eyes bright and intent on the man's heavy face. "The captain has to take our word for it, until he sees the ship. Even then he couldn't tell for sure—I'm the only drive engineer on the Station. We have the charts, we could work with them, try to find out where the ship came from; I already have an idea of how the drive is operated. Another look and I could make it work. Think of it, Johnny! What difference does it make where we went, or what we found? You're a misfit, too, you know that—this coarseness and bitterness is a shell, if you could only see it, a sham. You don't really believe in this world we're in—who cares where, if only we could go, get away? Oh, it's a chance, the wildest, freak chance, but we could take it—"

"If only to get away from *him*," said Sabo

in a muted voice. "Lord, how I hate him. I've seen smallness and ambition before—pettiness and treachery, plenty of it. But that man is our whole world knotted up in one little ball. I don't think I'd get home without killing him, just to stop that voice from talking, just to see fear cross his face one time. But if we took the ship, it would break him for good." A new light appeared in the big man's eyes. "He'd be through, Brownie. Washed up."

"And we'd be *free—*"

Sabo's eyes were sharp. "What about the acceleration? It killed those that came in the ship."

"But they were so frail, so weak. Light brittle bones and soft jelly. Our bodies are stronger, we could stand it."

Sabo sat for a long time, staring at Brownie. His mind was suddenly confused by the scope of the idea, racing in myriad twirling fantasies, parading before his eyes the long, bitter, frustrating years, the hopelessness of his own life, the dull aching feeling he felt deep in his stomach and bones each time he set back down on Earth, to join the teeming throngs of hungry people. He thought of the rows of drab apartments, the thin faces, the hollow, hunted eyes of the people he had seen. He knew that was why he was a soldier—because soldiers ate well, they had time to sleep, they were never allowed long hours to think, and wonder, and grow dull and empty. But he knew his life had been barren. The life of a mindless automaton, moving from place to place, never thinking, never daring to think or speak, hoping only to work without pain each day, and sleep without nightmares.

And then, he thought of the nights in his childhood, when he had lain awake, sweating with fear, as the airships screamed across the dark sky above, bound he never knew where; and then, hearing in the far distance the booming explosion, he had played that horrible little game with himself, seeing how high he could count before he heard the weary, plodding footsteps of the people on the road, moving on to another place. He had known, even as a little boy, that the only safe place was in those bombers, that the place for survival was in the striking armies, and his life had followed the hard-learned pattern, twisting him into the cynical mold of the mercenary soldier, dulling the quick and clever mind, drilling into him the ways and responses of order and obey, stripping him of his heritage of love and humanity. Others less thoughtful had been happier; they had succeeded in forgetting the life they had known before, they had been able to learn easily and well the lessons of the repudiation of the rights of men which had crept like a blight through the world.

But Sabo, too, was a misfit, wrenched into a mold he could not fit. He had sensed it vaguely, never really knowing when or how he had built the shell of toughness and cynicism, but also sensing vaguely that it was built, and that in it he could hide, somehow, and laugh at himself, and his leaders, and the whole world through which he plodded. He had laughed, but there had been long nights, in the narrow darkness of spaceship bunks, when his mind pounded at the shell, screaming out in nightmare, and he had wondered if he had really lost his mind.

His gray eyes narrowed as he looked at Brownie, and he felt his heart pounding in his chest, pounding with a fury that he could no longer deny. "It would have to be fast," he said softly. "Like lightning, tonight, tomorrow—very soon."

"Oh, yes, I know that. But we can do it—"

"Yes," said Sabo, with a hard, bitter glint in his eyes. "Maybe we can."

THE PREPARATION WAS TENSE. For the first time in his life, Sabo knew the meaning of real fear, felt the clinging aura of sudden death in every glance, every word of the men around him. It seemed incredible that the captain didn't notice the brief exchanges with the little engineer, or his own sudden appearances and disappearances about the Station. But

the captain sat in his cabin with angry eyes, snapping answers without even looking up. Still, Sabo knew that the seeds of suspicion lay planted in his mind, ready to burst forth with awful violence at any slight provocation. As he worked, the escape assumed greater and greater proportions in Sabo's mind; he knew with increasing urgency and daring that nothing must stop him. The ship was there, the only bridge away from a life he could no longer endure, and his determination blinded him to caution.

Primarily, he pondered over the charts, while Brownie, growing hourly more nervous, poured his heart into a study of his notes and sketches. A second look at the engines was essential; the excuse he concocted for returning to the ship was recklessly slender, and Sabo spent a grueling five minutes dissuading the captain from accompanying him. But the captain's eyes were dull, and he walked his cabin, sunk in a gloomy, remorseful trance.

The hours passed, and the men saw, in despair, that more precious, dangerous hours would be necessary before the flight could be attempted. And then, abruptly, Sabo got the call to the captain's cabin. He found the old man at his desk, regarding him with cold eyes, and his heart sank. The captain motioned him to a seat, and then sat back, lighting a cigar with painful slowness. "I want you to tell me," he said in a lifeless voice, "exactly what Brownie thinks he's doing."

Sabo went cold. Carefully he kept his eyes on the captain's face. "I guess he's nervous," he said. "He doesn't belong on a Satellite Station. He belongs at home. The place gets on his nerves."

"I didn't like his report."

"I know," said Sabo.

The captain's eyes narrowed. "It was hard to believe. Ships don't just happen out of space. They don't wander out interstellar by accident, either." An unpleasant smile curled his lips. "I'm not telling you anything new. I wouldn't want to accuse Brownie of lying, of course—or you either. But we'll know soon. A patrol craft will be here from the Triton supply base in an hour. I signaled as soon as I had your reports." The smile broadened maliciously. "The patrol craft will have experts aboard. Space drive experts. They'll review your report."

"An hour—"

The captain smiled. "That's what I said. In that hour, you could tell me the truth. I'm not a drive man, I'm an administrator, and organizer and director. You're the technicians. The truth now could save you much unhappiness—in the future."

Sabo stood up heavily. "You've got your information," he said with a bitter laugh. "The patrol craft will confirm it."

The captain's face went a shade grayer. "All right," he said. "Go ahead, laugh. I told you, anyway."

Sabo didn't realize how his hands were trembling until he reached the end of the corridor. In despair he saw the plan crumbling beneath his feet, and with the despair came the cold undercurrent of fear. The patrol would discover them, disclose the hoax. There was no choice left—ready or not, they'd *have* to leave.

Quickly he turned in to the central control room where Brownie was working. He sat down, repeating the captain's news in a soft voice.

"An *hour!* But how can we—"

"We've *got* to. We can't quit now, we're dead if we do."

Brownie's eyes were wide with fear. "But can't we stall them, somehow? Maybe if we turned on the captain—"

"The crew would back him. They wouldn't dare go along with us. We've got to run, nothing else." He took a deep breath. "Can you control the drive?"

Brownie stared at his hands. "I—I think so. I can only try."

"You've got to. It's now or never. Get down to the lock, and I'll get the charts. Get the

sleds ready."

He scooped the charts from his bunk, folded them carefully and bound them swiftly with cord. Then he ran silently down the corridor to the landing port lock. Brownie was already there, in the darkness, closing the last clamps on his pressure suit. Sabo handed him the charts, and began the laborious task of climbing into his own suit, panting in the darkness.

And then the alarm was clanging in his ear, and the lock was flooded with brilliant light. Sabo stopped short, a cry on his lips, staring at the entrance to the control room.

The captain was grinning, a nasty, evil grin, his eyes hard and humorless as he stood there flanked by three crewmen. His hand gripped an ugly power gun tightly. He just stood there, grinning, and his voice was like fire in Sabo's ears. "Too bad," he said softly. "You almost made it, too. Trouble is, two can't keep a secret. Shame, Johnny, a smart fellow like you. I might have expected as much from Brownie, but I thought you had more sense—"

Something snapped in Sabo's mind, then. With a roar, he lunged at the captain's feet, screaming his bitterness and rage and frustration, catching the old man's calves with his powerful shoulders. The captain toppled, and Sabo was fighting for the power gun, straining with all his might to twist the gun from the thin hand, and he heard his voice shouting, *"Run!* Go, Brownie, make it *go!"*

The lock was open, and he saw Brownie's sled nose out into the blackness. The captain choked, his face purple. "Get him! Don't let him get away!"

The lock clanged, and the screens showed the tiny fragile sled jet out from the side of the Station, the small huddled figure clinging to it, heading straight for the open port of the gray ship. "Stop him! The guns, you fools, the guns!"

The alarm still clanged, and the control room was a flurry of activity. Three men snapped down behind the tracer-guns, firing

levers on the war-head servos. Three of them shot out from the Satellite, like deadly bugs, careening through the intervening space, until one of them struck the side of the gray ship, and exploded in purple fury against the impervious hull. And the others nosed into the flame, and passed on through, striking nothing.

Like the blinking of a light, the alien ship had throbbed, and jerked, and was gone.

With a roar the captain brought his fist down on the hard plastic and metal of the control panel, kicked at the sheet of knobs and levers with a heavy foot, his face purple with rage. His whole body shook as he turned on Sabo, his eyes wild. "You let him get away! It was your fault, yours! But *you* won't get away! I've got you, and you'll pay, do you hear that?" He pulled himself up until his face was bare inches from Sabo's, his teeth bared in a frenzy of hatred. "Now we'll see who'll laugh, my friend. You'll laugh in the death chamber, if you can still laugh by then!" He turned to the men around him. "Take him," he snarled. "Lock him in his quarters, and guard him well. And while you're doing it, take a good look at him. See how he laughs now."

without aiming, in a frenzied attempt to catch the fleeing sled. The sled began zig-zagging, twisting wildly as the shells popped on either side of it. The captain twisted away from Sabo's grip with a roar, and threw one of the crewmen to the deck, wrenching the gun controls from his hands. "Get the big ones on the ship! Blast it! If it gets away you'll all pay."

Suddenly the sled popped into the ship's port, and the hatch slowly closed behind it. Raving, the captain turned the gun on the sleek, polished hull plates, pressed the firing

They marched him down to his cabin, stunned, still wondering what had happened. Something had gone in his mind in that second, something that told him that the choice had to be made, instantly. Because he knew, with dull wonder, that in that instant when the lights went on he could have stopped Brownie, could have saved himself. He could have taken for himself a piece of the glory and promotion due to the discoverers of an

Interstellar drive. But he had also known, somehow, in that short instant, that the only hope in the world lay in that one nervous, frightened man, and the ship which could take him away.

And the ship was gone. That meant the captain was through. He'd had his chance, the ship's coming had given him his chance, and he had muffed it. Now he, too, would pay. The Government would not be pleased that such a ship had leaked through his fingers. Captain Loomis was through.

And him? Somehow, it didn't seem to matter any more. He had made a stab at it, he had tried. He just hadn't had the luck. But he knew there was more to that. Something in his mind was singing, some deep feeling of happiness and hope had crept into his mind, and he couldn't worry about himself any more. There was nothing more for him; they had him cold. But deep in his mind he felt a curious satisfaction, transcending any fear and bitterness. Deep in his heart, he knew that *one* man had escaped.

And then he sat back and laughed.

"Derelict" first appeared in the May 1953 issue of If: Worlds of Science Fiction, *illustrated by Ed Emshwiller. Alan Edward Nourse was an American physician and author of nonfiction books about medical science, as well as SF (often focusing on medicine and/or paranormal phenomena in relation to the application of electronics). He initially wrote to help pay for his medical education, but after completing his internship and practicing for five years, Nourse chose to exclusively pursue his writing career. For more fiction by Nourse, be sure to read "Infinite Intruder" and "The Dark Door," in our last issue,* Black Infinity: Strange Dimensions.

(CONTINUED FROM PAGE 8)

This scary first-season episode of Gerry Anderson's 1975 series *Space: 1999* was inspired by the 11th-century legend of Saint George and the Dragon, and is yet another, *excellent* example of the derelict ship theme—undeniably a popular and intriguing staple of SF on film and in print.

Before signing off I wish to thank our readers (and writers) for faithfully supporting *Black Infinity* and helping the magazine to continue and grow. As an expression of our gratitude we've included a free music download with this issue. Readers will find more details about this exclusive selection of music from the popular *Space Adventures* series, prepared especially for *Black Infinity* by electronic musician **Mac of BIOnighT**, within these pages. (Subtle hint: peruse this issue's table of contents.)

Tom English
New Kent, VA

PHOTO CREDITS: left: "Dragon's Domain," *Space: 1999* © ITC Entertainment; page 3 (bottom): *2010: The Year We Make Contact* (1984) © MGM; p. 4: Allen Koszowski; p. 5: Gustave Doré (1887 *Rime* edition); p. 6 (top): "The Thirty-Fathom Grave" and "Death Ship," *The Twilight Zone* © CBS Studios; p. 6 (bottom): "The Mystery of the Lizard Men," *Jonny Quest* © Hanna-Barbera and Warner Bros; p. 7 (top): "Space Seed" and "The Doomday Machine," *Star Trek* © Paramount and CBS Studios; p. 7 (bottom): "The Phantom Strikes," *Voyage to the Bottom of the Sea* © 20th Century Fox; p. 8: "Condemned of Space," *Lost in Space* © 20th Century Fox.

BEHIND THE FIRST YEARS

by Stewart C Baker

FIVE SHORT HOURS TO PLANET-FALL, PETE SAT WATCHING MAGDA DIE. Her hands were thin and wrinkle-fine, the leathern colour of paper five hundred years old. She had been Archivist sixty years before him there in the great, silent bulk of the ship.

"But what am I to do when we land?" he asked. "I have only been Transcriber, Magda. I never—"

"You must look behind the shelf of the first years."

"The shelf of the first years is empty."

"Did I say *on*, foolish man?" Magda tsked. "How can you record history if you do not listen?" Her eyes were as sharp as her voice, clear and precise, honed from the long years of watching her duties entailed.

Pete flushed and bowed his head. "Behind the shelf, Magda. I understand."

How can she possibly die? he thought. Yet the grey-white walls of her quarters were hung with fresh-picked jasmine to hide the stink of it.

"You understand nothing, foolish man. Look at me." And again, kinder, when he did not. "Look at me."

"Yes, Magda."

"What lies behind the shelf of the first years is important, but does not change your duty. You must record all things, as I have. Record and preserve, Peter. In all these lifetimes under space, that has been our calling."

"Record and preserve. Yes, Magda."

He had first spoken the words fifteen years prior, when he became Transcriber. His parents cried during the ceremony, then left him to go back to Bottom. Magda had been old even then, and Pete used to go to bed terrified of finding her dead when he woke, and him still an untrained youth. Now she was going at last.

She coughed once, twice, making no move to clean the deep red flecks from her lips. Her eyes had gone dim.

"Peter," she said, "Peter."

She reached out with one frail hand and he took it: "Yes, Magda."

"You will be building the history of a world. Remember ... the first years."

Pete did not respond: she was gone. He placed her hand back on her stomach and wiped her lips one last time with the damp cloth the ship's doctor had left him. The man waited outside the door, polite and sympathetic.

"I know it's hard, but it may be for the best. The dispersal would have been hard on her."

Pete nodded, not trusting himself to speak, and left the doctor to his work. It was eighteen floors down to the archives, but instead of the express lift he took the stairs. Something Magda had said didn't sit right, but he could not put his finger on it. Walking helped him think.

'Remember the first years' was a strange directive. The people of that time had been content to track their history in transient digital form, with the result that little was left. Pete thought with regret of the few scraps of paper that *had* come down to them. Scrawled inventories, engineer-neat lists of meaningless names. In his darker moments, Pete felt the first people were mocking him, conspiring to erase all knowledge of why they had been sent away, what calamity had befallen Earth.

But what did it matter? Earth was a planet he would never see, and in just over four hours he would be walking the surface of a world untouched by human hands. A place to start anew. Even Magda's death could not entirely remove the thrill of it. She had died well, clear and alert until the last. And it was true the dispersal would have been hard on her.

Dispersal! Soon they would spread across the surface of the unsullied planet, down amidst the mottled green-and-black they had so far seen only on the vid-screens, where it hung in the middle distance between the ship and the system's star.

He came out on the archives level and picked up his pace. He had set up an interview with Captain McAllister-Xo the night before, the first part of his duty. He would not have long to examine the shelf of the first years. He was reaching for the panel to open the ever-dimmed rooms of the archives when he realized.

Under. Magda had said *under* space.

CAPTAINCY WAS IN MCALLISTER-XO'S BONES. His family had guided the ship since the time of the first people—or so it was said. He greeted Pete and spoke to him of approach vectors and automated systems, stopping occasionally to check in with an officer or to type arcane sequences of keys into the mem-pad before him.

In one of these pauses, Pete told him of Magda's death.

"That old witch," the captain said. "I always thought she'd live forever." He paused, coughed, scratched his temple with his middle finger. "Sorry. I know you were close."

"It was her time. But there was something she said before she passed that I thought you might be able to explain."

"Shoot."

"She was talking of the Archivists' Code: record and preserve."

"I've heard it."

"Um, yes. But it was how she described it: 'In all these lifetimes under space, that has been our calling.' She said 'under,' not 'in.' What do you make of that?"

The captain shrugged. "She was old. She was dying. A slip of the tongue, some missed connection between her brain and her lips. What's to make of it?"

The explanation made as much sense as any Pete could think of, but McAllister-Xo had not been there. Magda had been too alert, her voice too clear and strong for the word to be delirium or sickness. He remembered the way she had taken him to task for not listening clearly. There was something to what she had said, he was sure of it.

He thanked the captain and made his way to Bottom. Perhaps popular memory could tell him what high command could not.

BOTTOM, SO CALLED for its location at the lowest part of the ship, was a vast expanse of inspired agro-engineering which doubled as the ship's food supply and as a living space for most of its population. It was as large as the rest of the ship.

The express lift plunged from the light-specked ceiling and sank past moisture sprays and clouds. The rolling green landscape which sped to meet him was the same as he remembered from before he had been taken above to the archives. He could just make out the pale, blue-tinged metal of the inner bulkhead a kilometre or so away. Then the trees rushed up and overhead, and the lift doors hissed open.

The smell of Bottom was earthy and moist, as different from the paper-dry odours of the archives as possible. He strode past farms and villages he knew from his childhood, passing within metres of the homes where his family and friends still lived. But he did not have time for a visit today.

At last, he reached his destination. Old Jadwiga had been ancient when he was still a child and, unlike Magda, had lived the hard life of a Bottom woman. She walked with a cane, bent over and shuffling, and her hands trembled as she invited him to sit. Her eyes were rheumy, and he had to repeat Magda's dying words several times before she understood him.

"Under space, hmmm?"

She sat quiet for a few minutes after that, but Pete waited patiently. As slow as it was, even Old Jadwiga's memory would be faster than trying to find just the right Bottom lore in the archives' massive collection, which filled kilometres of shelving.

Just as Pete began to doubt his assessment, the old woman spoke again:

"I remember ... under the time of Captain Xo, there was a great anger among the people."

"Captain *Xo*?" But that was ridiculous—the last captain of that name had served almost one hundred years ago. Jadwiga couldn't possibly be that old, could she?

"Yes. Yes. People were angry, for the upper deck families took the best crops and we in Bottom had always to make do with their leavings. One year when I was a young girl...."

Jadwiga continued to speak, drawing out story after story of those long-dead and their actions. Pete let her voice fade into the background, half-listening for anything about the ship being 'under' space instead of in it. After an hour, he excused himself and left the old woman to her memories. They were fascinating enough, but of all she had said there were only two things relevant to Magda's words.

First, something he'd forgotten from his childhood: people here took the designation of 'Bottom' with pride. They were liable to refer to any other part of the ship as "above." But Magda had come from an upper deck family, and in any case, she had placed the entire ship under space, not just Bottom.

The second was a children's rhyme, cryptic to the point of uselessness:

Under space and over all,

Ship-bound people standing tall;
When they reach their destination,
They will build a new old nation.

He shook his head as he re-entered the lift. Even the stacks, with their information overload, would likely have given him more than that.

There were only two hours left to landing, and Captain McAllister-Xo expected Pete to make a record of the dispersal. He hoped there would still be time to make it to the shelf of the first years and retrieve whatever Magda had hidden there.

THE STACKS WERE DARK, but Pete did not bother with a light. The shelf of the first years was easy enough to find without looking: it was the only one empty.

He ran his hands over the smooth metal surface, then crouched down, feeling around behind the shelf with one awkward, outstretched arm. There was only open space. He wondered if he had, after all, put too much stock in the words of an old, dying woman.

Then, just as he was standing, giving up, something brushed the tips of his fingers. Something hard, with the texture of rough-spun cloth. He leaned his shoulder into the shelf, extending his arm until the muscles burned, and closed his hand around the item. A book.

Back in the lift, on the way to McAllister-Xo and the ceremony, he brushed dust off the cover and read the title, embossed in the spine: *The Book of the Ship*.

He had expected something grander from the way the book was hidden, and Magda's cryptic promises. He flipped to a random page, hoping it would make the book's purpose clear. It was in one of the old languages: "...extended isolation studies, which have shown the feasibility of interplanetary travel, were first carried out...." Other pages were filled with similar stuff. Exciting as it was from an archival point of view—it was clearly very old—how could any of it be important to him in the days to come?

Perhaps he was misunderstanding the text, he thought. He had never mastered the old languages as Magda had. But he remembered her words as she lay dying. *How can you record if you do not listen?*

The same must be true of reading, of observation in general. He would have to take the time to decipher it, but time was something he did not have—he would have to wait until the dispersal had begun.

McCALLISTER-Xo and a half-dozen officers were crammed into the control room with Pete, the captain going through the schedule one last time before the live broadcast began.

"First Officer Seong, you will say the words to set us on our way. I will then inform the ship about the dispersal order, and the dangers that may await them on the planet."

He had rehearsed these briefly already, his voice terse as he rattled off the items of a list apparently long memorized. The possibility of indigenous flora and fauna, dangerous or benign. Likely meteorological phenomena, dangerous or benign. How to handle riots from the people of Bottom, who were unused to change.

"We touched down three hours ago, ahead of schedule," the captain concluded. "All systems show a planet which matches the specifications from the few remaining scientific records of the first people. Oxygen content and purity is similar to Earth's and the ship's, and our exterior sensors show pressure well within comfort range."

Not for the first time, Pete marvelled at the shipbuilding genius of the first people. He had felt nothing whatsoever during the landing: the ship was silent and still as before. His regret for their missing records intensified, but at least he had the book.

The ceremony made up little more than a scant few words directed at the present, not the future. Vague and visionary things Pete did not bother to remember—the first moments of the dispersal would be infinitely more important, and anyway, an officer with

a vid crew was transmitting it all live to the entire ship.

They filed into the airlock, thick with the dry smell of centuries of stale emptiness. Pete, at the front of the crowd with the captain, watched the dull steel of the outer door. He wished the first people had put in windows—the scenes from the vid display had done little to whet his appetite for the new world. Yet as the door hissed open, he could not help closing his eyes tight, preparing poetic turns of phrase to use later when he wrote the events of this day, their first on the planet, the fruition of all their long labors.

But there was a black void beyond the ship when he did look, the only light a dim yellow which spilled from the airlock and illuminated little save a narrow, steel ledge jutting up against the ship. The vid-screen had shown hills, rock-strewn but wide and gentle. There was a sudden surge as the officers at the back tried to push forward out into the planet. Pete stumbled back, jostling against the press of bodies. He felt more than saw the newly empty space beside him—McCallister-Xo had fallen over the side of the ledge. His hoarse yells echoed down and away, punctuated in jerking thuds until at last all was silent.

That silenced them all, and one of the officers took out a maintenance flash-light. The stark white beam pulled fragments of horror out of the dark: bloody streaks left by the captain's fall on the side of the ship; the hull stretching endlessly down, juxtaposed not against some outcropping of rock or grass but hard, slick steel. Dust and mildewed greens.

Across the ledge was a vast platform, similar in design to the ship itself. The far wall was rough stone and stretched up into darkness beyond the range of their vision; set into it were two massive steel doors, the words *May God forgive us what we have done* scrawled rust-colored and huge above them in one of the ancient Earth languages. Pete translated for the others, his mind numb.

Captainless and bewildered—were they still on Earth? How? And why?—they wandered the platform in disarray, all thoughts of their grand journey's fated destination fallen away into the dark. Three of the officers joined McCallister-Xo, walking slow, deliberate steps off the ledge, their descent all the more harrowing for its silence. Pete and the others heard only soft thuds and scratches as they tumbled off the hull of the ship they had served.

At last Pete remembered the book, Magda's dying words. She had known—all the archivists had. His head felt loose on his shoulders as he staggered back to the airlock to read by its light.

It took a team of six rugged Bottom laborers several hours to shift the doors at the cavern's edge. While they worked, other teams walked its interior, measuring and probing, trying to find some sort of explanation.

Pete read.

The book turned out to hold two separate texts, joined who knew when. The first, older text was the shorter of the two, and so despite the difficulty of its language, Pete tackled it first. It was set on official looking paper and dated in the old style, which had not been used as far as Pete was aware since the second or third generation.

This was the portion of the book he had turned to when he first found it. The terminology seemed wilfully obscure at points, and even when the words were clear the grammar was strange to him, but eventually Pete determined that it was a study on simulated space travel, commissioned by some long-ago Earth government.

He had struggled through half of it before the team breached the door, revealing empty, winding caves which branched and joined in maze-like arrays. The ship crew abandoned their search of the cavern where the ship sat and spread outward. It was dispersal of a sort, but tethered and impermanent, a ranging into the caves which always returned to the bulk of the ship.

They found none of the promised meadows, no life of any sort save mildew and fungi.

There were streams, little trickling spots of damp which were clear and cool as promises on their tongue, filtered by the endless rock. The water tasted bitter in the dankness of their underground prison.

The teams were always careful to mark the way back to the ship, placing fluorescent strips from long-term storage on the walls or floors of the caves. But even so, some did not return. Other teams would come across markings which simply stopped, with no sign of life nearby and nobody to answer their calls.

When he was not ranging, Pete read the book. By now it was clear the ship had never left Earth, although the reason for this eluded them all. Pete skipped the rest of the first text and moved to the second, which was actually harder to read despite its language being more recognizably his own. It was technical in nature, describing systems the ship used to simulate space travel. Even though he didn't understand most of what it said, Pete continued to read.

Then one day Pete's team found the wall. It was at the end of a long passage which wound inexorably upwards, and it was made of brick. Pete watched, glad he had been there when it happened, as two Bottom men scrabbled at the caulking, hammered at the bricks with stalagmites they ripped from the cave floor, breaking down the dirt and rocks and scree beyond with equal fervor. He made no move to participate, caught up in fantasies of what they would find on the other side and readying what he would say when they returned to the ship.

All they found was ruin and stagnation, silence and death—an ash-choked swathe of land which stretched away beyond their new-made exit in the brick. Clouds of the dust blew past what must have once been a town, billowing out grey plumes from shattered buildings and tugging formless bundles of stuff.

The two men who had torn down the wall walked off into the dust, searching for life, supplies, or signs of what had happened. After an hour or two, with weak sunlight ribboning down, the other members of the party went too. Pete stayed: he would report back to the ship, he told them.

And so he watched and waited until the sun died a fiery red and the cold of evening set in. In the dim emptiness, he seemed to hear sounds in the distance, low sinuous hissings from the depths of history. The clouds of ash seemed to hide shadowy figures, but when they swirled away revealed only a shattered building, a rusting, useless metal hulk, or nothing at all. He shuddered and returned to the ship's resting place, alone.

When he arrived, they questioned him. Why had he returned alone? Where was his team? What of the time they had spent out in the caves? He only shook his head, filled with grief, and passed them by.

"The secrets of the ship?"

"Yes, Captain Seong. Nothing of why we're here, who the first people were or what purpose they hoped to achieve. But all the secrets of the ship's systems, everything we need to prolong the illusion."

"And we should do this even though you *found a way out*?"

"Just come with me, Captain. Come with me and you will understand. Hope, purpose, meaning, happiness of a sort—what we had in the years before was infinitely, unthinkably better than what awaits us without."

Captain Seong took little convincing once he had seen the desolation which lay beyond the caves. He and Pete took a few steps out down the hillside until the ash began to choke them, cold acrid fingers down their throats. They heard the sounds, saw things that were not there. Captain Seong swore he felt something brush his shoulder, though Pete was only a few feet away and saw nothing but ash. They turned back lest they lose sight of the entrance: Earth held nothing for them, and if it did they were terrified of it.

Inside the cave mouth, the other officers waited. At a shake of the head from Captain Seong, they began to rebuild the wall, working in silence. On the walk back to the ship, they tore up the guide-strips. Over the next few days, as Bottom teams tore up the other strips, removing all signs which pointed to their ship, Pete and the officers between them got the ship's systems rebooted.

When all was complete, they sealed the cavern doors and closed off the ship once more. The ship's journey was a lie, but it was one with promise—promise they would pass on to later generations.

Pete finished transcribing the last of the records from the dispersal and sat back, cracking his knuckles. It was only right, he thought, that he complete his duty as Archivist before betraying it. His generation would keep few records, and preserve none of them.

He lifted the paper from the desk and set it in the book he held, behind the two older sets of papers, then walked with it from the stacks, nodding to the two officers who stood at the ready with vid-cams and torches.

At the door, he stopped to watch. One last time, one last event: the fire-swept cleansing of all they had recorded, all their history and lore. He felt no regret at the destruction of their legends and dreams, their pasts and their futures.

After a while, he set the book firmly under his arm, turned on his heel, and walked to the express lift and the rich, verdant hills of Bottom. Behind him, the tongues of flame licked over everything but the shelf of the first years, already long since empty.

☻ ☻ ☻

"Behind the Years" first appeared at Cosmos Online, *May 28, 2013. Stewart C Baker is an academic librarian, speculative fiction writer and poet, and the editor-in-chief of* sub-Q Magazine. *His fiction has appeared in* Nature, Galaxy's Edge, *and* Flash Fiction Online, *among other places. Stewart was born in England, has lived in South Carolina, Japan, and California (in that order), and currently resides in Oregon with his family—although if anyone asks, he'll usually say he's from the Internet.*

LATECOMERS
by Vonnie Winslow Crist

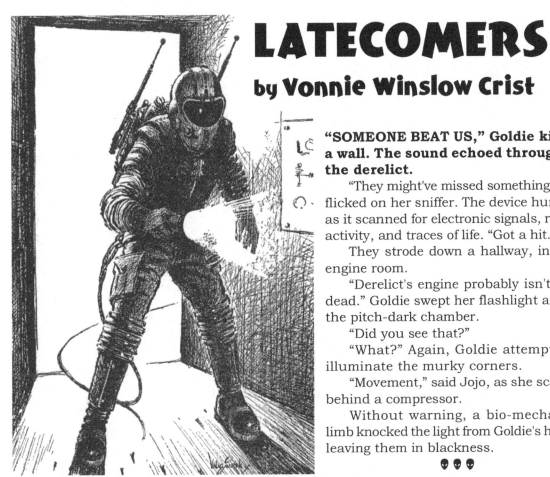

"SOMEONE BEAT US," Goldie kicked a wall. The sound echoed throughout the derelict.

"They might've missed something." Jojo flicked on her sniffer. The device hummed as it scanned for electronic signals, robotic activity, and traces of life. "Got a hit."

They strode down a hallway, into the engine room.

"Derelict's engine probably isn't quite dead." Goldie swept her flashlight around the pitch-dark chamber.

"Did you see that?"

"What?" Again, Goldie attempted to illuminate the murky corners.

"Movement," said Jojo, as she scanned behind a compressor.

Without warning, a bio-mechanical limb knocked the light from Goldie's hand—leaving them in blackness.

👽 👽 👽

The drabble "Latecomers" debuts in this issue accompanied by an illustration by Ed Valigursky. Vonnie Winslow Crist, SFWA, HWA, is author of The Enchanted Dagger, Owl Light, The Greener Forest, Murder on Marawa Prime, *and other award-winning books. Her fiction is included in* Amazing Stories, Cast of Wonders, Lost Signals of the Terran Republic, Defending the Future: Dogs of War, Best Speculative Indie Fiction: 2018, Outposts of Beyond, *and elsewhere. A clover-hand who has found so many four-leafed clovers that she keeps them in jars, Vonnie strives to celebrate the power of myth in her writing. Visit her at vonniewinslowcrist.com*

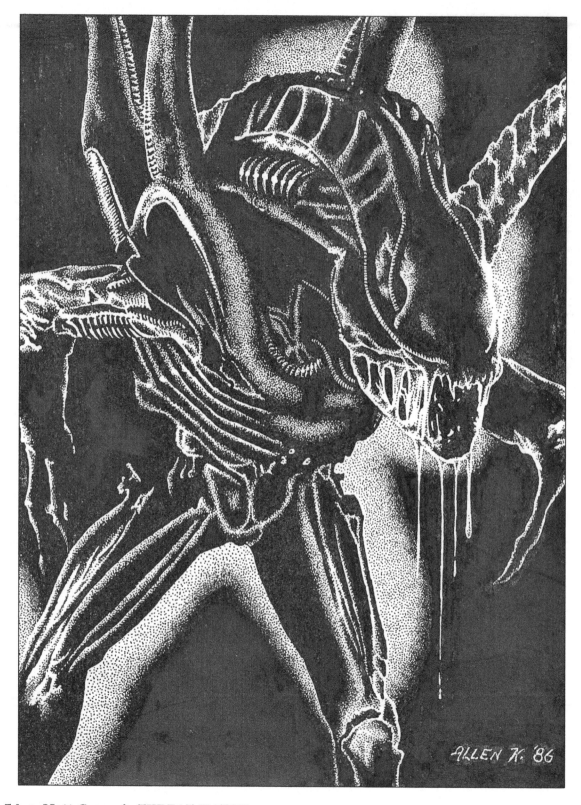

ALLEN K. '86

YOU MAY NOW ACCESS THE FILES. THESE FILES CONTAIN DATA MODULES COMPILED FROM EVIDENCE PRESENTED IN MOVIES AND TELEVISION. EACH MODULE FOCUSES ON A SPECIFIC THREAT: DEADLY PLANETS, HOSTILE ALIENS, SCIENTIFIC ABOMINATIONS, MURDEROUS COMPUTERS AND ...

ACCESSING ... ACCESSING.... OPENING MODULE 5:

DERELICT SHIPS

A SHIP ADRIFT, HER CREW GONE, YET ONWARD SHE ROAMS. Where has her crew gone? More importantly, what caused them to go? One can only presume that whatever it may have been must have been truly dire indeed. But, now a new contingent of unsuspecting voyagers have stumbled upon her as she silently stalks the icy, still byways, and of course they won't be able to resist the lure of exploring such an enticing enigma? They either forget, or disregard, the notion that a decision to cast aside such a valuable, expensive piece of property would never have come to easily; and whatever dire situation brought about her abandonment surely wouldn't still be there, slinking endlessly up and down her cavernous halls in hungry anticipation of new, fresh faces to terrorize.

The four films listed below each hinge on the discovery of some lost derelict, perhaps not upon the open sea, but that makes them no less deadly; and those who chance upon them soon learn some things are best left forgotten.

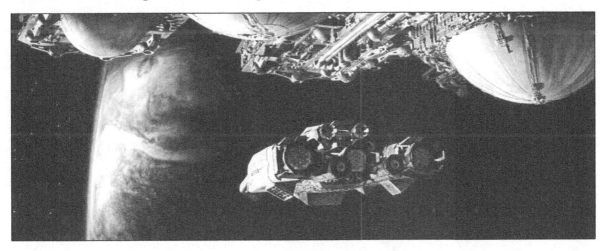

ALIEN (20th Century Fox, 1979)

Vessel's Name: Unknown
Classification: Derelict alien vessel

Location Discovered:
On a moon designated LV-426

Deadliness Factor: 8 out of 10
(The alien is quick, strong, instinctively smart and bleeds acidic blood when wounded—an absolute killing machine, yet it is capable of sustaining damage, so it's not invincible.)

Most Dangerous Condition:
The large field of alien eggs the derelict holds inside it which are designed to inject larva into other species

Necessities for Survival: The ability to effectively track, and isolate the creature. Lots of firepower is also helpful.

Favorite Scene: There's the chest-bursting scene of course, which would be in contention for me, but I'm going with the crew's

exploration of the alien spacecraft on LV-426. It perfectly sets the mood for the rest of the film.

Synopsis: All seven members of the crew of the commercial towing ship *Nostromo* are awakened early from their stasis sleep by *Mother,* the ships computerized operating system. She did so after receiving a distress signal from a moon designated as LV-426 which they pass near on their way home. Despite being a private vessel, they are legally required to investigate any such call.

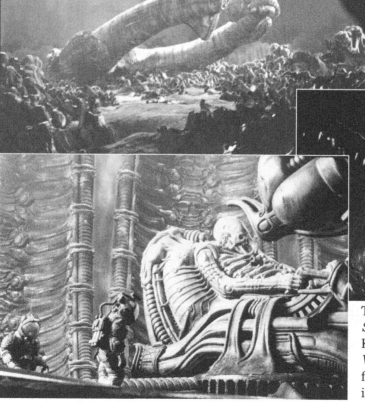

This forces Captain Dallas *(Tom Skerritt)* to take two other officers, Kane and Lambert *(John Hurt and Veronica Cartwright),* to the moon's fog-shrouded surface in search of its origin. There they discover it originated from an abandoned alien spacecraft—and alien-looking it is indeed, thanks to the design work of legendary artist H.R. Geiger. Inside they find an enormous, deceased creature reclining in a giant chair *(this harkens back to a similar scene in the 1965 film* Planet of the Vampires, *which I covered back in the first issue of* Black Infinity). Meanwhile, aboard the *Nostromo* the film's star, Warrant Officer Ripley *(played by Sigourney*

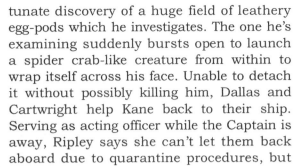

Weaver in her break-out role), deciphers part of the signal they received as being a warning rather than a call for help. They decide to continue on anyway, which turns out to be a poor decision as Kane makes the unfor-

tunate discovery of a huge field of leathery egg-pods which he investigates. The one he's examining suddenly bursts open to launch a spider crab-like creature from within to wrap itself across his face. Unable to detach it without possibly killing him, Dallas and Cartwright help Kane back to their ship. Serving as acting officer while the Captain is away, Ripley says she can't let them back aboard due to quarantine procedures, but Science Officer Ash ignores her and opens the doors to them anyway. This ends up allowing a vicious, swiftly transmorphing alien lifeform loose inside the ship. After eventually bursting out of Kane's chest as a small hatchet-headed creature which immediately skitters away, it soon grows to enormous proportions and begins methodically stalking the crew throughout the ship, attempting to kill them off one-by-one.

My Take: There's no question this original

Alien film is among the most seminal examples of science fiction/horror media of all time. It's tightly plotted, well-acted and looks great. It's easy to see why Sigourney Weaver's character Ripley is regarded as such an iconic figure. She's the one person who makes the right call at each turn. Take her refusal to allow her crewmates back aboard the ship while the face-hugger is attached to Kane, for example. Certainly, she wanted to, but she knew there was good reason the quarantine procedures were put in place. It's the rest of the crew's emotion-based decisions which put everyone at risk. Ultimately, she proves to be a far more effective leader than Dallas. I also liked the added mystery of Science Officer Ash's motivations simmering in the background. Dallas says he was a late addition to the crew, and his coldly detached way of observing everything leads Ripley to distrust him.

What more is there to say? *Alien* does a near-perfect job mixing the wonders of discovery in the deepest regions of space with the unspeakable horrors such discoveries are capable of unleashing. Containing an ample helping of surprise twists, while introducing a top-notch new heroine and one of the most terrifying, seemingly unbeatable monsters of its time, this is a truly riveting film.

Rating: 9 out of 10

THE BLACK HOLE
(Walt Disney Productions, 1979)

Vessel's Name: The *USS Cygnus*
Classification: A former space exploration ship which had gone missing for the past 20 years
Location Discovered: On the edge of a vast black hole

Deadliness Factor: 5 out of 10 *(If you go in ready and properly armed, you can survive.)*
Most Dangerous Condition: The hulking, deadly robot, Maximilian
Necessities for Survival: A well-armed force of stalwart sharp shooters and robots
Favorite Scene: The startling reveal to the mystery of the faceless robots near the film's end

Synopsis: The crew aboard the *USS Palomino* notice a large spaceship floating on the edge of a massive black hole without being pulled inside with everything else. They are

able to identify the ship as the *USS Cygnus* whose mission was the same as that of the *Palomino*, to discover other life in outer space. The *Cygnus* vanished 20 years ago along with the father of Dr. Kate McCrae *(Yvette Mimieux)* who is serving aboard the *Palomino* as science officer.

Captain of the *Palomino,* Dan Holland *(Robert Forster),* authorizes them to fly a single pass by the giant, derelict ship, but they must be careful to not get caught in the black

hole's gravitational pull. Their ship begins to take some damage in the process, but when they near the *Cygnus*, the force of the hole begins to ease and the *Cygnus'* lights suddenly turn on indicating it isn't derelict after all. Leaving Lieutenant Charlie Pizer *(Joseph Bottoms)* behind with their docked ship, the rest of the crew, made up of Captain Holland, Dr. McCrae, Dr. Alex Durant *(Anthony Perkins of* Psycho *fame),* journalist Harry Booth *(Earnest Borgnine)* and their mildly irritating robot V.I.N.CENT *(voiced by the great Roddy McDowall),* board the *Cygnus* where they discover an entire crew of faceless robots operating it for Dr. Hans Reinhardt *(Maximilian Schell),* a genius scientist who was aboard when the *Cygnus* originally vanished. He tells them the ship had been damaged after being struck by a meteor and that he ordered his crew to return back to Earth while he remained. He says Dr. McCrae's father elected to stay behind with him and ultimately ended up dying later on. He assumed his crew had

made it safely back but had no way to communicate with them for verification. Reinhardt is not particularly friendly with his unexpected guests and seems to have trouble suppressing anger boiling just beneath the surface. He offers them the equipment necessary to repair the damage to the *Palomino* but says he has no interest in returning with them.

The always intense Dr. Reinhardt later informs them over dinner that he intends to take the *Cygnus* into and through the black hole. Dr. McCrae, who possesses limited E.S.P. abilities, tells her crewmates that Reinhardt is teetering between genius and insanity. It soon becomes apparent Reinhardt is hiding some dark secret, and with the help of a beat up janitor robot called Old B.O.B. *(Slim Pickens)*, V.I.N.CENT discovers they are in more danger than they originally suspected.

My Take: There are some really cool designs here, particularly in the look of the *Cygnus* and the dreaded robot Maximilian. I always thought the Sentry robots had a neat aesthetic to them as well, with their unique twin-firing laser guns *(which apparently don't improve their aim any)*. I wanted to like V.I.N.CENT

(especially since he's voiced by Roddy McDowall), but I tend to find his constant snippy platitudes more groan-worthy than entertaining. That aside, there are plenty of interesting things going on throughout the movie, such as a secret robot funeral, the silent face-

less beings piloting the ship, and even a robotic shooting competition. I remember being very excited to see this film as a kid, thinking it would be similar to *Star Wars*, which was obviously the audience Disney was hoping to pull in, but it falls far short in that regard. There's just too much hokeyness in various spots, as well as a lot of stilted dialog, too, but I still think it's a fun watch. It has an interesting premise, a slew of neat-looking robots, serviceable special effects, and an underrated villain in the performance Maximilian Schell puts in as Dr. Reinhardt.

Rating: 6 out of 10

LEVIATHAN
(Paramount Pictures, 1989)

Vessel's Name: *Leviathan*
Classification: A huge Russian shipwreck
Location Discovered: Deep in the Atlantic Ocean—16,000 feet beneath the surface
Deadliness Factor: 6 out of 10
(The creature isn't particularly smart, but is extremely difficult to permanently kill.)

Most Dangerous Condition: The horrible, genetic mutating disease it has onboard

Necessities for Survival: The ability to completely eradicate the entirety of those infected, such as by burning with fire.

Favorite Scene: When Beck and Doc enter the medical lab to discover the corpses of two fellow crew members have merged into a single, disgustingly twisted form on the table

Synopsis: Submerged 16,000 feet below the water's surface in the Atlantic Ocean lies the base of the Tri Oceanic Mining Corporation. Its mission there is to extract silver and other precious metals. With just a few days left of their ninety-day shift, they look forward to returning to life back on-

shore. Steven Beck *(Peter Weller of* RoboCop *fame)* supervises the crew, often having to smooth out the tensions which arise from so many unique personalities being forced to live together in such confined quarters for three months.

When lecherous crewman Buzz 'Six Pack' Parrish stumbles into a deep underwater crevasse during a mission outside the base

while in his high-pressure suit, he discovers a large sunken ship called *Leviathan*, which a search reveals belongs to the Russians and is reported as active in the Baltic Sea at that very moment. When he and Elizabeth 'Willie' Williams *(Amanda Pays),* who was on the mission with him, return, they bring with them a safe they retrieved from inside the wrecked vessel. Opening it they find several

things, including the *Leviathan* Captain's videotaped log recordings and some vodka.

When Six Pack suddenly comes down with a serious skin rash, Beck tries to get him evacuated a day early but is discouraged from doing so by their surface superior Miss Martin *(Meg Foster).* A few hours later, Six Pack dies. Dr. Glen 'Doc' Thompson's *(Richard Crenna)* analysis of a tiny worm taken from his body indicates some form of genetic alteration is present.

Soon afterwards, Beck and the doctor go to investigate a sound in the medical lab, only to discover the bodies of Six Pack and fellow crewwoman Bridget Bowman *(Lisa Eilbacher),* who killed herself after becoming ill, have merged together into a monstrous, fleshy mass. It's soon discovered this abomination can move, and it soon sets about trying to infect

impressive as well. I also felt the abhorrent masses of mutated flesh-things were nasty and well-realized. The idea of how the original crew became infected with the disease is also a plus. There are a lot of obvious similarities to John Carpenter's masterpiece *The Thing*[6] in *Leviathan*. Both focus on a crew of hard-working people in an isolated location being stalked by a bizarre, somewhat similar-looking creature. Between the two, *The Thing* is unquestionably superior, but *Leviathan* is still an effective, worthwhile watch.

Rating: 7 out of 10

the rest of the crew. What follows are the survivors' attempts to evade and come up with some way to destroy this increasingly vast organic beast.

My Take: The cast is strong with Peter Weller, Richard Crenna, Ernie Hudson, Daniel Stern and Amanda Pays all playing memorable roles. The creature effects, designed by Academy Award-winning artist Stan Winston, are pretty

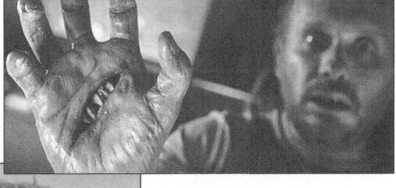

EVENT HORIZON
(Paramount Pictures, 1997)

Vessel's Name: The *Event Horizon*
Classification:
A deep-space research vessel
Location Discovered:
In orbit around Neptune
Deadliness Factor: 8 out of 10
(If the Gravitational Drive is off and you don't spend much time aboard, survival is possible.)
Most Dangerous Condition: The fact that the ship itself has been transformed into something horrible

---

[6] Previously discussed in Matt Cowan's Threat Watch, in *Black Infinity: Body Snatchers*.

beyond the planet Neptune. In 2047, U.S. Aerospace Command received a distress signal from that location, prompting them to dispatch a rescue ship designated the *Lewis and Clark* to retrieve it. It's led by Captain Miller *(Lawrence Fishburne),* who is unhappy that he and his crew have been ordered off leave to embark on this mission which is further out than is deemed safe. Dr. William Weir *(Sam Neill)* has been sent along with them. He informs the crew that the *Event Horizon* did not explode as the general public was told but actually vanished while attempting to initiate an experimental, top-secret engine called a *Gravity Drive,* which was designed to fold time and space in order to produce faster-than-light travel. Dr. Weir knows this because he is the engine's inventor. When a message from the *Event Horizon* is played, it sounds like a chorus of screams and someone crying *"Save me"* in Latin.

They come upon the *Event Horizon* drifting derelict, depowered and without internal gravity. Inside they find floating corpses, all with their eyes torn out. When young crew member Ensign Justin *(Jack Noseworthy)*

Necessities for Survival: Strong willpower and extremely limited time aboard

Favorite Scene: The hellish visions shown to Captain Miller by Dr. Weir of where the *Event Horizon* had been before they found it

Synopsis: The deep-space research vessel *Event Horizon* was launched in the year 2040 to explore the boundaries of our solar system. It mysteriously disappeared without a trace after it had passed

Technician Cooper *(Richard T. Jones),* but a shockwave pulses out from it, damaging the hull of the *Lewis and Clark* and forcing everyone to board the *Event Horizon* for survival.

With less than 24 hours of air available, Dr. Weir suggests using the *Event Horizon*'s Gravitational Drive to return home instantly. He explains that the drive works by creating a secure, artificial black hole, but the Captain does not like this option.

Then the entire crew begin to see and hear nightmarish things from their darkest fears, which leads some to attempt suicide as a result. As things get progressively worse, D.J., the ship's medic, tells

seeks to reinitiate power to the ship, the *Gravity Drive* activates, opening a portal that sucks him inside. He's pulled out by Rescue

Captain Miller he originally misinterpreted the Latin phrase on the recording. He now believes it translates to *"Save yourself from Hell."* With madness consuming some of the crew, who also seem transformed by the dark forces now inherent in the ship, they must try to work together to survive and escape back home.

crew aren't given much to do; this is especially glaring in regards to the female members of the cast, as most of their interactions seem tacked on. While it doesn't quite deliver on the whole "haunted house in space" aspect it was billed as, it's still a fun and often nightmarish ride.

Rating: 8 out of 10

My Take: First off, the ship itself looks awesome with its mammoth, spikey mace-head stretched out front before a run of long, narrow tubes which culminate in Klingon-style wings at the back. This looks like a haunted ship! The recording played for the crew sounds truly hellish as well, and having the voice on it speaking Latin is a nice touch due to how often that ancient language turns up in classic horror literature. Sam Neill and Lawrence Fishburne are always brilliant. Their performances here are no exception. Richard T. Jones is great as the brash, heroic Rescue Technician Cooper. The film does an excellent job creating an atmosphere of what a ship which has traveled to Hell and back might be like. The ending seems a bit rushed, and several members of the *Lewis and Clark*'s

MR. SPACESHIP

BY PHILIP K. DICK

KRAMER LEANED BACK. "YOU CAN SEE THE SITUATION. HOW CAN WE DEAL WITH A FACTOR LIKE THIS? THE PERFECT VARIABLE."

"Perfect? Prediction should still be possible. A living thing still acts from necessity, the same as inanimate material. But the cause-effect chain is more subtle; there are more factors to be considered. The difference is quantitative, I think. The reaction of the living organism parallels natural causation, but with greater complexity."

Gross and Kramer looked up at the board plates, suspended on the wall, still dripping, the images hardening into place. Kramer traced a line with his pencil.

"See that? It's a pseudopodium. They're alive, and so far, a weapon we can't beat. No mechanical system can compete with that, simple or intricate. We'll have to scrap the Johnson Control and find something else."

"Meanwhile the war continues as it is. Stalemate. Checkmate. They can't get to us, and we can't get through their living minefield."

Kramer nodded. "It's a perfect defense, for them. But there still might be one answer."

"What's that?"

"Wait a minute." Kramer turned to his rocket expert, sitting with the charts and files. "The heavy cruiser that returned this week. It didn't actually touch, did it? It came close but there was no contact."

"Correct." The expert nodded. "The mine was twenty miles off. The cruiser was in space-drive, moving directly toward Proxima, line-straight, using the Johnson Control, of course. It had deflected a quarter of an hour earlier for reasons unknown. Later it resumed its course. That was when they got it."

"It shifted," Kramer said. "But not enough. The mine was coming along after it, trailing it. It's the same old story, but I wonder about the contact."

"Here's our theory," the expert said. "We keep looking for contact, a trigger in the pseudopodium. But more likely we're witnessing a psychological phenomenon, a decision without any physical correlative. We're watching for something that isn't there. The mine *decides* to blow up. It sees our ship, approaches, and then decides."

"Thanks." Kramer turned to Gross. "Well, that confirms what I'm saying. How can a ship guided by automatic relays escape a mine that decides to explode? The whole theory of mine penetration is that you must avoid tripping the trigger. But here the trigger is a state of mind in a complicated, developed life-form."

"The belt is fifty thousand miles deep," Gross added. "It solves another problem for them, repair and maintenance. The damn things reproduce, fill up the spaces by spawning into them. I wonder what they feed on?"

"Probably the remains of our first-line. The big cruisers must be a delicacy. It's a game of wits, between a living creature and a ship piloted by automatic relays. The ship always loses." Kramer opened a folder. "I'll tell you what I suggest."

"Go on," Gross said. "I've already heard ten solutions today. What's yours?"

"Mine is very simple. These creatures are superior to any mechanical system, but only because they're alive. Almost any other life-form could compete with them, any higher life-form. If the yuks can put out living mines to protect their planets, we ought to be able to harness some of our own life-forms in a similar way. Let's make use of the same weapon ourselves."

"Which life-form do you propose to use?"

"I think the human brain is the most agile of known living forms. Do you know of any better?"

"But no human being can withstand outspace travel. A human pilot would be dead of heart failure long before the ship got anywhere near Proxima."

"But we don't need the whole body," Kramer said. "We need only the brain."

"What?"

"The problem is to find a person of high intelligence who would contribute, in the same manner that eyes and arms are volunteered."

"But a brain...."

"Technically, it could be done. Brains have been transferred several times, when body destruction made it necessary. Of course, to a spaceship, to a heavy outspace cruiser, instead of an artificial body, that's new."

The room was silent.

"It's quite an idea," Gross said slowly. His heavy square face twisted. "But even supposing it might work, the big question is *whose* brain?"

IT WAS ALL VERY CONFUSING, the reasons for the war, the nature of the enemy. The Yucconae had been contacted on one of the outlying planets of Proxima Centauri. At the approach of the Terran ship, a host of dark slim pencils had lifted abruptly and shot off into the distance. The first real encounter came between three of the yuk pencils and a single exploration ship from Terra. No Terrans survived. After that it was all out war, with no holds barred.

Both sides feverishly constructed defense rings around their systems. Of the two, the Yucconae belt was the better. The ring around Proxima was a living ring, superior to anything Terra could throw against it. The standard equipment by which Terran ships were guided in outspace, the Johnson Control, was not adequate. Something more was needed. Automatic relays were not good enough.

—Not good at all, Kramer thought to himself, as he stood looking down the hillside at the work going on below him. A warm wind blew along the hill, rustling the weeds and grass. At the bottom, in the valley, the mechanics had almost finished; the last elements of the reflex system had been removed from the ship and crated up.

All that was needed now was the new core, the new central key that would take the place of the mechanical system. A human brain, the brain of an intelligent, wary human being. But would the human being part with it? That was the problem.

Kramer turned. Two people were approaching him along the road, a man and a woman. The man was Gross, expressionless, heavy-set, walking with dignity. The woman was—He stared in surprise and growing annoyance. It was Dolores, his wife. Since they'd separated he had seen little of her....

"Kramer," Gross said. "Look who I ran into. Come back down with us. We're going into town."

"Hello, Phil," Dolores said. "Well, aren't you glad to see me?"

He nodded. "How have you been? You're looking fine." She was still pretty and slender in her uniform, the blue-grey of Internal Security, Gross' organization.

"Thanks." She smiled. "You seem to be doing all right, too. Commander Gross tells me that you're responsible for this project, Operation Head, as they call it. Whose head have you decided on?"

"That's the problem." Kramer lit a cigarette. "This ship is to be equipped with a human brain instead of the Johnson system.

We've constructed special draining baths for the brain, electronic relays to catch the impulses and magnify them, a continual feeding duct that supplies the living cells with everything they need. But—"

"But we still haven't got the brain itself," Gross finished. They began to walk back toward the car. "If we can get that we'll be ready for the tests."

"Will the brain remain alive?" Dolores asked. "Is it actually going to live as part of the ship?"

"It will be alive, but not conscious. Very little life is actually conscious. Animals, trees, insects are quick in their responses, but they aren't conscious. In this process of ours the individual personality, the ego, will cease. We only need the response ability, nothing more."

Dolores shuddered. "How terrible!"

"In time of war everything must be tried," Kramer said absently. "If one life sacrificed will end the war it's worth it. This ship might get through. A couple more like it and there wouldn't be any more war."

THEY GOT INTO THE CAR. As they drove down the road, Gross said, "Have you thought of anyone yet?"

Kramer shook his head. "That's out of my line."

"What do you mean?"

"I'm an engineer. It's not in my department."

"But all this was your idea."

"My work ends there."

Gross was staring at him oddly. Kramer shifted uneasily.

"Then who is supposed to do it?" Gross said. "I can have my organization prepare examinations of various kinds, to determine fitness, that kind of thing—"

"Listen, Phil," Dolores said suddenly.

"What?"

She turned toward him. "I have an idea. Do you remember that professor we had in college. Michael Thomas?"

Kramer nodded.

"I wonder if he's still alive." Dolores frowned. "If he is he must be awfully old."

"Why, Dolores?" Gross asked.

"Perhaps an old person who didn't have much time left, but whose mind was still clear and sharp—"

"Professor Thomas." Kramer rubbed his jaw. "He certainly was a wise old duck. But could he still be alive? He must have been seventy, then."

"We could find that out," Gross said. "I could make a routine check."

"What do you think?" Dolores said. "If any human mind could outwit those creatures—"

"I don't like the idea," Kramer said. In his mind an image had appeared, the image of an old man sitting behind a desk, his bright gentle eyes moving about the classroom. The old man leaning forward, a thin hand raised—

"Keep him out of this," Kramer said.

"What's wrong?" Gross looked at him curiously.

"It's because I suggested it," Dolores said.

"No." Kramer shook his head. "It's not that. I didn't expect anything like this, somebody I knew, a man I studied under. I remember him very clearly. He was a very distinct personality."

"Good," Gross said. "He sounds fine."

"We can't do it. We're asking his death!"

"This is war," Gross said, "and war doesn't wait on the needs of the individual. You said that yourself. Surely he'll volunteer; we can keep it on that basis."

"He may already be dead," Dolores murmured.

"We'll find that out," Gross said speeding up the car. They drove the rest of the way in silence.

FOR A LONG TIME the two of them stood studying the small wood house, overgrown with ivy, set back on the lot behind an enormous oak. The little town was silent and sleepy; once in awhile a car moved slowly along the distant highway, but that was all.

"This is the place," Gross said to Kramer.

He folded his arms. "Quite a quaint little house."

Kramer said nothing. The two Security Agents behind them were expressionless.

Gross started toward the gate. "Let's go. According to the check he's still alive, but very sick. His mind is agile, however. That seems to be certain. It's said he doesn't leave the house. A woman takes care of his needs. He's very frail."

They went down the stone walk and up onto the porch. Gross rang the bell. They waited. After a time they heard slow footsteps. The door opened. An elderly woman in a shapeless wrapper studied them impassively.

"Security," Gross said, showing his card. "We wish to see Professor Thomas."

"Why?"

"Government business." He glanced at Kramer.

Kramer stepped forward. "I was a pupil of the Professor's," he said. "I'm sure he won't mind seeing us."

The woman hesitated uncertainly. Gross stepped into the doorway. "All right, mother. This is war time. We can't stand out here."

The two Security agents followed him, and Kramer came reluctantly behind, closing the door. Gross stalked down the hall until he came to an open door. He stopped, looking in. Kramer could see the white corner of a bed, a wooden post and the edge of a dresser.

He joined Gross.

In the dark room a withered old man lay, propped up on endless pillows. At first it seemed as if he were asleep; there was no motion or sign of life. But after a time Kramer saw with a faint shock that the old man was watching them intently, his eyes fixed on them, unmoving, unwinking.

"Professor Thomas?" Gross said. "I'm Commander Gross of Security. This man with me is perhaps known to you—"

The faded eyes fixed on Kramer.

"I know him. Philip Kramer…. You've grown heavier, boy." The voice was feeble, the rustle of dry ashes. "Is it true you're married now?"

"Yes. I married Dolores French. You remember her." Kramer came toward the bed. "But we're separated. It didn't work out very well. Our careers—"

"What we came here about, Professor," Gross began, but Kramer cut him off with an impatient wave.

"Let me talk. Can't you and your men get out of here long enough to let me talk to him?"

Gross swallowed. "All right, Kramer." He nodded to the two men. The three of them left the room, going out into the hall and closing the door after them.

The old man in the bed watched Kramer silently. "I don't think much of him," he said at last. "I've seen his type before. What's he want?"

"Nothing. He just came along. Can I sit down?" Kramer found a stiff upright chair beside the bed. "If I'm bothering you—"

"No. I'm glad to see you again, Philip. After so long. I'm sorry your marriage didn't work out."

"How have you been?"

"I've been very ill. I'm afraid that my moment on the world's stage has almost ended." The ancient eyes studied the younger man reflectively. "You look as if you have been doing well. Like everyone else I thought highly of. You've gone to the top in this society."

Kramer smiled. Then he became serious. "Professor, there's a project we're working on that I want to talk to you about. It's the first ray of hope we've had in this whole war. If it works, we may be able to crack the yuk defenses, get some ships into their system. If we can do that the war might be brought to an end."

"Go on. Tell me about it, if you wish."

"It's a long shot, this project. It may not work at all, but we have to give it a try."

"It's obvious that you came here because of it," Professor Thomas murmured. "I'm becoming curious. Go on."

* * *

AFTER KRAMER FINISHED the old man lay back in the bed without speaking. At last he sighed.

"I understand. A human mind, taken out of a human body." He sat up a little, looking at Kramer. "I suppose you're thinking of me."

Kramer said nothing.

"Before I make my decision I want to see the papers on this, the theory and outline of construction. I'm not sure I like it. —For reasons of my own, I mean. But I want to look at the material. If you'll do that—"

"Certainly." Kramer stood up and went to the door. Gross and the two Security Agents were standing outside, waiting tensely. "Gross, come inside."

They filed into the room.

"Give the Professor the papers," Kramer said. "He wants to study them before deciding."

Gross brought the file out of his coat pocket, a manila envelope. He handed it to the old man on the bed. "Here it is, Professor. You're welcome to examine it. Will you give us your answer as soon as possible? We're very anxious to begin, of course."

"I'll give you my answer when I've decided." He took the envelope with a thin, trembling hand. "My decision depends on what I find out from these papers. If I don't like what I find, then I will not become involved with this work in any shape or form." He opened the envelope with shaking hands. "I'm looking for one thing."

"What is it?" Gross said.

"That's my affair. Leave me a number by which I can reach you when I've decided."

Silently, Gross put his card down on the dresser. As they went out Professor Thomas was already reading the first of the papers, the outline of the theory.

KRAMER SAT ACROSS FROM Dale Winter, his second in line. "What then?" Winter said.

"He's going to contact us." Kramer scratched with a drawing pen on some paper. "I don't know what to think."

"What do you mean?" Winter's good-natured face was puzzled.

"Look." Kramer stood up, pacing back and forth, his hands in his uniform pockets. "He was my teacher in college. I respected him as a man, as well as a teacher. He was more than a voice, a talking book. He was a person, a calm, kindly person I could look up to. I always wanted to be like him, someday. Now look at me."

"So?"

"Look at what I'm asking. I'm asking for his life, as if he were some kind of laboratory animal kept around in a cage, not a man, a teacher at all."

"Do you think he'll do it?"

"I don't know." Kramer went to the window. He stood looking out. "In a way, I hope not."

"But if he doesn't—"

"Then we'll have to find somebody else. I know. There would be somebody else. Why did Dolores have to—"

The vidphone rang. Kramer pressed the button.

"This is Gross." The heavy features formed. "The old man called me. Professor Thomas."

"What did he say?" He knew; he could tell already, by the sound of Gross' voice.

"He said he'd do it. I was a little surprised myself, but apparently he means it. We've already made arrangements for his admission to the hospital. His lawyer is drawing up the statement of liability."

Kramer only half heard. He nodded wearily. "All right. I'm glad. I suppose we can go ahead, then."

"You don't sound very glad."

"I wonder why he decided to go ahead with it."

"He was very certain about it." Gross sounded pleased. "He called me quite early. I was still in bed. You know, this calls for a celebration."

"Sure," Kramer said. "It sure does."

TOWARD THE MIDDLE OF AUGUST the project neared completion. They stood outside in the hot autumn heat, looking up at the sleek metal sides of the ship.

Gross thumped the metal with his hand. "Well, it won't be long. We can begin the test any time."

"Tell us more about this," an officer in gold braid said. "It's such an unusual concept."

"Is there really a human brain inside the ship?" a dignitary asked, a small man in a rumpled suit. "And the brain is actually alive?"

"Gentlemen, this ship is guided by a living brain instead of the usual Johnson relay-control system. But the brain is not conscious. It will function by reflex only. The practical difference between it and the Johnson system is this: a human brain is far more intricate than any man-made structure, and its ability to adapt itself to a situation, to respond to danger, is far beyond anything that could be artificially built."

Gross paused, cocking his ear. The turbines of the ship were beginning to rumble, shaking the ground under them with a deep vibration. Kramer was standing a short distance away from the others, his arms folded, watching silently. At the sound of the turbines he walked quickly around the ship to the other side. A few workmen were clearing away the last of the waste, the scraps of wiring and scaffolding. They glanced up at him and went on hurriedly with their work. Kramer mounted the ramp and entered the control cabin of the ship. Winter was sitting at the controls with a Pilot from Space-transport.

"How's it look?" Kramer asked.

"All right." Winter got up. "He tells me that it would be best to take off manually. The robot controls—" Winter hesitated. "I mean, the built-in controls, can take over later on in space."

"That's right," the Pilot said. "It's customary with the Johnson system, and so in this case we should—"

"Can you tell anything yet?" Kramer asked.

"No," the Pilot said slowly. "I don't think so. I've been going over everything. It seems to be in good order. There's only one thing I wanted to ask you about." He put his hand on the control board. "There are some changes here I don't understand."

"Changes?"

"Alterations from the original design. I wonder what the purpose is."

Kramer took a set of the plans from his coat. "Let me look." He turned the pages over. The Pilot watched carefully over his shoulder.

"The changes aren't indicated on your copy," the Pilot said. "I wonder—" He stopped. Commander Gross had entered the control cabin.

"Gross, who authorized alterations?" Kramer said. "Some of the wiring has been changed."

"Why, your old friend." Gross signaled to the field tower through the window.

"My old friend?"

"The Professor. He took quite an active interest." Gross turned to the Pilot. "Let's get going. We have to take this out past gravity for the test they tell me. Well, perhaps it's for the best. Are you ready?"

"Sure." The Pilot sat down and moved some of the controls around. "Any time."

"Go ahead, then," Gross said.

"The Professor—" Kramer began, but at that moment there was a tremendous roar and the ship leaped under him. He grasped one of the wall holds and hung on as best he could. The cabin was filling with a steady throbbing, the raging of the jet turbines underneath them.

The ship leaped. Kramer closed his eyes and held his breath. They were moving out into space, gaining speed each moment.

"WELL, WHAT DO YOU THINK?" Winter said nervously. "Is it time yet?"

"A little longer," Kramer said. He was sitting on the floor of the cabin, down by the control wiring. He had removed the metal covering-plate, exposing the complicated maze of relay wiring. He was studying it, comparing it to the wiring diagrams.

"What's the matter?" Gross said.

"These changes. I can't figure out what they're for. The only pattern I can make out is that for some reason—"

"Let me look," the Pilot said. He squatted down beside Kramer. "You were saying?"

"See this lead here? Originally it was switch-controlled. It closed and opened automatically, according to temperature change. Now it's wired so that the central control system operates it. The same with the others. A lot of this was still mechanical, worked by pressure, temperature, stress. Now it's under the central master."

"The brain?" Gross said. "You mean it's been altered so that the brain manipulates it?"

Kramer nodded. "Maybe Professor Thomas felt that no mechanical relays could be trusted. Maybe he thought that things would be happening too fast. But some of these could close in a split second. The brake rockets could go on as quickly as—"

"Hey," Winter said from the control seat. "We're getting near the moon stations. What'll I do?"

They looked out the port. The corroded surface of the moon gleamed up at them, a corrupt and sickening sight. They were moving swiftly toward it.

"I'll take it," the Pilot said. He eased Winter out of the way and strapped himself in place. The ship began to move away from the moon as he manipulated the controls. Down below them they could see the observation stations dotting the surface, and the tiny squares that were the openings of the underground factories and hangars. A red blinker winked up at them and the Pilot's fingers moved on the board in answer.

"We're past the moon," the Pilot said, after a time. The moon had fallen behind them; the ship was heading into outer space. "Well, we can go ahead with it."

Kramer did not answer.

"Mr. Kramer, we can go ahead any time."

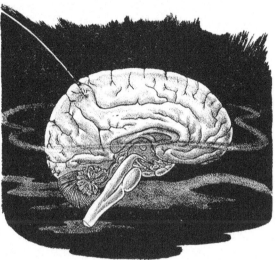

Kramer started. "Sorry. I was thinking. All right, thanks." He frowned, deep in thought.

"What is it?" Gross asked.

"The wiring changes. Did you understand the reason for them when you gave the okay to the workmen?"

Gross flushed. "You know I know nothing about technical material. I'm in Security."

"Then you should have consulted me."

"What does it matter?" Gross grinned wryly. "We're going to have to start putting our faith in the old man sooner or later."

The Pilot stepped back from the board. His face was pale and set. "Well, it's done," he said. "That's it."

"What's done?" Kramer said.

"We're on automatic. The brain. I turned the board over to it—to him, I mean. The Old Man." The Pilot lit a cigarette and puffed nervously. "Let's keep our fingers crossed."

THE SHIP WAS COASTING EVENLY, in the hands of its invisible pilot. Far down inside the ship, carefully armored and protected, a soft human brain lay in a tank of liquid, a thousand-minute electric charges playing over its surface. As the charges rose they were picked up and amplified, fed into relay systems, advanced, carried on through the entire ship—

Gross wiped his forehead nervously. "So *he* is running it, now. I hope he knows what he's doing."

Kramer nodded enigmatically. "I think he does."

"What do you mean?"

"Nothing." Kramer walked to the port. "I see we're still moving in a straight line." He picked up the microphone. "We can instruct the brain orally, through this." He blew against the microphone experimentally.

"Go on," Winter said.

"Bring the ship around half-right," Kramer said. "Decrease speed."

They waited. Time passed. Gross looked at Kramer. "No change. Nothing."

"Wait."

Slowly, the ship was beginning to turn. The turbines missed, reducing their steady beat. The ship was taking up its new course, adjusting itself. Nearby some space debris rushed past, incinerating in the blasts of the turbine jets.

"So far so good," Gross said.

They began to breathe more easily. The invisible pilot had taken control smoothly, calmly. The ship was in good hands. Kramer spoke a few more words into the microphone, and they swung again. Now they were moving back the way they had come, toward the moon.

"Let's see what he does when we enter the moon's pull," Kramer said. "He was a good mathematician, the old man. He could handle any kind of problem."

The ship veered, turning away from the moon. The great eaten-away globe fell behind them.

Gross breathed a sigh of relief. "That's that."

"One more thing." Kramer picked up the microphone. "Return to the moon and land the ship at the first space field," he said into it.

"Good Lord," Winter murmured. "Why are you—"

"Be quiet." Kramer stood, listening. The turbines gasped and roared as the ship swung full around, gaining speed. They were moving back, back toward the moon again. The ship dipped down, heading toward the great globe below.

"We're going a little fast," the Pilot said. "I don't see how he can put down at this velocity."

THE PORT FILLED UP, as the globe swelled rapidly. The Pilot hurried toward the board, reaching for the controls. All at once the ship jerked. The nose lifted and the ship shot out into space, away from the moon, turning at an oblique angle. The men were thrown to the floor by the sudden change in course. They got to their feet again, speechless, staring at each other.

The Pilot gazed down at the board. "It wasn't me! I didn't touch a thing. I didn't even get to it."

The ship was gaining speed each moment. Kramer hesitated. "Maybe you better switch it back to manual."

The Pilot closed the switch. He took hold of the steering controls and moved them experimentally. "Nothing." He turned around. "Nothing. It doesn't respond."

No one spoke.

"You can see what has happened," Kramer said calmly. "The old man won't let go of it, now that he has it. I was afraid of this when I saw the wiring changes. Everything in this ship is centrally controlled, even the cooling system, the hatches, the garbage release. We're helpless."

"Nonsense." Gross strode to the board. He took hold of the wheel and turned it. The ship continued on its course, moving away from the moon, leaving it behind.

"Release!" Kramer said into the microphone. "Let go of the controls! We'll take it back. Release."

"No good," the Pilot said. "Nothing." He spun the useless wheel. "It's dead, completely dead."

"And we're still heading out," Winter said, grinning foolishly. "We'll be going through the first-line defense belt in a few minutes. If they don't shoot us down—"

"We better radio back." The Pilot clicked the radio to *send*. "I'll contact the main bases, one of the observation stations."

"Better get the defense belt, at the speed we're going. We'll be into it in a minute."

"And after that," Kramer said, "we'll be in outer space. He's moving us toward outspace velocity. Is this ship equipped with baths?"

"Baths?" Gross said.

"The sleep tanks. For space-drive. We may need them if we go much faster."

"But good God, where are we going?" Gross said. "Where—where's he taking us?"

THE PILOT OBTAINED CONTACT. "This is Dwight, on ship," he said. "We're entering the defense zone at high velocity. Don't fire on us."

"Turn back," the impersonal voice came through the speaker. "You're not allowed in the defense zone."

"We can't. We've lost control."

"Lost control?"

"This is an experimental ship."

Gross took the radio. "This is Commander Gross, Security. We're being carried into outer space. There's nothing we can do. Is there any way that we can be removed from this ship?"

A hesitation. "We have some fast pursuit ships that could pick you up if you wanted to jump. The chances are good they'd find you. Do you have space flares?"

"We do," the Pilot said. "Let's try it."

"Abandon ship?" Kramer said. "If we leave now we'll never see it again."

"What else can we do? We're gaining speed all the time. Do you propose that we stay here?"

"No." Kramer shook his head. "Damn it, there ought to be a better solution."

"Could you contact *him*?" Winter asked. "The Old Man? Try to reason with him?"

"It's worth a chance," Gross said. "Try it."

"All right." Kramer took the microphone. He paused a moment. "Listen! Can you hear me? This is Phil Kramer. Can you hear me, Professor. Can you hear me? I want you to release the controls."

There was silence.

"This is Kramer, Professor. Can you hear me? Do you remember who I am? Do you understand who this is?"

Above the control panel the wall speaker made a sound, a sputtering static. They looked up.

"Can you hear me, Professor. This is Philip Kramer. I want you to give the ship back to us. If you can hear me, release the controls! Let go, Professor. Let go!"

Static. A rushing sound, like the wind. They gazed at each other. There was silence for a moment.

"It's a waste of time," Gross said.

"No—listen!"

The sputter came again. Then, mixed with the sputter, almost lost in it, a voice came, toneless, without inflection, a mechanical, lifeless voice from the metal speaker in the wall, above their heads.

"...Is it you, Philip? I can't make you out. Darkness.... Who's there? With you...."

"It's me, Kramer." His fingers tightened against the microphone handle. "You must release the controls, Professor. We have to get back to Terra. You must."

Silence. Then the faint, faltering voice came again, a little stronger than before. "Kramer. Everything so strange. I was right, though. Consciousness result of thinking. Necessary result. *Cognito ergo sum*. Retain conceptual ability. Can you hear me?"

"Yes, Professor—"

"I altered the wiring. Control. I was fairly certain.... I wonder if I can do it. Try...."

Suddenly the air-conditioning snapped into operation. It snapped abruptly off again. Down the corridor a door slammed. Something thudded. The men stood listening. Sounds came from all sides of them, switches shutting, opening. The lights blinked off; they were in darkness. The lights came back on, and at the same time the heating coils dimmed and faded.

"Good God!" Winter said.

Water poured down on them, the emergency fire-fighting system. There was a screaming rush of air. One of the escape hatches had slid back, and the air was roaring frantically out into space.

The hatch banged closed. The ship subsided into silence. The heating coils glowed into life. As suddenly as it had begun the weird exhibition ceased.

"I can do—everything," the dry, toneless voice came from the wall speaker. "It is all controlled. Kramer, I wish to talk to you. I've been—been thinking. I haven't seen you in many years. A lot to discuss. You've changed, boy. We have much to discuss. Your wife—"

The Pilot grabbed Kramer's arm. "There's a ship standing off our bow. Look."

THEY RAN TO THE PORT. A slender pale craft was moving along with them, keeping pace with them. It was signal-blinking.

"A Terran pursuit ship," the Pilot said. "Let's jump. They'll pick us up. Suits—"

He ran to a supply cupboard and turned the handle. The door opened and he pulled the suits out onto the floor.

"Hurry," Gross said. A panic seized them. They dressed frantically, pulling the heavy garments over them. Winter staggered to the escape hatch and stood by it, waiting for the others. They joined him, one by one.

"Let's go!" Gross said. "Open the hatch."

Winter tugged at the hatch. "Help me."

They grabbed hold, tugging together. Nothing happened. The hatch refused to budge.

"Get a crowbar," the Pilot said.

"Hasn't anyone got a blaster?" Gross looked frantically around. "Damn it, blast it open!"

"Pull," Kramer grated. "Pull together."

"Are you at the hatch?" the toneless voice came, drifting and eddying through the corridors of the ship. They looked up, staring around them. "I sense something nearby, outside. A ship? You are leaving, all of you? Kramer, you are leaving, too? Very unfortunate. I had hoped we could talk. Perhaps at some other time you might be induced to remain."

"Open the hatch!" Kramer said, staring up at the impersonal walls of the ship. "For God's sake, open it!"

There was silence, an endless pause. Then, very slowly, the hatch slid back. The air screamed out, rushing past them into space.

One by one they leaped, one after the other, propelled away by the repulsive material of the suits. A few minutes later they were being hauled aboard the pursuit ship. As the last one of them was lifted through the port, their own ship pointed itself suddenly upward and shot off at tremendous speed. It disappeared.

Kramer removed his helmet, gasping. Two sailors held onto him and began to wrap him in blankets. Gross sipped a mug of coffee, shivering.

"It's gone," Kramer murmured.

"I'll have an alarm sent out," Gross said.

"What's happened to your ship?" a sailor asked curiously. "It sure took off in a hurry. Who's on it?"

"We'll have to have it destroyed," Gross went on, his face grim. "It's got to be destroyed. There's no telling what it—what *he* has in mind." Gross sat down weakly on a metal bench. "What a close call for us. We were so damn trusting."

"What could he be planning," Kramer said, half to himself. "It doesn't make sense. I don't get it."

AS THE SHIP SPED BACK toward the moon base they sat around the table in the dining room, sipping hot coffee and thinking, not saying very much.

"Look here," Gross said at last. "What kind of man was Professor Thomas? What do you remember about him?"

Kramer put his coffee mug down. "It was ten years ago. I don't remember much. It's vague."

He let his mind run back over the years. He and Dolores had been at Hunt College together, in physics and the life sciences. The College was small and set back away from the momentum of modern life. He had gone there because it was his home town, and his father had gone there before him.

Professor Thomas had been at the College a long time, as long as anyone could remember. He was a strange old man, keeping to himself most of the time. There were many things that he disapproved of, but he seldom said what they were.

"Do you recall anything that might help us?" Gross asked. "Anything that would give us a clue as to what he might have in mind?"

Kramer nodded slowly. "I remember one thing...."

One day he and the Professor had been sitting together in the school chapel, talking leisurely.

"Well, you'll be out of school, soon," the Professor had said. "What are you going to do?"

"Do? Work at one of the Government Research Projects, I suppose."

"And eventually? What's your ultimate goal?"

Kramer had smiled. "The question is unscientific. It presupposes such things as ultimate ends."

"Suppose instead along these lines, then: What if there were no war and no Government Research Projects? What would you do, then?"

"I don't know. But how can I imagine a hypothetical situation like that? There's been war as long as I can remember. We're geared for war. I don't know what I'd do. I suppose I'd adjust, get used to it."

The Professor had stared at him. "Oh, you do think you'd get accustomed to it, eh? Well, I'm glad of that. And you think you could find something to do?"

Gross listened intently. "What do you infer from this, Kramer?"

"Not much. Except that he was against war."

"We're all against war," Gross pointed out.

"True. But he was withdrawn, set apart. He lived very simply, cooking his own meals. His wife died many years ago. He was born in Europe, in Italy. He changed his name when he came to the United States. He used to read Dante and Milton. He even had a Bible."

"Very anachronistic, don't you think?"

"Yes, he lived quite a lot in the past. He found an old phonograph and records, and he listened to the old music. You saw his house, how old-fashioned it was."

"Did he have a file?" Winter asked Gross.

"With Security? No, none at all. As far as we could tell he never engaged in political work, never joined anything or even seemed to have strong political convictions."

"No," Kramer, agreed. "About all he ever did was walk through the hills. He liked nature."

"Nature can be of great use to a scientist," Gross said. "There wouldn't be any science without it."

"Kramer, what do you think his plan is, taking control of the ship and disappearing?" Winter said.

"Maybe the transfer made him insane," the Pilot said. "Maybe there's no plan, nothing rational at all."

"But he had the ship rewired, and he had made sure that he would retain consciousness and memory before he even agreed to the operation. He must have had something planned from the start. But what?"

"Perhaps he just wanted to stay alive longer," Kramer said. "He was old and about to die. Or—"

"Or what?"

"Nothing." Kramer stood up. "I think as

soon as we get to the moon base I'll make a vidcall to earth. I want to talk to somebody about this."

"Who's that?" Gross asked.

"Dolores. Maybe she remembers something."

"That's a good idea," Gross said.

"WHERE ARE YOU calling from?" Dolores asked, when he succeeded in reaching her.

"From the moon base."

"All kinds of rumors are running around. Why didn't the ship come back? What happened?"

"I'm afraid he ran off with it."

"He?"

"The Old Man. Professor Thomas." Kramer explained what had happened.

Dolores listened intently. "How strange. And you think he planned it all in advance, from the start?"

"I'm certain. He asked for the plans of construction and the theoretical diagrams at once."

"But why? What for?"

"I don't know. Look, Dolores. What do you remember about him? Is there anything that might give a clue to all this?"

"Like what?"

"I don't know. That's the trouble."

On the vidscreen Dolores knitted her brow. "I remember he raised chickens in his back yard, and once he had a goat." She smiled. "Do you remember the day the goat got loose and wandered down the main street of town? Nobody could figure out where it came from."

"Anything else?"

"No." He watched her struggling, trying to remember. "He wanted to have a farm, sometime, I know."

"All right. Thanks." Kramer touched the switch. "When I get back to Terra maybe I'll stop and see you."

"Let me know how it works out."

He cut the line and the picture dimmed and faded. He walked slowly back to where Gross and some officers of the Military were sitting at a chart table, talking.

"Any luck?" Gross said, looking up.

"No. All she remembers is that he kept a goat."

"Come over and look at this detail chart." Gross motioned him around to his side. "Watch!"

Kramer saw the record tabs moving furiously, the little white dots racing back and forth.

"What's happening?" he asked.

"A squadron outside the defense zone has finally managed to contact the ship. They're maneuvering now, for position. Watch."

The white counters were forming a barrel formation around a black dot that was moving steadily across the board, away from the central position. As they watched, the white dots constricted around it.

"They're ready to open fire," a technician at the board said. "Commander, what shall we tell them to do?"

Gross hesitated. "I hate to be the one who makes the decision. When it comes right down to it—"

"It's not just a ship," Kramer said. "It's a man, a living person. A human being is up there, moving through space. I wish we knew what—"

"But the order has to be given. We can't take any chances. Suppose he went over to them, to the yuks."

Kramer's jaw dropped. "My God, he wouldn't do that."

"Are you sure? Do you know what he'll do?"

"He wouldn't do that."

Gross turned to the technician. "Tell them to go ahead."

"I'm sorry, sir, but now the ship has gotten away. Look down at the board."

Gross stared down, Kramer over his shoulder. The black dot had slipped through the white dots and had moved off at an abrupt angle. The white dots were broken up, dispersing in confusion.

"He's an unusual strategist," one of the officers said. He traced the line. "It's an ancient maneuver, an old Prussian device, but it worked."

The white dots were turning back. "Too many yuk ships out that far," Gross said. "Well, that's what you get when you don't act quickly." He looked up coldly at Kramer. "We should have done it when we had him. Look at him go!" He jabbed a finger at the rapidly moving black dot. The dot came to the edge of the board and stopped. It had reached the limit of the chartered area. "See?"

—Now what? Kramer thought, watching. So the Old Man had escaped the cruisers and gotten away. He was alert, all right; there was nothing wrong with his mind. Or with his ability to control his new body.

Body—The ship was a new body for him. He had traded in the old dying body, withered and frail, for this hulking frame of metal and plastic, turbines and rocket jets. He was strong, now. Strong and big. The new body was more powerful than a thousand human bodies. But how long would it last him? The average life of a cruiser was only ten years. With careful handling he might get twenty out of it, before some essential part failed and there was no way to replace it.

And then, what then? What would he do, when something failed and there was no one to fix it for him? That would be the end. Someplace, far out in the cold darkness of space, the ship would slow down, silent and lifeless, to exhaust its last heat into the eternal timelessness of outer space. Or perhaps it would crash on some barren asteroid, burst into a million fragments.

It was only a question of time.

"Your wife didn't remember anything?" Gross said.

"I told you. Only that he kept a goat, once."

"A hell of a lot of help that is."

Kramer shrugged. "It's not my fault."

"I wonder if we'll ever see him again." Gross stared down at the indicator dot, still hanging at the edge of the board. "I wonder if he'll ever move back this way."

"I wonder, too," Kramer said.

THAT NIGHT KRAMER lay in bed, tossing from side to side, unable to sleep. The moon gravity, even artificially increased, was unfamiliar to him and it made him uncomfortable. A thousand thoughts wandered loose in his head as he lay, fully awake.

What did it all mean? What was the Professor's plan? Maybe they would never know. Maybe the ship was gone for good; the Old Man had left forever, shooting into outer space. They might never find out why he had done it, what purpose—if any—had been in his mind.

Kramer sat up in bed. He turned on the light and lit a cigarette. His quarters were small, a metal-lined bunk room, part of the moon station base.

The Old Man had wanted to talk to him. He had wanted to discuss things, hold a conversation, but in the hysteria and confusion all they had been able to think of was getting away. The ship was rushing off with them, carrying them into outer space. Kramer set his jaw. Could they be blamed for jumping? They had no idea where they were being taken, or why. They were helpless, caught in their own ship, and the pursuit ship standing by waiting to pick them up was their only chance. Another half hour and it would have been too late.

But what had the Old Man wanted to say? What had he intended to tell him, in those first confusing moments when the ship around them had come alive, each metal strut and wire suddenly animate, the body of a living creature, a vast metal organism?

It was weird, unnerving. He could not forget it, even now. He looked around the small room uneasily. What did it signify, the coming to life of metal and plastic? All at once they had found themselves inside a *living* creature, in its stomach, like Jonah inside the whale.

It had been alive, and it had talked to

them, talked calmly and rationally, as it rushed them off, faster and faster into outer space. The wall speaker and circuit had become the vocal cords and mouth, the wiring the spinal cord and nerves, the hatches and relays and circuit breakers the muscles.

They had been helpless, completely helpless. The ship had, in a brief second, stolen their power away from them and left them defenseless, practically at its mercy. It was not right; it made him uneasy. All his life he had controlled machines, bent nature and the forces of nature to man and man's needs. The human race had slowly evolved until it was in a position to operate things, run them as it saw fit. Now all at once it had been plunged back down the ladder again, prostrate before a Power against which they were children.

Kramer got out of bed. He put on his bathrobe and began to search for a cigarette. While he was searching, the vidphone rang.

He snapped the vidphone on. "Yes?"

The face of the immediate monitor appeared. "A call from Terra, Mr. Kramer. An emergency call."

"Emergency call? For me? Put it through!" Kramer came awake, brushing his hair back out of his eyes. Alarm plucked at him.

From the speaker a strange voice came. "Philip Kramer? Is this Kramer?"

"Yes. Go on."

"This is General Hospital, New York City, Terra. Mr. Kramer, your wife is here. She has been critically injured in an accident. Your name was given to us to call. Is it possible for you to—"

"How badly?" Kramer gripped the vidphone stand. "Is it serious?"

"Yes, it's serious, Mr. Kramer. Are you able to come here? The quicker you can come the better."

"Yes." Kramer nodded. "I'll come. Thanks."

The screen died as the connection was broken. Kramer waited a moment. Then he tapped the button. The screen relit again. "Yes, sir," the monitor said.

"Can I get a ship to Terra at once? It's an emergency. My wife—"

"There's no ship leaving the moon for eight hours. You'll have to wait until the next period."

"Isn't there anything I can do?"

"We can broadcast a general request to all ships passing through this area. Sometimes cruisers pass by here returning to Terra for repairs."

"Will you broadcast that for me? I'll come down to the field."

"Yes sir. But there may be no ship in the area for a while. It's a gamble." The screen died.

Kramer dressed quickly. He put on his coat and hurried to the lift. A moment later he was running across the general receiving lobby, past the rows of vacant desks and conference tables. At the door the sentries stepped aside and he went outside, onto the great concrete steps.

The face of the moon was in shadow. Below him the field stretched out in total darkness, a black void, endless, without form. He made his way carefully down the steps and along the ramp along the side of the field, to the control tower. A faint row of red lights showed him the way.

Two soldiers challenged him at the foot of the tower, standing in the shadows, their guns ready.

"Kramer?"

"Yes." A light was flashed in his face.

"Your call has been sent out already."

"Any luck?" Kramer asked.

"There's a cruiser nearby that has made contact with us. It has an injured jet and is moving slowly back toward Terra, away from the line."

"Good." Kramer nodded, a flood of relief rushing through him. He lit a cigarette and gave one to each of the soldiers. The soldiers lit up.

"Sir," one of them asked, "is it true about the experimental ship?"

"What do you mean?"

"It came to life and ran off?"

"No, not exactly," Kramer said. "It had a new type of control system instead of the

Johnson units. It wasn't properly tested."

"But sir, one of the cruisers that was there got up close to it, and a buddy of mine says this ship acted funny. He never saw anything like it. It was like when he was fishing once on Terra, in Washington State, fishing for bass. The fish were smart, going this way and that—"

"Here's your cruiser," the other soldier said. "Look!"

An enormous vague shape was setting slowly down onto the field. They could make nothing out but its row of tiny green blinkers. Kramer stared at the shape.

"Better hurry, sir," the soldiers said. "They don't stick around here very long."

"Thanks." Kramer loped across the field, toward the black shape that rose up above him, extended across the width of the field. The ramp was down from the side of the cruiser and he caught hold of it. The ramp rose, and a moment later Kramer was inside the hold of the ship. The hatch slid shut behind him.

As he made his way up the stairs to the main deck the turbines roared up from the moon, out into space.

Kramer opened the door to the main deck. He stopped suddenly, staring around him in surprise. There was nobody in sight. The ship was deserted.

"Good God," he said. Realization swept over him, numbing him. He sat down on a bench, his head swimming. "Good God."

The ship roared out into space leaving the moon and Terra farther behind each moment.

And there was nothing he could do.

"SO IT WAS YOU who put the call through," he said at last. "It was you who called me on the vidphone, not any hospital on Terra. It was all part of the plan." He looked up and around him. "And Dolores is really—"

"Your wife is fine," the wall speaker above him said tonelessly. "It was a fraud. I am sorry to trick you that way, Philip, but it was all I could think of. Another day and you would have been back on Terra. I don't want to remain in this area any longer than necessary. They have been so certain of finding me out in deep space that I have been able to stay here without too much danger. But even the purloined letter was found eventually."

Kramer smoked his cigarette nervously. "What are you going to do? Where are we going?"

"First, I want to talk to you. I have many things to discuss. I was very disappointed when you left me, along with the others. I had hoped that you would remain." The dry voice chuckled. "Remember how we used to talk in the old days, you and I? That was a long time ago."

The ship was gaining speed. It plunged through space at tremendous speed, rushing through the last of the defense zone and out beyond. A rush of nausea made Kramer bend over for a moment.

When he straightened up the voice from the wall went on, "I'm sorry to step it up so quickly, but we are still in danger. Another few moments and we'll be free."

"How about yuk ships? Aren't they out here?"

"I've already slipped away from several of them. They're quite curious about me."

"Curious?"

"They sense that I'm different, more like their own organic mines. They don't like it. I believe they will begin to withdraw from this area, soon. Apparently they don't want to get involved with me. They're an odd race, Philip. I would have liked to study them closely, try to learn something about them. I'm of the opinion that they use no inert material. All their equipment and instruments are alive, in some form or other. They don't construct or build at all. The idea of *making* is foreign to them. They utilize existing forms. Even their ships—"

"Where are we going?" Kramer said. "I want to know where you are taking me."

"Frankly, I'm not certain."

"You're not certain?"

"I haven't worked some details out. There are a few vague spots in my program, still. But I think that in a short while I'll have them ironed out."

"What is your program?" Kramer said.

"It's really very simple. But don't you want to come into the control room and sit? The seats are much more comfortable than that metal bench."

Kramer went into the control room and sat down at the control board. Looking at the useless apparatus made him feel strange.

"What's the matter?" the speaker above the board rasped.

Kramer gestured helplessly. "I'm—powerless. I can't do anything. And I don't like it. Do you blame me?"

"No. No, I don't blame you. But you'll get your control back, soon. Don't worry. This is only a temporary expedient, taking you off this way. It was something I didn't contemplate. I forgot that orders would be given out to shoot me on sight."

"It was Gross' idea."

"I don't doubt that. My conception, my plan, came to me as soon as you began to describe your project, that day at my house. I saw at once that you were wrong; you people have no understanding of the mind at all. I realized that the transfer of a human brain from an organic body to a complex artificial space ship would not involve the loss of the intellectualization faculty of the mind. When a man thinks, he *is*.

"When I realized that, I saw the possibility of an age-old dream becoming real. I was quite elderly when I first met you, Philip. Even then my life-span had come pretty much to its end. I could look ahead to nothing but death, and with it the extinction of all my ideas. I had made no mark on the world, none at all. My students, one by one, passed from me into the world, to take up jobs in the great Research Project, the search for better and bigger weapons of war.

"The world has been fighting for a long time, first with itself, then with the Martians, then with these beings from Proxima Centauri, whom we know nothing about. The human society has evolved war as a cultural institution, like the science of astronomy, or mathematics. War is a part of our lives, a career, a respected vocation. Bright, alert young men and women move into it, putting their shoulders to the wheel as they did in the time of Nebuchadnezzar. It has always been so.

"But is it innate in mankind? I don't think so. No social custom is innate. There were many human groups that did not go to war; the Eskimos never grasped the idea at all, and the American Indians never took to it well.

"But these dissenters were wiped out, and a cultural pattern was established that became the standard for the whole planet. Now it has become ingrained in us.

"But if someplace along the line some other way of settling problems had arisen and taken hold, something different than the massing of men and material to—"

"What's your plan?" Kramer said. "I know the theory. It was part of one of your lectures."

"Yes, buried in a lecture on plant selection, as I recall. When you came to me with this proposition I realized that perhaps my conception could be brought to life, after all. If my theory were right that war is only a habit, not an instinct, a society built up apart from Terra with a minimum of cultural roots might develop differently. If it failed to absorb our outlook, if it could start out on another foot, it might not arrive at the same point to which we have come: a dead end, with nothing but greater and greater wars in sight, until nothing is left but ruin and destruction everywhere.

"Of course, there would have to be a Watcher to guide the experiment, at first. A crisis would undoubtedly come very quickly, probably in the second generation. Cain would arise almost at once.

"You see, Kramer, I estimate that if I remain at rest most of the time, on some small planet or moon, I may be able to keep functioning for almost a hundred years. That would be time enough, sufficient to see the direction of the new colony. After that— Well, after that it would be up to the colony itself.

"Which is just as well, of course. Man must take control eventually, on his own. One hundred years, and after that they will have control of their own destiny. Perhaps I am wrong, perhaps war is more than a habit. Perhaps it is a law of the universe, that things can only survive as groups by group violence.

"But I'm going ahead and taking the chance that it is only a habit, that I'm right, that war is something we're so accustomed to that we don't realize it is a very unnatural thing. Now as to the place! I'm still a little vague about that. We must find the place, still."

"That's what we're doing now. You and I are going to inspect a few systems off the beaten path, planets where the trading prospects are low enough to keep Terran ships away. I know of one planet that might be a good place. It was reported by the Fairchild Expedition in their original manual. We may look into that, for a start."

The ship was silent.

KRAMER SAT FOR A TIME, staring down at the metal floor under him. The floor throbbed dully with the motion of the turbines. At last he looked up.

"You might be right. Maybe our outlook is only a habit." Kramer got to his feet. "But I wonder if something has occurred to you?"

"What is that?"

"If it's such a deeply ingrained habit, going back thousands of years, how are you going to get your colonists to make the break, leave Terra and Terran customs? How about *this* generation, the first ones, the people who found the colony? I think you're right that the next generation would be free of all this, if there were an—" He grinned. "—An Old Man Above to teach them something else instead."

Kramer looked up at the wall speaker. "How are you going to get the people to leave Terra and come with you, if by your own theory, this generation can't be saved, it all has to start with the next?"

The wall speaker was silent. Then it made a sound, the faint dry chuckle.

"I'm surprised at you, Philip. Settlers can be found. We won't need many, just a few." The speaker chuckled again. "I'll acquaint you with my solution."

At the far end of the corridor a door slid open. There was sound, a hesitant sound. Kramer turned.

"Dolores!"

Dolores Kramer stood uncertainly, looking into the control room. She blinked in amazement. "Phil! What are you doing here? What's going on?"

They stared at each other.

"What's happening?" Dolores said. "I received a vidcall that you had been hurt in a lunar explosion—"

The wall speaker rasped into life. "You see, Philip, that problem is already solved. We don't really need so many people; even a single couple might do."

Kramer nodded slowly. "I see," he murmured thickly. "Just one couple. One man and woman."

"They might make it all right, if there were someone to watch and see that things went as they should. There will be quite a few things I can help you with, Philip. Quite a few. We'll get along very well, I think."

Kramer grinned wryly. "You could even help us name the animals," he said. "I understand that's the first step."

"I'll be glad to," the toneless, impersonal voice said. "As I recall, my part will be to bring them to you, one by one. Then you can do the actual naming."

"I don't understand," Dolores faltered. "What does he mean, Phil? Naming animals. What kind of animals? Where are we going?"

Kramer walked slowly over to the port and stood staring silently out, his arms folded. Beyond the ship a myriad fragments of light gleamed, countless coals glowing in the dark void. Stars, suns, systems. Endless, without number. A universe of worlds. An infinity of planets, waiting for them, gleaming and winking from the darkness.

He turned back, away from the port. "Where are we going?" He smiled at his wife, standing nervous and frightened, her large eyes full of alarm. "I don't know where we are going," he said. "But somehow that doesn't seem too important right now.... I'm beginning to see the Professor's point, it's the result that counts."

And for the first time in many months he put his arm around Dolores. At first she stiffened, the fright and nervousness still in her eyes. But then suddenly she relaxed against him and there were tears wetting her cheeks.

"Phil ... do you really think we can start over again—you and I?"

He kissed her tenderly, then passionately.

And the spaceship shot swiftly through the endless, trackless eternity of the void....

"Mr. Spaceship" first appeared in the January 1953 issue of Imagination Stories of Science and Fantasy (with an uncredited illustration). The illustration at left is by Ed Emshwiller.

Award-winning American author Philip K. Dick is perhaps better known to film buffs for several movies adapted from his inventive SF tales, most notably Blade Runner and Total Recall. Dick often explored philosophical, social and political themes in a body of work encompassing 44 novels and 121 short stories. Dick was greatly interested in metaphysics, religion and, as this tale exemplifies, the nature of identity.

THE GRAVEYARD OF SPACE

BY MILTON LESSER

H E LIT A CIGARETTE, THE LAST ONE THEY HAD, AND ASKED HIS WIFE "WANT TO SHARE IT?"

"No. That's all right." Diane sat at the viewport of the battered old Gormann '87, a small figure of a woman hunched over and watching the parade of asteroids like tiny slow-moving incandescent flashes.

Ralph looked at her and said nothing. He remembered what it was like when she had worked by his side at the mine. It had not been much of a mine. It had been a bust, a first-class, sure-as-hell bust, like everything else in their life together. And it had aged her. Had it only been three years? he thought. Three years on asteroid 4712, a speck of cosmic dust drifting on its orbit in the asteroid belt between Jupiter and Mars. Uranium potential, high—the government had said. So they had leased the asteroid and prospected it and although they had not finished the job, they were finished. They were going home and now there were lines on Diane's face although she was hardly past twenty-four. And there was a bitterness, a bleakness, in her eyes.

The asteroid had ruined them, had taken something from them and given nothing in return. They were going home and, Ralph Meeker thought, they had left more than their second-hand mining equipment on asteroid 4712. They had left the happy early days of their marriage as a ghost for whomever tried his luck next on 4712. They had never mentioned the word divorce; Diane had merely said she would spend some time with her sister in Marsport instead of going on to Earth....

"We'd be swinging around to sunward on 4712," Ralph mused.

"Please. That's over. I don't want to talk about the mine."

"Won't it ever bother you that we never finished?"

"We finished," Diane said.

He smoked the cigarette halfway and offered it to her. She shook her head and he put the butt out delicately, to save it.

Then a radar bell clanged.

"What is it?" Ralph asked, immediately alert, studying the viewport. You had to be alert on an old tub like the Gormann '87. A hundred tonner, it had put in thirty years and a billion and some miles for several owners. Its warning devices and its reflexes—it was funny, Ralph thought, how you ascribed something human like reflexes to a hundred tons of battered metal—were unpredictable.

"I don't see anything," Diane said.

He didn't either. But you never knew in the asteroid belt. It was next to impossible to thread a passage without a radar screen—and completely impossible with a radar screen on the blink and giving you false information. You could shut it off and pray—but the odds would still be a hundred to one against you.

"There!" Diane cried. "On the left! The left,

Ralph—"

He saw it too. At first it looked like a jumble of rocks, of dust as the asteroid old-timers called the gravity-held rock swarms which pursued their erratic, dangerous orbits through the asteroid belt.

But it was not dust.

"Will you look at that," Diane said.

The jumble of rocks—which they were ready to classify as dust—swam up toward them. Ralph waited, expecting the automatic pilot to answer the radar warning and swing them safely around the obstacle. So Ralph watched and saw the dark jumble of rocks—silvery on one side where the distant sunlight hit it—apparently spread out as they approached it. Spread out and assuming tiny shapes, shapes in miniature.

"Spaceships," Diane said. "Spaceships, Ralph. Hundreds of them."

They gleamed like silver motes in the sun or were black as the space around them. They tumbled slowly, in incredible slow motion, end over end and around and around each other, as if they had been suspended in a slowly boiling liquid instead of the dark emptiness of space.

"That's the sargasso," Ralph said.

"But—"

"But we're off course. I know it. The radar was probably able to miss things in our way, but failed to compensate afterwards and bring us back to course. Now—"

Suddenly Ralph dived for the controls. The throbbing rockets of the Gormann '87 had not responded to the radar warning. They were rocketing on toward the sargasso, rapidly, dangerously.

"Hold on to something!" Ralph hollered, and punched full power in the left rockets and breaking power in the right forward rockets simultaneously, attempting to stand the Gormann '87 on its head and fight off the deadly gravitational attraction of the sargasso.

The Gormann '87 shuddered like something alive and Ralph felt himself thrust to the left and forward violently. His head struck the radar screen and, as if mocking him the radar bell clanged its warning. He thought he heard Diane scream. Then he was trying to stand, but the gravity of sudden acceleration gripped him with a giant hand and he slumped back slowly, aware of a wetness seeping from his nose, his ears—

All of space opened and swallowed him and he went down, trying to reach for Diane's hand. But she withdrew it and then the blackness, like some obscene mouth as large as the distance from here to Alpha Centauri, swallowed him.

"ARE YOU ALL RIGHT, DIANE?" he asked.

He was on his knees. His head ached and one of his legs felt painfully stiff, but he had crawled over to where Diane was down, flat on her back, behind the pilot chair. He found the water tank unsprung and brought her some and in a few moments she blinked her eyes and looked at him.

"Cold," she said.

He had not noticed it, but he was still numb and only half conscious, half of his faculties working. It *was* cold. He felt that now. And he was giddy and growing rapidly more so—as if they did not have sufficient oxygen to breathe.

Then he heard it. A slow steady hissing, probably the sound feared most by spacemen. Air escaping.

Diane looked at him. "For God's sake, Ralph," she cried. "Find it."

He found it and patched it—and was numb with the cold and barely conscious when he had finished. Diane came to him and squeezed his hand and that was the first time they had touched since they had left the asteroid. Then they rested for a few moments and drank some of the achingly cold water from the tank and got up and went to the viewport. They had known it, but confirmation was necessary. They looked outside.

They were within the sargasso.

The battered derelict ships rolled and tumbled and spun out there, slowly, unhurried, in a mutual gravitational field which their own Gormann '87 had disturbed. It was a sargasso like the legendary Sargasso Seas of Earth's early sailing days, becalmed seas, seas without wind, with choking Sargasso weed, seas that snared and entrapped....

"Can we get out?" Diane asked.

He shrugged. "That depends. How strong the pull of gravity is. Whether the Gormann's rocket drive is still working. If we can repair the radar. We'd never get out without the radar."

"I'll get something to eat," she said practically. "You see about the radar."

Diane went aft while he remained there in the tiny control cabin. By the time she brought the heated cans back with her, he knew it was hopeless. Diane was not the sort of woman you had to humor about a thing like that. She offered him a can of pork and beans and looked at his face, and when he nodded she said:

"It's no use?"

"We couldn't fix it. The scopes just wore out, Diane. Hell, if they haven't been replaced since this tub rolled off the assembly line, they're thirty years old. She's an '87."

"Is there anything we can do?"

He shrugged. "We're going to try. We'll check the air and water and see what we have. Then we start looking."

"Start looking? I don't understand."

"For a series eighty Gormann cruiser."

Diane's eyes widened. "You mean—out there?"

"I mean out there. If we find a series eighty cruiser—and we might—and if I'm able to transfer the radarscopes after we find out they're in good shape, then we have a chance."

Diane nodded slowly. "If there are any other minor repairs to make, I could be making them while you look for a series eighty Gormann."

But Ralph shook his head. "We'll probably have only a few hours of air to spare, Diane. If we both look, we'll cover more ground.

I hate to ask you, because it won't be pretty out there. But it might be our only chance."

"I'll go, of course. Ralph?"

"Yes?"

"What is this sargasso, anyway?"

He shrugged as he read the meters on the compressed air tanks. Four tanks full, with ten hours of air, for two, in each. One tank half full. Five hours. Five plus forty. Forty-five hours of air.

They would need a minimum of thirty-five hours to reach Mars.

"No one knows for sure about the sargasso," he said, wanting to talk, wanting to dispel his own fear so he would not communicate it to her as he took the spacesuits down from their rack and began to climb into one. "They don't think it's anything but the ships, though. It started with a few ships. Then more. And more. Trapped by mutual gravity. It got bigger and bigger and I think there are almost a thousand derelicts here now. There's talk of blasting them clear, of salvaging them for metals and so on. But so far the planetary governments haven't co-operated."

"But how did the first ships get here?"

"It doesn't make a hell of a lot of difference. One theory is ships only, and maybe a couple of hunks of meteoric debris in the beginning. Another theory says there may be a particularly heavy small asteroid in this maze of wrecks somewhere—you know, super-heavy stuff with the atoms stripped of their electrons and the nuclei squeezed together, weighing in the neighborhood of a couple of tons per square inch. That could account for the beginning, but once the thing got started, the wrecked ships account for more wrecked ships and pretty soon you have—a sargasso."

Diane nodded and said, "You can put my helmet on now."

"All right. Don't forget to check the radio with me before we go out. If the radio doesn't work, then you stay here. Because I want us in constant radio contact if we're both out there. Is that understood?"

"Yes, sir, captain," she said, and grinned.

It was her old grin. He had not seen her grin like that for a long time. He had almost forgotten what that grin was like. It made her face seem younger and prettier, as he had remembered it from what seemed so long ago but was only three years. It was a wonderful grin and he watched it in the split-second which remained before he swung the heavy helmet up and in place over her shoulders.

Then he put on his own helmet awkwardly and fingered the outside radio controls. "Hear me?" he said.

"I can hear you." Her voice was metallic but very clear through the suit radios.

"Then listen. There shouldn't be any danger of getting lost. I'll leave a light on inside the ship and we'll see it through the ports. It will be the only light, so whatever you do, don't go out of range. As long as you can always see it, you'll be OK. Understand?"

"Right," she said as they both climbed into the Gormann '87's airlock and waited for the pressure to leave it and the outer door to swing out into space. "Ralph? I'm a little scared, Ralph."

"That's all right," he said. "So am I."

"What did you mean, it won't be pretty out there?"

"Because we'll have to look not just for series eighty Gormanns but for any ships that look as old as ours. There ought to be plenty of them and any one of them could have had a Gormann radarscope, although it's unlikely. Have to look, though."

"But what—won't be pretty?"

"We'll have to enter those ships. You won't like what's inside."

"Say, how will we get in? We don't have blasters or weapons of any kind."

"Your suit rockets," Ralph said. "You swing around and blast with your suit rockets. A porthole should be better than an airlock if it's big enough to climb through. You won't have any trouble."

"But you still haven't told me what—"

"Inside the ships. People. They'll all be dead. If they didn't lose their air so far, they'll lose it when we go in. Either way, of course, they'll be dead. They've all been dead for years, with no food. But without air—"

"What are you stopping for?" Diane said. "Please go on."

"A body, without air. Fifteen pounds of pressure per square inch on the inside, and zero on the outside. It isn't pretty. It bloats."

"My God, Ralph."

"I'm sorry, kid. Maybe you want to stay back here and I'll look."

"You said we only have ten hours. I want to help you."

All at once, the airlock swung out. Space yawned at them, black, enormous, the silent ships, the dead sargasso ships, floating slowly by, eternally, unhurried....

"Better make it eight hours," Ralph said over the suit radio. "We'd better keep a couple of hours leeway in case I figured wrong. Eight hours, and remember, don't get out of sight of the ship's lights and don't break radio contact under any circumstances. These suit radios work like miniature radar sets, too. If anything goes wrong, we'll be able to track each other. It's directional beam radio."

"But what can go wrong?"

"I don't know," Ralph admitted. "Nothing probably." He turned on his suit rockets and felt the sudden surge of power drive him clear of the ship. He watched Diane rocketing away from him to the right. He waved his hand in the bulky spacesuit. "Good luck," he called. "I love you, Diane."

"Ralph," she said. Her voice caught. He heard it catch over the suit radio. "Ralph, we agreed never to—oh, forget it. Good luck, Ralph. Good luck, oh good luck. And I—"

"You what."

"Nothing, Ralph. Good luck."

"Good luck," he said, and headed for the first jumble of space wrecks.

IT WOULD PROBABLY have taken them a month to explore all the derelicts which were old enough to have Gormann series eighty radarscopes. Theoretically, Ralph realized, even a newer ship could have one. But it wasn't likely, because if someone could afford a newer ship then he could afford a better radarscope. But that, he told himself, was only half the story. The other half was this: with a better radarscope a ship might not have floundered into the sargasso at all....

So it was hardly possible to pass up any ship if their life depended on it—and the going was slow.

Too slow.

He had entered some dozen ships in the first four hours, turning, using his shoulder rockets to blast a port hole out and climbing in through there. He had not liked what he saw, but there was no preventing it. Without a light it wasn't so bad, but you needed a light to examine the radarscope....

THEY WERE DEAD. They had been dead for years, but of course there would be no decomposition in the airless void of space and very little even if air had remained until he blasted his way in, for the air was sterile canned spaceship air. They were dead, and they were bloated. All impossibly fat men, with white faces like melons and gross bodies like Tweedle Dee's and limbs like fat sausages.

By the fifth ship he was sick to his stomach, but by the tenth he had achieved the necessary detachment to continue his task. Once—it was the eighth ship—he found a Gormann series eighty radarscope, and his heart pounded when he saw it. But the scope was hopelessly damaged, as bad as their own. Aside from that one, he did not encounter any, damaged or in good shape, which they might convert to their own use.

Four hours, he thought. Four hours and twelve ships. Diane reported every few moments by intercom. In her first four hours she had visited eight ships. Her voice sounded funny. She was fighting it every step of the way he thought. It must have been hell to her, breaking into those wrecks with their dead men with faces like white, bloated melons—

In the thirteenth ship he found a skeleton.

He did not report it to Diane over the intercom. The skeleton made no sense at all. The flesh could not possibly have decomposed. Curious, he clomped closer on his magnetic boots. Even if the flesh had decomposed, the clothing would have remained. But it was a skeleton picked completely clean, with no clothing, not even boots—

As if the man had been stripped of his clothing first.

He found out why a moment later, and it left him feeling more than a little sick. There were other corpses aboard the ship, a battered Thompson '81 in worse shape than their own Gormann. Bodies, not skeletons. But when they had entered the sargasso they had apparently struck another ship. One whole side of the Thompson was smashed in and Ralph could see the repair patches on the wall. Near them and thoroughly destroyed, were the Thompson's spacesuits.

The galley lockers were empty when Ralph found them. All the food gone—how many years ago? And one of the crew, dying before the others.

Cannibalism.

Shuddering, Ralph rocketed outside into the clear darkness of space. That was a paradox, he thought. It was clear, all right, but it was dark. You could see a great way. You could see a million million miles but it was darker than anything on Earth. It was almost an extra-dimensional effect. It made the third dimension on earth, the dimension of depth, seem hopelessly flat.

"Ralph!"

"Go ahead, kid," he said. It was their first radio contact in almost half an hour.

"Oh, Ralph. It's a Gormann. An eighty-five. I think. Right in front of me. Ralph, if its scopes are good—oh, Ralph."

"I'm coming," he said. "Go ahead inside. I'll pick up your beam and be along." He could feel his heart thumping wildly. Five hours now. They did not have much time. This ship—this Gormann eighty-five which

Diane had found—might be their last chance. Because it would certainly take him all of three hours to transfer the radarscope, using the rockets from one of their spacesuits, to their own ship.

He rocketed along now, following her directional beam, and listened as she said: "I'm cutting through the porthole now, Ralph. I—"

Her voice stopped suddenly. It did not drift off gradually. It merely ceased, without warning, without reason. "Diane!" he called. "Diane, can you hear me?"

HE TRACKED THE BEAM in desperate silence. Wrecks flashed by, tumbling slowly in their web of mutual gravitation. Some were molten silver if the wan sunlight caught them. Some were black, but every rivet, every seam was distinct. The impossible clarity of blackest space....

"Ralph?" Her voice came suddenly.

"Yes, Diane. Yes. What is it?"

"What a curious thing. I stopped blasting at the port hole. I'm not going in that way. The airlock, Ralph."

"What about the airlock?"

"It opened up on me. It swung out into space, all of a sudden. I'm going in, Ralph."

Fear, unexpected, inexplicable, gripped him. "Don't," he said. "Wait for me."

"That's silly, Ralph. We barely have time. I'm going in now. There. I'm closing the outer door. I wonder if the pressure will build up for me. If it doesn't, I'll blast the outer door with my rockets and get out of here.... Ralph! The light's blinking. The pressures building. The inner door is beginning to open, Ralph. I'm going inside now."

He was still tracking the beam. He thought he was close now, a hundred miles perhaps. A hundred miles by suit rocket was merely a few seconds but somehow the fear was still with him. It was that skeleton, he thought. That skeleton had unnerved him.

"Ralph. It's here, Ralph. A radarscope just like ours. Oh, Ralph, it's in perfect shape."

"I'm coming," he said. A big old Bartson Cruiser tumbled by end over end, a thousand tonner, the largest ship he had seen in here so far. At some of the portholes as he flashed by he could see faces, dead faces staring into space forever.

Then Diane's voice suddenly: "Is that you, Ralph?"

"I'm still about fifty miles out," he said automatically, and then cold fear, real fear, gripped him. *Is that you, Ralph?*

"Ralph, is that—oh, Ralph. Ralph—" she screamed, and was silent.

"Diane! Diane, answer me."

Silence. She had seen someone—something. Alive? It hardly seemed possible. He tried to notch his rocket controls further toward full power, but they were straining already—

The dead ships flashed by, scores of them, hundreds, with dead men and dead dreams inside, waiting through eternity, in no hurry to give up their corpses and the corpses of their dreams.

He heard Diane again then, a single agonized scream. Then there was silence, absolute silence.

Time seemed frozen, frozen like the faces of the dead men inside the ships, suspended, unmoving, not dropping into the well of the past. The ships crawled by now, crawled. And from a long way off he saw the Gormann eighty-five. He knew it was the right ship because the outer airlock door had swung open again. It hung there in space, the lock gaping—

But it was a long way off.

He hardly seemed to be approaching it at all. Every few seconds he called Diane's name, but there was no answer. No answer. Time crawled with the fear icy now, as cold as death, in the pit of his stomach, with the fear making his heart pound rapidly, with the fear making it impossible for him to think. Fear—for Diane. I love you, Di, he thought. I love you. I never stopped loving you. We were wrong. We were crazy wrong. It was like a sargasso, inside of us, an emptiness which needed filling—but we were wrong. Diane—

He reached the Gormann and plunged inside the airlock, swinging the outer door shut behind him. He waited. Would the pressure build up again, as it had built up for Diane? He did not know. He could only wait—

A red light blinked over his head, on and off, on and off as pressure was built. Then it stopped.

Fifteen pounds of pressure in the airlock, which meant that the inner door should open. He ran forward, rammed his shoulder against it, tumbled through. He entered a narrow companionway and clomped awkwardly toward the front of the ship, where the radarscope would be located.

He passed a skeleton in the companionway, like the one he had seen in another ship. For the same reason, he thought. He had time to think that. And then he saw them.

Diane. On the floor, her spacesuit off her now, a great bruise, blue-ugly bruise across her temple. Unconscious.

And the thing which hovered over her.

At first he did not know what it was, but he leaped at it. It turned, snarling. There was air in the ship and he wondered about that.

But he did not have time to wonder. The thing was like some monstrous, misshapen creature, a man—yes, but a man to give you nightmares. Bent and misshapen, gnarled, twisted like the roots of an ancient tree, with a wild growth of beard, white beard, heavy across the chest, with bent limbs powerfully muscled and a gaunt face, like a death's head. And the eyes—the eyes were wild, staring vacantly, almost glazed as in death. The eyes stared at him and through him and then he closed with this thing which had felled Diane.

It had incredible strength. The strength of the insane. It drove Ralph back across the cabin and Ralph, encumbered by his spacesuit, could only fight awkwardly. It drove him back and it found something on the floor, the metal leg of what once had been a chair, and slammed it down across the faceplate of Ralph's spacesuit.

Ralph staggered, fell to his knees. He had absorbed the blow on the crown of his skull through the helmet of the suit, and it dazed

him. The thing struck again, and Ralph felt himself falling....

Somehow, he climbed to his feet again. The thing was back over Diane's still form again, looking at her, its eyes staring and vacant. Spittle drooled from the lips—

Then Ralph was wrestling with it again. The thing was almost protean. It all but seemed to change its shape and writhe from Ralph's grasp as they struggled across the cabin, but this time there was no weapon for it to grab and use with stunning force.

Half-crazed himself now, Ralph got his

fingers, gauntleted in rubberized metal, about the sinewy throat under the tattered beard. His fingers closed there and the wild eyes went big, and he held it that way a long time, then finally thrust it away from him.

The thing fell but sprang to its feet. It looked at Ralph and the mouth opened and closed, but he heard no sound. The teeth were yellow and black, broken, like fangs.

Then the thing turned and ran.

Ralph followed it as far as the airlock. The inner door was slammed between them. A light blinked over the door.

Ralph ran to a port hole and watched.

The thing which once had been a man floated out into space, turning, spinning slowly. The gnarled twisted body expanded outward, became fat and swollen, balloon-like. It came quite close to the porthole, thudding against the ship's hull, the face—dead now— like a melon.

Then, after he was sick for a moment there beside the airlock, he went back for Diane.

THEY WERE BACK ABOARD the Gormann '87 now, their own ship. Ralph had revived Diane and brought her back—along with the other Gormann's radarscope—to their battered tub. The bruise on her temple was badly discolored and she was still weak, but she would be all right.

"But what was it?" Diane asked. She had hardly seen her attacker.

"A man," Ralph said. "God knows how long that ship was in here. Years, maybe. Years, alone in space, here in the sargasso, with dead men and dead ships for company. He used up all the food. His shipmates died. Maybe he

killed them. He needed more food—"

"Oh, no. You don't mean—"

Ralph nodded. "He became a cannibal. Maybe he had a spacesuit and raided some of the other ships too. It doesn't matter. He's dead now."

"He must have been insane like that for years, waiting here, never seeing another living thing...."

"Don't talk about it," Ralph said, then smiled. "Ship's ready to go, Diane."

"Yes," she said.

He looked at her. "Mars?"

She didn't say anything.

"I learned something in there," Ralph said. "We were like that poor insane creature in a way. We were too wrapped up in the asteroid and the mine. We forgot to live from day to day, to scrape up a few bucks every now and then maybe and take in a show on Ceres or have a weekend on Vesta. What the hell, Di, everybody needs it."

"Yes," she said.

"Di?"

"Yes, Ralph?"

"I—I want to give it another try, if you do."

"The mine?"

"The mine eventually. But the mine isn't important. Us, I mean." He paused, his hands still over the controls. "Will it be Mars?"

"No," she said, and sat up and kissed him. "A weekend on Vesta sounds very nice. Very, very nice, darling."

Ralph smiled and punched the controls. Minutes later they had left the sargasso—both sargassos—behind them.

"The Graveyard of Space" first appeared in the April 1956 issue of Imagination, with illustrations by H. W. McCauley. Prolific American novelist Stephen Marlowe (born Milton Lesser) once stated, "At the age of eight I wanted to be a writer and I never changed my mind." In 1950, shortly after celebrating his 23rd birthday, Marlowe sold his first story to Amazing, launching a writing life that stretched across six decades. He wrote SF under a variety of pseudonyms, including Adam Chase, C. H. Thames, and Stephen Marlowe, the name he took legally in the 1950s. Marlowe soon turned to writing mostly hardboiled crime and suspense novels, and, eventually, to well-researched (and well-received) biographical novels, including one about Edgar Allan Poe, The Lighthouse at the End of the World. In 1997 he received the Private Eye Writers of America's Life Achievement Award.

THE STAR JUMPERS

BY DAVID VONALLMEN

FROM WHERE MASTER SERGEANT TAU GWEMBE STOOD, ELECTROMAGNET BOOTS THE ONLY THING KEEPING HIM FROM FLOATING OFF THE HULL OF HIS SQUAD'S TRANSPORT, the freighter was nothing more than a massive black space where no background stars could be seen. The readout on his helmet's HUD told him his transport had matched the freighter's trajectory and they were holding steady at a velocity of eight kilometers per second, 200 meters off the freighter's starboard side.

But it couldn't tell him what was waiting for them inside.

"Go," he whispered.

Two of his soldiers jumped, their leap accelerated by the vacuum wave thrusters in the soles of their boots. The vibration of vacuum waves—what they called "yume" for short—conducted through the hull and rattled Tau's spacesuit. The soldiers' slim, shadow-gray suits disappeared into the blackness.

"Alpha Dog, I have a question," Yaz said, her voice almost too quiet to hear. "Why are we whispering?"

"Cut it out, Yaz," Tau said.

"It's standard operating procedure," the sniper they called Jab whispered in his light Indian accent. He lay with his back magnetically secured to the hull so he didn't have to awkwardly aim his long Yume-C rifle directly over his head.

"Is it?" Yaz asked. "Did they give us like a handbook or something?"

"Special forces are supposed to be quiet when sneaking up on the enemy," Jab said.

"Are we?"

"Yeah. I think it's so they don't hear us coming."

"Oh, that's important. I guess. Wait. Did the bad guys figure out how to intercept narrow-beam transmissions?"

"No, but voices carry, you know."

"Voices carry across a couple hundred meters of vacuum?"

"Yours does."

Tau flicked off his microphone. He was

left in utter silence save the huffs of breath against the inside of his face shield. He'd never minded his squad joking around in the past, their job had become so routine it hardly mattered. Whether they were called in to take care of pirates, smugglers, or separatists, when a squad of Star Jumpers boarded a ship, the bad guys floated their guns and put their hands in the air. The Jumpers' reputation did the work for them. No one had fought back in years.

But something was different this time. Smugglers always took roundabout routes to avoid being spotted. Pirates always sold their stolen cargo outside of Sol System. Separatists always made friendly radio chatter to appear like just another commercial ship. But this freighter was on a direct trajectory to enter Earth orbit within a half hour and had been ignoring all attempts to communicate. Comm pings had shown the freighter's communications equipment was functioning, so it wasn't a technical problem. Tau had been trying to make sense of it for the handful of hours since they'd been ordered to fly out and intercept. He couldn't figure any way the facts added up.

Tau switched his microphone back on. "Sitrep," he said.

The reply crackled into Tau's helmet comm. "Almost there…. Locked." There was a moment of pause before the soldier spoke again. "Clear."

"Second pair, go," Tau ordered.

Two more soldiers jumped.

"Alpha … I can't really cover them when I can't see anything," Jab said.

Tau stared into the black void half his squad had already disappeared into. Jab was right, standard cover tactics didn't make sense when you couldn't get eyes on the team members you were meant to be covering.

"Second pair?" Tau said.

"Locked," came the reply, heavy with static.

"Fireteam Bravo you're jumping with me," Tau said.

Jab used a couple orienting bursts from the yume thrusters in the palms of his gloves to get his feet mag-locked to the surface and handed his sniper rifle to Yaz, who secured it to his back.

"Go," Tau said, leaping in synch with a quick thrust from his boots. The buzz of yume waves raced up his legs. The four members of Yaz's fireteam followed him.

The starless patch of sky above him grew larger until his entire field of vision was pure black save the blue glow of numbers in the lower corner of his visor. The digits rushed downward, counting off the meters until he hit the side of the freighter. With a few bursts from his gloves, Tau reoriented himself, flying feet-first.

"Alpha, are we really breaking standard procedure?" Jab asked.

"I didn't like the situation," Tau replied.

"Since when do you care about standard procedure?" Yaz asked.

The pop and hiss of comm static grew thicker as they approached the freighter.

"I didn't say I did," Jab said, "I'm just giddy that for once, Alpha decided—"

"The Star Jumpers need to evolve," Tau said. His HUD showed a couple dozen meters. He let out a decelerating thrust from his boots, just enough for his legs to absorb the last of his momentum as he landed against the freighter's hull. "I keep telling the brass—"

"We don't know how the pirates and the terrorists will adapt," Yaz said in the gruff tone and cadence she used for imitating him. She continued in an uptight voice, mocking the man they called Colonel Larry, "Training for every outlandish scenario your mind can dream up is a waste of our most precious resource: time." She touched down next to Tau and continued in his voice, "Those people *live* in space, they'll improvise new tactics faster than we can keep up." The faint glow of her HUD provided just enough light to put a gleam in her eye as she finished the argument in Colonel Larry's voice, "Gwembe, sometimes I think you didn't ever really want to be a squad leader. Now why would that be?"

She'd taken the joke too far, but if she hadn't, she wouldn't be Yaz. If they hadn't been in the middle of a mission he would have dressed her down for that. No, he wouldn't have. Somehow, she managed to be charming even when she was intentionally irritating.

"Be a smartass all you want, Yaz, you know I'm right," Tau said.

"I hope you *are* right," Jab said through static strong enough that his words were hard to make out. He pulled the short Yume-10 rifle off his back. "Someone trying to pull a new trick on us is the only thing that's gonna keep me from falling asleep on the job."

"Alpha Dog, you only put Jab on my fireteam because he's Indian, didn't you?" Yaz asked.

"I put him on your team because he's the only soldier I got who's a bigger pain in the ass than you," Tau replied. He crouched down next to Dizzy, their breach specialist, who was working on overriding the freighter's outer airlock door. Dizzy held a laser torch at the ready because the easy way never actually worked.

"I'm not even Indian, you know," Yaz said. "My father's from Bangladesh. Entirely different country."

"You know I already know that, Yaz," Tau said. "Everybody quiet."

The outer airlock door slid open, which was unexpected. Hijackers always locked out manual airlock controls. The mission was already too easy, and Tau didn't like it one bit. An airlock opening would pop up on all the control screens on the freighter's bridge. If whoever was in control of this ship didn't know Tau's squad was coming before, they sure knew it now.

For all their joking, the squad moved tactically and efficiently when it counted. Dizzy yanked himself through the hatch first to begin work on overriding the inner airlock door. The rest of Fireteam Charlie followed in order. By the time Tau pulled himself into the airlock, Dizzy was ready, but held off until the

four members of Fireteam Bravo squeezed in and the outer door closed.

Tau took a quick look through the inner airlock window. Beyond it lay an industrial corridor typical of freighters: metal on all sides, grated to reduce mass, the floor only distinguished by its lack of support beams, the ceiling only distinguished by the cold-white glow of circular lights evenly spaced down its length.

The inner door opened with a gasp, air rushing into the airlock. Dizzy lead Fireteam Charlie through feet first, one at a time, locking their boots to the wall opposite. Two of the soldiers trained their Yume-10 rifles down the corridor to the left, the other two to the right.

Someone tried to speak but static overwhelmed their words. Commercial vessels were lined with jamming equipment so pirates or terrorists couldn't have an inside man using his own communication device to help coordinate a hijacking. Dizzy, realizing his words weren't getting through, looked up at Tau and signaled "clear."

Tau jumped through the airlock door and locked his boots to the wall. Half the light panels had been smashed out and the far end of the corridor disappeared into uneven lighting. Black scorch marks darkened the wall in multiple places. A cardboard box and bits of trash floated in the air.

Dizzy flipped open his face shield. "Something went down here," he said, voice low.

Tau and the first four soldiers stepped down from the wall and onto the floor. He signaled Bravo team to enter.

While Yaz led Fireteam Bravo through the inner airlock door, Tau pulled up the schematics for this model of freighter on his HUD. Standard operating procedure was to take control of the ship's bridge, that gave you as much control of the situation as you were going to get. His HUD would show him the quickest route.

With comms non-functional, the squad members raised their face shields. Tau silently pointed and the squad set off, Dizzy taking point, all rifles at high ready—pressed against their shoulders, eyes trained down the sights, scanning the corridor's shadows for any hint of movement. Their helmet computers read the pressure on the soles of their boots and automatically switched the electromagnets off and on, allowing the soldiers to creep forward just as quickly as they could have under gravity. Yaz's Bravo Team walked backwards to cover the squad's rear. Dizzy had to knock the occasional bit of floating trash aside as he stalked forward. The broken lighting gave occasional glimpses of dents and scrapes on the walls.

Company workers were given detailed training on what to do in the event of a hijacking, and foremost among their orders was "don't try to fight." Their best chance of survival was to cooperate and let the professionals handle the bad guys. This freighter was either full of men with testosterone problems, or whatever happened here spooked the crew badly enough that they panicked.

A soft sound, like a trickle of water, caught Tau's attention. He held up a fist to halt his squad. As the noise grew louder, it resolved into endless distinct clacks, like hundreds of fingernails tapping against each other without rhythm or pattern.

Yaz looked at Tau and mouthed the words, "What the hell?"

Something leapt out of the darkness and wrapped itself around Dizzy.

"You're soldiers!" the figure exclaimed in a breathless voice. It was a man in a maintenance outfit, hair disheveled, a week's worth of stubble on his face, cheeks sunken and eyes strained as if he hadn't slept in days. "You gotta get me off the ship!"

Dizzy shoved the man off of him. "What the hell's going on here?" he demanded.

A second figure flew out of the shadows, throwing itself at Dizzy. Tau had just enough time to see the thing was an inhuman shape, spinning like a disk, before it ripped straight through Dizzy's clavicle, spraying blood into the air.

Dizzy's anguished scream overpowered the soldiers' shouts. Tau thrust his rifle against his shoulder and spun to get a read on the form. Tau's eyes struggled to make sense of the thing's shape, now floating nearly motionless in the better lit part of the corridor. It was a blob, maybe twice the diameter of a human head, with jellyfish tentacles streaming out from the center mass in every dimension, some as long as a man's arm. The body and tentacles were so dark in their aqua color they were nearly charcoal gray, with an iridescent sheen of aqua flashing off their surfaces. Droplets of Dizzy's dark-red blood painted its tentacles and floated in the air. The thing hung in the middle of the soldiers, a placement that prevented them from firing on it for fear of hitting each other in the crossfire.

"Jab!" Tau yelled.

"On it!" he called back. Tau kept his eye trained on the thing, but the sounds coming from behind told him Jab had opened his backpack med kit and set into stopping Dizzy's blood loss even before Tau had opened his mouth.

A twitch of the thing's tentacles made the soldiers flinch back. Its movements brought the same clacking noise they'd heard before. The thing had curled the top of a tentacle around a gap in the grating. Across its body, fist-sized holes opened and closed, the surface drawing back to an interior dark enough that no details could be seen. Whether they were eyes or mouths or something else entirely, Tau had no idea.

The thing flung itself at Yaz. Its body flattened and elongated, warped by the centrifugal force of its spin, all of the tentacles aligning to whip in circles like the teeth of a buzz saw. Yaz arched her upper body to one side, throwing her rifle up to block the attack. The whirling limbs clanged against her Yume-10 with a sound like a piece of metal shoved into a fan, cutting the rifle in half. She floated the rifle and engaged her boot and glove thrusters, rippling the air with the deep rumble of yume waves, throwing herself one way and the creature the other.

Tau tracked the thing down the sights of his rifle. He got a clear shot and took it.

The instant Tau pulled the trigger, the thing slapped a tentacle against the wall and changed its momentum. The blur of Tau's yume beam shot past the creature, the beam's deep buzz disappearing down the corridor. Tau fired again and again, his beam's heavy vibrations echoing off the walls. The thing seemed to know its survival depended on never continuing in a straight line for more than a fraction of a second. It dodged every shot.

Tau floated his rifle, stomped one boot behind him, mag-locked his feet to the surface, and fired his glove thrusters. The waves knocked the thing far enough down the corridor to present an open shot for his entire squad. None of them hesitated. A half-dozen yume rifles fired in quick succession, warping the air, overwhelming Tau's ears with their chest-rumbling buzz. They ripped the creature apart.

As the reverberation of the last shot faded away, Tau drew and exhaled a long breath. The corridor before him was littered with chunks of the thing's body and globs of fluids in black, dark yellow, green, and off-white. Which, if any, of those was the thing's blood, Tau had no idea. One piece of the creature, a nearly intact tentacle, began to wiggle, as if alive and still looking to attack. As it floated past him, Tau got just close enough to see that the tentacle's surface was not pliable, continuous skin, but rather looked to be thousands of interlocking triangular pieces, each rigid like a crab shell.

The squad stayed alert, half aiming their rifles down the corridor in one direction, half in the other.

"Alpha...."

Tau turned. From the look on Jab's face he knew straight away—Dizzy was dead.

Yaz started toward him, "Dizzy ... dammit, no. Dizzy!"

"I'm sorry," Jab said.

Tau sucked in a breath, fighting to keep his throat from closing into a sob. His squad needed him to keep his head on straight. Grieving would have to wait.

Yaz spun, seized the worker by the collar, and slammed him against the wall.

"What the hell was that thing?" she yelled through her teeth. "Are there more of them?"

"Yes," the worker said.

"How many?"

"No idea. Could be hundreds by now. You gotta get me off this ship."

"Hundreds?" Jab said.

"How could you not know?" Yaz asked.

"Every time one of those jellyfish things feeds, it pops off a couple of tentacles and those grow into new jellyfish creatures," he said. "I hadn't left that closet for days until I heard you."

"Feed on what?" Yaz asked.

The man started at her. "When this started a few days ago, there was only one jellyfish and more than a hundred crew. I'm probably the only one left."

Yaz's mouth twisted down in revulsion.

The ship had to be on autopilot, which meant that if they didn't stop it, the freighter would enter Earth orbit in less than twenty minutes and land at Achebe Port, Kenya a handful of minutes after that. Images of the jellyfish creatures running wild through downtown Nairobi flashed through Tau's mind. People ripped apart in the streets by the thousands, the creatures feeding and replicating until they became an endless swarm that devoured every living thing on the continent.

Earth had to be warned. If the Star Jumpers couldn't get control of the ship, the freighter needed to be shot out of the sky. Tau opened a channel to their transport ship's pilot. Static squawked back at him. That left one clear tactical objective.

"We take the bridge," Tau said.

"Master Sergeant, are you serious?" Jab asked.

"We run this same as any other mission," Tau said. "Take the bridge, control the ship, control the situation."

"Roger that," Yaz said. She snatched Dizzy's rifle out of the air. Jab put Dizzy's body over one shoulder, holding it down with one arm and wielding a rifle with the other. Tau placed the worker's hand on his shoulder and motioned his squad forward.

"Please," the man said, holding on to Tau, his body trailing behind. "Can't you get me off the ship, first? I don't want to get eaten by the jellies. I've seen it. It's horrible. Please."

Tau shook his head. "No time. What's your name?"

"Oliver," the man replied.

"How'd that jellyfish thing get on your ship?" Tau asked.

"Don't know," Oliver said. "We were in deep space, between systems, when it first attacked."

The clacking noise of another creature yanked a gasp from Oliver's throat.

Monk, the squad's heavy gunner, pulled the wide-barreled Yume-A2 from her back and looked at Tau, who shook his head.

"The corridor's too tight," he said. "The bounceback will knock us all on our butts."

"Rather be on my butt than six feet under," she said.

"Keep it ready," Tau said. "But no firing unless I give the say so and make damn sure it's aimed directly down the corridor."

The squad continued forward, moving as quickly and quietly as possible, rifles at high ready. Tau signaled directions until they reached the final dark corridor before the passageway that would give them a direct line of sight to the bridge. He faced his squad.

"We can't let them get to Earth," he said, careful to keep emotion out of his voice. "No matter what it takes ... not one of those things gets off this ship. No matter what it takes."

In turn, Tau met the eyes of the seven remaining members of his squad. Each nodded.

"You understand what I'm saying?" Tau asked. "You understand what I'm asking of you right now?"

"Tau...." Yaz said. "Everyone understands."

"But there's gotta be more of those jellyfish somewhere out there," Jab said. "Even if we keep this horde from getting to Earth, if none of us are left alive to warn everyone what's waiting out there between the stars.... Sooner or later they take another ship and find their way to Earth."

Yaz slowly nodded. "The next Jumper squad to come across them won't be any more prepared than us." She looked at Tau with a grim smile. "You officially won your argument with Colonel Larry."

For a moment, the enormity of it all overwhelmed Tau. He clenched his teeth and said, "We don't have to kill every jellyfish on this ship, we just have to take the bridge and get a message out. Whatever happens after that, at least Earth will know." Tau removed Oliver's hand from his shoulder. "Stay here. We'll get you when the bridge is clear."

Jab thrust Dizzy's dead body onto Oliver. "And hold onto Dizzy."

Oliver reeled back, face twisting.

"Hey, this man gave his life to rescue you and your crew," Jab said. "We're not gonna leave him behind."

Tau pressed his back to the wall. He thrust his head around the corner just long enough to get a glimpse. Like the other corridors, the broken lighting and hard shadows made it difficult to see clearly. A number of jellyfish hung onto the series of archways leading to the door of the bridge, some half the size of the first creature they encountered, some more than twice as large. Tau yanked his head back.

"There's eight or so of them," he whispered. "All different sizes. They're around the door, but it's open. About two dozen meters between us and them."

Yaz cursed in whatever language people spoke in Bangladesh. "Open door sounds like a lure," she said.

"If this was a trap they wouldn't be out in the open where we could see them," Jab said.

"Flashbang," Tau said, sticking out his hand. Yaz pulled one of the small silver cylinders off her belt and handed it to him. Tau activated it and stepped out just far enough to toss it underhand. It floated through the air, timer silently counting down, drifting into the center of the mass of jellyfish. Tau jumped back behind the wall. A blinding flare and clap of thunder erupted from the intersection.

The soldiers stormed the corridor, sighting creatures and firing as fast as their fingers could pull the triggers. The jellyfish seemed stunned by the flashbang, floating in the air with little movement and no direction. The barrage of howling yume beams ripped the creatures apart, bits of flesh shredding and globs of fluid scattering until none of the jellyfish were left in one piece.

"Cease fire," Tau called out.

The air stilled as the last of the beams dissipated. There were no more jellyfish, just chunks of their limbs and pieces of their innards floating in the corridor. Tau signaled Bravo Team to cover the rear. He fought to keep his breath calm in hopes he'd hear if any more of the creatures were coming their way.

"Why haven't more come out of the bridge?" Yaz whispered.

"They might have gotten enough of the flashbang that they're stunned, too," Jab said.

"Or they're smart enough to know better than to charge armed soldiers," Yaz said.

The idea that the jellyfish might be intelligent enough to think tactically froze Tau, but only for a moment. He didn't really have a choice. They needed to press their advantage, and do it quickly.

"Forward. Double time," he ordered.

The soldiers advanced as a team, fast walking, rifles at high ready, quietly as they could without sacrificing speed. Tau, in the middle, strained to look past the globs of jellyfish parts and the heads of the three soldiers in front of him, eyes searching for any sign of movement in the small bit of the bridge he could see. Monk slowed just as she reached the entrance to the bridge and looked back over her shoulder for the go signal. As soon as she turned her head, her eyes grew wide.

Instantly, Tau realized his mistake.

The monstrous creatures leapt out from behind the corridor's arches, attacking the squad from all sides, the clack of their tentacles like the rush of a river.

Soldiers screamed in surprise and fear and pain. Rifle beams and thruster waves rippled the air, overwhelming Tau's ears. A shredding pain gouged deep across his thigh, another across his back. Soldiers flailed and threw their bodies in every direction, desperately trying to get away from the swarm of thrashing jellyfish tentacles. In the choppy light, warp of yume waves, and frenetic movement, Tau's eyes couldn't sort out what was what. Pieces of dead jellyfish, lives ones on the attack, the bodies of his teammates, streams of blood from both humans and jellyfish—it all spun around him too fast.

A jellyfish leapt for his face. Tau jerked backward and threw a blast from his glove on pure instinct. The wave knocked the creature back and cleared the air in front of him just enough for Tau to get his bearings. More of the things crawled out of the door to the bridge. It made his tactical decision easy.

"Fall back!" he yelled.

Tau punched and shot and kicked jellyfish back with boot thrusters, but he could not make progress. His soldiers were trying to fight their way back, but it was all they could do just to stay alive. One of them floated in the air, no longer fighting, while jellyfish ripped open the soldier's suit and attached to his body. The soldier was dead and the creatures were feeding. The tentacles of one of the feeding jellyfish ballooned grotesquely in places, like a snake that had swallowed a rabbit that was bigger around than its body. Tau shot the creature full of holes.

A yume beam punched through the stomach of one of the soldiers, spraying blood out the man's back.

"Check your targets! Check your targets!" Tau screamed. He doubted anyone could hear him through the commotion.

Monk, one jellyfish wrapped around her chest and another around her arm, fought to raise her bulky Yume-A2 rifle.

"No!" Tau yelled.

In Monk's struggle with the jellyfish, the rifle wound up pointed directly at the wall when the tip of the creature's tentacle reached inside the trigger guard.

The explosive wave shattered all of Tau's senses. He must have been thrown by the blast, but his eyes were shocked into blindness and his ears could hear nothing save the buzzing of his skull. He could get no feeling for anything around him. He might be dead, crushed against a wall, for all he could tell.

Tau had no idea how long he floated, stunned, before a voice broke through the muffle of his ears, screaming, "Tau! Tau!"

He forced his eyes open. Yaz was yanking him through the air. They were still in the corridor. The bodies of soldiers and jellyfish lay scattered through the air, half of them struggling to move, half not moving at all. Yaz grabbed another soldier by his backpack and yume-kicked off the wall. Two more men managed to get away with them.

Oliver floated in the air, curled into a ball with his head ducked down, eyes squeezed tight, hands over his ears. Jab grabbed him by the shoulder and Oliver flinched in fear.

"What was that explosion?" Oliver said. "Are they dead?"

Jab grabbed Oliver under the armpits and squatted horizontally, feet against a wall in preparation to jump.

"What about Dizzy's body?" Oliver said. "You said we weren't gonna leave him behind."

"We're gonna leave him behind," Jab said.

He yume-jumped off the wall, the two racing away down the corridor. Yaz did the same, groaning under the strain of keeping her grip as the inertia of two grown men pulled against her sudden acceleration. They slammed into the wall at the end of the corridor. Yaz didn't let go of either man, quickly recovering and yume-jumping again. She zigzagged through the corridors, putting as much distance as possible between them and the horde of creatures.

"We're clear," Tau said, gently pulling free of Yaz's grip. "We gotta regroup."

Tau had four soldiers left: Jab and Bad Hand, who were his two snipers, Swank, and, thank God, Yaz. She had drops of blood floating out of a gash on her cheek and the A2 tucked under one armpit. Dangerous as it was, they might need it yet. It was impressive that she'd had the presence of mind to snatch it out of the air while pulling her teammates to safety. It was a hell of an odd time for Tau to find himself lamenting that he was ten years too old for her.

"What now?" Yaz asked.

"We gotta hope we can get to one of the airlocks," Tau said. "We gotta get to the transport and relay a message to Earth to shoot this freighter out of the sky."

"Whoa, what?" Oliver said. "We're still *on* this freighter."

Tau led the way on foot, following the directions of his HUD, snaking from one corridor to the next, rifle at high ready, finger tense against the trigger. They reached an airlock at the intersection of three corridors. Not a defendable position. At least all the corridors were a few dozen meters long. If the jellyfish attacked, they'd see it coming. As Yaz worked the inner door controls, her teammates covered each of the corridors at the end of their rifles.

"Swank, you're jumping," Tau said.

Movement drew his eye. At the end of one corridor, a jellyfish crawled around the corner and hung from the ceiling. Jab fired a shot that blew off one of the creature's tentacles. It reeled back but did not retreat. A second jellyfish joined it.

"Yaz!" Tau yelled.

"I know!" she replied.

The inner airlock door slid open and

Swank leapt in. Yaz shut it behind him and spun with her weapon up, sighting the creatures and firing off her first shot in the space of a breath. More of the jellyfish joined the two at the end of the corridor. One of the jellyfish flung itself at them. It became a vertical whirling disk, seen edge-on. Yaz and Jab fired on it, but their shots missed its thin profile until it was almost on top of them. Their last few shots tore the creature apart an instant before it reached them. They spun away to avoid the chunks of flesh and liquid carried forward by momentum.

Tau glanced through the airlock window just in time to see thruster waves fire against the glass and Swank shoot into space, the Star Jumper transport ship in the distance behind him. With some luck they might be able to hold off the creatures long enough for their pilot to dock with the airlock and move Oliver across to their ship. If there were any other survivors still on the freighter there was nothing more that could be done for them.

Tau huffed out a relieved breath. At the very least, their transport ship would send out a warning. Earth would know—

A jellyfish came flying in from the left side of Tau's view and slammed into Swank, wrapping its long tentacles around his body and knocking him off trajectory. Blood sprayed into the vacuum of space. Swank and the creature spun out of sight.

"No!" Tau yelled. He flipped on his comm. "Swank! Swank!"

All that came back to Tau was static.

A jellyfish leapt into the airlock from the outside, coming straight at Tau and ramming the tip of one tentacle through the window. Tau threw himself back in surprise. The high hiss of air escaping through the hole in the glass was overpowered by the soldiers opening fire again. Tau spun and jammed the stock of this rifle against his shoulder. What little remained of his squad were shooting in different directions. The jellyfish were coming at them from two corridors now.

Tau fired off a few shots before yelling,

"Fall back!"

His squad scampered backward, continuing to fire. As Yaz pulled even with the airlock window, the jellyfish inside ripped its tentacle back, shattering the glass outward. Air whipped past the soldiers and out the airlock with a hollow whoosh. Yaz spun just in time to see the creature lunge for her, but its attack was slowed fighting the rush of wind. She hit it with a dozen beams, shredding it into fragments.

The squad continued back, firing at the handful of jellyfish that crawled across the ceiling and leapt from wall to wall. Tau pulled the freighter plans up on his HUD and searched for any other airlocks they might be able to reach. None. It was just as well, Tau suspected if they made it outside they'd just be walking into the same ambush that had been waiting for Swank.

What could they do to get a message out? There must have been a half-dozen places on the ship with long-distance communication ability, but none they were likely to get to. They were being pushed to the rear of the ship, cut off from everything save the cargo holds and the engine room.

"Oliver!" Tau yelled. "If we can get to the engine room, can we shut down the magnetic coils?"

"What? No!" Oliver yelled back. "The entire ship would turn into a nuclear fireball!"

"That's the idea," Tau said.

"No, they've got safeguards against crap like that."

"Damn," Tau said. "But we could disable the fusion reactor, right?"

"Yeah, we could disable it or alter the thrust," Oliver said.

"We can alter thrust? Including trajectory? You're sure of that?"

"Won't have navigation instruments so our steering won't be too precise, but yeah."

Tau yelled to his three remaining soldiers. "With me, fast as you can!"

He didn't have to tell them what he really meant was "fast as you can move backwards while firing." The creatures kept coming, more and more of them crawling into the corridor, covering the walls and ceiling and floor. There were too many, the squad wouldn't make it to the engine room before being overrun.

"Flashbang!" Yaz called out, and whipped one of the small cylinders down the hallway. Everyone spun, covering their eyes and ears against the blinding snap of light and ear-splitting crack of thunder. Tau glanced at Yaz's belt—she only had one flashbang left.

The team made some distance before the jellyfish regained their senses and charged again. By the time the soldiers reached the door to the engine room, the corridor was so thick with them that any rifle shot could hardly help but hit one of the creatures.

Tau hauled Oliver into the cavernous engine room while Yaz, Jab, and Bad Hand stood just inside the doorway, filling the corridor with the rumble of yume beams. He could make no sense of the jumble of machinery that made up the ship's reactor, interwoven into the rough shape of a column stretching the entire twenty meters to the ceiling and eight meters in diameter, filling up a third of the room. The space was dimly lit by lights shining up from the handful of walkways that circled the column and what little fusion flickered out of the reactor while the ship was not thrusting.

"Can you crash the ship?" Tau asked.

"Into what?" Oliver asked.

"The Earth."

"Okay, but then ... how do we get off?"

"We don't."

Oliver's face twisted. "But ... I could steer us away from Earth," he said. "How long until another team of Star Jumpers comes?"

"Too long," Tau said. "We'd get overrun long before they got here and then the autopilot would steer this thing back to Earth."

"But you said there's more of those things somewhere out there," Oliver said. "Even if we kill all these...."

Tau nodded. "I know. But there's nothing we can do about that. We have to take care of the immediate threat and pray the next time this happens someone finds a way to send out a warning."

Oliver's mouth opened and closed, no words coming out.

"There is no way off this ship," Tau said. "We are either going to be the heroes who saved humanity or the cowards who doomed it, but no matter what, we will not survive."

Oliver's chin trembled, but Tau could see it in the man's eyes—he was starting to accept that Tau was right.

Tau said, "Before we die, we have one last job to do: point this ship toward the Earth and fire those engines."

Oliver nodded, tears forming.

Tau said, "What do you need from me?"

Oliver shook his head. He looked up at an instrument panel in the middle of a walkway five meters above them. "Even after I fire the engines, if they wreck the control panel or damage the engines too much it throws off our trajectory and we miss the Earth. You have to keep them out of here until we crash. Understand?"

"Roger that," Tau said.

Oliver leapt for the walkway, grabbed hold of a railing, and pulled himself to the panel.

"Tau!" Yaz yelled. "A-two!"

Jab and Bad Hand had already turned away and covered their ears. Yaz had her body halfway behind the doorway, the Yume-A2 in her hands, carefully levelling it to aim directly down the corridor. She thrust the end of the barrel as far out of the engine room as she could manage. Tau spun and covered his ears.

The thunder of the wave shook Tau's entire body. He turned to see the first dozen meters of the corridor had been cleared of jellyfish, their innards smeared across the walls. But those further along the corridor had only been knocked back and were regaining their wits. They rushed forward, tumbling over each other to get at the soldiers.

"Damn," Yaz said. She floated the A2 and lifted her Yume-10. Jab and Bad Hand joined her, opening fire with their sniper rifles. The A2 only had so many shots until it ran dry. Yaz could pull that trick a handful more times, but after that there'd be nothing left to do but try to pick off the creatures one by one.

"Hey!" Oliver yelled. "Hey Alpha … guy…!"

Tau jumped, grabbed a railing and pulled himself down onto the walkway where Oliver floated in front of the control panel.

"It's not working," Oliver said, voice raised to be heard above the deep screech of yume beams.

"What? Why not?" Tau asked.

"There's safeguards against crashes built into the bridge controls," Oliver said, "It's auto-rejecting the trajectory."

"Is there any way—?"

"We can cut the data lines," Oliver said. "Between here and the bridge."

"Show me where."

Oliver tilted his head up and swiveled it back and forth, searching.

"Uh … jeez," he said.

"A-two!" Yaz yelled from below.

Tau and Oliver covered their ears. A deep roar shook the entire room.

"We don't got a lot of time," Tau said.

"Just rip out all that," Oliver said, sweeping his hand across dozens of colored pipes that blanketed the ceiling twenty meters above their heads.

Tau muttered a curse and leapt. He reoriented and landed with his feet against the ceiling, magnetically locking his boots against the metal pipes. The Yume-10's beams were designed to dissipate over distance to avoid breaching the hull of a ship, but close up the beam was concentrated enough to puncture metal. Tau fired a shot. It punched a hole clean through the pipe, but a small one.

"Bad Hand!" Tau yelled. "Get up here!"

Bad Hand looked back and forth between the corridor and Tau.

"Go!" Yaz yelled.

Bad Hand jumped, flipping himself over in mid-air and landing next to Tau.

"We need to shred the wires inside all these pipes," Tau said.

The pair opened fire, Bad Hand's sniper rifle doing a more effective job than Tau's weapon. Still, it was taking too long. The jellyfish threatened to overrun the engine room at any second.

"A-two!" Yaz called again.

Tau didn't stop to cover his ears. He kept firing into the pipes as the blast shook the metal under his feet. When he'd cut through all the pipes directly under him, Tau looked up. Bad Hand was almost through the last set. Yaz and Jab were holding the door. They might make it yet.

Bad Hand's sniper rifle had blasted clear through the pipes and the ceiling in a jagged line. He stopped firing.

"Good. Get back to—" Tau began.

Jellyfish tentacles erupted through the crack and seized Bad Hand, crushing him against the ceiling before he could utter anything more than a gasp. The soldier's bones cracked and blood gushed from his body. Tau opened fire into the tangle of arms.

The ceiling ruptured, a dozen jellyfish spinning out in all directions, filling the air with the clack of their tentacles. Tau yume-kicked away, rifle aimed between his feet, firing wildly, howling in warning to his team. One of the creatures flung itself directly at him. Just before it would have shredded his leg, he managed to shove one boot in its path and fire a thruster wave to knock it back, sending himself spinning. He bounced off the floor shoulder-first. For a second he could do nothing but try to draw air into his lungs as he slowly drifted upward.

Still struggling to breathe, Tau snatched the last flashbang off Yaz's belt. She spun to look at him.

"What…?" she began.

Tau flung the flashbang up into a cloud of jellyfish.

"Oh hell," Yaz said, then spun away, clamping her eyes shut.

The explosion carried little concussive force, but the burst of light shone through

Tau's eyelids. When he looked back up, every jellyfish in the room was floating aimlessly, stunned. But it would only last for a second.

More jellyfish poured out of the crack in the ceiling. Yaz punched Jab in the chest, nodded up at the creatures and yelled, "Go! I'm right behind you!"

Jab leapt upward with a yume-jump, aiming along his rifle sight and picking off jellyfish as he flew. Tau followed, doing the same. An instant later, the thunder of the A2 vibrated him right down to the teeth.

A reactor panel shattered under a creature's tentacles, sparks and metal debris exploding outward. Were they attacking the reactor on purpose? The thought would have shocked Tau with fear if he'd had even one second between trigger pulls to register an emotion.

Somehow Tau managed to spot Bad Hand's sniper rifle floating through the middle of the room. He snatched it and kicked off the reactor structure, directing himself back to the control panel.

Tau landed directly behind Oliver, doing the best he could to shield the man's body with his own. Wielding a rifle in each hand, he filled the air around them with yume beams.

"You got it or not?" Tau yelled.

"Just need a minute...." Oliver said, eyes locked on the control panel, fingers moving frantically.

"It look to you like we got a minute?" Tau said.

He fired both rifles up at a jellyfish spinning directly for them. A second jellyfish targeted them. Then a third and a fourth. He'd never get them all in time.

Yaz shouldered him aside and unleashed a boom from the A2. The jellyfish flying for them were crushed and flung backward. Even in the massive engine room, the bounce-back still rattled Tau's skull.

"Thank y—" Tau began.

Yaz grabbed the back of his helmet, pulled him down, and kissed him.

"Well," she said, "we've pretty much run out of time for you to make a move on me, so I had to take matters into my own hands."

"But ... I'm your superior officer," Tau said.

Yaz floated the A2 and whipped a Yume-10 up against her shoulder, opening fire. "Sorry, it's too late to talk dirty to me now."

Tau put his back against Yaz's and fired into the swirl of jellyfish spinning past in every direction.

"Whoa...." Oliver muttered.

"What?" Tau yelled. "You got it?"

"I can launch the black box from here. With all the flight data and video recordings. It won't survive our impact with Earth but I could eject it before we crash. It's got a beacon. They'll find it, they'll see the jellies."

"So do it."

"I'll have to back out of this control set...."

"No! We got less than five minutes before this ship enters orbit and starts landing procedure. Fire the engines first. Then the black box. Got it?"

"Alpha!" Jab hollered.

Tau stopped firing just long enough to look down. A jellyfish was entering the room, a creature so large it had to thrust two of its tentacles through the door before squeezing its body through. The bulk of its mass expanded as it pushed clear of the doorway. The giant slapped arms against the floor to pull itself forward, each impact rattling the walkway.

Jab fired at the creature, every shot popping a hole that spurted fluid. The wounds were tiny on the monstrous jellyfish. It continued forward, swinging a tentacle that barely missed the soldier. Tau and Yaz directed their shots at the giant. It lumbered forward as if their yume beams were beneath its notice.

Jab backed away, shooting as fast as his rifle could fire. A jellyfish struck him from behind, knocking the rifle from his hand and opening a bloody gash across his back. He threw himself forward, snatching his rifle out of the air, spinning, and opening fire on the creature that had wounded him. The tentacle of the giant jellyfish snapped tight around his chest.

Yaz pulled herself over the side of the walkway and kicked off. She pulled the A2 up and took aim at the center of the giant's mass. The instant she got close enough that Jab was outside the weapon's blast cone, she pulled the trigger.

Nothing happened. The A2 had run dry.

Yaz floated the weapon and fired all four glove and boot thrusters, but the maneuver didn't get her far enough fast enough. One of the giant's tentacles swatted her out of the air, throwing her across the room and bouncing her off the far wall.

The giant slammed Jab against the floor. The soldier's body broke in too many ways. He went limp. The surface of the giant's body opened in multiple places at once as the tentacles ripped Jab into two pieces. It scooped Jab's body halves into the openings.

The giant lunged forward, slamming an enormous tentacle against the walkway, crushing it into a V shape. Tau, still maglocked, was jerked down, awkwardly attached to one slope. Oliver, who floated free, startled to see the walkway bend beneath him. Tau concentrated his fire on the giant's tentacle, causing the limb to flinch back. A jellyfish came spinning down at Oliver from above. Tau was forced to refocus his aim, his beams cutting it apart just in time. Only chunks of flesh and blood remained, momentum splattering those pieces across the control panel. Oliver wiped a hand across the screen and kept working.

Below, the giant's tentacle swung for Yaz again. She yume-kicked off the ground and riddled the limb with holes.

"Yaz!" Tau yelled.

Continuing upward, Yaz looked at Tau, who held up a gloved fist, the hum of a charge building. She nodded without hesitation, though a flash of emotion played itself across the twist of her lips. Yaz shoved off a walkway and flew past the giant, just out of reach, shooting into its core. With his free hand, Tau took shots at every jellyfish that caught his eye.

Tau's HUD warned him that his left glove was building up a dangerous charge, indicator light changing from yellow to orange. He pushed it into the red, the vibration in his glove deepening until it numbed his hand straight down to the bones.

A yelp from below yanked Tau's attention back to the giant. It had Yaz in one tentacle and was about to crush her. Tau yume-jumped at a downward angle off the railing, directly at the giant, praying it would expose its mouth again. It did.

With a howl of rage and fear, Tau flew with his left arm straight out, ramming it as deep as he could into the giant's open mouth and letting go of the glove's charge.

The yume explosion stunned Tau's brain, disrupting all of his senses. His mind barely registered that he'd been pitched backward. His back slammed against an unmoving beam, sending him spiraling off. He triggered his suit's auto-stabilize function. Some malfunction signal lit on his HUD and it took longer than expected for him to stop spinning. When he regained enough control of his thoughts to check if his body was all in one piece, he realized it was not. His left forearm was misshapen, the bones of his hand crushed to the point it was unrecognizable. Somewhere in his mind he knew he should be in pain, but he felt nothing.

A groan from Yaz pulled his attention up. She floated, her body slowly regaining movement, the limp tentacle of the giant hovering lifelessly next to her. The beast was still in one piece, but its body bulged in odd disfigurations and fluids flowed from its mouth.

"Tau?" Yaz said, her lungs fighting to squeeze out the single word.

Tau only managed to grunt in reply.

"Thanks," Yaz said.

A roar filled Tau's ears. His body slammed to the floor. He opened his eyes to see the room filled with brightly dancing flickers of warm light. Dozens of jellyfish rained down on him. His brain registered gravity pushing him against the ground. The ship was accelerating.

One of the jellyfish fell directly toward Tau's face. He rolled out of the way as the thing thudded against the floor. It hopped back up and sprung off its tentacles, leaping for his face. He knocked it back with his remaining glove thruster. It wouldn't take but a second to recover and come back for him. Where the hell was his rifle?

Oliver screamed. The acceleration had knocked him off the sloped walkway and onto the floor. By the time Tau spotted him, the jellyfish had already ripped him apart.

Tau struggled to get off the floor. He still needed to keep the jellyfish from doing too much damage before the ship crashed. He still needed to launch the black box. He had to find his rifle and climb up to the control panel.

The buzz of yume beams made his head swivel. Yaz was on her feet, picking off jellyfish as they climbed the reactor. Tau fought to get up, but the ship was under more than one gravity of acceleration—or at least it felt like it. As beat up and exhausted as Tau was, he had no way to judge what a gravity should feel like. He pulled up gravity on his HUD. It read 1.4 g and climbing.

Tau yume-jumped, thankful that his suit was designed to read the force of gravity against his boot soles and auto-adjust thrust. He stumbled down onto the section of walkway that was still mostly horizontal, falling to his knees. A jellyfish dropped next to him and bounced right back up, spinning forward, its clacking tentacles lashing out. A yume beam from below punched through the dead center of its body. The creature's momentum threw it against Tau, knocking him over, but the slack tentacles didn't cut any deeper than his suit fabric.

"What the hell are you doing?" Yaz yelled up at him.

"I can launch the black box from here!" Tau yelled back. "We can warn Earth!"

Yaz yume-jumped up to the walkway, rifle firing the whole way. Tau yanked the glove off his one useable hand with his teeth and worked the control panel as Yaz stood with her back to his, firing an endless volley of shots. The roar of the fusion engine grew louder, the strain on Tau's muscles heavier, by the second. They were almost at double Earth gravity.

"You figure it out?" Yaz yelled.

"Yeah," Tau answered.

"Include a message. Tell Colonel Larry, 'Kiss my ass.'"

Tau pressed the record button, "This message is for Colonel Anton Lawrence. Yaz says kiss her ass."

"No! Kiss *your* ass."

"Kiss both our asses," Tau yelled into the control panel. "And the ass of every member of Jump Team Red who died today. That's 18 butt cheeks—kiss 'em all!"

Tau mashed the launch button with his thumb. The control panel indicated the freighter's black box had been jettisoned into space.

Jellyfish toppled from the side of the reactor, crashing off the walkway, thudding to the floor. Acceleration passed two and a half g. Tau collapsed to his knees, laboring to draw breath. The creatures continued to lumber forward, fighting with all they had to climb the walkway, but they made no progress. Yaz's rifle went silent.

She dropped down in front of Tau, bringing the two face to face.

"You *do* have a sense of humor," she said. "Always knew it."

"Thank you," he said. "For everything."

An overwhelming rumble shook the room like an earthquake. They'd hit Earth's atmosphere. Tau and Yaz floated up off the walkway as the decelerating force of air resistance balanced the acceleration of the ship's thrust and they became weightless again.

It would only be a few seconds, now.

Tau wrapped Yaz in a hug. She clung to him, gripping with all her strength, helmet pressed against his shoulder.

"Love you, Yasmine," he said.

"Love you, too, Sarge."

"The Star Jumpers" debuts in this issue. Accompanying llustration by Allen Koszowski.

It wasn't until David VonAllmen's high school professor decided one of his short stories was suspiciously high in literary merit and threatened to have him expelled for plagiarism that he realized he just might have the talent to be a real writer. David's writing has appeared in Marvel Comics, Galaxy's Edge, Writers of the Future, and other professional publications. David is the Grand Prize winner for the 2018 Baen Fantasy Adventure Award. He lives in his hometown of St. Louis with his wife, Ann, and children, Lucas and Eva, who write some pretty darn good stories of their own. Links to his other works can be found at davidvonallmen.com (ILLUSTRATION BELOW BY ALLEN KOSZOWSKI)

LOST and FOUND:
REMEMBERING LOST IN SPACE

By Gregory L. Norris

IT DIDN'T TAKE LONG FOR TV VIEWERS TUNING TO CBS ON THE EVENING OF SEPTEMBER 15, 1965 TO FIGURE OUT THAT THEY WERE IN FOR SOMETHING BIG. Energy builds. The space vehicle's powerful deutronium-fueled engines strobe and pulse, the heartbeat signaling the *Jupiter 2* is nearing takeoff. Then the saucer-shaped colony ship glows, turns her prow spaceward, and ascends.

"This is the beginning. This is the day," an announcer's voice boomed out as the cameras panned across a futuristic control room. "You are watching the unfolding of one of history's great adventures: man's colonization of space beyond the stars..."

That great adventure was coming to weekly television audiences courtesy of producer Irwin Allen, who had conquered the deep one season earlier with *Voyage to the Bottom of the Sea*. Allen's new series would depict a voyage of another kind—one that would leave a futuristic family lost in space.

The series chronicled the adventures of the Robinson clan, who bid goodbye to an overcrowded Earth in the then far-off year of 1997. The Robinsons never made it to their

promised land, a planet in the solar system Alpha Centauri, though they spent eighty-three episodes trying to get there. But for legions of impressionable young fans, being lost was half the fun.

"TV at the time was designed more for kids as opposed to adults. *Lost in Space* was clever without being mean-spirited or cynical," recalls Kevin Burns, a former Fox executive and first generation *LiS* fan who spent thousands of dollars of his own money collecting and restoring various artifacts from the series. "It was much more visual and inventive, less topical, which is why shows like *Lost in Space* still play today. *Lost in Space* wasn't made only for the time. It was made to be timeless."

It was also very expensive to produce. The pilot episode, "No Place to Hide", cost a then-staggering $700,000. That budget bought plenty of intergalactic thrills and chills, including meteor storms, a breathtaking spaceship crash landing on an uncharted planet, and a race of giant Cyclops creatures. It also gave Allen the chance to create a large ensemble cast for the show. Guy Williams, best known to TV audiences as the swashbuckling Zorro, was cast as the family patriarch, Professor John Robinson. *Lassie* co-star June Lockhart came aboard as his wife, biologist Maureen Robinson. Playing the ship's pilot, Major Donald West, was *The Detectives* heart-throb, Mark Goddard. Marta Kristen was cast as Judy, the family's golden-haired elder daughter, while *The Sound of Music*'s Angela Cartwright played middle child, Penny.

Rounding out the clan was ten-year-old Bill Mumy, already a genre vet thanks to his appearance in the classic *Twilight Zone* episode "It's a Good Life," as boy genius Will Robinson. The Robinsons also picked up an intergalactic hitchhiker in the form of an alien monkey with exaggerated ears known as Debbie the Bloop. Despite crowded accommodations, CBS insisted that the Robinson's spaceship needed two more passengers.

"Perry Lafferty, one of the network execs, felt the show could use a recurring villain," Goddard remembers. "They were smart enough to also create a robot along with the villain to knock us off course and get us lost."

A rebooted and recut pilot, "The Reluctant Stowaway," was shot, introducing the sinister Doctor Zachary Smith. Also added to the cast was a barrel-chested robot, which Smith reprogrammed to destroy the ship eight hours after takeoff. When last minute tampering trapped Smith onboard, he too went along for the voyage. Footage from the original pilot was used over four of the first five episodes of Season One. For *LiS*'s second

(and considered by many fans among its best), the crew of *Jupiter 2* encounters a massive derelict spaceship that draws them into its maw and leads to their first encounter with the galaxy's numerous forms of alien life. Those early episodes combine gothic horror, the ticking clock element of danger, and classic science fiction adventure with the perfect doses of elegance in crisp black and white detail.

"Those early episodes were terrific," says Tom Kerr, a professional actor and lifelong fan of the series. "Doctor Smith had not yet become a buffoon and was actually quite a menacing character. And since the robot was

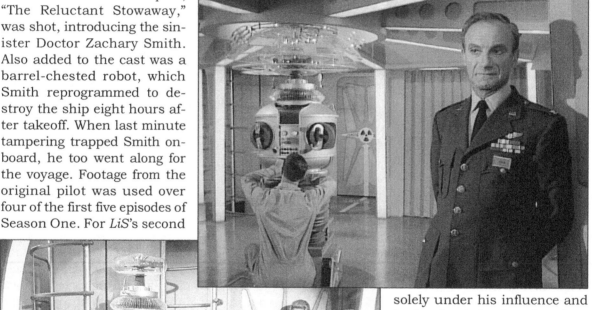

solely under his influence and had not yet developed a close attachment to the rest of the family, it was often quite frightening. The first journeys out of the spacecraft with John and Maureen Robinson floating in space were tense and filled with real danger. When the Robinsons crash on their first planet, the fight for survival is presented quite realistically and the stakes couldn't be

boulders being thrown by the one-eyed giant? The show hadn't become slapstick yet and was instead a genuine look at the struggles in an alien world."

Master of snark Jonathan Harris was cast as the villainous Smith, while it took two actors to bring the robot to life. Five-foot-seven Bob May got the more physically demanding half of the role. He was the poor soul who was jammed into all that metal week after week.

higher. Who can forget the blinding sun almost burning them to a crisp or the raging seas tossing the Chariot around like a dog's chew toy? And the Cyclops monster—wow! What kid doesn't remember those giant

"In the opening episodes, I had to make the robot walk using my own legs," the late actor told me during a 2001 conversation. "Doing that cut me up pretty bad. When Irwin saw how bloody I got, they bolted the robot's legs together and

post-production and called in voice-over expert Dick Tufeld, whom he'd hired to be the show's announcer.

"I remember saying to Irwin, 'I presume you're looking for a mechanical, robotian kind of sound,'" the late actor recalled during that same conversation in 2001. "He said, 'My dear boy, that is exactly what I don't want.' So in a very low-key

pulled it along by hidden cables." But that wasn't the end of May's robotic woes. "Film in those days wasn't as fast, so more lights were used on the set. Plus, the robot suit radiated its own heat from all the electrical cables in it. I'm the only actor in Hollywood

voice, I said, 'This will not compute. Danger, warning.' After about ten minutes, he told me he just wasn't hearing what he wanted and said he'd have to look further. I thanked him and started toward the door. One foot from leaving, I turned back and asked to try something else. Then in my best mechanical voice, I bellowed, "Danger! Warning! That will not compute!" He said, 'Jesus Christ! What took you so long?' And that's how I became the voice of the robot."

Though little more than a sinister prop in those first episodes, the robot moved to center stage as his friendship with young Will Robinson was developed by the show's writers. The Doctor Smith character, meanwhile, underwent its own transformation.

who ever had his own jacuzzi and sauna built into his wardrobe."

Though May memorized and performed all of the robot's lines, he ended up sounding like what he was: a man stuck in a tin can. Allen needed to have the lines redone during

"Jonathan wisely recognized that a villain

of that darkness had nowhere to go, so he very subtly started to seed humor into the character, ultimately making him more buffoonish, somebody you loved to hate," Mumy told me in 2001. Mumy only lived five minutes from the studio and used to ride his bike to the set each day. "For all three seasons, half of the cast played it straight while Jonathan and the robot were flying at comedy. It was an interesting blend, a recipe of madness that somehow seemed to work."

Episodes in the first season often explored the mysteries of outer space with a noirish tone as the Robinsons discovered alien mausoleums, ancient starships, even werewolves. Standout episodes for dark, gothic tone include

"My Friend, Mr. Nobody," "Invaders from the Fifth Dimension," "War of the Robots" (guest starring Robby the Robot from the 1956

climbed through the stomach and intestines."

During the series' second season, that prankish, kid-friendly energy made the transition from set to screen. The show, now shot in vibrant color instead of moody black and white, came to focus almost exclusively on what Mumy calls "The Three Stooges of *Lost in Space*": Will, Dr. Smith, and the robot. The plots took on a kooky, manic flavor, with the Robinsons encountering intergalactic circuses, pirates, cowboys and, most memorably, a yodeling Norse goddess in the episode "The Space Vikings."

classic *Forbidden Planet*), "Follow the Leader," and the aforementioned "The Derelict." As with any series, the production pace was often grueling for those involved, but the show's far-out plots helped the work seem more like play, according to Lockhart.

"It was a very hectic schedule and we spent a lot of time on our feet, but it was also like going out in the backyard to play in the sand," she says.

Meanwhile, Harris did his part to keep the mood light.

"Every day around 4, he'd climb up into the rafters above the set and throw Tootsie Rolls down to us," Angela Cartwright recalls. "He called it our candy lift for the day, which was really sweet of him. It came to be a tradition."

When not being entertained by Harris, the show's youngest cast members came up with other ways to break the monotony of long workdays.

"Bill and I used to get into mischief together," Cartwright admits. "When we weren't needed, we investigated other sets. They were filming the Sci-Fi movie classic *Fantastic Voyage* on the same lot. We snuck over there and

"A lot of it had to do with that very interesting, mid-1960s decade we were working in. Pop art was really big, and not only was *Batman* on the same lot, it was our competition on network TV," Mumy says. "*Batman* was an extremely campy, colorful show and

initially it was a huge success. Irwin Allen wanted to jump on that bandwagon."

Not everyone wanted to make that jump with the producer.

"That second season, Doctor Smith and the robot sort of muscled June and Guy out," Goddard says. "Not me as much, because I had my stuff to do with Jonathan and the rest of the Robinson family. But it got hairy sometimes, with some strange feelings among the cast."

Lost in Space's third season saw a shift back toward more serious story-lines, with such excellent fare as the claustrophobic "The Space Creature" and the truly creepy and disturbing "The Anti-Matter Man." Even so, more silliness was in store for the Robinsons in the form of space hippies, mambo-dancing cavemen, and the series' most infamous low moment of high camp, the penultimate episode "The Great Vegetable Rebellion," featuring a nefarious alien carrot that turns Smith into a stalk of poetry-spouting celery. Whether the

this personally at a CBS gathering in Hawaii. *Lost in Space* was not dropped because of ratings. We were never outside the top twenty shows on TV, and often we were in the top ten. It was cancelled because Irwin delayed coming up with any ideas for a new season, which is a real shame."

Though the fourth season never materialized, the Robinsons' journey to reach Alpha Centauri didn't end at the close of Season Three. The show lived on through a one-shot Saturday Morning Cartoon in 1973, a big-budget movie reboot in 1998 starring William Hurt, Matt Leblanc, Mimi Rogers, and Heather Graham, and a failed 2003 pilot revival. In 2018, Netflix reimagined the series as a ten-part event, produced by lifelong fan Kevin Burns. A second season is in production.

original *Lost in Space* writing cast could have topped the sheer lunacy of that plotline will never be known—although the show was given a verbal green light, a forth season wasn't made.

"I remember getting a call from my agent saying, 'Guess what? You're not going back.' I was fourteen and I'll admit it. I cried," Mumy says of the show's abrupt cancellation. "None of us thought it would end when we finished the third season, so nobody said goodbye. We all went on our little vacations planning to see each other again on the set. We were told in no uncertain terms that we were coming back."

Why the series—a ratings success from the start—was axed has been a mystery ever since. But Lockhart has a theory.

"Irwin simply never turned in his synopsis for a fourth season," she says. "Perry Lafferty pushed him to get an outline for twenty-six new episodes in front of the network because they were planning for the fall schedule. Perry told me

robot, and D) Will Robinson," says Kerr. "The scripts centered on these four elements/individuals, and indeed there is a reason why people most often say, 'Danger, Will Robinson!' when remembering the original series. That really does sum up what the show was about and there is a comfort in the familiarity and predictability. What mess are those three getting into this week and how will Doctor Smith foul things up this time? Those three were the Lucy/Ricky/Fred/Ethel[7] of Science Fiction shows and we can't help watching their exploits over and over again. That's just my opinion. I'm sure others would point out their love of spaceships and aliens."

And decades of syndicated reruns introduced the series to new generations of viewers.

"I think the show has lasting appeal because of A) the humor, B) Doctor Smith, C) the

Adds Burns, "*Lost in Space* was an adventure told from a kid's point of view. It was every kid's fantasy." 👽 👽 👽

---

[7] The featured characters of the wildly popular, pioneering American television comedy series *I Love Lucy* (1951-1957).

Lost in Space *was appointment viewing during Gregory L. Norris' boyhood. Every autumn, the series ran on UHF, starting with those fantastic black and white episodes, at early dusk, and fueled his imagination in readiness for a life as a professional writer. In 2001, it was his privilege to interview the surviving cast. During a 2013 TV segment about his writing career, Norris played the audio tape of Dick Tufeld who, in the robot's voice, said, "Danger, Danger! Gregory Norris is on the line, and he always does compute!" Norris recently novelized the classic made-for-TV movie by Gerry Anderson,* The Day After Tomorrow: Into Infinity *and penned its sequel,* Planetfall, *for Anderson Entertainment. Follow his literary adventures at www.gregorylnorris.blogspot.com*

Lost in Space and all photos on pages 108-117 are copyright 20th Century Fox Television and CBS. Above illustration by Allen Koszowski.

SHIP OF DOOM

by Ray Cummings

I FIRST SAW THE SHIP FROM OUR FORWARD TURRET WINDOW. IT HAD BEEN OBSERVED, ELECTRO-TELESCOPICALLY, FOR AN HOUR PAST BUT I HAD NO OPPORTUNITY TO SEE IT. Then to the naked eye it became visible—a tiny black dot at first, so small amid the blazing gems strewn on the great concave velvet of the firmament, that one might blink and wonder if it were a vision. Then it was a blob of formless shape, faintly illumined on one side by the dim light from distant suns.

The interior of our vessel clanged with the signals to stop our flight. The heavens swung in a great pendulum arc; and presently we were hovering, and the Ship of Doom—as always in my mind I shall term it—lay close before us.

I recall now with what strangely awed emotion I gazed through the glassite bullseye of that turret window. Around me was the torrent of excited questions of my companions; the clang of bells; the tramp of feet. But I scarcely heard it as I stared at this derelict we had come upon so suddenly, lying so silent and alone in the trackless infinitude of interstellar space. Millions upon millions of miles of nothingness were here. Behind us the sun of our solar system was a mere point of light, so far distant that most of its planets were lost in the stars, with only Apollo, that tenth and last outpost, near enough now to cast a faint reflected light upon us.

And here in this eternity of emptiness where we had thought ourselves the first of humans ever to penetrate, lay the derelict Ship of Doom. It hung now no more than a mile away. It seemed, from this viewpoint, to resemble an old-time spaceship of the sort which once attempted the Moon journey and failed to do more than rise out of Earth's atmosphere.

Yet, when soon we were approaching still closer, I saw that this could be no spaceship at all. It showed itself to be in form like a ball, flattened well down at its poles so that it had the aspect of a disc. I could not tell at first how large it might be. But Ranee was steadily maneuvering us closer to it.

I saw at last that it was a coppery metal disc perhaps a hundred feet in diameter, with bulging convex bottom and top to give an interior height of some thirty feet. A deck encircled its outer rim—a narrow deck of what might have been glassite panes and with a row of bullseye windows. And in the center, upon the top of the disc a curiously bulging little conning tower was bravely set.

As we drew forward I saw that the tower was a woven mesh of wire strands. The disc seemed slowly rotating upon a polar axis so that all its deck windows passed our line of vision in a silent review. And between two of the bullseyes there was a small door-port.

Ranee called at me: "Good Lord, Allerton, see that door! It's partly open! There's no air in the damned thing! No one can be on it alive!'

I did not answer. Was anyone, dead or alive, within this strange little derelict? It seemed not. No face was at any of the bullseyes. And what was this little thing doing out here? It was not a spaceship. Even with my limited technical knowledge, I could not fail now to see that there was no visible means by which this strange affair could navigate space. Then how came it here? What human had devised it? And how had he brought it here? And where was he, with his little mechanism poised here in the vast eternal silences?

Or perhaps the thing had not come from Earth at all. Realization of my own fatuousness rushed upon me. To each human mind himself is the pivot of the Universe. Why should I so childishly assume that this little thing had come from our tiny Earth when so many other worlds were closer?

Yet it had come from Earth. As though to answer the flood of my unspoken questions, a hand gripped my shoulder. It was old man Dorrance, father of our present commander. At seventy now, for all his white hair and the weight of his years there was not a man among us more capable of coping with the unknown. It was he who had brought us out here—he who seemingly would never turn back if a mystery lay ahead.

hearsay. Years ago, to an incredulous world, a scientist named Ronald Deely announced that he had found the secret of time-traveling. He had procured funds and built his little ve-

HIS HAND GRIPPED ME. His voice brought me out of my thoughts. "That thing, I know what it is! I remember it, forty odd years ago, lad—that was before your time! So this was its end."

And as he told me, I too recalled it by

hicle—this same disc-like vehicle which now lay so strangely inert before us. Old Dorrance poured out the tale to me now. There was Deely and his wife Hilda—and the commander was one Gerald Vane. With three other men, these dabblers into the unknown had one day entered their burnished disc for a time-flight fifty years into the future.

Ten thousand people—so old Dorrance said, and he had been one of them—had breathlessly stood and watched this disc depart. The current went into it. The thing hummed. The solid, burnished coppery shape grew tenuous. An instant and it was a wraith—the shimmering ghost of a disc. Imponderable, intangible—yet for a brief instant, visible. Then it was gone, speeding forward into time.

Yet, as Dorrance told me now, that time-traveling disc was not equipped to move in space. The concrete platform where it rested, to the eye of the beholder seemed empty when it departed. For *that* time it *was* empty. The disc presumably had gone fifty years ahead—yet it should have remained upon its platform, so that in fifty years the platform would again have caught up with it and possessed it.

Then why was the disc hanging out here now, in space billions of miles from Earth? What trick had nature played upon these brash scientists who had dared to pry into her secrets?

A group of our men were around me and old Dorrance. Young Dorrance was saying: "No air in it! Did you see that door-port? Partly open—I can make contact there. We'll board it—"

Somebody else exclaimed: "So it's the Deely time-ship? Out here, by God, forty years ago—"

"And if any of you men want to go aboard it with me, get into your pressure suits. We'll see what's there—no one alive, of course—this weird thing—" Young Dorrance's voice faded as he dashed from our turret.

"Wait!" said old Dorrance, "but I know why it's here. These young scientists—scatter-brained, always rushing to do something—let them get our suits ready."

I paused while he told me his theory; meanwhile Ranee's brother was assembling our pressure suits. This strange thing—yet so simple.

The Deely time-ship had gone fifty years into the future. But Ronald Deely, coping thus with nature, had failed to make adjustments of time, with space. His little ship, once in the stream of time, plunging forward, became wholly disconnected from Earth. And Earth is not at rest in space, but swiftly moving. How fast, with absolute motion, who can tell? It follows our Sun, which in turn is drifting—and all the stars, all the Universe plunges—somewhere.

Deely had either overlooked this, or had been unable to make the necessary adjustments. His ship was whirled away into the infinity of interstellar space, fifty years ahead of the motion of our solar system—to wait fifty years for the arrival of our little planet to make a space and time contact.

I listened, amazed, as old man Dorrance explained it. Something undoubtedly had gone wrong with Deely's time-mechanism. He had reached his fifty-year goal, but could not, or at least did not, return. And here was his ship, with forty odd of those fifty years now past, waiting out its predestined meeting with Earth.

Awesome idea! Yet who could doubt its rationality? This then was where Earth would be in some ten years more. I stared at the Ship of Doom with a new amazement. It seemed very slowly rotating on its vertical axis. But was it? Was that not perhaps a mere visual illusion. Perhaps all the great firmament, with me in it, was endowed with that slow spin. Our turret instruments, trained now upon the little derelict and measuring its angles with the far-distant sun of the solar system, showed that the derelict had a perceptible drift in that direction.

Thoughts are swift-flying things. They thronged me. Deely's ship, lying here, was drifting toward Earth. But of course! Why not? The proximity of the solar system—its total mass—was slowly, very slowly drawing the derelict toward it. That was understandable. That was reconcilable with the known laws of celestial mechanics.

2: THE DERELICT

BUT WAS IT? Was this derelict drifting back home—or was Earth merely approaching their predestined meeting place. As I envisaged this commingling of time and space, it seemed to me that here might be the secret of gravity itself. And as I stared at the Ship of Doom I saw in it suddenly *absolute rest.* In all this great starry Universe, was this little time-ship which had tampered with nature, the only thing unmoving? I think so. Poised here for its fifty years, *unmoving*—like a pivot around which flowed the ceaseless changes of the cosmos.

"Perhaps that is so," old man Dorrance was saying. "So many things we think we know and find we know nothing.... Yes, young friend, I want my pressure suit! Do you think the old man is likely to sit here doing nothing?"

There were four of us who went aboard the Ship of Doom. Our space-flyer came up to it very slowly. The silence and the motionlessness hung like a spell upon it. No faces at its little windows. Nothing moving on its little deck; no sign of life in its little turret. We could sense that death was here. The four of us went across the void. We leaped from our ship, spanning emptiness and landing gently on the Ship of Doom.

"Got it!" exulted young Dorrance. "Put on your helmets.... You, Jake, watch the valves—don't exhaust the lock too fast."

I fastened down my goggling metal helmet to the heavy collar, and started the mechanism of the suit. The fabric bloated. Upon my shoulders the small oxygen tanks and the sponge-like absorbers of the carbon-dioxide sat like a hunchback's lump.

Through the visor pane my companions showed as gaping monsters from some strange planet, shapeless, puffed human forms. Old Dorrance touched a metal finger against the metal contact plate of my arm. My audiphone tinkled and I heard his voice in my ear. "Be sure you maintain a fairly even pressure, lad. Keep it at about fifteen pounds."

I could see his eyes staring at me through his visor. "Right," I said. "Don't worry—I've done this before."

We crowded into the small pressure chamber and the inner door slid closed. The valves opened. The air in the lock slowly rushed out into space and then at last we slid aside the outer panel.

Young Dorrance was first to bridge the small yawning gap between the two ships. His bloated, gloved hand seized the partly open door and drew it aside. We crowded forward with the dim starlit little deck of the Ship of Doom curving before us.

What would we see? Wreckage? Carnage? There was nothing. A few small metal chairs stood neatly in a row. The curving deck was four feet wide and twice as high. A nearby inner door to the circular interior was closed. Nothing here.

But as I turned from this instant glance, I saw slumped here on the deck, a human form. A man, hunched forward with his arms wrapped around his up-drawn knees.

"Dead!" said the voice of old Dorrance in my ear. "Dead, of course, these many years. No air—body marvelously preserved. Look at him—I remember him. Brown, the mechanic. Odd sort of fellow—I had a talk with him once."

He sat here by the opened outer door, as though he were on guard. Or perhaps watching the rush of air as it went out. His attitude seemed so calm, so resigned. Philosophical. The word hit me. This fellow here in his work-stained garments—philosophically watching death stalk upon him.

The body fell forward to the deck as my companions pulled at it like prowling ghouls. He was a man about thirty. A rough-hewn, good-natured looking face, now pulled up.... bulging blue eyes.

But there were others on this Ship of Doom not so smiling...

The central portion of the circular disc

was divided into two horizontal floors, and into several rooms on each. It was a dark and a silent interior of woven metal gridwork and metal furnishings. Our small torchlights flashed their tiny white beams around it.

The rooms were segments of a circle like a pie cut into quarters. Four on the lower tier; a little circular stairway leading upward to four other chambers, and a circular ladder into the upper tower. On the lower tier were the mechanism and control rooms; a storeroom of food; and a sort of general lounge. The sleeping rooms were upstairs; and in the tower were the observation instruments.

I gave little thought to these details. It was the dead which fascinated me.

The inner connecting doors were all tightly closed as though these doomed travelers had realized their danger and sealed themselves in to hold the precious air as long as possible. And we saw them now as they had chosen to be when death came upon them.

We chanced to enter first the room where the food was stored. Here was evidence of strife! Death had not been faced with utter calmness by them all. The storeroom was wrecked as though by some desperate struggle. And on the floor lay another man's body. How different from the calmness of Brown the mechanic. This man lay contorted. And under our lights his head and face showed gruesome where some heavy instrument had smashed it with a murderous blow.

Murdered, this one—a struggle here, over the food doubtless.

Four other human bodies were on the ship—all of them were in the lounge room.

Upon a chair, with a small table before him, a young man sat slumped over a notebook and pencil as though he had been assiduously writing, almost at the last. A handsome young fellow, with sensitive features. The face of a dreamer. Staring dark eyes, which one could fancy looked at life always with amused wonderment. Above the almost girlish face there was a shock of waving black hair.

I gazed at the notebook in which he had been writing; its cover was inscribed:

The Chronicle of Philip Thomasson.

Old Dorrance touched me. "He had more money than was good for him. Prominent social family. Only thing he ever did in life was finance Deely. And this Hilda Deely was mad with passion—but not for her husband. Everybody knew it—except the husband. That's Hilda Deely over there—look at her!"

Strange contrasts! Thomasson sat so calmly. But across the lounge there lay the body of a man who had not had the courage to die. His hands were tearing at his throat; an agony of terror was on his face; his thick tongue protruded. One could fancy that he had met his end screaming.

There were two others—a man and a woman. The woman was young and slim and very beautiful, with a mouth that seemed made for love, and eyes which even now in death seemed to hold love like a torch to burn eternally.

This was Hilda Deely. She lay on a couch wrapped in a man's arms, with the long tresses of her black hair falling disheveled to envelope them both, and his arms protectingly holding her. Together, never to be separated, death had come to these two. And upon both of them, with the prospect of death, it seemed that there must have come a strange tranquility of spirit.

But what had happened on this doomed little vessel? What tragic scenes had been enacted of which we now were seeing the mere final tableau? What turgid, philosophical and exalted human emotions must have swept this half dozen humans in those last moments of their lives?

I can try to picture it. There is what we saw on the ship to guide me. And Thomasson's Chronicle, which with an ironical determination he seemed to have written in detail until almost at the last... And there is my own fancy, weaving it together; impressionistically perhaps, and with lapses—but weaving it nevertheless until I think that after all it may be a fairly true picture.

3: FIRST MOMENTS

THE MOMENT OF departure was at hand. In the lower mechanism room of the Deely time-vehicle, Brown the mechanic sat at his controls. Outside his glassite window he could see the awed and excited crowd which had assembled to witness the departure. But Brown wasn't interested in the crowd. That sort of thing meant nothing to him. This was a job he had to do. The risk, the danger—he was getting paid extra for that; he wanted no applause; there was no reason, he felt, that anyone should applaud him. Besides, waving flags and shouting and throwing hats in the air was childish.

Brown, with his stocky figure encased in a greasy work-suit, stood at his window for a moment, puffing at his pipe. The throng was cheering, gazing up to the tower of the time-vehicle. Brown knew that Professor Deely and his wife were up there, with Gerald Vane, commander of this time-flight. Brown, though he could not see them, knew that they were smiling and bowing to the multitude. He grinned ironically to himself. Deely was a fatuous ass to bring his wife in this close contact with a man like Gerald Vane.

Brown shrugged and turned away. It was no concern of his. For all of him, the woman could stand up there clutching roses to her breast, bowing and smiling, looking like the soul of purity—and yet have in her heart and mind nothing but duplicity. To Brown—who was a bachelor—it was of no importance.

AND AT THAT MOMENT Hilda Deely and her husband were indeed in the tower, answering the plaudits of the crowd.

"Hilda, dear, isn't it wonderful." Deely's arm went around his wife. He was a frail, studious looking man of forty. His shock of prematurely gray hair made him seem older. His face always bore the look of a man far away in spirit. He was an unworldly fellow, this Deely. He passed by the evil in the world without seeing it, for his gaze was always fixed on the stars.

His mind, learned, erudite, profound, was in worldly things that of an innocent child. He sought for so many long hours each day to delve into the mysteries of Nature that the beauty of his young wife and her love for him became things he took for granted. Her inner life, her desires—the myriad illusions upon which a woman builds romance—all those were mysteries of nature to which Deely never gave a thought.

"Isn't it wonderful," Hilda?" he repeated. "Listen to them cheering us." He tightened his arms around his wife's shoulders. "This is the happiest moment of my life."

He did not notice that she involuntarily drew away from his encircling arm. Gerald Vane stood close behind them darkly handsome, of flashing dark eyes, bold features and strong cleft chin, and with his broad athletic shoulders so trim now in the uniform with gold braid. Whatever his inner character, outwardly Gerald Vane was the sort of man upon which a woman may build her dreams.

And the earnest, tremblingly happy Ronald Deely did not notice that his wife's free hand went behind her so that in this moment while the crowd applauded, Vane gripped her hand and briefly held it with a tender pressure while between them passed unspoken a reassurance of their love.

"Well," said Vane, "we're getting the publicity, Deely. Every newscaster in the world is blaring of this. Shall we make another speech for the microphones?"

"No! No, I'm too excited. Hilda dear, isn't this wonderful? All these years I have worked for this—"

"Then let's get started," Vane interrupted. "This is a good dramatic time. Close that port."

"Yes, we'll start now. Hilda and I will sit here. There will be a starting shock, Hilda. Don't be afraid—I'll hold you."

Vane closed all the ports. In effect the little vehicle was a spaceship now, almost capable of withstanding an outer vacuum. "All ready?"

"Yes! Yes, Vane." Deely did not see the look which passed between his wife and Vane. For them this was a moment of crisis also. A moment of triumph. Hilda shrank against her husband; but to her mind it was Gerald Vane she was clutching. They would fling themselves out into the future. And in that world of the future, she and Gerald would escape from the ship ... facing the future together.

Gerald Vane pulled at a lever. Down in the lower control room the phlegmatic Brown calmly and efficiently responded. The little vehicle glowed and hummed, and was flung into time...

In the lower lounge the two other men sat gripping their seats against the shock of starting.

"You all right, Thomasson?"

"Yes, I—I'm still here!"

"My God—this weird thing—where—where are we?"

PHIL THOMASSON half rose out of his chair, but sank dizzily back. The floor window-port of the lounge room showed a gray luminous blur. The door to the little deck stood open, but nothing could be seen out there save the reflected glow of a small deck light.

William Mink repeated, "Where—where are we?"

The pale, byronic Thomasson smiled. "Just passing through day after tomorrow, I should fancy."

It was romance to young Phil Thomasson. He knew nothing of the science of it, nor cared. With his inherited money he had financed all this. An adventure. Freedom from the boredom of being a too-rich young man with nothing to do in life save dissipate wealth.

To the perspiring, frightened William Mink it was an adventure also. Mink was a thick-set, paunchy man of fifty. At forty he had thought to conquer the financial world. But now at fifty he was a pauper. His banks had failed and shattered his mind. His mentality now was far from normal, though he did not know it. Perhaps it never had been normal. One cannot work with the obsession of unbounded wealth, desiring nothing else in life but money, and be of normal mind.

Mink was a good friend of Gerald Vane. He had indeed, upon many occasions loaned Vane money. He would have financed this Deely expedition—for the publicity which in many ways he could have turned to financial profit—had not his fortunes crashed and Phil Thomasson come forward and financed it instead.

And so Mink was here as an escape from his troubles. But Mink had also another idea. There were secrets in the future of the world which he could learn. Secrets which when he brought them back would speedily make him rich again.

But now he was terrified, so that Phil Thomasson gazed at him with a sarcastic smile. "You're not much of an adventurer, are you? Brace up, Mink! We've started and we're still alive. That's a triumph, anyway."

Thomasson climbed to his feet unsteadily. "Jove, it's weird. Come on out on the deck, let's see what next year looks like. We're omnipotent, Mink. Little gods, with clay feet..."

To gaze and see what next year looks like! But Nature was to play a sudden, sardonic trick to confound this band of necromancers, so that when they learned of it they were to gather, jammed, terror stricken into the upper little tower room, and even the stolid Brown was startled.

* * *

THE REALIZATION of what the destiny of the flight might be came to them apparently hours after the flight had started. It came with a shock, but then the thing was wholly understandable to Deely and to Vane. Deely indeed, had thought of it as a possibility, but hoped it would not come to pass since he could see no way of changing it. The realization that finally came, that while they were whirling through Time, they were also hurtling through Space, brought to each of them a secret confounding. Their secret plans were awry. *The vehicle had actually separated from Earth*: and what they gazed at now through the turret bullseyes, was a luminous blurring vista of a starry firmament all in movement!

To Phil Thomasson it was less of a disappointment. He had thought to observe the follies of future generations and be amused; but after all it was amusing also to see these crazy swaying stars. And it was amusing to see the baffled, lustful Gerald Vane, and the baffled woman.

"But it's all right," Deely was trying to assure them, when the realization that they were in interstellar space, had finally penetrated.

"We'll go into the future and then turn back. We cannot land anywhere—except back on Earth in what will always be the present time. The experiment is a success, Vane! Think of what an advance for science—look at those worlds out there!"

It was a blurred crazy Universe endowed optically with strange motion. The sun was drawing away. Saturn with its brilliant rings was coming forward.

"Don't you realize, my friends," Deely went on vehemently. "We're explorers into the unknown of space and time. You think we're moving? We're not. This vehicle of ours has found absolute rest."

He gazed at the bank of dials before him, with their whirring indicators. "We are in the future now. This is where Earth will be at this time which we have already reached. And we are going fifty years into the future! What realms of starry space we will see—where Earth will be fifty years from now! Think of it—no man has ever penetrated those realms—"

"A space trip!" murmured Thomasson. "Jove, we start for a time-trip and it turns out to be a voyage among the stars! That's funny."

"And what a trip," exclaimed Deely. "Think of it—"

Thomasson was smiling ironically. "I *am*

thinking of it. We can't gaze into the future of Earth! Don't you realize, man, this is the Almighty's little joke? You think with your science you can do everything, but you can't. The future has always been hidden from us, and it always will be."

"We—we're in no danger then," stammered Mink. "Nothing has gone wrong with your mechanism?"

"Of course not," Deely reassured excitedly. "My time mechanisms are working perfectly. I have conquered the secret of time. When we return, think what new facts we will have to add to science. Why, this involves gravity itself. It involves the cause of all movement. It shows that time is indeed the fundamental pivot upon which everything swings."

"Well," said Brown, "if everything's all right, I better get back to work. Them batteries maybe need renewin' already."

He tamped out his pipe and clambered down the ladder. "Chief," he called, "if Mrs. Deely needs any help gettin' the lunch, I'm ready any time."

"Hungry," said Deely, "of course we all must be hungry. Hilda dear, you go down and start things. I must stay here and make notes."

"Yes. Yes, Ronald."

"I'll help her," said Vane. "Come, Hilda."

In the small tower, crowded with the six of them, Hilda Deely had found herself pressed close against Gerald Vane. It seemed that everyone must hear the thumping of her heart. She and Gerald standing so close that it seemed she could feel the rhythm of his heart against her breast. Every beat of that strong heart of his was for her.

They descended the ladder and he turned suddenly in the empty lounge and flung his arms around her. "Hilda!"

"Gerald, not so loud!"

"They can't hear us. Kiss me—"

"Brown may see us!"

"No! And what difference? He knows how to keep his mouth shut. Kiss me. He knows he'd lose his work with us.... It drove me frantic up there in the turret, Hilda. The warmth of you...."

"Gerald, dear one...."

They snatched, like this, another moment of madness. Or ecstasy? Or love? To Hilda, it was all of those. "Gerald, I love you! Oh, take me away! Far away from everyone, Gerald—everyone but you."

And so the strange journey went on. A little world of itself, this Deely time-vehicle, hurtling into the future and out into the uncharted realms of interplanetary space. A world of six inhabitants. They went fifty years from their starting point. Then sixty years. The journey consumed days of their life. And then Deely reversed the mechanism. Retrograding through time so that all the universe was adjusting itself, and to the observers from the little tower it seemed that the solar system now so distant was again approaching.

Deely's mechanisms worked perfectly. For him it was a triumph. The dials recorded the passage of absolute time. Sixty years forward. Then the return. With what instruments he had at his command, Deely charted the apparent movements of the stellar universe. And his mind flung ahead. With a larger—a more powerful vehicle—the time transition could be greatly accelerated. Those sixty years had seemed about a week to the travelers now. Deely envisaged an apparatus which would penetrate sixty hundred, or sixty thousand years while the humans on it were experiencing only a few days.

Sixty thousand years! To what infinite realms of space such a ship would reach! The point where Earth will be sixty thousand years from now! Perhaps such a ship could land somewhere....

4: THE DISCOVERY!

BUT DEELY NOW, with the care and the precision of a true scientist, was heading back for a landing upon Earth. The time the voyagers had experienced would be about two weeks. And Deely knew that the laws of nature—unnameable laws, but inexorable—would allow

him successfully to land at a point of time on Earth that same two weeks *after* his departure. He would have lived those two weeks, and those on Earth would have lived them. All devised by nature into rationality.

Deely was a careful man. No amount of enthusiasm now led him to want to take unnecessary chances. Two weeks was long enough for them to chance upon this voyage. They had brought food and water for a comfortable two weeks. It had seemed wholly adequate since they had intended to land in a future time-world of Earth where supplies would be available. And the batteries, too, were safely adequate for no longer an operation than that.

"We'd better turn back," Deely had said to Vane. "Don't you think...."

"Yes, I do. Stick to safety—always my idea, in everything."

Even in those stolen moments—safety in everything for Vane.

So they turned. It was just after they had passed the point at which they were still fifty years ahead of Earth when....

Gerald Vane and Hilda had been alone so much during this week of the outward trip, that Vane—playing always for safety—forgot his motto. Brown was generally in the lower mechanism room. Mink was always abstracted, brooding and morose. Thomasson was gay when there was anyone to listen—or if not that, he was immersed in an interminable chronicle for his own amusement; and Deely slept, ate and worked upon his scientific data.

It left Hilda and Vane with many stolen moments. A sweet intimacy—not yet cloying—for it made Gerald Vane ever more bold....

And then came that moment of the return flight when Deely received his crushing blow. It chanced to be, in the living routine of this little world, after the evening meal. One might call it "nearly midnight." Deely at this time was ordinarily sleep, worn to the point of exhaustion by his mathematics.

But this night he awakened. Hilda was

not in their sleeping room, but it caused Deely no second thought for Hilda often remained up after he retired, sitting in the lower lounge with Mink and Vane. Deely suddenly found himself strangely wakeful. The problem on which he had been working after supper was unfinished, and now the solution of it seemed ready to be found.

He slipped from his bed, into slippers and outer robe and left the small triangular room. It was glowing with the strange iridescence of the time-current. The humming which always pervaded the interior of the disc was like music to Deely's ears. Outside his cabin window, through the bullseye pane, he saw the familiar vista of the stars—all blurred and unreal and flowing with a silent movement (in retrograde now) which marked the changing positions of the heavens with the years.

The upper tier of the small vehicle with its four cabins, had a narrow corridor bisecting it like a diameter line. The corridor was unlighted, save for the glowing metal walls. Deely, in his gray cloth gown and his rumpled white hair, moved along the corridor toward the spiral ladder leading to the tower where he knew Phil Thomasson would be on watch. He mounted the ladder. He might have heard soft voices from one of the rooms off the corridor had he stopped to listen, but he did not.

Thomasson greeted him. "Well, Deely, shouldn't you be asleep?"

"I couldn't—I can't sleep. I woke up with that accursed problem tormenting me. Stay where you are, Phil—I'll sit here. Or would you rather go to bed? I shall be here several hours, I imagine."

"I'll stay," said Thomasson. "What is sleep to me? I've been watching those crazy lurching stars. I say, one might read his destiny in them if he were clever enough, mightn't he? And then he'd be worse off—realizing what hell lay ahead of him."

But Deely was already immersed in his formulae, with Thomasson watching him thoughtfully. A nice fellow, this Deely. Too impractical for a hard world of reality. A fellow who was bound to get hurt. It occurred to Thomasson rather too bad that one must be destined for disillusionment and heartache.

By some trick of fate; it seemed to Thomasson that there was a sudden stillness about the vehicle. Voices in a soft murmur came floating up the ladder to the tower room.

"Gerald dear, I must go—if he should awaken—"

"Nonsense, Hilda—you know he sleeps for hours."

"Gerald, please...."

"But I won't let you go now."

Thomasson was about to speak—to say something, anything to drown the damning sounds. He had thought that Deely had not heard, but he saw Deely's face and its expression struck him dumb.

And again the voice of Hilda floated up to them. "Gerald—darling, I'm going. But kiss me once more—oh hold me close—I don't want to leave you."

There seemed a strange blankness on Deely's face as though all his reasoning were paralyzed to leave him blankly staring. And slowly the blood was draining so that he was white to the lips.

"I say—" began Thomasson. But Deely's vague gesture silenced him as effectively as if it had been a roaring command. The murmuring had ceased momentarily. There was an interval while Deely stared blankly with his pencil still poised over the paper. Then the pencil dropped with a little thud and Deely was fumbling with his chair, trying to rise to his feet.

Thomasson found his voice. "Where are you going?"

"Downstairs. I guess—I think I want to go down...."

"But I say, I wouldn't do that." He put a hand on Deely's thin shoulder. "Take it easy, old fellow. Give it thought. I say—damn it, I'm sorry for you. Look here—don't go down there now."

Deely sank back. "I guess you're right.

Give it thought.... I guess you're right."

Mercifully, there came no more of the horrible words. For minutes Deely sat staring, with Thomasson regarding him. What was there to say? Thomasson could think of nothing. It is a tragic thing to sit and watch a man stricken by a knife thrust into his heart by the woman he loves. Deely seemed to realize it very slowly, as though the thing were impossible, and all his faculties were numbed, groping with it. His pale blue eyes had been staring through the metal walls of the little tower; then at last they came and focussed upon Thomasson.

"You knew—this thing?"

"Yes. I knew it."

"And you did not tell me!"

"But how could I, old fellow? One does not go like a cad and tell his—"

"No. That's right. And Mink—he knew it?"

"I suppose so."

"And even Brown? So everybody knew it—everybody but me."

"But I say, Deely, look here—"

"And now I know it—at last. I guess you're right—give it thought—give it thought.... You'll go down to bed now, won't you, Thomasson?" It was a gentle plea. "I want to stay here alone—to give it thought."

And Thomasson was glad enough to escape, for it was an awkward thing to sit helplessly and watch a man whose castle is clattering down into bits of broken glass at his feet.

"Yes, I'll go." He touched Deely. "I say, I'm sorry as hell. You know that."

"Yes—thanks."

Deely's gentle white face was vaguely staring with a confused stricken wonderment as Thomasson went down the ladder. The sleeping rooms were quiet. Thomasson, seeking his own, peered into the opened door-oval of Deely's as he passed it. Hilda lay there on her own couch, apparently asleep. Her black braids were on her breast. The pale, slim beauty of her face seemed so pure. Thomasson sighed, entered his own room and drifted,

after an interval, into uneasy slumber.

A sudden, lurching shock awakened him. Something was wrong with the ship. He realized there was no humming, no vibration, no iridescent glow to the room-walls. The time-mechanism was not operating!

As he gained his feet Thomasson heard the distant shouts of his companions. In the corridor he ran into Hilda, a white spectre in her long filmy night robe. "Oh, what is it, Mr. Thomasson? What's wrong? Where is Ronald? I woke up—"

Gerald Vane dashed toward them. "Where is Deely? What in hell has happened?"

There was only wan starlight in the narrow upper corridor from its end windows. Vane was as white as the woman.

"Gerald!" She clutched at him, but he flung her off.

"Don't do that, you fool! Thomasson, where is Deely?"

In a nearby door-oval Mink appeared. "What is it? We're not—not wrecked? Are we in danger, Vane? In danger...." His voice shrilled and broke. He clutched at the door casement. In danger...."

FROM DOWN ON the lower tier Brown was shouting: "It's gone dead! Everything's off! What'll I do? The signals won't work to the tower—nobody answers."

Vane was rushing toward the tower ladder, and slowly the figure of Deely came down. He pulled his dressing gown around his thin shoulders and with a shaking hand smoothed his rumpled hair. But his voice was calm. "Don't get excited. No danger—I stopped our time-flight."

Brown arrived. "But Professor, them controls...."

"What matter, Brown? Come down to the lounge, all of you. I want to show you the stars through the window there. The firmament is rational—at last. The stars are very beautiful."

His gaze went to his wife. "Ah, Hilda—have you slept well? Too bad to awaken you."

"Look here," shouted Vane. "What are you

talking about? Stopped our time flight? Why? And no one on guard in the turret—"

In Deely's drab, mild eyes a sudden fire came. "Do as I tell you, Vane. All of you—come down to the lounge. Stop that sniveling, Mink. Hilda, you go ahead with Gerald. Don't let her fall, Vane. She looks so frightened...."

The strange force of Deely made them gather silently in the lounge. The vehicle was at rest, poised in the void of infinite space. Through the windows they could all see the motionless firmament, freed now from the distortion of their time flight. A vast bowl of black velvet—a hollow interior of unfathomable capacity with themselves hanging in its center—and everywhere now the motionless blazing worlds.

Brown found his voice. "Are we all crazy? We can't stop here like this! We haven't air or water to stop. We'll be killed."

Vane gasped: "Start the mechanism, Brown. You damn fool, don't stay here...."

"But I can't! Nothin' works! He...."

Vane turned upon Deely. "What have you done, you...."

Deely suddenly backed away. He faced them all, with even a greater calmness. "I thought it would be a wise thing to smash the mechanism. I have no need of it any longer—so I smashed it."

"Death...." Only Mink could find voice—the words came with a shrill ascending scream. "Death! "Death—Oh, my God...."

As though all the scene were sharpened and reduced to miniature, Thomasson saw Mink clutching at his throat and screaming; Hilda, white as a beautiful wraith; and Gerald Vane, staring with dumb amazement, and then leaping upon Deely.

"Wrecked us? You—you—" His thickened tongue refused him. "You—wrecked—"

"Not I? It was you who wrecked us." Deely sat down on the couch, with pale eyes surveying them all. "You and the woman—wrecked us. All of you saw it—all but me, and no one bothered to tell me.... Go to him, Hilda. There's nothing to stop you now. Go and take comfort in his loving arms."

But she only stood staring. Mink, still screaming, rushed away. And Brown, cursing to himself, dashed for his control room. Vane took a step, and whirled. "You—crazy—fool..."

"I was—but I'm not now. Hold her in your arms, Vane. Don't you see she's frightened?" Thomasson gasped. "But I say, the wall might explode—hadn't we better try to repair the controls? Vane, come up to the tower. That's where he—"

"No use," Deely interrupted. And now he spoke vehemently. "You can't repair it. The walls won't explode—but our air is leaking out. We've a few hours—two or three. Sit down—if you've anything to do before death—any things to think about.... Hilda, you belong in his arms. I shouldn't waste time if I were you. A few hours isn't very long for loving—like yours and his."

It seemed to the stricken Thomasson that she would fall. She swayed toward Vane, but his terrified hysterical glare and his words stopped her.

"You brought this on me! You with your pale face—your kisses—"

"Gerald—"

"You rotten little—"

Vile epithet, so vile that as Vane turned and staggered from the room Thomasson was impelled to take a menacing step toward him. But Deely said, "Come back, Thomasson! Don't bother." Deely was vaguely smiling. "She isn't—she didn't mean to be—quite that. Sit down, Hilda—it's too bad if you're going to lack the comfort of his love at the end—but I guess you are."

5: LAST MOMENTS

IT ALL BLURRED for a moment to Thomasson's shocked senses. One cannot be struck with the realization of death's inevitable nearness and maintain normality. It occurred vaguely to Thomasson that there was nothing to do. He found himself seated at the little table where he had done most of his writing, and on it before him was his notebook and pencil.

Nothing he could do, and death was coming. He heard, vaguely, the running footsteps of Vane and Brown as they dashed around the ship. They were trying to accomplish the impossible. And shouting frantically about it. Like struggling rats in a cage immersed in water. That was an amusing thought.

Thomasson stared across the starlit lounge at Deely and his wife. They sat numbly gazing at each other. Perhaps they were thinking of all the happy moments they had once had together.... Thomasson felt himself like a man dazed by drink. This little ship was a tiny world in the silent void of interplanetary space, and because death was coming, madness stalked it.

All of them were mad.... It was an amusing thought. Thomasson contemplated that this proximity of death was intoxicating. Perhaps they were all their real selves for the first time since childhood. Alcohol does that. The man of low breeding becomes more vulgar. The gentleman is punctiliously polite.

Thomasson was aware of a turmoil outside the room. The shouts of Vane and Brown. Thudding blows of metal against metal. Then a horrible agonized scream from Mink.

"He's locked himself in the food room!" Vane gasped. "Brown, get him out of there! Eating our food—more than his share—keeping it from us...."

They stood by the closed metal door. Mink was inside. They could hear him moving. Vane put his ear to the door. Mink was babbling to himself. "All this for me. Nobody can have any of it, but me. Food and drink—that's life. Nobody can die with all this food and drink."

Stark mad! Vane heard him fall over a cask of water. The gurgle as it spilled sounded horribly plain. Their precious water spilling, with this madman wasting it.

Vane's fist thudded against the door. "Mink, open here! Let us in!"

Brown shouted, "Say, you, open this door!"

But there was only silence as though Mink were crouching like a trapped animal.

Vane pounded harder. The door resounded with the blows of the heavy iron wrench which Brown was carrying. Then it suddenly occurred to Vane that there was no lock on the inside of this door.

"He's got things piled against it, Brown! Only that. Help me shove."

With their shoulders they heaved. The door yielded a little; there was an inch of space. And now, in the silence as momentarily they rested, they could hear Mink scuttling back and forth around the little room. An animal, trapped, in a frenzy of fear and hate. The boxes of food were clattering as he scattered them. And they heard his mouthing, mumbling words: "Food and drink. Nobody can die in here...."

"Harder, Brown! Damn it—shove...."

The door suddenly went inward as the water casks and boxes which were piled against it were shoved backward. Over the litter, Vane and Brown tumbled forward. The dark, triangular room was scattered with broken boxes of food, and wet with spilled water. The light from the corridor shone on Mink as he crouched in his white night-robe. His hands were before him, with clawing fingers; his lips snarled with bared teeth and his eyes were blazing with maniacal fury. "You—go 'way! Get away from me!"

And as Vane recovered his balance the frenzied Mink was on him, clawing at him, gouging at his eyes, and the bared teeth closed on the flesh of his throat.

"Brown! Good God—help!"

Brown saw the two swaying forms in the blue tube-light glow from the doorway. Vane stumbled and fell. Brown raised his heavy wrench, crashed it upon Mink's head, and Brown staggered back, staring as Vane lifted himself from the gruesome thing on top of him.

"Did it, Brown! Good enough! He's dead—what of it? We've saved the food and water."

But Brown had never killed a man before. He stammered, "That—looks awful. Them brains—that...."

"Come on outside."

"Yes."

They stumbled to the corridor. Brown found himself still holding the wrench. He dropped it with a shudder. "I'm goin' to the deck. Cool off. That looked awful—that blood an' them brains...." He wavered away, muttering to himself.

Vane dashed to the lounge. Thomasson was at his little table. Hilda was in a chair, and Deely still sat on the couch.

Vane gasped, "Mink went crazy. Wrecked our storeroom—Brown killed him with a wrench—look where he bit me. Stark, raving mad—the fool."

There was blood on Vane's neck and on his chalk-white face—some of it his own, and some Mink's. He wiped his face with his sleeve. "The crazy fool...."

Deely barely moved. "Sit down, Vane. No—close that door first. You're wise to come in here—this is the best place. We can hold the air a little longer in here."

Thomasson could feel that the air was going. His cheeks were hot and prickling as though the blood were trying to ooze out through the skin. His head was humming— or was the roar in his ears?

Vane slammed the door. "I don't want to die! Deely, can't you do something? Good God, we've got to do something—not just let ourselves die like this! Deely, for God's sake...."

"Nothing I can do, now," Deely said calmly.

"The control mechanism...."

"Didn't you see it, Vane?"

"Yes, I saw it. Brown and I saw it. You— you smashed it."

"Yes. I told you that."

"But Deely, please—you can fix it. You know more about it than Brown or me."

Vane was whimpering like a child. "Hilda, tell him to fix it. Tell him, Hilda...."

But Hilda Deely only stared; and it seemed to the watching, fascinated Thomasson that there was a faint, very queer smile on her vivid lips.

"You'd better sit down," Deely said. "Save your strength—the air is getting very thin. Losing pressure fast...."

And just at that moment the air began escaping still faster. From a thousand places around the little disc-like vehicle as it hung poised in the vacuum of space, the precious air was leaking out. Brown, clinging to a chair on the curved starlit deck-corridor, could hear the silence of everything broken by the faint hiss and whine of the air as it went out.

He found himself sitting on the deck by the small outer door-port. Mink was dead. Soon the others would be dead. All of them, slowly dying.... That was a good thing for Mink, dying so quickly. He hadn't lived to know that his brains were scattered like that and his skull like an eggshell. It was nice to die all at once. From inside he could hear the whimpering Gerald Vane. "I don't want to die! Deely, please...." But he was going to die.

Brown thought again how much better it would be to die all at once. He found that the door-port lever was beside him. His hand had accidentally touched it; his fingers were gripping it. The air was going out so slowly with this door-port closed. It was awful to die, just a little at a time.

Brown's hand very slowly pulled at the lever. The door slid partly open. The rush of wind as the deck-air went out seemed like a graceful summer breeze. And then a gale. It blew so strong it took your breath away. He had to grasp a support with all his might to keep from being blown into interstellar space.

Brown's head slumped down on his up-drawn knees.

DEELY GAZED ACROSS the lounge toward the closed corridor door. "Going fast now. Listen to it whine. Something outside must have broken."

Vane was collapsed in a chair, whimpering; and then he began screaming. "Stop it! Don't let it go! You fool—you murderer—don't let it go! I don't want to die."

Thomasson thought how foolish it was to

rail like that. Vane was coughing, choking. He was a pitiable object—the man who had once been strong, handsome, so virile-looking—so romantic. He was a pitiable object now. No, not pitiable—no one should pity Gerald Vane. He looked stricken of all his manhood now. Or perhaps he had never had any manhood.

Under the gaze of Hilda's calm eyes, and that faint queer smile on her white lips, Gerald Vane screamed his protests—choking and gasping in the rarefied air until suddenly he had fainted. "Hilda—" On the couch Deely himself was gasping now. "Hilda—in a moment we'll be gone—"

"I know—" She tried to rise to her feet, but the room must have whirled before her. "Ronald! Where—are you? I—I can't seem to see you."

"I just thought, Hilda—now at the last—you might have something to say to me. If you—have something...."

She wavered, with hands outstretched, across the few feet that separated them. And on the couch his eager arms caught her. "Hilda—my wife again...."

"I want to say—if only you could forgive me, Ronald."

"I do! I do, Hilda."

The roaring in Thomasson's head seemed to drown their murmured words. The triangle of metal with its concave, low ceiling was pale and wan with starlight. But it roared—as Thomasson's head was roaring.

And the door was straining with the outgoing, whining sucking wind.

Every breath was an effort. Trying to breathe, and there was nothing to breathe. Vane's dead body seemed so hideous, over there in the chair. But on the couch Deely and Hilda were lying together wrapped in each other's arms. They were tranquil, peaceful in death.

It was all swiftly blurring before Thomasson's fading senses. Roaring and blurring, and then it slid away into a great and everlasting silence....

Thomasson had fallen forward over his little table.

AND THUS WE FOUND THEM, with the air gone so that their frozen bodies were preserved through the years and the final tableau of this drama, or comedy, or tragedy—call it what you will—was clear before us.

We did not attempt to take the Deely timeship back to Earth; but left it there, with its six passengers untouched. As young Dorrance turned us back and set our course toward Apollo and the Earth, I was at a rear turret window. The little disc-like vehicle, with its small tower bravely set on top, seemed hung askew. Little Ship of Doom. I watched until it was lost among the blazing stars.

"Ship of Doom" first appeared in the Fall 1931 issue of Wonder Stories Quarterly, *under the title "The Derelict of Space." The story was accompanied by an illustration by Frank R. Paul.*

Following an adventurous early life that included searching for gold in British Columbia, and striking oil in Wyoming, Raymond King Cummings (1887-1957) served five years as personal assistant to the inventor Thomas Edison before turning to fiction writing. According to an article in Argosy-Allstory Weekly *(February 8, 1930), "Cummings' success as a writer [was] meteoric"; his "stories gripped the popular imagination and they 'clicked.'" As one of the most popular early 20th-century writers of "scientific fiction," Ray Cummings was hailed as an American H.G. Wells, and is now considered one of the founding fathers of the SF genre. His best-known work is the 1922 novel* The Girl in the Golden Atom, *which Cummings later recycled as a two-part Timely Comics story, "The Princess of the Atom" (*Captain America #25 and 26*). The story introduced the concept that eventually developed into the Marvel Comics Microverse.*

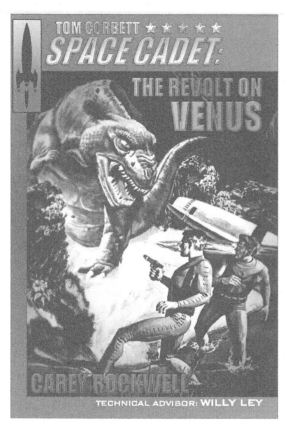

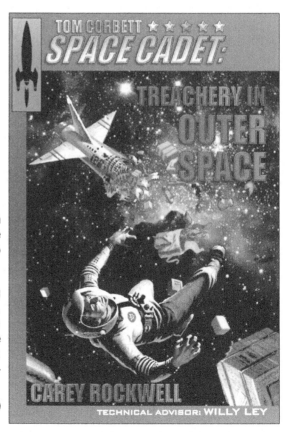

ALL CATS ARE GRAY
by Andre Norton

STEENA OF THE SPACEWAYS—THAT SOUNDS JUST LIKE A CORNY TITLE FOR ONE OF THE STELLAR-VEDO SPREADS. I ought to know, I've tried my hand at writing enough of them. Only this Steena was no glamour babe. She was as colorless as a Lunar plant—even the hair netted down to her skull had a sort of grayish cast and I never saw her but once draped in anything but a shapeless and baggy gray space-all.

Steena was strictly background stuff and that is where she mostly spent her free hours —in the smelly smoky background corners of any stellar-port dive frequented by free spacers. If you really looked for her you could spot her—just sitting there listening to the talk—listening and remembering. She didn't open her own mouth often. But when she did spacers had learned to listen. And the lucky few who heard her rare spoken words—these will never forget Steena.

She drifted from port to port. Being an expert operator on the big calculators, she found jobs wherever she cared to stay for a time. And she came to be something like the master-minded machines she tended—smooth, gray, without much personality of her own.

But it was Steena who told Bub Nelson about the Jovan moon-rites—and her warning saved Bub's life six months later. It was Steena who identified the piece of stone Keene Clark was passing around a table one night, rightly calling it unworked Slitite. That started a rush which made ten fortunes overnight for men who were down to their last jets. And, last of all, she cracked the case of the *Empress of Mars*.

All the boys who had profited by her queer store of knowledge and her photographic memory tried at one time or another to balance the scales. But she wouldn't take so much as a cup of Canal water at their expense, let alone the credits they tried to push on her. Bub Nelson was the only one who got around her refusal. It was he who brought her Bat.

About a year after the Jovan affair he walked into the Free Fall one night and dumped Bat down on her table. Bat looked at Steena and growled. She looked calmly back at him and nodded once. From then on they traveled together—the thin gray woman and the big gray tom-cat. Bat learned to know the inside of more stellar bars than even most spacers visit in their lifetimes. He developed a liking for Vernal juice, drank it neat and quick, right out of a glass. And he was always at home on any table where Steena elected to drop him.

This is really the story of Steena, Bat, Cliff Moran and the *Empress of Mars*, a story which is already a legend of the spaceways. And it's a damn good story too. I ought to know, having framed the first version of it myself.

For I was there, right in the Rigel Royal, when it all began on the night that Cliff Moran blew in, looking lower than an antman's belly and twice as nasty. He'd had a spell of luck foul enough to twist a man into a slug-snake and we all knew that there was an attachment out for his ship. Cliff had fought his way up from the back courts of Venaport. Lose his ship and he'd slip back there—to rot. He was at the snarling stage that night when he picked out a table for himself and set out to drink away his troubles.

However, just as the first bottle arrived, so did a visitor. Steena came out of her corner, Bat curled around her shoulders stole-wise, his favorite mode of travel. She crossed over and dropped down without invitation at Cliff's side. That shook him out of his sulks. Because Steena never chose company when she could be alone. If one of the man-stones on Ganymede had come stumping in, it wouldn't have made more of us look out of the corners of our eyes.

She stretched out one long-fingered hand and set aside the bottle he had ordered and said only one thing, "It's about time for the *Empress of Mars* to appear again."

Cliff scowled and bit his lip. He was tough, tough as jet lining—you have to be granite inside and out to struggle up from Venaport to a ship command. But we could guess what was running through his mind at that moment. The *Empress of Mars* was just about the biggest prize a spacer could aim for. But in the fifty years she had been following her queer derelict orbit through space many men had tried to bring her in—and none had succeeded.

A pleasure-ship carrying untold wealth, she had been mysteriously abandoned in space by passengers and crew, none of whom had ever been seen or heard of again. At intervals thereafter she had been sighted, even boarded. Those who ventured into her either vanished or returned swiftly without any believable explanation of what they had seen—wanting only to get away from her as quickly as possible. But the man who could bring her in—or even strip her clean in space—that man would win the jackpot.

"All right!" Cliff slammed his fist down on the table. "I'll try even that!"

Steena looked at him, much as she must have looked at Bat the day Bub Nelson brought him to her, and nodded. That was all I saw. The rest of the story came to me in pieces, months later and in another port half the System away.

Cliff took off that night. He was afraid to risk waiting—with a writ out that could pull the ship from under him. And it wasn't until he was in space that he discovered his passengers—Steena and Bat. We'll never know

what happened then. I'm betting that Steena made no explanation at all. She wouldn't.

It was the first time she had decided to cash in on her own tip and she was there—that was all. Maybe that point weighed with Cliff, maybe he just didn't care. Anyway the three were together when they sighted the *Empress* riding, her dead-lights gleaming, a ghost ship in night space.

She must have been an eerie sight because her other lights were on too, in addition to the red warnings at her nose. She seemed alive, a Flying Dutchman of space. Cliff worked his ship skillfully alongside and had no trouble in snapping magnetic lines to her lock. Some minutes later the three of them passed into her. There was still air in her cabins and corridors. Air that bore a faint corrupt taint which set Bat to sniffing greedily and could be picked up even by the less sensitive human nostrils.

Cliff headed straight for the control cabin but Steena and Bat went prowling. Closed doors were a challenge to both of them and Steena opened each as she passed, taking a quick look at what lay within. The fifth door opened on a room which no woman could leave without further investigation.

I don't know who had been housed there when the *Empress* left port on her last lengthy cruise. Anyone really curious can check back on the old photo-reg cards. But there was a lavish display of silks trailing out of two travel kits on the floor, a dressing table crowded with crystal and jeweled containers, along with other lures for the female which drew Steena in. She was standing in front of the dressing table when she glanced into the mirror—glanced into it and froze.

Over her right shoulder she could see the spider-silk cover on the bed. Right in the middle of that sheer, gossamer expanse was a sparkling heap of gems, the dumped contents of some jewel case. Bat had jumped to the foot of the bed and flattened out as cats will, watching those gems, watching them and—something else!

Steena put out her hand blindly and

caught up the nearest bottle. As she unstoppered it she watched the mirrored bed. A gemmed bracelet rose from the pile, rose in the air and tinkled its siren song. It was as if an idle hand played.... Bat spat almost noiselessly. But he did not retreat. Bat had not yet decided his course.

She put down the bottle. Then she did something which perhaps few of the men she had listened to through the years could have done. She moved without hurry or sign of disturbance on a tour about the room. And, although she approached the bed she did not touch the jewels. She could not force herself to that. It took her five minutes to play out her innocence and unconcern. Then it was Bat who decided the issue.

He leaped from the bed and escorted something to the door, remaining a careful distance behind. Then he mewed loudly twice. Steena followed him and opened the door wider.

Bat went straight on down the corridor, as intent as a hound on the warmest of scents. Steena strolled behind him, holding her pace to the unhurried gait of an explorer. What sped before them both was invisible to her but Bat was never baffled by it.

They must have gone into the control cabin almost on the heels of the unseen—if the unseen had heels, which there was good reason to doubt—for Bat crouched just within the doorway and refused to move on. Steena looked down the length of the instrument panels and officers' station-seats to where Cliff Moran worked. On the heavy carpet her boots made no sound and he did not glance up but sat humming through set teeth as he tested the tardy and reluctant responses to buttons which had not been pushed in years.

To human eyes they were alone in the cabin. But Bat still followed a moving something with his gaze. And it was something which he had at last made up his mind to distrust and dislike. For now he took a step or two forward and spat—his loathing made plain by every raised hair along his spine. And in that same moment Steena saw a flicker—a flicker of vague outline against Cliff's hunched shoulders as if the invisible one had crossed the space between them.

But why had it been revealed against Cliff and not against the back of one of the seats or against the panels, the walls of the corridor or the cover of the bed where it had reclined and played with its loot? What could Bat see?

The storehouse memory that had served Steena so well through the years clicked open a half-forgotten door. With one swift motion she tore loose her space-all and flung the baggy garment across the back of the nearest seat.

Bat was snarling now, emitting the throaty rising cry that was his hunting song. But he was edging back, back toward Steena's feet, shrinking from something he could not fight but which he faced defiantly. If he could draw it after him, past that dangling space-all.... He had to—it was their only chance.

"What the...." Cliff had come out of his seat and was staring at them.

What he saw must have been weird enough. Steena, bare-armed and shouldered, her usually stiffly-netted hair falling wildly down her back; Steena watching empty space with narrowed eyes and set mouth, calculating a single wild chance. Bat, crouched on his belly, retreating from thin air step by step and wailing like a demon.

"Toss me your blaster." Steena gave the order calmly—as if they still sat at their table in the Rigel Royal.

And as quietly Cliff obeyed. She caught the small weapon out of the air with a steady hand—caught and leveled it.

"Stay just where you are!" she warned. "Back, Bat, bring it back!"

With a last throat-splitting screech of rage and hate, Bat twisted to safety between her boots. She pressed with thumb and forefinger, firing at the space-alls. The material turned to powdery flakes of ash—except for certain bits which still flapped from the scorched seat —as if something had protected them from the force of the blast. Bat sprang straight up in the air with a scream that tore their ears.

"What...?" began Cliff again.

Steena made a warning motion with her left hand. *"Wait!"*

She was still tense, still watching Bat. The cat dashed madly around the cabin twice, running crazily with white-ringed eyes and flecks of foam on his muzzle. Then he stopped abruptly in the doorway, stopped and looked back over his shoulder for a long silent moment. He sniffed delicately.

Steena and Cliff could smell it too now, a thick oily stench which was not the usual odor left by an exploding blaster-shell.

Bat came back, treading daintily across the carpet, almost on the tips of his paws. He raised his head as he passed Steena and then he went confidently beyond to sniff, to sniff and spit twice at the unburned strips of the space-all. Having thus paid his respects to the late enemy he sat down calmly and set to washing his fur with deliberation. Steena sighed once and dropped into the navigator's seat.

"Maybe now you'll tell me what in the hell's happened?" Cliff exploded as he took the blaster out of her hand.

"Gray," she said dazedly, "it must have been gray—or I couldn't have seen it like that. I'm colorblind, you see. I can see only shades of gray—my whole world is gray. Like Bat's—his world is gray too—all gray. But he's been compensated, for he can see above and below our range of color vibrations and—apparently—so can I!"

Her voice quavered and she raised her chin with a new air Cliff had never seen before—a sort of proud acceptance. She pushed back her wandering hair, but she made no move to imprison it under the heavy net again.

"That is why I saw the thing when it crossed between us. Against your space-all it was another shade of gray—an outline. So I put out mine and waited for it to show against that—it was our only chance, Cliff.

"It was curious at first, I think, and it knew we couldn't see it—which is why it waited to attack. But when Bat's actions gave it away it moved. So I waited to see that flicker against the space-all and then I let him have it. It's really very simple...."

Cliff laughed a bit shakily. "But what was this gray thing? I don't get it."

"I think it was what made the *Empress* a derelict. Something out of space, maybe, or from another world somewhere." She waved her hands. "It's invisible because it's a color beyond our range of sight. It must have stayed in here all these years. And it kills—it must—when its curiosity is satisfied." Swiftly she described the scene in the cabin and the strange behavior of the gem pile which had betrayed the creature to her.

Cliff did not return his blaster to its holder. "Any more of them on board, d'you think?" He didn't look pleased at the prospect.

Steena turned to Bat. He was paying particular attention to the space between two front toes in the process of a complete bath. "I don't think so. But Bat will tell us if there are. He can see them clearly, I believe."

BUT THERE WEREN'T ANY MORE, and two weeks later Cliff, Steena and Bat brought the *Empress* into the Lunar quarantine station. And that is the end of Steena's story because, as we have been told, happy marriages need no chronicles. And Steena had found someone who knew of her gray world and did not find it too hard to share with her—someone besides Bat. It turned out to be a real love match.

The last time I saw her she was wrapped in a flame-red cloak from the looms of Rigel and wore a fortune in Jovan rubies blazing on her wrists. Cliff was flipping a three-figure credit bill to a waiter. And Bat had a row of Vernal juice glasses set up before him. Just a little family party out on the town. ♥ ♥ ♥

"All Cats Are Gray" first appeared pseudonymously, as by Andrew North, in the August–September 1953 issue of Fantastic Universe Science Fiction.

Popular American author Andre Norton (née Alice Mary Norton) spent two decades shelving books as a librarian before finally deciding to write them instead. In the end, she produced over a hundred SF novels, the earliest of which were primarily marketed as young adult ... (CONTINUED ON NEXT PAGE)

(CONTINUED FROM PREVIOUS PAGE) *...fiction. Later in her career, Norton was embraced by more mature SF readers, inducted into the Science Fiction Hall of Fame, and honored with the SFWA Grand Master Award (1984). Apropos to this issue's theme, Norton features or references derelicts in several of her SF novels, including* Sargasso of Space *(1955),* Plague Ship *('57),* Galactic Derelict *('59) and* Derelict for Trade *('97).*

SARGASSO OF SPACE

BY EDMOND HAMILTON

CAPTAIN CRAIN FACED HIS CREW CALMLY. "We may as well face the facts, men," he said. "The ship's fuel-tanks are empty and we are drifting through space toward the dead-area."

The twenty-odd officers and men gathered on the middle-deck of the freighter *Pallas* made no answer, and Crain continued: "We left Jupiter with full tanks, more than enough fuel to take us to Neptune. But the leaks in the starboard tanks lost us half our supply, and we had used the other half before discovering that. Since the ship's rocket-tubes cannot operate without fuel, we are simply drifting. We would drift on to Neptune if the attraction of Uranus were not pulling us to the right. That attraction alters our course so that in three ship-days we shall drift into the dead-area."

Rance Kent, first-officer of the *Pallas*, asked a question: "Couldn't we raise Neptune with the radio, sir, and have them send out a fuel-ship in time to reach us?"

"It's impossible, Mr. Kent," Crain answered. "Our main radio is dead without fuel to run its dynamotors, and our auxiliary set hasn't the power to reach Neptune."

"Why not abandon ship in the space-suits," asked Liggett, the second-officer, "and trust to the chance of some ship picking us up?"

The captain shook his head. "It would be quite useless, for we'd simply drift on through space with the ship into the dead-area."

The score of members of the crew, bronzed space-sailors out of every port in the solar system, had listened mutely. Now, one of them, a tall tube-man, stepped forward a little.

"Just what is this dead-area, sir?" he asked. "I've heard of it, but as this is my first outer-planet voyage, I know nothing about it."

"I'll admit I know little more," said Liggett, "save that a good many disabled ships have drifted into it and have never come out."

"The dead area," Crain told them, "is a region of space ninety thousand miles across within Neptune's orbit, in which the ordinary gravitational attractions of the solar system are dead. This is because in that region the pulls of the sun and the outer planets exactly balance each other. Because of that, anything in the dead-area, will stay in there until time ends, unless it has power of its own. Many wrecked space-ships have drifted into it at one time or another, none ever emerging; and it's believed that there is a great mass of wrecks somewhere in the area, drawn and held together by mutual attraction."

"And we're drifting in to join them," Kent said. "Some prospect!"

"Then there's really no chance for us?" asked Liggett keenly.

Captain Crain thought. "As I see it, very little," he admitted. "If our auxiliary radio can reach some nearby ship before the *Pallas* enters the dead-area, we'll have a chance. But it seems a remote one."

He addressed himself to the men: "I have laid the situation frankly before you because I consider you entitled to the truth. You must remember, however, that while there is life there is hope.

"There will be no change in ship routine, and the customary watches will be kept. Half-rations of food and water will be the rule from now on, though. That is all."

As the men moved silently off, the captain looked after them with something of pride.

"They're taking it like men," he told Kent and Liggett. "It's a pity there's no way out for them and us."

"If the *Pallas* does enter the dead-area and join the wreck-pack," Liggett said, "how long will we be able to live?"

"Probably for some months on our present condensed air and food supplies," Crain answered. "I would prefer, myself, a quicker end."

"So would I," said Kent. "Well, there's nothing left but to pray for some kind of ship to cross our path in the next day or two."

KENT'S PRAYERS were not answered in the next ship-day, nor in the next. For, though one of the *Pallas'* radio-operators was constantly at the instruments under Captain Crain's orders, the weak calls of the auxiliary set raised no response.

Had they been on the Venus or Mars run, Kent told himself, there would be some chance, but out here in the vast spaces, between the outer planets, ships were fewer and farther between. The big, cigar-shaped freighter drifted helplessly on in a broad curve toward the dreaded area, the green light-speck of Neptune swinging to their left.

On the third ship-day Kent and Captain Crain stood in the pilot-house behind Liggett, who sat at the now useless rocket-tube controls. Their eyes were on the big glass screen of the gravograph. The black dot on it that represented their ship was crawling steadily toward the bright red circle that stood for the dead-area....

They watched silently until the dot had crawled over the circle's red line, heading toward its center.

"Well, we're in at last," Kent commented. "There seems to be no change in anything, either."

Crain pointed to the instrument-panel. "Look at the gravitometers."

"All dead!" said Kent. "No gravitational pull from any direction—no, that one shows a slight attraction from ahead!"

"Then gravitational attraction of some sort does exist in the dead-area after all!" Liggett exclaimed.

"You don't understand," said Crain. "That attraction from ahead is the pull of the wreck-pack at the dead-area's center."

"And it's pulling the *Pallas* toward it?" Kent asked.

Crain nodded. "We'll probably reach the wreck-pack in two more ship-days."

THE NEXT TWO SHIP-DAYS seemed to Kent drawn out endlessly. A moody silence had grown upon the officers and men of the ship. All seemed oppressed by the strange forces of fate that had seized the ship and were carrying it, smoothly and soundlessly, into this region of irrevocable doom.

The radio-operators' vain calls had ceased. The *Pallas* drifted on into the dreaded area like some dumb ship laden with damned souls. It drifted on, Kent told himself, as many a wrecked and disabled ship had done before it, with the ordinary activities and life of the solar system forever behind it, and mystery and death ahead.

It was toward the end of the second of those two ship-days that Liggett's voice came down from the pilot-house:

"Wreck-pack in sight ahead!"

"We've arrived, anyway!" Kent cried, as he and Crain hastened up into the pilot house. The crew was running to the deck-windows.

"Right ahead there, about fifteen degrees left," Liggett told Kent and Crain, pointing. "Do you see it?"

Kent stared; nodded. The wreck-pack was a distant, disk-like mass against the star-flecked heavens, a mass that glinted here and there in the feeble sunlight of space. It did not seem large, but, as they drifted steadily closer in the next hours, they saw that in reality the wreck-pack was tremendous, measuring at least fifty miles across.

Its huge mass was a heterogeneous heap, composed mostly of countless cigar-like spaceships in all stages of wreckage. Some appeared smashed almost out of all recognizable shape, while others were, to all appearances unharmed. They floated together in this dense mass in space, crowded against one another by their mutual attraction.

There seemed to be among them every type of ship known in the solar system, from small, swift mail-boats to big freighters. And, as they drifted nearer, the three in the pilot-house could see that around and between the ships of the wreck-pack floated much other matter—fragments of wreckage, meteors, small and large, and space-debris of every sort.

The *Pallas* was drifting, not straight toward the wreck-pack, but in a course that promised to take the ship past it.

"We're not heading into the wreck-pack!" Liggett exclaimed. "Maybe we'll drift past it, and on out the dead-area's other side!"

Captain Crain smiled mirthlessly. "You're forgetting your space-mechanics, Liggett. We will drift along the wreck-pack's edge, and then will curve in and go round it in a closing spiral until we reach its edge."

"Lord, who'd have thought there were so many wrecks here!" Kent marveled. "There must be thousands of them!"

"They've been collecting here ever since

the first interplanetary rocket-ships went forth," Crain reminded him. "Not only meteor-wrecked ships, but ships whose mechanisms went wrong—or that ran out of fuel like ours—or that were captured and sacked, and then set adrift by space-pirates."

The *Pallas* by then was drifting along the wreck-pack's rim at a half-mile distance, and Kent's eyes were running over the mass.

"Some of those ships look entirely undamaged. Why couldn't we find one that has fuel in its tanks, transfer it to our own tanks, and get away?" he asked.

Crain's eyes lit. "Kent, that's a real chance! There must be some ships in that pack with fuel in them, and we can use the space-suits to explore for them!"

"Look, we're beginning to curve in around the pack now!" Liggett exclaimed.

The *Pallas*, as though loath to pass the wreck-pack, was curving inward to follow its rim. In the next hours it continued to sail slowly around the great pack, approaching closer and closer to its edge.

In those hours Kent and Crain and all in the ship watched with a fascinated interest that even knowledge of their own peril could not kill. They could see swift-lined passenger-ships of the Pluto and Neptune runs shouldering against small space-yachts with the insignia of Mars or Venus on their bows. Wrecked freighters from Saturn or Earth floated beside rotund grain-boats from Jupiter.

The debris among the pack's wrecks was just as varied, holding fragments of metal, dark meteors of differing size—and many human bodies. Among these were some clad in insulated space-suits, with their transparent glassite helmets. Kent wondered what wreck they had abandoned hastily in those suits, only to be swept with it into the dead-area, to die in their suits.

By the end of that ship-day, the *Pallas*, having floated almost completely around the wreck-pack, finally struck the wrecks at its edge with a jarring shock; then bobbed for a while and lay still. From pilothouse and deck windows the men looked eagerly forth.

THEIR SHIP FLOATED at the wreck-pack's edge. Directly to its right floated a sleek, shining Uranus-Jupiter passenger-ship whose bows had been smashed in by a meteor. On their left bobbed an unmarked freighter of the old type with projecting rocket-tubes, apparently intact. Beyond them in the wreck-pack lay another Uranus craft, a freighter, and, beyond it, stretched the countless other wrecks.

Captain Crain summoned the crew together again on the middle-deck.

"Men, we've reached the wreck-pack at the dead-area's center, and here we'll stay until the end of time unless we get out under our own power. Mr. Kent has suggested a possible way of doing so, which I consider highly feasible.

"He has suggested that in some of the ships in the wreck-pack may be found enough fuel to enable us to escape from the dead-area, once it is transferred to this ship. I am going to permit him to explore the wreck-pack with a party in space suits, and I am asking for volunteers for this service."

The entire crew stepped quickly forward. Crain smiled. "Twelve of you will be enough," he told them. "The eight tube-men and four of the cargo-men will go, therefore, with Mr. Kent and Mr. Liggett as leaders. Mr. Kent, you may address the men if you wish."

"Get down to the lower airlock and into your space-suits at once, then," Kent told them. "Mr. Liggett, will you supervise that?"

As Liggett and the men trooped down to the airlock, Kent turned back toward his superior.

"There's a very real chance of your becoming lost in this huge wreck-pack, Kent," Crain said, "so be very careful to keep your bearings at all times. I know I can depend on you."

"I'll do my best," Kent was saying, when Liggett's excited face reappeared suddenly at the stair.

"There are men coming toward the *Pallas* along the wreck-pack's edge!" he reported— "a half-dozen men in space-suits!"

"You must be mistaken, Liggett!" exclaimed Crain. "They must be some of the bodies in space-suits we saw in the pack."

"No, they're living men!" Liggett cried. "They're coming straight toward us—come down and see!"

CRAIN AND KENT followed Liggett quickly down to the airlock room, where the men who had started donning their space-suits were now peering excitedly from the windows. Crain and Kent looked where Liggett pointed, along the wreck-pack's edge to the ship's right.

Six floating shapes, men in space-suits, were approaching along the pack's border. They floated smoothly through space, reaching the wrecked passenger-ship beside the *Pallas*. They braced their feet against its side and propelled themselves on through the void like swimmers under water, toward the *Pallas*.

"They must be survivors from some wreck that drifted in here as we did!" Kent exclaimed. "Maybe they've lived here for months!"

"It's evident that they saw the *Pallas* drift into the pack, and have come to investigate," Crain estimated. "Open the airlock for them, men, for they'll want to come inside."

Two of the men spun the wheels that slid aside the airlock's outer door. In a moment the half-dozen men outside had reached the ship's side, and had pulled themselves down inside the airlock.

When all were in, the outer door was closed, and air hissed in to fill the lock. The airlock's inner door then slid open and the newcomers stepped into the ship's interior, unscrewing their transparent helmets as they did so. For a few moments the visitors silently surveyed their new surroundings.

Their leader was a swarthy individual with sardonic black eyes who, on noticing Crain's captain-insignia, came toward him with outstretched hand. His followers seemed to be cargo-men or deck-men, looking hardly intelligent enough to Kent's eyes to be tube-men.

"Welcome to our city!" their leader exclaimed as he shook Crain's hand. "We saw your ship drift in, but hardly expected to find anyone living in it."

"I'll confess that we're surprised ourselves to find any life here," Crain told him. "You're living on one of the wrecks?"

The other nodded. "Yes, on the *Martian Queen*, a quarter-mile along the pack's edge. It was a Saturn-Neptune passenger ship, and about a month ago we were at this cursed dead-area's edge, when half our rocket-tubes exploded. Eighteen of us escaped the explosion, the ship's walls still being tight; and we drifted into the pack here, and have been living here ever since."

"My name's Krell," he added, "and I was a tube-man on the ship. I and another of the tube-men, named Jandron, were the highest in rank left, all the officers and other tube-men having been killed, so we took charge and have been keeping order."

"What about your passengers?" Liggett asked.

"All killed but one," Krell answered. "When the tubes let go they smashed up the whole lower two decks."

Crain briefly explained to him the *Pallas'* predicament. "Mr. Kent and Mr. Liggett were on the point of starting a search of the wreck-pack for fuel when you arrived," he said, "With enough fuel we can get clear of the dead-area."

Krell's eyes lit up. "That would mean a getaway for all of us! It surely ought to be possible!"

"Do you know whether there are any ships in the pack with fuel in their tanks?" Kent asked. Krell shook his head.

"We've searched through the wreck-pack a good bit, but never bothered about fuel, it being no good to us. But there ought to be some, at least; there's enough wrecks in this cursed place to make it possible to find almost anything.

"You'd better not start exploring, though," he added, "without some of us along as guides, for I'm here to tell you that you can lose yourself in this wreck-pack without knowing it. If you wait until tomorrow, I'll come over myself and go with you."

"I think that would be wise," Crain said to Kent. "There is plenty of time."

"Time is the one thing there's plenty of in this damned place," Krell agreed. "We'll be getting back to the *Martian Queen* now and give the good news to Jandron and the rest."

"Wouldn't mind if Liggett and I came along, would you?" Kent asked. "I'd like to see how your ship's fixed—that is, if it's all right with you, sir," he added to his superior.

Crain nodded. "All right if you don't stay long," he said. But, to Kent's surprise Krell seemed reluctant to endorse his proposal.

"I guess it'll be all right," he said slowly, "though there's nothing much on the *Martian Queen* to see."

Krell and his followers replaced their helmets and returned into the airlock. Liggett followed them, and, as Kent struggled hastily into a space-suit, he found Captain Crain at his side.

"Kent, look sharp when you get over on that ship," Crain told him. "I don't like the look of this Krell, and his story about all the officers being killed in the explosion sounds fishy to me."

"To me, too," Kent agreed. "But Liggett and I will have the suit-phones in our space-suits and can call you from there in case of need."

Crain nodded, and Kent, with space-suit on and transparent helmet screwed tight, stepped into the airlock with the rest. The airlock's inner door closed, the outer one opened, and as the air puffed out into space, Kent and Krell and Liggett leapt out into the void, the others following.

It was no novelty to Kent to float in a space-suit in the empty void. He and the others now floated as smoothly as though under water toward a wrecked liner at the *Pallas'* right. They reached it, pulled themselves around it, and, with feet braced against its side, propelled themselves on through space along the border of the wreck-pack.

They passed a half-dozen wrecks thus, before coming to the *Martian Queen*. It was a silvery, glistening ship whose stern and lower walls were bulging and strained, but not cracked. Kent told himself that Krell had spoken truth about the exploding rocket-tubes, at least.

They struck the *Martian Queen's* side and entered the upper-airlock open for them. Once through the airlock they found themselves on the ship's upper-deck. And when Kent and Liggett removed their helmets with the others they found a full dozen men confronting them, a brutal-faced group who exhibited some surprise at sight of them.

Foremost among them stood a tall, heavy individual who regarded Kent and Liggett with the cold, suspicious eyes of an animal.

"My comrade and fellow-ruler here, Wald Jandron," said Krell. To Jandron he explained rapidly. "The whole crew of the *Pallas* is alive, and they say if they can find fuel in the wreck-pack their ship can get out of here."

"Good," grunted Jandron. "The sooner they can do it, the better it will be for us."

Kent saw Liggett flush angrily, but he ignored Jandron and spoke to Krell. "You said one of your passengers had escaped the explosion?"

To Kent's amazement a girl stepped from behind the group of men, a slim girl with pale face and steady, dark eyes. "I'm the passenger," she told him. "My name's Marta Mallen."

Kent and Liggett stared, astounded. "Good Lord!" Kent exclaimed. "A girl like you on this ship!"

"Miss Mallen happened to be on the upper-deck at the time of the explosion and, so, escaped when the other passengers were killed," Krell explained smoothly. "Isn't that so, Miss Mallen?"

The girl's eyes had not left Kent's, but at Krell's words she nodded. "Yes, that is so," she said mechanically.

Kent collected his whirling thoughts. "But wouldn't you rather go back to the *Pallas* with us?" he asked. "I'm sure you'd be more comfortable there."

"She doesn't go," grunted Jandron. Kent

turned in quick wrath toward him, but Krell intervened.

"Jandron only means that Miss Mallen is much more comfortable on this passenger-ship than she'd be in your freighter." He shot a glance at the girl as he spoke, and Kent saw her wince.

"I'm afraid that's so," she said, "but I thank you for the offer, Mr. Kent."

Kent could have sworn that there was an appeal in her eyes, and he stood for a moment, indecisive, Jandron's stare upon him. After a moment's thought he turned to Krell.

"You were going to show me the damage the exploding tubes did," he said, and Krell nodded quickly.

"Of course; you can see from the head of the stair back in the after-deck."

He led the way along a corridor, Jandron and the girl and two of the men coming with them. Kent's thoughts were still chaotic as he walked between Krell and Liggett. What was this girl doing amid the men of the *Martian Queen*? What had her eyes tried to tell him?

Liggett nudged his side in the dim corridor, and Kent, looking down, saw dark splotches on its metal floor. Bloodstains! His suspicions strengthened. They might be from the bleeding of those wounded in the tube-explosions. But were they?

THEY REACHED the after-deck whose stair's head gave a view of the wrecked tube-rooms beneath. The lower decks had been smashed by terrific forces. Kent's practiced eyes ran rapidly over the shattered rocket-tubes.

"They've back-blasted from being fired too fast," he said. "Who was controlling the ship when this happened?"

"Galling, our second-officer," answered Krell. "He had found us routed too close to the dead-area's edge and was trying to get away from it in a hurry, when he used the tubes too fast, and half of them back-blasted."

"If Galling was at the controls in the pilot-house, how did the explosion kill him?" asked Liggett skeptically.

Krell turned quickly. "The shock threw him against the pilothouse wall and fractured his skull—he died in an hour," he said. Liggett was silent.

"Well, this ship will never move again," Kent said. "It's too bad that the explosion blew out your tanks, but we ought to find fuel somewhere in the wreck-pack for the *Pallas*. And now we'd best get back."

As they returned up the dim corridor Kent managed to walk beside Marta Mallen, and without being seen, he contrived to detach his suit-phone—the compact little radiophone case inside his space-suit's neck—and slip it into the girl's grasp. He dared utter no word of explanation, but, apparently, she understood, for she had concealed the suit-phone by the time they reached the upper-deck.

Kent and Liggett prepared to don their space-helmets, and before entering the air-lock, Kent turned to Krell.

"We'll expect you at the *Pallas* first hour tomorrow, and we'll start searching the wreck-pack with a dozen of our men," he said.

He then extended his hand to the girl. "Goodbye, Miss Mallen. I hope we can have a talk soon."

He had said the words with double meaning, and saw understanding in her eyes. "I hope we can, too," she said.

Kent's nod to Jandron went unanswered, and he and Liggett adjusted their helmets and entered the airlock.

Once out of it, they kicked rapidly away from the *Martian Queen*, floating along with the wreck-pack's huge mass to their right, and only the star-flecked emptiness of infinity to their left. In a few minutes they reached the airlock of the *Pallas*.

THEY FOUND Captain Crain awaiting them anxiously. Briefly Kent reported everything.

"I'm certain there has been foul play aboard the *Martian Queen*," he said. "Krell you saw for yourself, Jandron is pure brute, and their men seem capable of anything.

"I gave the suit-phone to the girl, however,

and if she can call us with it, we can get the truth from her. She dared not tell me anything there in the presence of Krell and Jandron."

Crain nodded, his face grave. "We'll see whether or not she calls," he said.

Kent took a suit-phone from one of their space-suits and rapidly, tuned it to match the one he had left with Marta Mallen. Almost at once they heard her voice from it, and Kent answered rapidly.

"I'm so glad I got you!" she exclaimed. "Mr. Kent, I dared not tell you the truth about this ship when you were here, or Krell and the rest would have killed you at once."

"I thought that was it, and that's why I left the suit-phone for you," Kent said. "Just what *is* the truth?"

"Krell and Jandron and these men of theirs are the ones who killed the officers and passengers of the *Martian Queen*! What they told you about the explosion was true enough, for the explosion did happen that way; and because of it, the ship drifted into the dead-area. But the only ones killed by it were some of the tube-men and three passengers.

"Then, while the ship was drifting into the dead-area, Krell told the men that the fewer aboard, the longer they could live on the ship's food and air. Krell and Jandron led the men in a surprise attack and killed all the officers and passengers, and threw their bodies out into space. I was the only passenger they spared, because both Krell and Jandron— want me!"

There was a silence, and Kent felt a red anger rising in him. "Have they dared harm you?" he asked after a moment.

"No, for Krell and Jandron are too jealous of each other to permit the other to touch me. But it's been terrible living with them in this awful place."

"Ask her if she knows what their plans are in regard to us," Crain told Kent.

Marta had apparently overheard the question. "I don't know that, for they shut me in my cabin as soon as you left," she said. "I've heard them talking and arguing excitedly, though. I know that if you do find fuel, they'll try to kill you all and escape from here in your ship."

"Pleasant prospect," Kent commented. "Do you think they plan an attack on us now?"

"No. I think that they'll wait until you've refueled your ship, if you are able to do that, and then try treachery."

"Well, they'll find us ready. Miss Mallen, you have the suit-phone: keep it hidden in your cabin and I'll call you first thing tomorrow. We're going to get you out of there, but we don't want to break with Krell until we're ready. Will you be all right until then?"

"Of course I will," she answered. "There's another thing, though. My name isn't Miss Mallen—it's Marta."

"Mine's Rance," said Kent, smiling. "Goodbye until tomorrow, then, Marta."

"Goodbye, Rance."

Kent rose from the instrument with the smile still in his eyes, but with his lips compressed. "Damn it, there's the bravest and finest girl in the solar system!" he exclaimed. "Over there with those brutes!"

"We'll have her out, never fear," Crain reassured him. "The main thing is to determine our course toward Krell and Jandron."

Kent thought. "As I see it, Krell can help us immeasurably in our search through the wreck-pack for fuel," he said. "I think it would be best to keep on good terms with him until we've found fuel and have it in our tanks. Then we can turn the tables on them before they can do anything."

Crain nodded thoughtfully. "I think you're right. Then you and Liggett and Krell can head our search party tomorrow."

Crain established watches on a new schedule, and Kent and Liggett and the dozen men chosen for the exploring party of the next day ate a scanty meal and turned in for some sleep.

WHEN KENT WOKE and glimpsed the massed wrecks through the window he was for the moment amazed, but rapidly remembered. He and Liggett were finishing their morning ration when Crain pointed to a window.

"There comes Krell now," he said, indicating the single space-suited figure approaching along the wreck-pack's edge.

"I'll call Marta before he gets here," said Kent hastily.

The girl answered on the suit-phone immediately, and it occurred to Kent that she must have spent the night without sleeping. "Krell left a few minutes ago," she said.

"Yes, he's coming now. You heard nothing of their plans?"

"No, they've kept me shut in my cabin. However, I did hear Krell giving Jandron and the rest directions. I'm sure they're plotting something."

"We're prepared for them," Kent assured her. "If all goes well, before you realize it you'll be sailing out of here with us in the *Pallas*."

"I hope so," she said. "Rance, be careful with Krell in the wreck-pack. He's dangerous."

"I'll be watching him," he promised. "Goodbye, Marta."

Kent reached the lower-deck just as Krell entered from the airlock, his swarthy face smiling as he removed his helmet. He carried a pointed steel bar. Liggett and the others were donning their suits.

"All ready to go, Kent?" Krell asked.

Kent nodded. "All ready," he said shortly. Since hearing Marta's story he found it hard to dissimulate with Krell.

"You'll want bars like mine," Krell continued, "for they're damned handy when you get jammed between wreckage masses. Exploring this wreck-pack is no soft job: I can tell you from experience."

Liggett and the rest had their suits adjusted, and with bars in their grasp, followed Krell into the airlock. Kent hung back for a last word with Crain, who, with his half-dozen remaining men, was watching.

"Marta just told me that Krell and Jandron have been plotting something," he told the captain; "so I'd keep a close watch outside."

"Don't worry, Kent. We'll let no one inside the *Pallas* until you and Liggett and the men get back."

IN A FEW MINUTES they were out of the ship, with Krell and Kent and Liggett leading, and the twelve members of the *Pallas'* crew following closely.

The three leaders climbed up on the Uranus-Jupiter passenger-ship that lay beside the *Pallas*, the others moving on and exploring the neighboring wrecks in parties of two and three. From the top of the passenger-ship, when they gained it, Kent and his two companions could look far out over the wreck-pack. It was an extraordinary spectacle, this stupendous mass of dead ships floating motionless in the depths of space, with the burning stars above and below them.

His companions and the other men clambering over the neighboring wrecks seemed weird figures in their bulky suits and transparent helmets. Kent looked back at the *Pallas*, and then along the wreck-pack's edge to where he could glimpse the silvery side of the *Martian Queen*. But now Krell and Liggett were descending into the ship's interior through the great opening smashed in its bows, and Kent followed.

They found themselves in the liner's upper navigation-rooms. Officers and men lay about, frozen to death at the instant the meteor-struck vessel's air had rushed out, and the cold of space had entered. Krell led the way on, down into the ship's lower decks, where they found the bodies of the crew and passengers lying in the same silent death.

The salons held beautifully-dressed women, distinguished-looking men, lying about as the meteor's shock had hurled them. One group lay around a card-table, their game interrupted. A woman still held a small child, both seemingly asleep. Kent tried to shake off the oppression he felt as he and Krell and Liggett continued down to the tank-rooms.

They found their quest there useless, for the tanks had been strained by the meteor's shock, and were empty. Kent felt Liggett grasp his hand and heard him speak, the sound-vibrations coming through their contacting suits.

"Nothing here; and we'll find it much the same through all these wrecks, if I'm not wrong. Tanks always give at a shock."

"There must be some ships with fuel still in them among all these," Kent answered.

They climbed back, up to the ship's top, and leapt off it toward a Jupiter freighter lying a little farther inside the pack. As they floated toward it, Kent saw their men moving on with them from ship to ship, progressing inward into the pack. Both Kent and Liggett kept Krell always ahead of them, knowing that a blow from his bar, shattering their glassite helmets, meant instant death. But Krell seemed quite intent on the search for fuel.

The big Jupiter freighter seemed intact from above, but when they penetrated into it, they found its whole under-side blown away, apparently by an explosion of its tanks. They moved on to the next ship, a private space-yacht, small in size, but luxurious in fittings. It had been abandoned in space, its rocket-tubes burst and tanks strained.

They went on, working deeper into the wreck-pack. Kent almost forgot the paramount importance of their search in the fascination of it. They explored almost every known type of ship—freighters, liners, cold-storage boats, and grain-boats. Once Kent's hopes ran high at sight of a fuel-ship, but it proved to be in ballast, its cargo-tanks empty and its own tanks and tubes apparently blown simultaneously.

Kent's muscles ached from the arduous work of climbing over and exploring the wrecks. He and Liggett had become accustomed to the sight of frozen, motionless bodies.

As they worked deeper into the pack, they noticed that the ships were of increasingly older types, and at last Krell signaled a halt. "We're almost a mile in," he told them, gripping their hands. "We'd better work back out, taking a different section of the pack as we do."

Kent nodded. "It may change our luck," he said.

It did, for when they had gone not more than a half-mile back, they glimpsed one of their men waving excitedly from the top of a Pluto liner.

They hastened at once toward him, the other men gathering also; and when Kent grasped the man's hand he heard his excited voice.

"Fuel-tanks here are more than half-full, sir!"

They descended quickly into the liner, finding that though its whole stern had been sheared away by a meteor, its tanks had remained miraculously unstrained.

"Enough fuel here to take the *Pallas* to Neptune!" Kent exclaimed.

"How will you get it over to your ship?" Krell asked. Kent pointed to great reels of flexible metal tubing hanging near the tanks.

"We'll pump it over. The *Pallas* has tubing like this ship's, for taking on fuel in space, and by joining its tubing to this, we'll have a tube-line between the two ships. It's hardly more than a quarter-mile."

"Let's get back and let them know about it," Liggett urged, and they climbed back out of the liner.

They worked their way out of the wreck-pack with much greater speed than that with which they had entered, needing only an occasional brace against a ship's side to send them floating over the wrecks. They came to the wreck-pack's edge at a little distance from the *Pallas*, and hastened toward it.

They found the outer door of the *Pallas'* airlock open, and entered, Krell remaining with them. As the outer door closed and air hissed into the lock, Kent and the rest removed their helmets. The inner door slid open as they were doing this, and from inside almost a score of men leapt upon them!

Kent, stunned for a moment, saw Jandron among their attackers, bellowing orders to them, and even as he struck out furiously he comprehended. Jandron and the men of the *Martian Queen* had somehow captured the *Pallas* from Crain and had been awaiting their return!

THE STRUGGLE was almost instantly over, for, outnumbered and hampered as they were by their heavy space-suits, Kent and Liggett and their followers had no chance. Their hands, still in the suits, were bound quickly behind them at Jandron's orders.

Kent heard an exclamation, and saw Marta starting toward him from behind Jandron's men. But a sweep of Jandron's arm brushed her rudely back. Kent strained madly at his bonds. Krell's face had a triumphant look.

"Did it all work as I told you it would, Jandron?" he asked.

"It worked," Jandron answered impassively. "When they saw fifteen of us coming from the wreck-pack in space-suits, they opened right up to us."

Kent understood, and cursed Krell's cunning. Crain, seeing the fifteen figures approaching from the wreck-pack, had naturally thought they were Kent's party, and had let them enter to overwhelm his half-dozen men.

"We put Crain and his men over in the *Martian Queen*," Jandron continued, "and took all their helmets so they can't escape. The girl we brought over here. Did you find a wreck with fuel?"

Krell nodded. "A Pluto liner a quarter-mile back, and we can pump the fuel over here by connecting tube-lines. What the devil—"

Jandron had made a signal at which three of his men had leapt forward on Krell, securing his hands like those of the others.

"Have you gone crazy, Jandron?" cried Krell, his face red with anger and surprise.

"No," Jandron replied impassively, "but the men are as tired as I am of your bossing ways, and have chosen me as their sole leader."

"You dirty double-crosser!" Krell raged. "Are you men going to let him get away with this?"

The men paid no attention, and Jandron motioned to the airlock. "Take them over to the *Martian Queen* too," he ordered, "and make sure there's no space-helmet left there. Then get back at once, for we've got to get the fuel into this ship and make a getaway."

The helmets of Kent and Krell and the other helpless prisoners were put upon them, and, with hands still bound, they were herded into the airlock by eight of Jandron's men attired in space-suits also. The prisoners were then joined one to another by a strand of metal cable.

Kent, glancing back into the ship as the airlock's inner door closed, saw Jandron giving rapid orders to his followers, and noticed Marta held back from the airlock by one of them. Krell's eyes glittered venomously through his helmet. The outer door opened, and their guards jerked them forth into space by the connecting cable.

They were towed helplessly along the wreck-pack's rim toward the *Martian Queen*. Once inside its airlock, Jandron's men removed the prisoners' space-helmets and then used the duplicate-control inside the airlock itself to open the inner door. Through this opening they thrust the captives, those inside the ship not daring to enter the airlock. Jandron's men then closed the inner door, reopened the outer one, and started back toward the *Pallas* with the helmets of Kent and his companions.

Kent and the others soon found Crain and his half-dozen men who rapidly undid their bonds. Crain's men still wore their space-suits but, like Kent's companions, were without space-helmets.

"Kent, I was afraid they'd get you and your men too!" Crain exclaimed. "It's all my fault, for when I saw Jandron and his men coming from the wreck-pack I never doubted but that it was you."

"It's no one's fault," Kent told him. "It's just something that we couldn't foresee."

Crain's eyes fell on Krell. "But what's he doing here?" he exclaimed. Kent briefly explained Jandron's treachery toward Krell, and

Crain's brows drew ominously together.

"So Jandron put you here with us! Krell, I am a commissioned captain of a space-ship, and as such can legally try you and sentence you to death here without further formalities."

Krell did not answer, but Kent intervened. "There's hardly time for that now, sir," he said. "I'm as anxious to settle with Krell as anyone, but right now our main enemy is Jandron, and Krell hates Jandron worse than we do, if I'm not mistaken."

"You're not," said Krell grimly. "All I want right now is to get within reach of Jandron."

"There's small chance of any of us doing that," Crain told them. "There's not a single space-helmet on the *Martian Queen*."

"You've searched?" Liggett asked.

"Every cubic inch of the ship," Crain told him. "No, Jandron's men made sure there were no helmets left here, and without helmets this ship is an inescapable prison."

"Damn it, there must be some way out!" Kent exclaimed. "Why, Jandron and his men must be starting to pump that fuel into the *Pallas* by now! They'll be sailing off as soon as they do it!"

Crain's face was sad. "I'm afraid this is the end, Kent. Without helmets, the space between the *Martian Queen* and the *Pallas* is a greater barrier to us than a mile-thick wall of steel. In this ship we'll stay, until the air and food give out, and death releases us."

"Damn it, I'm not thinking of myself!" Kent cried. "I'm thinking of Marta! The *Pallas* will sail out of here with her in Jandron's power!"

"The girl!" Liggett exclaimed. "If she could bring us over space-helmets from the *Pallas* we could get out of here!"

Kent was thoughtful. "If we could talk to her—she must still have that suit-phone I gave her. Where's another?"

Crain quickly detached the compact suit-phone from inside the neck of his own space-suit, and Kent rapidly tuned it to the one he had given Marta Mallen. His heart leapt as her voice came instantly from it:

"Rance! Rance Kent—"

"Marta—this is Rance!" he cried.

He heard a sob of relief. "I've been calling you for minutes! I was hoping that you'd remember to listen!

"Jandron and ten of the others have gone to that wreck in which you found the fuel," she added swiftly. "They unreeled a tube-line behind them as they went, and I can hear them pumping in the fuel now."

"Are the others guarding you?" Kent asked quickly.

"They're down in the lower deck at the tanks and airlocks. They won't allow me down on that deck. I'm up here in the middle-deck, absolutely alone.

"Jandron told me that we'd start out of here as soon as the fuel was in," she added, "and he and the men were laughing about Krell."

"Marta, could you in any way get space-helmets and get out to bring them over here to us?" Kent asked eagerly.

"There's a lot of space-suits and helmets here," she answered, "but I couldn't get out with them, Rance! I couldn't get to the airlocks with Jandron's seven or eight men down there guarding them!"

Kent felt despair; then as an idea suddenly flamed in him, he almost shouted into the instrument:

"Marta, unless you can get over here with helmets for us, we're all lost. I want you to put on a space-suit and helmet at once!"

There was a short silence, and then her voice came, a little muffled. "I've got the suit and helmet on, Rance. I'm wearing the suit-phone inside it."

"Good! Now, can you get up to the pilot-house? There's no one guarding it or the upper-deck? Hurry up there, then, at once."

Crain and the rest were staring at Kent. "Kent, what are you going to have her do?" Crain exclaimed. "It'll do no good for her to start the *Pallas*; those guards will be up there in a minute!"

"I'm not going to have her start the

Pallas," said Kent grimly. "Marta, you're in the pilothouse? Do you see the heavy little steel door in the wall beside the instrument-panel?"

"I'm at it, but it's locked with a combination-lock," she said.

"The combination is 6–34–77–81," Kent told her swiftly. "Open it as quickly as you can."

"Good God, Kent!" cried Crain. "You're going to have her—?"

"Get out of there the only way she can!" Kent finished fiercely. "You have the door open, Marta?"

"Yes, there are six or seven control-wheels inside."

"Those wheels control the *Pallas'* exhaust-valves," Kent told her. "Each wheel opens the valves of one of the ship's decks or compartments and allows its air to escape into space. They're used for testing leaks in the different deck and compartment divisions. Marta, you must turn all those wheels as far as you can to the right."

"But all the ship's air will rush out; the guards below have no suits on, and they'll be—" she was exclaiming.

Kent interrupted, "It's the only chance for you, for all of us. Turn them!"

There was a moment of silence, and Kent was going to repeat the order when her voice came, lower in tone, a little strange: "I understand, Rance. I'm going to turn them."

There was silence again, and Kent and the men grouped round him were tense. All were envisioning the same thing—the air rushing out of the *Pallas'* valves, and the unsuspecting guards in its lower deck smitten suddenly by an instantaneous death.

Then Marta's voice, almost a sob: "I turned them, Rance. The air puffed out all around me."

"Your space-suit is working all right?"

"Perfectly," she said.

"Then go down and tie together as many space-helmets as you can manage, get out of the airlock, and try to get over here to the *Martian Queen* with them. Do you think you can do that, Marta?"

"I'm going to try," she said steadily. "But I'll have to pass those men in the lower-deck I just—killed. Don't be anxious if I don't talk for a little."

Yet her voice came again almost immediately. "Rance, the pumping has stopped! They must have pumped all the fuel into the *Pallas!*"

"Then Jandron and the rest will be coming back to the *Pallas* at once!" Kent cried. "Hurry, Marta!"

The suit-phone was silent; and Kent and the rest, their faces closely pressed against the deck-windows, peered intently along the wreck-pack's edge. The *Pallas* was hidden from their view by the wrecks between, and there was no sign as yet of the girl.

Kent felt his heart beating rapidly. Crain and Liggett pressed beside him, the men around them. Krell's face was a mask as he, too, gazed. Kent was rapidly becoming convinced that some mischance had overtaken the girl when an exclamation came from Liggett. He pointed excitedly.

She was in sight, unrecognizable in space-suit and helmet, floating along the wreck-pack's edge toward them. A mass of the glassite space-helmets tied together was in her grasp. She climbed bravely over the stern of a projecting wreck and shot on toward the *Martian Queen*.

The airlock's door was open for her, and when she was inside it, the outer door closed and air hissed into the lock. In a moment she was in among them, still clinging to the helmets. Kent grasped her swaying figure and removed her helmet.

"Marta, you're all right?" he cried. She nodded a little weakly.

"I'm all right. It was just that I had to go over those guards that were all frozen.... Terrible!"

"Get these helmets on!" Crain was crying. "There's a dozen of them, and twelve of us can stop Jandron's men if we get back in time!"

and they leapt forth into space, floating smoothly along the wreck-pack's border with bars in their grasp, thirteen strong.

Kent found the slowness with which they floated forward torturing. He glimpsed Crain and Liggett ahead, Marta beside him, Krell floating behind him to the left. They reached the projecting freighters, climbed over and around them, braced against them and shot on. They sighted the *Pallas* ahead now. Suddenly they discerned another group of eleven figures in space-suits approaching it from the wreck-pack's interior, rolling up the tube-line that led from the *Pallas* as they did so. Jandron's party!

JANDRON AND HIS MEN had seen them and were suddenly making greater efforts to reach the *Pallas*. Kent and his companions, propelling themselves frenziedly on from another wreck, reached the ship's side at the same time as Jandron's men. The two groups mixed and mingled, twisted and turned in a mad space-combat.

Kent and Liggett and the nearer of their men were swiftly donning the helmets. Krell grasped one and Crain sought to snatch it.

"Let that go! We'll not have you with us when we haven't enough helmets for our own men!"

"You'll have me or kill me here!" Krell cried, his eyes hate-mad. "I've got my own account to settle with Jandron!"

"Let him have it!" Liggett cried. "We've no time now to argue!"

Kent reached toward the girl. "Marta, give one of the men your helmet," he ordered; but she shook her head.

"I'm going with you!" Before Kent could dispute she had the helmet on again, and Crain was pushing them into the airlock. The nine or ten left inside without helmets hastily thrust steel bars into the men's hands before the inner door closed. The outer one opened

Kent had been grasped by one of Jandron's men and raised his bar to crack the other's glassite helmet. His opponent caught the bar, and they struggled, twisting and turning over and over far up in space amid a half-score similar struggles. Kent wrenched his bar free at last from the other's grasp and brought it down on his helmet. The glassite cracked, and he caught a glimpse of the man's hate-distorted face frozen instantly in death.

Kent released him and propelled himself toward a struggling trio nearby. As he floated toward them, he saw Jandron beyond them making wild gestures of command, and saw Krell approaching Jandron with upraised bar. Kent, on reaching the three combatants, found them to be two of Jandron's men overcoming Crain. He shattered one's helmet as he reached them, but saw the other's bar go up for a blow.

Kent twisted frantically, uselessly, to escape it, but before the blow could descend a bar shattered his opponent's helmet from behind. As the man froze in instant death Kent saw that it was Marta who had struck him from behind. He jerked her to his side. The struggles in space around them seemed to be ending.

Six of Jandron's party had been slain, and three of Kent's companions. Jandron's four other followers were giving up the combat, floating off into the wreck-pack in clumsy, hasty flight. Someone grasped Kent's arm, and he turned to find it was Liggett.

"They're beaten!" Liggett's voice came to him! "They're all killed but those four!"

"What about Jandron himself?" Kent cried. Liggett pointed to two space-suited bodies twisting together in space, with bars still in their lifeless grasp.

Kent saw through their shattered helmets the stiffened faces of Jandron and Krell, their helmets having apparently been broken by each other's simultaneous blows.

Crain had gripped Kent's arm also. "Kent, it's over!" he was exclaiming. "Liggett and I will close the *Pallas'* exhaust-valves and release new air in it. You take over helmets for the rest of our men in the *Martian Queen.*"

IN SEVERAL MINUTES Kent was back with the men from the *Martian Queen.* The *Pallas* was ready, with Liggett in its pilothouse, the men taking their stations, and Crain and Marta awaiting Kent.

"We've enough fuel to take us out of the dead-area and to Neptune without trouble!" Crain declared. "But what about those four of Jandron's men that got away?"

"The best we can do is leave them here," Kent told him. "Best for them, too, for at Neptune they'd be executed, while they can live indefinitely in the wreck-pack."

"I've seen so many men killed on the *Martian Queen* and here," pleaded Marta. "Please don't take them to Neptune."

"All right, we'll leave them," Crain agreed, "though the scoundrels ought to meet justice." He hastened up to the pilot-house after Liggett.

In a moment came the familiar blast of the rocket-tubes, and the *Pallas* shot out cleanly from the wreck-pack's edge. A scattered cheer came from the crew. With gathering speed the ship arrowed out, its rocket-tubes blasting now in steady succession.

Kent, with his arm across Marta's shoulders, watched the wreck-pack grow smaller behind. It lay as when he first had seen it, a strange great mass, floating forever motionless among the brilliant stars. He felt the girl beside him shiver, and swung her quickly around.

"Let's not look back or remember now, Marta!" he said. "Let's look ahead."

She nestled closer inside his arm. "Yes, Rance. Let's look ahead."

"The Sargasso of Space" first appeared in the September 1931 issue of Astounding Stories.

Spinning dozens of interstellar adventure stories—many of which were published in Weird Tales—*as well as novels such as* The Star Kings *(1949), versatile American author* Edmond Hamilton, *along with E. E. "Doc" Smith and Jack Williamson, helped to create and popularize the SF sub-genre known as Space Opera. Hamilton also penned horror and thriller stories, was the principal writer of the Captain Future pulp novels, and scripted countless comic book tales for such DC Comics characters as Batman, Superman, and the Legion of Superheroes. During his time writing for DC, Hamilton co-created the heroes Batwoman and Space Ranger.*   (Accompanying illustrations from *Astounding* by H. W. Wesso.)

Todd Treichel's

HOW WEIRD IS THAT?

THE NOTION OF A DERELICT VESSEL SEEMS TO SPEAK TO A DEEP, PRIMAL PART OF OUR IMAGINATION. We experience a frisson of fear when contemplating how the people onboard were humbled by the unthinkably mighty, indifferent sea as she collected her price of passage, especially when there is a mystery as to the fate of the crew. The derelict may be seen after decades of untracked wandering, thousands of miles away from its last spotting, and no logbook records its experiences in between.

Derelicts are as old as sea travel. Ships that were becalmed, or trapped in ice, or severely damaged in storms, had little prospect of reaching harbor. All accepted that the sea would claim a certain number of ships, but derelicts seemed to live on in a sort of limbo. Those that were boarded might carry a dead crew, wizened in the sun and fallen victim to unknown threats. Others might carry no crew, and no sign of why they abandoned ship, nor what became of them.

Sailors, being superstitious in all eras, didn't have to hear many stories of crewless ships, or ships full of skeletons, before sleepless nights would be given over to pondering these mysteries, and eventually to the beginnings of a large body of folklore. It would have been clear to many men of the sea that some-

thing supernatural lay behind these mysteries. Ships full of skeletons became ships crewed by skeletons, and drifting ships became ships forced to sail endlessly and randomly under a curse.

The truth was chilling enough. The *Mary Celeste*, the HMS *Resolute*, the *Governor Parr*—many cases were fully confirmed by authorities. Some had wandered for many years, or had been frozen in ice for decades, dooming their passengers, until breaking free and drifting into the paths of ships. But in other cases, they had been abandoned recently, with fresh food on plates and coffee boiling, yet no sign of crew.

These creepy legends inspired similarly haunted literature. "The Rime of Ancient Mariner" features an encounter with a derelict bearing Death and the pale lady Life-in-Death, a meeting which results in the Mariner sailing alone on his own derelict, later manned by specters. The narrator of Edgar Allan Poe's "The Narrative of Arthur Gordon Pym of Nantucket" relates the tale of a ship approaching with a sailor in the rigging nodding in greeting, revealed on closer view to be a corpse with a gull pulling at its head. William Hope Hodgson was a master at evoking the horror of being stranded in the Sargasso Sea, vulnerable to whatever strange things may approach at night ("The Thing in the Weeds"), or otherwise becalmed or stranded ("The Voice in the Night").

Hodgson wasn't entirely exaggerating about the Sargasso Sea. Surrounded by some of the strongest currents in the world, the Sargasso encompasses thousands of square miles that are mostly still and windless, and covered by a continuous mat of seaweed that can tangle small propellers or the oars of a

lifeboat. When Christopher Columbus encountered the Sargasso, he found that its depth was beyond what he could measure (he was far above the Nares Abyssal Plain, some of the deepest sea in the world). The popular imagination was captured: art and news coverage of the 19th century depicted the Sargasso as clogged with weed-strewn derelicts, modern craft with those of all eras, trapped side by side forever. In 1881, the schooner *Ellen Austin* came upon a derelict schooner, in fine shape but apparently hurriedly abandoned by its crew. A portion of her own crew were transferred, to bring the find home as salvage. En route, a storm separated the two ships, and when the *Ellen Austin* closed with the derelict, once again she was without crew and drifting erratically. Is it a coincidence that the Sargasso Sea encompasses the infamous Bermuda Triangle, where 1,600 ships were abandoned or lost at sea in the 19th century alone?

Derelicts and their horrors were not left behind with the 19th century. In 2012 it was reported that the cruise ship *Lyubov Orlova* was drifting towards Scotland or Ireland, full of desperate "cannibal rats" ready to devour whatever unfortunate town she washed up on. She had been anchored off of Newfoundland until sold for scrap, and then broke free while under tow; and even in the era of modern surveillance, went in and out of sight on her way east. In 2013, emergency signals came in that are only sent by lifeboats upon contact with water, leading to the conclusion that she had finally sunk—unless of course the rats had figured out how to operate the launchers. (It sounds horrific, but wouldn't cannibal rats actually be a good thing? They conduct their own pest control!)

Beginning in 2015, Japanese coastal authorities began to receive reports of abandoned fishing boats, at first a few, and then dozens per year. The boats were unidentified, and the crews were dead, so it was a mystery where they originated and what was happening to them. Clues found aboard began to reveal that the boats came from North Korea. Although the boats were poorly equipped for fishing, it became evident that they were manned by North Korean soldiers pressed into fishing, perhaps because of the food crisis there, or to bring in hard currency. The boats were in poor condition, under-powered, and had no GPS or other navigation equipment. The untrained and under-provisioned soldiers perished, and their boats drifted over 600 miles.

Derelicts have their uses. Some are claimed for salvage, and others have contributed to science. In the early days of sail, drifters were observed for information on currents. In the 19th century, previously unknown currents called subtropical gyres were revealed in the northern Atlantic and Pacific. Inspired by that history, scientists track flotsam from spills and wrecks, such as container loads of Nike shoes and children's plastic toys that have drifted in revealing patterns, and even demonstrated that "global conveyer belt" currents allowed them to circumnavigate the earth, in roughly 20 years.

Not all derelicts are ships. The Chesapeake Bay has a problem with abandoned crab pots. These continue to catch crabs, which then attract more crabs, fish and other creatures to be trapped as well. The idea of a trap that continues to be effective long after those who placed it leave the scene has been used in science fiction a number of times, such as the *Star Trek: The Next Generation* episode "Booby Trap."

In the age of sail, there was always a concern that the unlighted derelicts would cause collisions in the night. Today this continues in a new context: worries about colliding with space junk in the "night" of space, or falling rockets landing on your town. Space serves some of the same purpose in our imaginations as the sea did in previous centuries. What we can see is a tiny fraction of its vastness. Life and travel in both are inherently hazardous, and failing equipment or a careless mistake can leave a crew's fate to the mercy of deadly and uncaring nature. And in both, some of these calamities result in derelicts.

In space, this is not just science fiction. There are abandoned spacecraft circling us now, and it's a problem. Space seems far too vast to pollute, just as the sea once did. Not so.

Space agencies estimate that over 120 million pieces of debris are orbiting Earth, both natural and man-made, and over 30,000 are at least four inches wide. Furthermore, these are not gently drifting—those in low-Earth orbit can exceed 17,000 mph. At those speeds, even flakes of paint can damage a spacecraft, and they regularly do. Space shuttles and other returning material show a range of damage from "sandblasting," nicks and pinholes to significant dents. And when two satellites collide, the destruction is thorough—but the resulting plentiful debris lives on as further space junk, ready to damage additional craft. George Jetson is going to have very high insurance premiums on his flying car, as he will be driving through a constant meteor shower.

And some of the craft up there are already manned. The Russian *Mir* experienced a dent deep enough to deform the inner surface of the crew compartment. The International Space Station is large enough that the odds of a significant collision are unnervingly non-trivial.

Items in low orbit eventually fall, burning up in the atmosphere or occasionally striking the surface. But higher objects may remain indefinitely, unless struck or designed to be maneuvered out of orbit when their useful lives are done. Thousands of objects are tracked by space agencies, so that some collisions can be predicted, and those satellites and other craft that are maneuverable can dodge out of the way. But the vast majority are too small to track, and many collisions come as an unwelcome surprise to the owners of equipment worth billions of dollars.

To some degree, the equipment can be protected by a surprising device, the Whipple shield. This is merely a piece of foil (or recently, specially-designed fabric), installed at a standoff from the craft itself. The light weight is ideal, and even the low-strength barrier is enough to liquefy particles striking it at high speeds. The International Space Station is shielded in this way, but is maneuvered if the chance of a collision is estimated at 0.0001 or more.

Some of the flotsam is unusual. During the first U.S. space walk, astronaut Ed White lost a glove, which continues to circle and wave as it goes by. Other space walkers have lost their grip on cameras. Cosmonauts on the *Mir* discarded bags of trash. Several sorts of hand tools have gotten away, including a toothbrush.

Before anyone had thought about this much (although scientist and writer Willy Ley gave warnings in the 1950s), objects were strewn about with impunity. In 1963 the U.S. Air Force put 400 million needle-sized bits of metal into orbit as part of an experiment. The results are long since obsolete, but the needles remain. Fuel tanks were left in orbit, to be deteriorated by debris until residue fuel exploded, creating still more debris.

In addition to shielding and avoidance maneuvers, there are other strategies under development to address this problem. In an airless environment, lasers can be used to

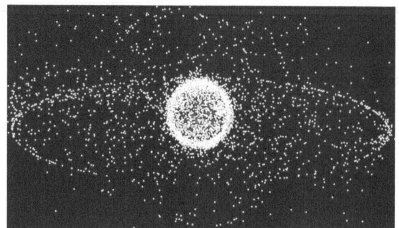

the atmosphere enough that Skylab's planned re-entry in 1979 happened earlier and in a different part of the world than intended. But the main protective measure is creating public awareness. The *Mir*, which weighed as much as a loaded railroad freight car, went full Icarus in 2001, and burning pieces rained down on Fiji. The remains of the space shuttle *Columbia*, 83,000 pieces, landed in at least six states.

push pieces around. Small specially-equipped remote-control vehicles can capture objects and force them to earth. (One of these attaches to the debris with a device inspired by Pac-Man.) Potentially sunlight might be concentrated to incinerate some objects, like space-ants under a magnifying glass. Anti-satellite missiles (ASATs) have been tested since the 1960s, with some success. Unfortunately, the physical destruction of a satellite creates substantial new debris. With enough of this, low-earth orbit or other useful orbits could become unusable. In fact, this could occur anyhow: scientists worry about the Kessler Syndrome, which is the possibility that a certain density of debris will begin a runaway process of objects smashing others into multiple still-potent objects until there is no survivable portion of the orbit. Many thousands of new satellites will be launched in the next decade, and smaller satellites that are easier to launch in quantity are on the verge of deployment. The number of active satellites will increase by orders of magnitude. Where is the Kessler threshold? We may find out. One imagines a future ad campaign urging clean-up, accentuated by a sad alien with a single, purple teardrop running down his face.

Derelict spacecraft don't stick to striking each other. They also strike earth. In fact, about one tracked object strikes earth per day, year after year. Fortunately, this can usually be predicted, although solar conditions changed

Luckily, injuries have been few thus far. They may include psychological damage. In 2007, people on a plane flying over the Pacific saw portions of a Russian spy satellite whiz by, within five miles of the aircraft. They don't show that in the beautiful skies in airline ads.

One further hazard of space junk is the possibility of war. When a spacecraft suddenly goes silent or explodes, its owner may not be able to tell whether the cause was natural, or an attack. If they conclude the latter, they might respond, and conflict could spread to the surface as well.

Space probes such as the Voyagers are now the ghost ships of our time, bound to journey away from our ken, until defunct and beyond, perhaps to collide with another object and spawn more deathless objects, perhaps to arrive at a distant civilization and raise mysteries and folktales about its nature. Perhaps one day manned Earth craft will follow, and some will be abandoned by their crews, or trap them in hopeless inertia, "as idle as a painted ship upon a painted ocean."

JIGSAW

BY DOUGLAS SMITH

STILL IN SHOCK, CASSIE MORANT SLUMPED IN THE COCKPIT OF THE EMPTY HOPPER, STARING AT THE TWO VIEWPLATES BEFORE HER.

In one, the planet Griphus, a blue, green and brown marble wrapped in belts of cloud, grew smaller. Except for the shape of its land masses, it could have been Earth.

But it wasn't. Griphus was an alien world, light-years from Sol System.

A world where nineteen of her shipmates were going to die.

And one of them was Davey.

On the other viewplate, the segmented, tubular hull of the orbiting Earth wormship, the *Johannes Kepler*, grew larger. Cassie tapped a command, and the ship's vector appeared, confirming her fears.

The ship's orbit was still decaying. She opened a comm-link.

"Hopper two to the *Kepler*," she said. "Requesting docking clearance."

Silence. Then a male voice crackled over the speaker, echoing cold and metallic in the empty shuttle. "Acknowledged, Hopper two. You are clear to dock, segment beta four, port nine."

Cassie didn't recognize the voice, but that wasn't surprising. The *Kepler* held the population of a small city, and Cassie was something of a loner. But she had no trouble identifying the gruff rumble she heard next.

"Pilot of hopper, identify yourself. This is Captain Theodor."

Cassie took a breath. "Sir, this is Dr. Cassandra Morant, team geologist."

Pause. "Where's team leader Stockard?" Theodor asked.

Davey. "Sir, the rest of the surface team was captured by the indigenous tribe inhabiting the extraction site. The team is..." Cassie stopped, her throat constricting.

"Morant?"

She swallowed. "They're to be executed at sunrise."

Another pause.

"Did you get the berkelium?" Theodor finally asked.

Cassie fought her anger. Theodor wasn't being heartless. The team below was secondary to the thousands on the ship.

"Just a core sample, sir," she said. "But it confirms that the deposit's there."

Theodor swore. "Dr. Morant, our orbit decays in under twenty hours. Report immediately after docking to brief the command team." Theodor cut the link.

Cassie stared at the huge wormship, suddenly hating it, hating its strangeness. Humans would never build something like that, she thought.

Consisting of hundreds of torus rings strung along a central axis like donuts on a stick, the ship resembled a giant metallic worm. A dozen rings near the middle were slowly rotating, providing the few inhabited sections with an artificial gravity. The thousands of humans on the ship barely filled a fraction of it.

This wasn't meant for us, she thought. *We*

shouldn't be here.

Humans had just begun to explore their solar system, when Max Bremer and his crew had found the wormships, three of them, outside the orbit of Pluto.

Abandoned? Lost? Or left to be found?

Found by the ever curious, barely-out-of-the-trees man-apes of Earth. Found with charted wormholes in Sol System. Found with still-only-partly-translated, we-think-this-button-does-this libraries and data-bases, and we-can't-fix-it-so-it-better-never-break technology. Incredibly ancient yet perfectly functioning Wormer technology.

Wormers. The inevitable name given to Earth's unknown alien benefactors.

Five years later, humanity was here, exploring the stars, riding like toddlers on the shoulders of the Wormers.

But Cassie no longer wanted to be here. She wished she was back on Earth, safely cocooned in her apartment, with Vivaldi playing, lost in one of her jigsaw puzzles.

She shifted uncomfortably in the hopper seat. Like every Wormer chair, like the ship itself, it almost fit a human. But not quite.

It was like forcing a piece to fit in a jigsaw—it was always a cheat, and in the end, the picture was wrong. Humans didn't belong here. They had forced themselves into a place in the universe where they didn't fit. *We cheated*, she thought, *and we've been caught. And now we're being punished.*

They faced a puzzle that threatened the entire ship. She'd had a chance to solve it on the planet.

And she'd failed.

Cassie hugged herself, trying to think. She was good at puzzles, but this one had a piece missing. She thought back over events since they'd arrived through the wormhole four days ago. The answer had to be there...

* * *

FOUR DAYS AGO, Cassie had sat in her quarters on the *Kepler*, hunched over a jigsaw puzzle covering her desk. The desk, like anything Wormer, favored unbroken flowing contours, the seat sweeping up to chair back wrapping around to desk surface. Viewplates on the curved walls showed telescopic shots of Griphus. The walls and ceiling glowed softly.

Lieutenant David Stockard, Davey to Cassie, lay on her bunk watching her.

"Don't you get tired of jigsaws?" he asked.

She shrugged. "They relax me. It's my form of meditation. Besides, I'm doing my homework."

Davey rolled off the bunk. She watched him walk over, wondering again what had brought them together. If she could call what they had being "together"—sometimes friendship, sometimes romance, sometimes not-talking-to-each-other.

They seemed a case study in "opposites attract." She was a scientist, and Davey was military. She was dark, short and slim, while he was fair, tall and broad. She preferred spending her time quietly, reading, listening to classical music—and doing jigsaw puzzles. Davey always had to be active.

But the biggest difference lay in their attitudes to the Wormers. Davey fervently believed that the alien ships were meant to be found by humans, that the Universe wanted them to explore the stars.

To Cassie, the Universe wasn't telling them everything it knew. She felt that they didn't understand Wormer technology enough to be risking thousands of lives.

He looked at the puzzle. "Homework?"

"I printed a Mercator projection of topographic scans of Griphus onto plas-per, and the computer cut it into a jigsaw."

The puzzle showed the planet's two major continents, which Dr. Xu, head geologist and Cassie's supervisor, had dubbed Manus and Pugnus. *Hand and fist.* The western continent, Pugnus, resembled a clenched fist and forearm, punching across an ocean at Manus, which resembled an open hand, fingers and thumb curled ready to catch the fist. Colored dots, each numbered, speckled the map.

"What are the dots?" Davey asked.

"Our shopping list. Deposits of rare minerals. That is, if you believe Wormer archives and Wormer scanners—"

"Cassie, let's not start—"

"Davey, these ships are at least ten thousand years old—"

"With self-healing nanotech—"

"That we don't understand—"

"Cassie..." Davey sighed.

She glared, then folded her arms. "Fine."

Davey checked the time on his per-comm unit. "Speaking of homework, Trask wants surface team rescue procedures by oh-eight-hundred. Gotta go." He kissed Cassie and left.

Cassie bit back a comment that this was a scientific, not a military, expedition. The likely need for Trask's "procedures" was low in her opinion.

She would soon change her mind.

An hour later, Cassie was walking along the busy outer corridor of the ring segment assigned to the science team. Suddenly, the ship shuddered, throwing Cassie and others against one curving wall.

The ship lurched again, and the light from the glowing walls blinked out. People screamed. Cassie stumbled and fell. And kept falling, waiting for the impact against the floor that never came, until she realized what had happened.

The ring's stopped rotating, she thought. *We've lost artificial gravity.*

She floated in darkness for maybe thirty minutes, bumping into others, surrounded by whispers, shouts, and sobbing. Suddenly, the lights flicked back on. Cassie felt gravity returning like an invisible hand tugging at her guts, followed by a sudden heaviness in her limbs. Hitting the floor, she rolled then rose on shaky legs. People stood dazed, looking like scattered pieces in a jigsaw that before had been a coherent picture of normality.

What had happened?

The intercom broke through the rising babble of conversations. "The following personnel report immediately to port six, segment beta four for surface team detail." Twenty names followed. One was Davey's.

One was hers. What was going on?

An hour later, her questions still unanswered, she and nineteen others sat in a hopper as it left the *Kepler*. Hoppers were smaller Wormer craft used for ship-to-surface trips and exploration. With a tubular hull, a spherical cockpit at the head, and six jointed legs allowing them to rest level on any terrain, they resembled grasshoppers.

The team faced each other in two rows of seats in the main cabin. Cassie only knew two others besides Davey. Manfred Mubuto, balding, dark and round, was their xeno-anthropologist. Liz Branson, with features as sharp as her sarcasm, was their linguist. Four were marines. But the rest, over half the team, were mining techs. Why?

Davey addressed them. She'd never seen him so serious.

"The Kepler's power loss resulted from the primary fuel cell being purged. Engineering is working to swap cells, but that requires translating untested Wormer procedures. We may need to replenish the cell, which means extracting berkelium from Griphus for processing."

That's why I'm here, Cassie thought. Berkelium, a rare trans-uranium element, was the favored Wormer energy source. It had never been found on Earth, only manufactured. Her analysis of Griphus had shown possible deposits.

"Like every planet found via the wormholes," Davey said, "Griphus is incredibly Earth-like: atmosphere, gravity, humanoid populations—"

Liz interrupted. "We purged a fuel cell? Who screwed up?"

Davey reddened. "That's not relevant—"

"Operator error, I hear," Manfred said. "A tech misread Wormer symbols on a panel, punched an incorrect sequence—"

Liz swore. "I knew it! We're like kids trying to fly Daddy's flitter—"

Cassie started to agree, but Davey cut

them off.

"We've no time for rumors," he snapped, looking at Cassie, Liz, and Manfred. "Our orbit decays in three days. I remind you that this team's under my command—including science personnel."

Manfred nodded. Liz glared, but said nothing.

Davey tapped the computer pad on his seat. A holo of Griphus appeared. "Dr. Morant, please locate the berkelium."

Cassie almost laughed at being called "Dr. Morant" by Davey, but then she caught his look. She tapped some keys, and two red dots blinked onto the holo, one in the ocean mid-way between Pugnus and Manus, and another offshore of Manus. The second site was circled.

"Wormer sensors show two sites. I've circled my recommendation," Cassie said.

"Why not the other site?" a mining tech asked.

A network of lines appeared, making the planet's surface look like a huge jigsaw puzzle.

"As on Earth," Cassie said, "the lithosphere or planetary crust of Griphus is broken into tectonic plates, irregular sections ranging from maybe fifteen kilometers thick under oceans to a hundred under continents. This shows the plate pattern on Griphus.

"Plates float on the denser, semi-molten asthenosphere, the upper part of the mantle. At 'transform' boundaries, they slide along each other, as in the San Andreas Fault on Earth. At 'convergent' boundaries, they collide, forming mountains such as the Himalayas."

A line splitting the ocean between Pugnus and Manus glowed yellow. The line also ran through the other berkelium site.

"But at 'divergent' boundaries," Cassie continued, "such as this mid-oceanic trench, magma pushes up from the mantle, creating new crust, forcing the plates apart. The other site is deep in the trench, below our sub's crush depth."

Davey nodded. "So we hit the site offshore of Manus. Any indigenous population along that coast?"

"Yes," Manfred said. "From orbital pictures, they appear tribal, agrarian, definitely pre-industrial. Some large stone structures and primitive metallurgy."

"Then defending ourselves shouldn't be a problem." Davey patted the *stinger* on his belt. The Wormer weapon was non-lethal, temporarily disrupting voluntary muscular control.

"Could we try talking before we shoot them?" Liz said.

Davey just smiled. "Which brings us to communication, Dr. Branson."

Liz sighed. "Wormer translator units need a critical mass of vocabulary, syntax, and context samples to learn a language. Given the time we have, I doubt they'll help much."

"With any luck, we won't need them," Davey said. "We'll locate the deposit, send in the mining submersible, and be out before they know we're there."

Looking around her, Cassie guessed that no one felt lucky.

The hopper landed on the coast near the offshore deposit. The team wore light body suits and breathing masks to prevent ingesting anything alien to human immune systems.

Cassie stepped onto a broad beach of gray sand lapped by an ocean too green for Earth, under a sky a touch too blue. The beach ran up to a forest of trees whose black trunks rose twenty meters into the air. Long silver leaves studded each trunk, glinting like sword blades in the sun. She heard a high keening that might have been birds or wind in the strange trees.

Southwards, the beach ran into the distance. But to the north, it ended at a cliff rising up to a low mesa. Cassie walked over to Davey, who was overseeing the marines unloading the submersible and drilling equipment.

"Cool, eh?" he said, looking around them.

She pointed at the mesa. "That's cooler to a rock nut."

He looked up the beach. "Okay. But keep your per-comm on."

Cassie nodded and set out. The cliff was an hour's walk. Cassie didn't mind, enjoying the exercise and strange surroundings. She took pictures of the rock strata and climbed to get samples at different levels. Then she walked back.

They captured Cassie just as she was wondering why the hopper seemed deserted. The natives appeared so quickly and silently, they seemed to rise from the sand. Cassie counted about forty of them, all remarkably human-like, but taller, with larger eyes, longer noses, and greenish skin. All were male, bare-chested, wearing skirts woven from sword-blade tree leaves, and leather sandals.

They led Cassie to stand before two women. One was dressed as the men were, but with a headdress of a coppery metal. The other was older and wore a cape of cloth and feathers. Her head was bare, her hair long and white. Beside them, pale but unharmed, stood Liz Branson, flanked by two warriors.

The older woman spoke to Liz in a sing-song melodic language. Cassie saw that the linguist wore a translator earplug. Liz sat down, motioning Cassie to do the same. The male warriors sat circling them. The two native women remained standing.

Cassie realized she was trembling. "What happened?"

Liz grimaced. "We've stepped in it big time. The Chadorans—our captors—believe a sacred object called "the third one" lies underwater here. Only a priestess may enter these waters. When our techs launched the sub, the natives ambushed us from the trees with blowguns. They grabbed the techs when they surfaced."

"Where's Davey?" Cassie asked, then added, "...and everyone?"

"Taken somewhere. They seemed okay."

"Why not you, too?"

"The tribe's matriarchal," Liz said. "The old woman is Cha-kay, their chief. The younger one, Pre-nah, is their priestess. Because I'm female and knew their language, Cha-kay assumed I was our leader. But I said you were."

"You what?" Cassie cried.

"Cassie, we need someone they'll respect," Liz said, her face grim. "That means a female who didn't defile the site. That means you."

"God, Liz—wait, how can you talk to them?"

Liz frowned. "It's weird. The translator produced understandable versions within minutes, pulling from Wormer archives of other worlds. That implies all those languages share the same roots. The Wormers may have seeded all these worlds."

Cassie didn't care. "What can I do?"

"Convince Cha-kay to let us go."

"How?" Cassie asked.

"She wants to show you something. It's some sort of test."

"And if I fail?"

Liz handed Cassie the translator. "Then they'll kill us."

Cassie swallowed. "I won't let that happen."

They led Cassie to a long boat with a curving prow powered by a dozen rowers. Cha-kay rode in a chair near the stern, Cassie at her feet. Pre-nah and six warriors stood beside them.

They traveled up a winding river through dense jungle. Conversation was sparse, but sufficient to convince Cassie that the translator unit worked. After three hours, they landed at a clearing. Cassie climbed out, happy to move and stretch. She blinked.

Blue cubes, ranging from one to ten meters high, filled the clearing. They were hewn from stone and painted. The party walked past the cubes to a path that switch-backed up a low mountain. They began to climb.

Cassie groaned but said nothing, since the aged Cha-kay didn't seem bothered by the climb. As they went, Cassie noticed smaller cubes beside the path.

Night had fallen when they reached the top and stepped onto a tabletop of rock about eighty meters across. Cassie gasped.

A huge cube, at least fifty meters on each side nearly filled the plateau. It was blue. It was glowing.

And it was hovering a meter off the ground.

Cha-kay led Cassie to it, and Cassie received another shock. On its smooth sides, Cassie saw familiar symbols.

The artifact, whatever its purpose, was Wormer.

Cha-kay prostrated herself, telling Cassie to do the same. As Cassie did so, she peeked underneath the cube. A column of pulsating blue light shone from a crevice to touch the base of the artifact at its center. Reaching down to her belt, Cassie activated her scanner. She'd check the readings later.

Rising, Cha-kay indicated a large diagram on the artifact. In it, a cube, a sphere, and a tetrahedron formed points of an equilateral triangle.

"It is a map. We are here," Cha-kay said, pointing to the cube. "The gods left three artifacts, but hid one. The third will appear when the gods return and lay their hands on the other two." Then, pointing to the outline of a hand on the artifact, Cha-kay looked at Cassie.

"Touch," she said.

With a sudden chill, Cassie understood. *They think we're the Wormers, finally returning*, she thought.

This was the test, on which the lives of her shipmates, of the entire ship, depended.

Reaching out a trembling hand, Cassie felt resistance from some invisible barrier and a warm tingling, then her hand slipped through onto the outline on the artifact.

Nothing happened.

Murmurs grew behind her. Feeling sick, Cassie looked at Cha-kay. To her surprise, the old woman smiled.

"Perhaps," Cha-kay said, "it rises even now."

Cassie understood. Cha-kay hoped to find that the third artifact had emerged from the sea when they returned to the beach. Cassie didn't share her hope.

They spent the night there. Pretending to sleep, Cassie checked her scanner readings. They confirmed her suspicions. The column of light showed berkelium emissions. The artifact was connected to a deposit as an energy source.

The next day, a similar journey brought them to the second artifact, located on another flat mountain peak. The only difference was the artifact itself, a huge glowing red tetrahedron. Cassie again saw a column of light underneath and detected berkelium. She touched the artifact, again with no apparent effect, and the party began the trip back.

Cha-kay seemed to have grown genuinely fond of Cassie. She told Cassie how her people found the artifacts generations ago, eventually realizing that the drawing was a map. They learned to measure distances and angles, and determined that the third artifact lay in the coastal waters. Priestesses had dived there for centuries but found nothing. Still they believed.

Cassie did some calculations, and found the Chadoran estimate remarkably accurate. Still, she wondered why the Wormers would locate two artifacts in identical settings on mountain plateaus, yet place the third underwater. Perhaps the third location had subsided over the years. But her scans showed no sunken mountains off the coast.

Cassie enjoyed Cha-kay's company, but as they neared the coast, her fear grew. Cha-kay fell silent as well. As the boat reached the beach, they stood at the railing, clasping each other's hand, scanning the waters for the third artifact.

Nothing.

Cries arose among the warriors. Pre-nah approached Cha-kay. "The strangers are false gods," the priestess said. "They must die."

Cha-kay stared across the ocean. Finally, she nodded. Cassie's legs grew weak as two warriors moved toward her.

Cha-kay raised her hand. "No. This one

goes free. She did not defile the sacred place."

Pre-nah didn't look pleased, but she bowed her head.

They landed, and Cha-kay walked with Cassie to the hopper.

"When?" Cassie asked, her voice breaking.

"At sunrise, child," Cha-kay said. "I am sorry."

Cassie boarded the hopper. She engaged the auto-launch, then slumped in her seat, as the planet and her hopes grew smaller.

* * *

AFTER DOCKING, CASSIE WENT immediately to the briefing room, as Captain Theodor had ordered. She quickly took a seat in one of a dozen Wormer chairs around a holo display unit. Dr. Xu gave her a worried smile. Commander Trask glared.

Theodor cleared his throat, a rumble that brought everyone's gaze to his stocky form.

"I'll be brief. Our orbit collapses in nineteen hours. Attempts to swap fuel cells were unsuccessful. The team sent to extract the berkelium has been captured and faces execution. Only Dr. Morant escaped."

Everyone looked at Cassie. All she could think of was how she'd failed.

Theodor continued. "Dr. Morant will summarize events on the planet. Then I need ideas."

Cassie told her story, then answered questions, mostly dealing with the artifacts. Will Epps, their expert on Wormer texts and writing, after analyzing her scans, agreed that the artifacts were Wormer.

The team began reviewing and discarding proposals. Finally, Theodor made his decision. A platoon of marines would drop outside the Chadoran city. Three squads would act as a diversion, drawing warriors from the city, while one squad slipped in for a search and rescue. One hour later, a hopper would drop two mining subs at the berkelium site.

"Sir, the priestess dives there daily," Cassie said. "When they see our subs, they'll kill the team."

"That's why I'm giving the rescue squads an hour head start," Theodor replied. "It's not much, but our priority is to replenish our fuel before our orbit decays. I can't delay the berkelium extraction any longer."

Cassie slumped in her seat. Davey, Liz, the others. They were all going to die.

Trask stood. "If Dr. Morant could provide a topographical display of the area, I'll outline the attack plan."

Cassie tapped some keys, and the planetary view of Griphus appeared, including the pattern of tectonic plates.

Like a jigsaw puzzle, Cassie thought. Why can't this be that simple?

"Zoom in to the landing site," Trask said.

Freezing the rotation over Pugnus and Manus, Cassie started to zoom in, then stopped, staring at the display. No, she thought, it's too wild. But maybe... She began tapping furiously, and calculations streamed across the holo.

"What the hell's going on?" Trask asked.

Theodor frowned. "Dr. Morant?"

Cassie looked at her results. My god, it fits. But the time span...

"Dr. Morant!" Theodor barked.

Cassie's head jerked up. Everyone was staring. It's wild, she thought, but it fits. And she liked things that fit. "Captain, what if we proved to the Chadorans that the deposit site is not sacred?"

Theodor frowned. "Discredit their religion? I don't—"

"No," Cassie said. "I mean, prove that it isn't sacred because..." She stopped. What if she was wrong? But it was Davey and the team's only chance. "...because the third artifact isn't there," she finished.

Trask snorted. "Then why will they kill to protect the site?"

"Because they think it's there, based entirely on the diagrams on the artifacts."

"And you think those diagrams are wrong?" Theodor asked, but his voice held none of Trask's derision.

"I think they were correct once," she said. "But not any more."

"So where's the artifact?" Theodor asked.

Cassie's hand trembled as she tapped more keys. Two green lights appeared inland on the western coast of Manus, followed by a red light just off the same coast, forming the triangular pattern diagrammed on the artifacts.

"The two green lights are the known artifacts. The red light is both the supposed underwater location of the third and our targeted berkelium site."

She swallowed. *Here goes*, she thought.

"And this, I believe, is the actual location of the third artifact." A third green light appeared.

Everyone started talking at once. Theodor silenced them with a wave of his hand. He stared at the display.

On the eastern coast of Pugnus, on a separate continent and an entire ocean away from the underwater site, blinked the third green light.

Theodor turned to Cassie. "Explain."

"It involves tectonic plate theory—" she began.

"I know the theory. What's the relevance?"

Cassie tapped a key. The mid-oceanic trench between Pugnus and Manus glowed yellow.

"That trench is a 'divergent' boundary," Cassie said, "where new crust is being formed, pushing Manus and Pugnus further apart every year. But that also means that sometime in the past, they looked like this." The plates began to shift. The two large continents moved closer until the fist of Pugnus slipped into the open hand of Manus like a piece in a puzzle. Someone gasped, as the third green light on Pugnus aligned itself over the red light offshore of Manus.

Theodor nodded. "You're saying the Wormers originally placed the three artifacts as the diagrams show, but the missing one moved relative to the other two as the continents separated."

Xu shook his head. "Cassie..."

Cassie sighed. "I know. The time frame is...difficult to believe."

"How old are the artifacts if your theory is true?" Theodor asked.

Xu answered. "At least as old as the core sample from the deposit site, which formed as the trench started to spread. Cassie, what was the isotopic clock dating on the sample?"

Cassie hesitated. "Its age was thirty, uh..." She swallowed. "...million years."

The eruption of exclamations made Cassie want to slink from the room. Theodor again waved for silence.

In desperation, Cassie turned to Will Epps. "We know that these ships are at least ten thousand years old. But couldn't they be much older?"

Several people squirmed. Their situation was bad enough without being reminded that they were relying on alien technology at least a hundred centuries old.

Will shrugged. "There's so much self-healing nano-tech, we can't estimate their age accurately."

"So any Wormer technology could be much older as well, right?" Cassie asked.

"But thirty million years..." Xu shook his head, as did others. Cassie was losing them.

She turned to Theodor.

"Captain, it all fits. It explains why the Chadorans have never found the artifact. Why our sub didn't see it. Why Wormers placed two artifacts on mountains, but supposedly put the third underwater. They didn't. They put it on land too."

"Can't we scan for the artifact?" Trask said.

"The other two don't show on scanners," Epps said. "They're shielded somehow."

"So the third artifact *could* be where the Chadorans say it is," Trask replied.

Cassie sat back, feeling defeated. Then something struck her.

"Both artifacts I saw are located over berkelium deposits, yet neither site appears on the mineral scans. The artifacts shield the berkelium too."

"So?" Theodor said.

"We detected berkelium at the underwater site. That means nothing's shielding it. The third artifact isn't there."

Trask started to protest, but Theodor raised a hand. "I agree with Dr. Morant. It fits." He stood up. "Cassie, I'll give you the same lead time. Take a hopper down now."

Cassie was already sprinting for the door.

* * *

ON A MOUNTAIN PLATEAU, across an ocean from where they had first landed on Griphus, Cassie and Davey stood, arms around each other's waist.

"So you saved me, the team, the entire ship," Davey said, "and made one of the most important discoveries in history. Not a bad day."

Cassie grinned. "Actually, the toughest part was convincing Cha-kay to fly in the hopper. Now she wants a world tour."

Beside them, happiness lighting her face, Cha-kay gazed at a huge glowing yellow sphere hovering above the ground.

The third artifact.

With one difference. A beam of energy shone from the sphere into the sky. The beam had begun the moment Cassie had touched the sphere.

Cassie's per-comm beeped. It was Theodor. "Dr. Morant, all three artifacts now appear on scanners, all beaming to the same point in space—"

"A new wormhole," Cassie interrupted.

Pause. "How'd you know?" Theodor asked.

Cassie grinned. "I'm good at puzzles, sir."

"Hmm. Anyway, Earth's sending a second wormship. We'll all have the option of returning home or exploring the wormhole. Once again, good work, Morant." Theodor signed off.

"You didn't mention your theory," Davey said.

"That the wormhole leads to the Wormers' home world? Just a hunch."

"Explain it to me then."

Cassie nodded at the sphere. "I think the artifacts were a puzzle—and the wormhole the prize."

"For us or the Chandorans?"

"For us. Another bread crumb in the trail the Wormers left us." She shrugged and laughed. "It just fits."

Davey nodded. "So what about you? Back to Earth or through the wormhole?"

"Wormhole," she said.

He raised an eyebrow. "Okay, that surprised me."

Cassie grinned. "Hey, if the Wormers liked puzzles, they couldn't have been that bad." She stared at the artifact. "Besides, we solved their puzzle, saved ourselves, became heroes to the Chadorans…" Her eyes followed the beam up towards the heavens.

"Maybe we fit out here after all," she said softly.

👽 👽 👽

"Jigsaw" first appeared in 2004, in the anthology Odyssey. *The story was a finalist for the 2005 Aurora Award for Best Short Fiction.*

Douglas Smith is an award-winning Canadian author described by Library Journal *as "one of Canada's most original writers of speculative fiction." His fiction has been published in twenty-six languages and thirty-two countries. His work includes the urban fantasy novel,* The Wolf at the End of the World, *and the collections* Chimerascope, Impossibilia, *and* La Danse des Esprits. *His non-fiction guide for writers,* Playing the Short Game: How to Market & Sell Short Fiction, *is a must read for any short story writer.*

Doug is a three-time winner of Canada's Aurora Award, and has been a finalist for the John W. Campbell Award, CBC's Bookies Award, Canada's juried Sunburst Award, and France's juried Prix Masterton and Prix Bob Morane.

His website is www.smithwriter.com and he tweets at twitter.com/smithwritr

THE MYSTERY OF THE DERELICT

by William Hope Hodgson

"IT'S THE *MATERIAL*," SAID THE OLD SHIP'S DOCTOR…. "THE MATERIAL, plus the Conditions; and, maybe," he added slowly, "a third factor—yes, a third factor; but there, there…." He broke off his half-meditative sentence, and began to charge his pipe.

"Go on, Doctor," we said, encouragingly, and with more than a little expectancy. We were in the smoke-room of the *Sand-a-lea*, running across the North Atlantic; and the Doctor was a character. He concluded the charging of his pipe, and lit it; then settled himself, and began to express himself more fully.

"The Material," he said, with conviction, "is inevitably the medium of expression of the Life-Force—the fulcrum, as it were; lacking which, it is unable to exert itself, or, indeed, to express itself in any form or fashion that would be intelligible or evident to us.

"So potent is the share of the Material in the production of that thing which we name Life, and so eager the Life-Force to express itself, that I am convinced it would, if given the right Conditions, make itself manifest even through so hopeless-seeming a medium as a simple block of sawn wood; for I tell you, gentlemen, the Life-Force is both as fiercely urgent and as indiscriminate as Fire—the Destructor; yet which some are now growing to consider the very essence of Life rampant…. There is a quaint seeming paradox there," he concluded, nodding his old grey head.

"Yes, Doctor," I said. "In brief, your argument is that Life is a thing, state, fact, or element, call-it-what-you-like, which requires the Material through which to manifest itself, and that given the Material, plus the Conditions, the result is Life. In other words, that Life is an evolved product, manifested through Matter and bred of Conditions—eh?"

"As we understand the word," said the old Doctor. "Though, mind you, there may be a third factor. But, in my heart, I believe that it is a matter of chemistry; Conditions and a suitable medium; but given the Conditions, the Brute is so almighty that it will seize upon anything through which to manifest itself. It is a Force generated by Conditions; but nevertheless this does not bring us one iota nearer to its explanation, any more than to the explanation of Electricity or Fire. They are, all three, of the Outer Forces—Monsters of the Void. Nothing we can do will create any one of them; our power is merely to be able, by providing the Conditions, to make each one of them manifest to our physical senses. Am I clear?"

"Yes, Doctor, in a way you are," I said. "But I don't agree with you; though I think I understand you. Electricity and Fire are both what I might call natural things; but Life is an abstract something—a kind of all-permeating Wakefulness. Oh, I can't explain it; who could! But it's spiritual; not just a thing bred out of a Condition, like Fire, as you say, or Electricity. It's a horrible thought of yours. Life's a kind of spiritual mystery…."

"Easy, my boy!" said the old Doctor, laughing gently to himself; "or else I may be asking you to demonstrate the spiritual mystery of life of the limpet, or the crab, shall we say."

He grinned at me, with ineffable perverseness. "Anyway," he continued, "as I suppose you've all guessed, I've a yarn to tell you in support of my impression that Life is no more a mystery or a miracle than Fire or Electricity. But, please to remember, gentlemen, that because we've succeeded in naming and making good use of these two Forces, they're just as much mysteries, fundamentally, as ever. And, anyway, the thing I'm going to tell you, won't explain the mystery of Life; but only give you one of my pegs on which I hang my feeling that Life is, as I have said, a Force made manifest through Conditions (that is to say, natural Chemistry), and that it can take for its purpose and Need, the most incredible and unlikely Matter; for without Matter, it cannot come into existence—it cannot become manifest...."

"I don't agree with you, Doctor," I interrupted. "Your theory would destroy all belief in life after death. It would...."

"Hush, sonny," said the old man, with a quiet little smile of comprehension. "Hark to what I've to say first; and, anyway, what objection have you to material life, after death; and if you object to a material framework, I would still have you remember that I am speaking of Life, as we understand the word in this our life. Now do be a quiet lad, or I'll never be done.

"IT WAS WHEN I was a young man, and that is a good many years ago, gentlemen. I had passed my examinations; but was so run down with overwork, that it was decided that I had better take a trip to sea. I was by no means well off, and very glad, in the end, to secure a nominal post as Doctor in a sailing passenger-clipper, running out to China.

"The name of the ship was the *Bheotpte*, and soon after I had got all my gear aboard, she cast off, and we dropped down the Thames, and next day were well away out in the Channel.

"The Captain's name was Gannington, a very decent man; though quite illiterate. The First Mate, Mr. Berlies, was a quiet, sternish, reserved man, very well-read. The Second Mate, Mr. Selvern, was, perhaps by birth and upbringing, the most socially cultured of the three; but he lacked the stamina and indomitable pluck of the two others. He was more of a sensitive; and emotionally and even mentally, the most alert man of the three.

"On our way out, we called at Madagascar, where we landed some of our passengers; then we ran Eastward, meaning to call at North West Cape; but about a hundred degrees East, we encountered very dreadful weather, which carried away all our sails and sprung the jibboom and fore t'gallant mast.

"The storm carried us Northward for several hundred miles, and when it dropped us finally, we found ourselves in a very bad state. The ship had been strained, and had taken some three feet of water through her seams; the main topmast had been sprung, in addition to the jibboom and fore t'gallant mast; two of our boats had gone, as also one of the pigsties (with three fine pigs), this latter having been washed overboard but some half hour before the wind began to ease, which it did quickly; though a very ugly sea ran for some hours after.

"The wind left us just before dark, and when morning came, it brought splendid weather; a calm, mildly undulating sea, and a brilliant sun, with no wind. It showed us also that we were not alone; for about two miles away to the Westward, was another vessel, which Mr. Selvern, the Second Mate, pointed out to me.

"'That's a pretty rum looking packet, Doctor,' he said, and handed me his glass. I looked through it, at the other vessel, and saw what he meant; at least, I thought I did.

"'Yes, Mr. Selvern,' I said, 'she's got a pretty old-fashioned look about her.'

"He laughed at me, in his pleasant way.

"'It's easy to see you're not a sailor, Doctor,' he remarked. 'There's a dozen rum things about her. She's a derelict, and has been floating round, by the look of her, for many a score of years. Look at the shape of her counter, and the bows and cutwater. She's as old as the hills, as you might say, and ought to have gone down to Davy Jones a long time ago. Look at the growths on her, and the thickness of her standing rigging;

experience had taught him. He lacked the book-knowledge which the Second Mate had, of vessels previous to his day, which it appeared the derelict was.

"'She's an old 'un, Doctor' was the extent of his observations in this direction.

"Yet, when I mentioned to him that it would be interesting to go aboard, and give her a bit of an overhaul, he nodded his head, as if the idea had been already in his mind, and accorded with his own inclinations.

"'When the work's over, Doctor,' he said. 'Can't spare the men now, ye know. Got to get all shipshape an' ready as smart as we can. But we'll take my gig, an' go off in the Second Dog Watch. The glass is steady, an' it'll be a bit of gam for us.'

that's all salt encrustations, I fancy, if you notice the white colour. She's been a small barque; but don't you see she's not a yard left aloft. They've all dropped out of the slings; everything rotted away; wonder the standing rigging hasn't gone too. I wish the Old Man would let us take the boat, and have a look at her; she'd be well worth it.'

"There seemed little chance, however, of this; for all hands were turned-to and kept hard at it all day long, repairing the damage to the masts and gear, and this took a long while, as you may think. Part of the time, I gave a hand, heaving on one of the deck-capstans; for the exercise was good for my liver. Old Captain Gannington approved, and I persuaded him to come along and try some of the same medicine, which he did; and we grew very chummy over the job.

"We got talking about the derelict, and he remarked how lucky we were not to have run full tilt on to her, in the darkness; for she lay right away to leeward of us, according to the way that we had been drifting in the storm. He also was of the opinion that she had a strange look about her, and that she was pretty old; but on this latter point, he plainly had far less knowledge than the Second Mate; for he was, as I have said, an illiterate man, and knew nothing of sea-craft, beyond what

"THAT EVENING, after tea, the captain gave orders to clear the gig and get her overboard. The Second Mate was to come with us, and the Skipper gave him word to see that two or three lamps were put into the boat, as it would soon fall dark. A little later, we were pulling across the calmness of the sea, with a crew of six at the oars, and making very good speed of it.

"Now, gentlemen, I have detailed to you with great exactness, all the facts, both big and little, so that you can follow step by step each incident in this extraordinary affair; and I want you now to pay the closest attention.

"I was sitting in the stern-sheets, with the Second Mate, and the Captain, who was steering; and as we drew nearer and nearer to the stranger, I studied her with an ever growing attention, as, indeed, did Captain Gannington and the Second Mate. She was, as you know, to the Westward of us, and the sunset was making a great flame of red light to the back of her, so that she showed a little blurred and indistinct, by reason of the halation of the light, which almost defeated the eye in any attempt to see her rotting spars and standing-rigging, submerged as they were in the fiery glory of the sunset.

"It was because of this effect of the sunset, that we had come quite close, comparatively, to the derelict, before we saw that she was all surrounded by a sort of curious scum, the colour of which was difficult to decide upon, by reason of the red light that was in the atmosphere; but which afterwards we discovered to be brown. This scum spread all about the old vessel for many hundreds of yards, in a huge, irregular patch, a great stretch of which reached out to the Eastward, upon our starboard side, some score, or so, fathoms away.

"'Queer stuff,' said Captain Gannington, leaning to the side, and looking over. 'Something in the cargo as 'as gone rotten an' worked out through 'er seams.'

"'Look at her bows and stern,' said the Second Mate; 'just look at the growth on her.'

"There were, as he said, great clumpings of strange-looking sea-fungi under the bows and the short counter astern. From the stump of her jibboom and her cutwater, great beards of rime and marine-growths hung downward into the scum that held her in. Her blank starboard side was presented to us, all a dead, dirtyish white, streaked and mottled vaguely with dull masses of heavier colour.

"'There's a steam or haze rising off her,' said the Second Mate, speaking again; 'you can see it against the light. It keeps coming and going. Look!'

"I saw then what he meant—a faint haze or steam, either suspended above the old vessel, or rising from her; and Captain Gannington saw it also.

"'Spontaneous combustion!' he exclaimed. 'We'll 'ave to watch w'en we lift the 'atches; 'nless it's some poor devil that's got aboard of 'er; but that ain't likely.'

"We were now within a couple of hundred yards of the old derelict, and had entered into the brown scum. As it poured off the lifted oars, I heard one of the men mutter to himself: 'dam treacle!' and, indeed, it was some-

thing like it. As the boat continued to forge nearer and nearer to the old ship, the scum grew thicker and thicker; so that, at last, it perceptibly slowed us.

"'Give way, lads! Put some beef to it!' sung out Captain Gannington; and thereafter there was no sound, except the panting of the men, and the faint, reiterated *suck, suck,* of the sullen brown scum upon the oars, as the boat was forced ahead. As we went, I was conscious of a peculiar smell in the evening air, and whilst I had no doubt that the puddling of the scum, by the oars, made it rise, I felt that in some way, it was vaguely familiar; yet I could give it no name.

"We were now very close to the old vessel, and presently she was high above us, against the dying light. The Captain called out then to 'in with the bow oars, and stand-by with the boat-hook,' which was done.

"'Aboard there! Ahoy! Aboard there! Ahoy!' shouted Captain Gannington; but there came no answer, only the flat sound of his voice going lost into the open sea, each time he sung out.

"'Ahoy! Aboard there! Ahoy!' he shouted, time after time; but there was only the weary silence of the old hulk that answered us; and, somehow as he shouted, the while that I stared up half expectantly at her, a queer little sense of oppression, that amounted almost to nervousness, came upon me. It passed; but I remember how I was suddenly aware that it was growing dark. Darkness comes fairly rapidly in the tropics; though not so quickly as many fiction-writers seem to think; but it was not that the coming dusk had perceptibly deepened in that brief time, of only a few moments, but rather that my nerves had made me suddenly a little hypersensitive. I mention my state particularly; for I am not a nervy man, normally; and my abrupt touch of nerves is significant, in the light of what happened.

"'There's no one aboard there!' said Captain Gannington. 'Give way, men!' For the boat's crew had instinctively rested on their oars, as the Captain hailed the old craft. The men gave way again; and then the Second Mate called out excitedly, 'Why, look there, there's our pigsty! See, it's got *Bheotpte* painted on the end. It's drifted down here, and the scum's caught it. What a blessed wonder!'

"It was, as he had said, our pigsty that had been washed overboard in the storm; and most extraordinary to come across it there.

"'We'll tow it off with us, when we go,' remarked the Captain, and shouted to the crew to get-down to their oars; for they were hardly moving the boat, because the scum was so thick, close in around the old ship, that it literally clogged the boat from going ahead. I remember that it struck me, in a half-conscious sort of way, as curious that the pigsty, containing our three dead pigs, had managed to drift in so far, unaided, whilst we could scarcely manage to *force* the boat in, now that we had come right into the scum. But the thought passed from my mind; for so many things happened within the next few minutes.

"The men managed to bring the boat in alongside, within a couple of feet of the derelict, and the man with the boat-hook, hooked on.

"''Ave ye got 'old there, forrard?' asked Captain Gannington.

"'Yessir!' said the bow-man; and as he spoke, there came a queer noise of tearing.

"'What's that?' asked the Captain.

"'It's tore, Sir. Tore clean away!' said the man; and his tone showed that he had received something of a shock.

"'Get a hold again then!' said Captain Gannington, irritably. 'You don't s'pose this packet was built yesterday! Shove the hook into the main chains.'

The man did so, gingerly, as you might say; for it seemed to me, in the growing dusk, that he put no strain on to the hook; though, of course, there was no need; you see, the boat could not go very far, of herself, in the stuff in which she was embedded. I remember thinking this, also, as I looked up at the bulging side of the old vessel. Then I heard Captain Gannington's voice:

"'Lord! but she's old! An' what a colour, Doctor! She don't half want paint, do she! ... Now then, somebody, one of them oars.'

"An oar was passed to him, and he leant it up against the ancient, bulging side; then he paused, and called to the Second Mate to light a couple of the lamps, and stand-by to pass them up; for darkness had settled down now upon the sea.

"The Second Mate lit two of the lamps, and told one of the men to light a third, and keep it handy in the boat; then he stepped across, with a lamp in each hand, to where Captain Gannington stood by the oar against the side of the ship.

"'Now, my lad,' said the Captain, to the man who had pulled stroke, 'up with you, an' we'll pass ye up the lamps.'

"The man jumped to obey; caught the oar, and put his weight upon it, and as he did so, something seemed to give a little.

"'Look!' cried out the Second Mate, and pointed, lamp in hand. 'It's sunk in!'

"This was true. The oar had made quite an indentation into the bulging, somewhat slimy side of the old vessel.

"'Mould, I reckon,' said Captain Gannington, bending towards the derelict, to look. Then, to the man, 'Up you go, my lad, and be smart.... Don't stand there waitin'!'

"At that, the man, who had paused a moment as he felt the oar give beneath his weight, began to shin up, and in a few seconds he was aboard, and leant out over the rail for the lamps. These were passed up to him, and the Captain called to him to steady the oar. Then Captain Gannington went, calling to me to follow, and after me the Second Mate.

"As the Captain put his face over the rail, he gave a cry of astonishment, 'Mould, by gum! Mould.... Tons of it! Good Lord!'

"As I heard him shout that, I scrambled the more eagerly after him, and in a moment or two, I was able to see what he meant—

everywhere that the light from the two lamps struck, there was nothing but smooth great masses and surfaces of a dirty white mould.

"I climbed over the rail, with the Second Mate close behind, and stood upon the mould-covered decks. There might have been no planking beneath the mould, for all that our feet could feel. It gave under our tread, with a spongy, puddingy feel. It covered the deck-furniture of the old ship, so that the shape of each article and fitment was often no more than suggested through it.

"Captain Gannington snatched a lamp from the man, and the Second Mate reached for the other. They held the lamps high, and we all stared. It was most extraordinary, and, somehow, most abominable. I can think of no other word, gentlemen, that so much describes the predominant feeling that affected me at the moment.

"'Good Lord!' said Captain Gannington, several times. 'Good Lord!' But neither the Second Mate nor the man said anything, and for my part I just stared, and at the same time began to smell a little at the air; for there was again a vague odour of something half familiar, that somehow brought to me a sense of half-known fright.

"I turned this way and that, staring, as I have said. Here and there, the mould was so heavy as to entirely disguise what lay beneath; converting the deck-fittings into indistinguishable mounds of mould, all dirty-white, and blotched and veined with irregular, dull purplish markings.

"There was a strange thing about the mould, which Captain Gannington drew attention to—it was that our feet did not crush into it and break the surface, as might have been expected; but merely indented it.

"'Never seen nothin' like it before! Never!' said the Captain, after having stooped with his lamp to examine the mould under our feet. He stamped with his heel, and the stuff gave out a dull, puddingy sound. He stooped again, with a quick movement, and stared, holding the lamp close to the deck. 'Blest, if it ain't a reg'lar skin to it!' he said.

"The Second Mate and the man and I all stooped, and looked at it. The Second Mate prodded it with his forefinger, and I remember I rapped it several times with my knuckles, listening to the dead sound it gave out, and noticing the close, firm texture of the mould.

"'Dough!' said the Second Mate. 'It's just like blessed dough! ... Pouf!' He stood up with a quick movement. 'I could fancy it stinks a bit,' he said.

"As he said this, I knew suddenly what the familiar thing was, in the vague odour that hung about us—It was that the smell had something animal-like in it; something of the same smell, only heavier, that you will smell in any place that is infested with mice. I began to look about with a sudden very real uneasiness.... There might be vast numbers of hungry rats aboard.... They might prove exceedingly dangerous, if in a starving condition; yet, as you will understand, somehow I hesitated to put forward my idea as a reason for caution; it was too fanciful.

"Captain Gannington had begun to go aft, along the mould-covered main-deck, with the Second Mate; each of them holding his lamp high up, so as to cast a good light about the vessel. I turned quickly and followed them, the man with me keeping close to my heels, and plainly uneasy. As we went, I became aware that there was a feeling of moisture in the air, and I remembered the slight mist, or smoke, above the hulk, which had made Captain Gannington suggest spontaneous combustion, in explanation.

"And always, as we went, there was that vague, animal smell; and, suddenly, I found myself wishing we were well away from the old vessel.

"Abruptly, after a few paces, the Captain stopped and pointed at a row of mould-hidden shapes on either side of the maindeck ... 'Guns,' he said. 'Been a privateer in the old days, I guess; maybe worse! We'll 'ave a look below, Doctor; there may be something worth touchin'. She's older than I thought. Mr.

Selvern thinks she's about three hundred year old; but I scarce think it.'

"We continued our way aft, and I remember that I found myself walking as lightly and gingerly as possible; as if I were subconsciously afraid of treading through the rotten, mould-hid decks. I think the others had a touch of the same feeling, from the way that they walked. Occasionally, the soft mould would grip our heels, releasing them with a little, sullen suck.

"The Captain forged somewhat ahead of the Second Mate; and I know that the suggestion he had made himself, that perhaps there might be something below, worth the carrying away, had stimulated his imagination. The Second Mate was, however, beginning to feel somewhat the same way that I did; at least, I have that impression. I think, if it had not been for what I might truly describe as Captain Gannington's sturdy courage, we should all of us have just gone back over the side very soon; for there was most certainly an unwholesome feeling abroad, that made one feel queerly lacking in pluck; and you will soon perceive that this feeling was justified.

"Just as the Captain reached the few, mould-covered steps, leading up on to the short half-poop, I was suddenly aware that the feeling of moisture in the air had grown very much more definite. It was perceptible now, intermittently, as a sort of thin, moist, fog-like vapour, that came and went oddly, and seemed to make the decks a little indistinct to the view, this time and that. Once, an odd puff of it beat up suddenly from somewhere, and caught me in the face, carrying a queer, sickly, heavy odour with it, that somehow frightened me strangely, with a suggestion of a waiting and half-comprehended danger.

"We had followed Captain Gannington up the three, mould-covered steps, and now went slowly aft along the raised after-deck.

"By the mizzenmast, Captain Gannington paused, and held his lantern near to it....

"'My word, Mister,' he said to the Second Mate, 'it's fair thickened up with the mould;

why, I'll g'antee it's close on four foot thick.' He shone the light down to where it met the deck. 'Good Lord!' he said, 'look at the sea-lice on it!' I stepped up; and it was as he had said; the sea-lice were thick upon it, some of them huge; not less than the size of large beetles, and all a clear, colourless shade, like water, except where there were little spots of grey in them, evidently their internal organisms.

"'I've never seen the like of them, 'cept on a live cod!' said Captain Gannington, in an extremely puzzled voice. 'My word! but they're whoppers!' Then he passed on; but a few paces farther aft, he stopped again, and held his lamp near to the mould-hidden deck.

"'Lord bless me, Doctor!' he called out, in a low voice, 'did ye ever see the like of that? Why, it's a foot long, if it's a hinch!'

"I stooped over his shoulder, and saw what he meant; it was a clear, colourless creature, about a foot long, and about eight inches high, with a curved back that was extraordinarily narrow. As we stared, all in a group, it gave a queer little flick, and was gone.

"'Jumped!' said the Captain. 'Well, if that ain't a giant of all the sea-lice that ever I've seen! I guess it's jumped twenty-foot clear.' He straightened his back, and scratched his head a moment, swinging the lantern this way and that with the other hand, and staring about us. 'Wot are *they* doin' aboard 'ere!' he said. 'You'll see 'em (little things) on fat cod, an' suchlike.... I'm blowed, Doctor, if I understand.'

"He held his lamp towards a big mound of the mould, that occupied part of the after portion of the low poop-deck, a little fore-side of where there came a two-foot high 'break' to a kind of second and loftier poop, that ran away aft to the taffrail. The mound was pretty big, several feet across, and more than a yard high. Captain Gannington walked up to it.

"'I reck'n this's the scuttle,' he remarked, and gave it a heavy kick. The only result was a deep indentation into the huge, whitish hump of mould, as if he had driven his foot into a mass of some doughy substance. Yet,

I am not altogether correct in saying that this was the only result; for a certain other thing happened—from a place made by the Captain's foot, there came a little gush of a purplish fluid, accompanied by a peculiar smell, that was, and was not, half-familiar. Some of the mould-like substance had stuck to the toe of the Captain's boot, and from this, likewise, there issued a sweat, as it were, of the same colour.

"'Well!' said Captain Gannington, in surprise; and drew back his foot to make another kick at the hump of mould; but he paused, at an exclamation from the Second Mate:

"'Don't, Sir!' said the Second Mate.

"I glanced at him, and the light from Captain Gannington's lamp showed me that his face had a bewildered, half-frightened look, as if he were suddenly and unexpectedly half-afraid of something, and as if his tongue had given away his sudden fright, without any intention on his part to speak.

"The Captain also turned and stared at him.

"'Why, Mister?' he asked, in a somewhat puzzled voice, through which there sounded just the vaguest hint of annoyance. 'We've got to shift this muck, if we're to get below.'

"I looked at the Second Mate, and it seemed to me that, curiously enough, he was listening less to the Captain, than to some other sound.

"Suddenly, he said in a queer voice, 'Listen, everybody!'

"Yet, we heard nothing, beyond the faint murmur of the men talking together in the boat alongside.

"'I don't hear nothin',' said Captain Gannington, after a short pause. 'Do you, Doctor?'

"'No,' I said.

"'Wot was it you thought you heard?' asked the Captain, turning again to the Second Mate. But the Second Mate shook his head, in a curious, almost irritable way; as if the Captain's question interrupted his listening. Captain Gannington stared a moment at him; then held his lantern up, and glanced

about him, almost uneasily. I know I felt a queer sense of strain. But the light showed nothing, beyond the greyish dirty-white of the mould in all directions.

"'Mister Selvern,' said the Captain at last, looking at him, 'don't get fancying things. Get hold of your bloomin' self. Ye know ye heard nothin'?'

"'I'm quite sure I heard something, Sir!' said the Second Mate. 'I seemed to hear—' He broke off sharply, and appeared to listen, with an almost painful intensity.

"'What did it sound like?' I asked.

"'It's all right, Doctor,' said Captain Gannington, laughing gently. 'Ye can give him a tonic when we get back. I'm goin' to shift this stuff.'

"He drew back, and kicked for the second time at the ugly mass, which he took to hide the companion-way. The result of his kick was startling; for the whole thing wobbled sloppily, like a mound of unhealthy-looking jelly.

"He drew his foot out of it, quickly, and took a step backward, staring, and holding his lamp towards it.

"'By gum!' he said; and it was plain that he was genuinely startled, 'the blessed thing's gone soft!'

"The man had run back several steps from the suddenly flaccid mound, and looked horribly frightened. Though, of what, I am sure he had not the least idea. The Second Mate stood where he was, and stared. For my part, I know I had a most hideous uneasiness upon me. The Captain continued to hold his light towards the wobbling mound, and stare.

"It's gone squashy all through!' he said. 'There's no scuttle there. There's no bally woodwork inside that lot! *Phoo!* what a rum smell!'

"He walked round to the after-side of the strange mound, to see whether there might be some signs of an opening into the hull at the back of the great heap of mould-stuff. And then:

"'*Listen!*' said the Second Mate, again, in the strangest sort of voice.

"Captain Gannington straightened himself upright, and there succeeded a pause of the most intense quietness, in which there was not even the hum of talk from the men alongside in the boat. We all heard it—a kind of dull, soft *Thud! Thud! Thud! Thud!* somewhere in the hull under us; yet so vague that I might have been half doubtful I heard it, only that the others did so, too.

"Captain Gannington turned suddenly to where the man stood.

"'Tell them—' he began. But the fellow cried out something, and pointed. There had come a strange intensity into his somewhat unemotional face; so that the Captain's glance followed his action instantly. I stared, also, as you may think. It was the great mound, at which the man was pointing. I saw what he meant.

"From the two gapes made in the mould-like stuff by Captain Gannington's boot, the purple fluid was jetting out in a queerly regular fashion, almost as if it were being forced out by a pump. My word, but I stared! And even as I stared, a larger jet squirted out, and splashed as far as the man, spattering his boots and trouser-legs.

"The fellow had been pretty nervous before, in a stolid, ignorant sort of way; and his funk had been growing steadily; but, at this, he simply let out a yell, and turned about to run. He paused an instant, as if a sudden fear of the darkness that held the decks, between him and the boat, had taken him. He snatched at the Second Mate's lantern; tore it out of his hand, and plunged heavily away over the vile stretch of mould.

"Mr. Selvern, the Second Mate, said not a word; he was just standing, staring at the strange-smelling twin streams of dull purple, that were jetting out from the wobbling mound. Captain Gannington, however, roared an order to the man to come back; but the man plunged on and on across the mould, his feet seeming to be clogged by the stuff, as if it had grown suddenly soft. He zigzagged, as he ran, the lantern swaying in wild circles, as he

wrenched his feet free, with a constant *plop, plop*; and I could hear his frightened gasps, even from where I stood.

"'Come back with that lamp!' roared the Captain again; but still the man took no notice, and Captain Gannington was silent an instant, his lips working in a queer, inarticulate fashion; as if he were stunned momentarily by the very violence of his anger at the man's insubordination. And in the silence, I heard the sounds again: *Thud! Thud! Thud! Thud!* Quite distinctly now, beating, it seemed suddenly to me, right down under my feet, but deep.

"I stared down at the mould on which I was standing, with a quick, disgusting sense of the terrible all about me; then I looked at the Captain, and tried to say something, without appearing frightened. I saw that he had turned again to the mound, and all the anger had gone out of his face. He had his lamp out towards the mound, and was listening. There was a further moment of absolute silence; at least, I know that I was not conscious of any sound at all, in all the world, except that extraordinary *Thud! Thud! Thud! Thud!* down somewhere in the huge bulk under us.

"The Captain shifted his feet, with a sudden, nervous movement; and as he lifted them, the mould went *plop, plop*. He looked quickly at me, trying to smile, as if he were not thinking anything very much about it. 'What do you make of it, Doctor?' he said.

"'I think—' I began. But the Second Mate interrupted with a single word; his voice pitched a little high, in a tone that made us both stare instantly at him.

"'Look!' he said, and pointed at the mound. The thing was all of a slow quiver. A strange ripple ran outward from it, along the deck, like you will see a ripple run inshore out of a calm sea. It reached a mound a little fore-side of us, which I had supposed to be the cabin-skylight; and in a moment, the second mound sank nearly level with the surrounding decks, quivering floppily in a most extraordinary fashion. A sudden, quick tremor took the mould, right under the Second Mate, and he gave out a hoarse little cry, and held his arms out on each side of him, to keep his balance. The tremor in the mould, spread, and Captain Gannington swayed, and spread his feet, with a sudden curse of fright. The Second Mate jumped across to him, and caught him by the wrist.

"'The boat, Sir!' he said, saying the very thing that I had lacked the pluck to say. 'For God's sake—'

"But he never finished; for a tremendous, hoarse scream cut off his words. They hove themselves round, and looked. I could see without turning. The man who had run from us, was standing in the waist of the ship, about a fathom from the starboard bulwarks. He was swaying from side to side, and screaming in a dreadful fashion. He appeared to be trying to lift his feet, and the light from his swaying lantern showed an almost incredible sight. All about him the mould was in active movement. His feet had sunk out of sight. The stuff appeared to be *lapping* at his legs; and abruptly his bare flesh showed.

The hideous stuff had rent his trouser-legs away, as if they were paper. He gave out a simply sickening scream, and, with a vast effort, wrenched one leg free. It was partly destroyed. The next instant he pitched face downward, and the stuff heaped itself upon him, as if it were actually alive, with a dreadful savage life. It was simply infernal. The man had gone from sight. Where he had fallen was now a writhing, elongated mound, in constant and horrible increase, as the mould appeared to move towards it in strange ripples from all sides.

"Captain Gannington and the Second Mate were stone silent, in amazed and incredulous horror; but I had begun to reach towards a grotesque and terrific conclusion, both helped and hindered by my professional training.

"From the men in the boat alongside, there was a loud shouting, and I saw two of their faces appear suddenly above the rail. They showed clearly, a moment, in the light from the lamp which the man had snatched from Mr. Selvern; for, strangely enough, this lamp was standing upright and unharmed on the deck, a little way fore-side of that dreadful, elongated, growing mound, that still swayed and writhed with an incredible horror. The lamp rose and fell on the passing ripples of the mould, just—for all the world—as you will see a boat rise and fall on little swells. It is of some interest to me now, psychologically, to remember how that rising and falling lantern brought home to me, more than anything, the incomprehensible, dreadful strangeness of it all.

"The men's faces disappeared, with sudden yells, as if they had slipped, or been suddenly hurt; and there was a fresh uproar of shouting from the boat. The men were calling to us to come away; to come away. In the same instant, I felt my left boot drawn suddenly and forcibly downward, with a horrible, painful grip. I wrenched it free, with a yell of angry fear. Forrard of us, I saw that the vile surface was all a-move; and abruptly I found myself shouting in a queer frightened voice:

"'The boat, Captain! The boat, Captain!'

"Captain Gannington stared round at me, over his right shoulder, in a peculiar, dull way, that told me he was utterly dazed with bewilderment and the incomprehensibleness of it all. I took a quick, clogged, nervous step towards him, and gripped his arm and shook it fiercely.

"'The boat!' I shouted at him. 'The boat! For God's sake, tell the men to bring the boat aft!'

"Then the mould must have drawn his feet down; for, abruptly, he bellowed fiercely with terror, his momentary apathy giving place to furious energy. His thick-set, vastly muscular body doubled and writhed with his enormous effort, and he struck out madly, dropping the lantern. He tore his feet free, something ripping as he did so. The reality and necessity of the situation had come upon him, brutishly real, and he was roaring to the men in the boat:

"'Bring the boat aft! Bring 'er aft! Bring 'er aft!'

"The Second Mate and I were shouting the

same thing, madly.

"For God's sake be smart, lads!' roared the Captain, and stooped quickly for his lamp, which still burned. His feet were gripped again, and he hove them out, blaspheming breathlessly, and leaping a yard high with his effort. Then he made a run for the side, wrenching his feet free at each step. In the same instant, the Second Mate cried out something, and grabbed at the Captain.

"'It's got hold of my feet! It's got hold of my feet!' he screamed. His feet had disappeared up to his boot-tops; and Captain Gannington caught him round the waist with his powerful left arm, gave a mighty heave, and the next instant had him free; but both his boot-soles had almost gone.

"For my part, I jumped madly from foot to foot, to avoid the plucking of the mould; and suddenly I made a run for the ship's side. But before I could get there, a queer gape came in the mould, between us and the side, at least a couple of feet wide, and how deep I don't know. It closed up in an instant, and all the mould, where the gape had been, went into a sort of flurry of horrible ripplings, so that I ran back from it; for I did not dare to put my foot upon it. Then the Captain was shouting at me:

"'Aft, Doctor! Aft, Doctor! This way, Doctor! Run!' I saw then that he had passed me, and was up on the after, raised portion of the poop. He had the Second Mate thrown like a sack, all loose and quiet, over his left shoulder; for Mr. Selvern had fainted, and his long legs flopped, limp and helpless, against the Captain's massive knees as the Captain ran. I saw, with a queer, unconscious noting of minor details, how the torn soles of the Second Mate's boots flapped and jigged, as the Captain staggered aft.

"'Boat ahoy! Boat ahoy! Boat ahoy!' shouted the Captain; and then I was beside him, shouting also. The men were answering with loud yells of encouragement, and it was plain they were working desperately to force the boat aft, through the thick scum about the ship.

"We reached the ancient, mould-hid taffrail, and slewed about, breathlessly, in the half-darkness, to see what was happening. Captain Gannington had left his lantern by the big mound, when he picked up the Second Mate; and as we stood, gasping, we discovered suddenly that all the mould between us and the light was full of movement. Yet, the part on which we stood, for about six or eight feet forrard of us, was still firm.

"Every couple of seconds, we shouted to the men to hasten, and they kept on calling to us that they would be with us in an instant. And all the time, we watched the deck of that dreadful hulk, feeling, for my part, literally sick with mad suspense, and ready to jump overboard into that filthy scum all about us.

"Down somewhere in the huge bulk of the ship, there was all the time that extraordinary, dull, ponderous *Thud! Thud! Thud! Thud!* growing ever louder. I seemed to feel the whole hull of the derelict beginning to quiver and thrill with each dull beat. And to me, with the grotesque and monstrous suspicion of what made that noise, it was, at once, the most dreadful and incredible sound I have ever heard.

"As we waited desperately for the boat, I scanned incessantly so much of the grey-white bulk as the lamp showed. The whole of the decks seemed to be in strange movement. Forrard of the lamp, I could see, indistinctly, the moundings of the mould swaying and nodding hideously, beyond the circle of the brightest rays. Nearer, and full in the glow of the lamp, the mound which should have indicated the skylight, was swelling steadily. There were ugly, purple veinings on it, and as it swelled, it seemed to me that the veinings and mottlings on it, were becoming plainer—rising, as though embossed upon it, like you will see the veins stand out on the body of a powerful, full-blooded horse. It was most extraordinary. The mound that we had supposed to cover the companionway, had sunk flat with the surrounding mould, and I could not see that it jetted out any more of the purplish fluid.

"'A quaking movement of the mould

began, away forrard of the lamp, and came flurrying away aft towards us; and at the sight of that, I climbed up on to the spongy-feeling taffrail, and yelled afresh for the boat. The men answered with a shout, which told me they were nearer; but the beastly scum was so thick that it was evidently a fight to move the boat at all. Beside me, Captain Gannington was shaking the Second Mate furiously, and the man stirred and began to moan. The Captain shook him again.

"Wake up! Wake up, Mister!' he shouted.

"The Second Mate staggered out of the Captain's arms, and collapsed suddenly, shrieking, 'My feet! Oh, God! My feet!' The Captain and I lugged him up off the mould, and got him into a sitting position upon the taffrail, where he kept up a continual moaning.

"'Hold 'im, Doctor,' said the Captain, and whilst I did so, he ran forrard a few yards, and peered down over the starboard quarter rail. 'For God's sake, be smart, lads! Be smart! Be smart!' he shouted down to the men; and they answered him, breathless, from close at hand; yet still too far away for the boat to be any use to us on the instant.

"I was holding the moaning, half-unconscious officer, and staring forrard along the poop decks. The flurrying of the mould was coming aft, slowly and noiselessly. And then, suddenly, I saw something closer:

"'Look out, Captain!' I shouted; and even as I shouted, the mould near to him gave a sudden peculiar slobber. I had seen a ripple stealing towards him through the horrible stuff. He gave an enormous, clumsy leap, and landed near to us on the sound part of the mould; but the movement followed him. He turned and faced it, swearing fiercely. All about his feet there came abruptly little gapings, which made horrid sucking noises.

"'Come back, Captain!' I yelled. 'Come back, quick!'

"As I shouted, a ripple came at his feet—lipping at them; and he stamped insanely at it, and leaped back, his boot torn half off his foot. He swore madly with pain and anger,

and jumped swiftly for the taffrail.

"'Come on, Doctor! Over we go!' he called. Then he remembered the filthy scum, and hesitated; roaring out desperately to the men to hurry. I stared down, also.

"'The Second Mate?' I said.

"'I'll take charge, Doctor,' said Captain Gannington, and caught hold of Mr. Selvern. As he spoke, I thought I saw something beneath us, outlined against the scum. I leaned out over the stern, and peered. There was something under the port quarter.

"'There's something down there, Captain!' I called, and pointed in the darkness.

"He stooped far over, and stared.

"'A boat, by gum! A *Boat!*' he yelled, and began to wriggle swiftly along the taffrail, dragging the Second Mate after him. I followed.

"'A boat it is, sure!' he exclaimed, a few moments later; and, picking up the Second Mate clear of the rail, he hove him down into the boat, where he fell with a crash into the bottom.

"'Over ye go, Doctor!' he yelled at me, and pulled me bodily off the rail, and dropped me after the officer. As he did so, I felt the whole of the ancient, spongy rail give a peculiar, sickening quiver, and begin to wobble. I fell on to the Second Mate, and the Captain came after, almost in the same instant; but fortunately, he landed clear of us, on to the fore thwart, which broke under his weight, with a loud crack and splintering of wood.

"'Thank God!' I heard him mutter. 'Thank God! ... I guess that was a mighty near thing to goin' to hell.'

"He struck a match, just as I got to my feet, and between us we got the Second Mate straightened out on one of the after thwarts. We shouted to the men in the boat, telling them where we were, and saw the light of their lantern shining round the starboard counter of the derelict. They called back to us, to tell us they were doing their best; and then, whilst we waited, Captain Gannington struck another match, and began to overhaul the boat we had dropped into. She was a modern, two-bowed boat, and on the stern, there was painted 'Cyclone Glasgow.' She was in pretty fair condition, and had evidently drifted into the scum and been held by it.

"Captain Gannington struck several matches, and went forrard towards the derelict. Suddenly he called to me, and I jumped over the thwarts to him.

"'Look, Doctor,' he said; and I saw what he meant—a mass of bones, up in the bows of the boat. I stooped over them, and looked. There were the bones of at least three people, all mixed together, in an extraordinary fashion, and quite clean and dry. I had a sudden thought concerning the bones; but I said nothing; for my thought was vague, in some ways, and concerned the grotesque and incredible suggestion that had come to me, as to the cause of that ponderous, dull *Thud! Thud! Thud! Thud!* that beat on so infernally within the hull, and was plain to hear even now that we had got off the vessel herself. And all the while, you know, I had a sick, horrible, mental-picture of that frightful wriggling mound aboard the hulk.

"As Captain Gannington struck a final match, I saw something that sickened me, and the Captain saw it in the same instant. The match went out, and he fumbled clumsily for another, and struck it. We saw the thing again. We had not been mistaken.... A great lip of grey-white was protruding in over the edge of the boat—a great lappet of the mould was coming stealthily towards us; a live mass of the very hull itself. And suddenly Captain Gannington yelled out, in so many words, the grotesque and incredible thing I was thinking:

"'*She's Alive!*'

"I never heard such a sound of comprehension and terror in a man's voice. The very horrified assurance of it, made actual to me the thing that, before, had only lurked in my subconscious mind. I knew he was right; I knew that the explanation, my reason and my training, both repelled and reached towards, was the true one.... I wonder whether anyone can possibly understand our feelings in that moment.... The unmitigable horror of it, and the incredibleness.

"As the light of the match burned up fully, I saw that the mass of living matter, coming towards us, was streaked and veined with purple, the veins standing out, enormously distended. The whole thing quivered continuously to each ponderous *Thud! Thud! Thud! Thud!* of that gargantuan organ that pulsed within the huge grey-white bulk. The flame of the match reached the Captain's fingers, and there came to me a little sickly whiff of burned flesh; but he seemed unconscious of any pain. Then the flame went out, in a brief sizzle; yet at the last moment, I had seen an extraordinary raw look, become visible upon the end of that monstrous, protruding lappet. It had become dewed with a hideous, purplish sweat. And with the darkness, there came a sudden charnel-like stench.

"I heard the match-box split in Captain Gannington's hands, as he wrenched it open. Then he swore, in a queer frightened voice; for he had come to the end of his matches. He turned clumsily in the darkness, and tumbled over the nearest thwart, in his eagerness to get to the stern of the boat; and I after him; for we knew that thing was coming towards us through the darkness; reaching over that piteous mingled heap of human bones, all jumbled together in the bows. We shouted madly to the men, and for answer saw the bows of the boat emerge dimly into view, round the starboard counter of the derelict.

"'Thank God!' I gasped out; but Captain Gannington yelled to them to show a light. Yet this they could not do; for the lamp had just been stepped on, in their desperate efforts to force the boat round to us.

"'Quick! Quick!' I shouted.

"'For God's sake be smart, men!' roared the Captain; and both of us faced the darkness under the port counter, out of which we knew (but could not see) the thing was coming towards us.

"'An oar! Smart now; pass me an oar!' shouted the Captain; and reached out his hands through the gloom towards the on-coming boat. I saw a figure stand up in the bows, and hold something out to us, across the intervening yards of scum. Captain Gannington swept his hands through the darkness, and encountered it.

"'I've got it. Let go there!' he said, in a quick, tense voice.

"In the same instant, the boat we were in, was pressed over suddenly to starboard by some tremendous weight. Then I heard the Captain shout: 'Duck y'r head, Doctor,' and directly afterwards he swung the heavy, fourteen-foot ash oar round his head, and struck into the darkness. There came a sudden squelch, and he struck again, with a savage grunt of fierce energy. At the second blow, the boat righted, with a slow movement, and directly afterwards the other boat bumped gently into ours.

"Captain Gannington dropped the oar, and springing across to the Second Mate, hove him up off the thwart, and pitched him with knee and arms clear in over the bows among the men; then he shouted to me to follow, which I did, and he came after me, bringing the oar with him. We carried the Second Mate aft, and the Captain shouted to the men to back the boat a little; then they got her bows clear of the boat we had just left, and so headed out through the scum for the open sea.

"'Where's Tom 'Arrison?' gasped one of the men, in the midst of his exertions. He happened to be Tom Harrison's particular chum; and Captain Gannington answered him briefly enough:

"'Dead! Pull! Don't talk!'

"Now, difficult as it had been to force the boat through the scum to our rescue, the difficulty to get clear seemed tenfold. After some five minutes pulling, the boat seemed hardly to have moved a fathom, if so much; and a quite dreadful fear took me afresh; which one of the panting men put suddenly into words:

"'It's got us!' he gasped out; 'same as poor Tom!' It was the man who had inquired where Harrison was.

"'Shut y'r mouth an' *pull!*' roared the Captain. And so another few minutes passed. Abruptly, it seemed to me that the dull, ponderous *Thud! Thud! Thud! Thud!* came more plainly through the dark, and I stared intently over the stern. I sickened a little; for I could almost swear that the dark mass of the monster was actually *nearer* ... that it was coming nearer to us through the darkness. Captain Gannington must have had the same thought; for after a brief look into the darkness, he made one jump to the stroke-oar, and began to double-bank it.

"'Get forrid under the thwarts, Doctor!' he said to me, rather breathlessly. 'Get in the bows, an' see if you can't free the stuff a bit round the bows.'

"I did as he told me, and a minute later I was in the bows of the boat, puddling the scum from side to side with the boat-hook, and trying to break up the viscid, clinging muck. A heavy, almost animal-like odour rose off it, and all the air seemed full of the deadening smell. I shall never find words to tell any one the whole horror of it all—the threat that seemed to hang in the very air around us; and, but a little astern, that incredible thing, coming, as I firmly believe, nearer, and the scum holding us like half-melted glue.

The minutes passed in a deadly, eternal fashion, and I kept staring back astern into the darkness; but never ceasing to puddle that filthy scum, striking at it and switching it from side to side, until I sweated.

"Abruptly, Captain Gannington sang out:

"'We're gaining, lads. *Pull!* 'And I felt the boat forge ahead perceptibly, as they gave way, with renewed hope and energy. There was soon no doubt of it; for presently that hideous *Thud! Thud! Thud! Thud!* had grown quite dim and vague somewhere astern, and I could no longer see the derelict; for the night had come down tremendously dark, and all the sky was thick overset with heavy clouds. As we drew nearer and nearer to the edge of the scum, the boat moved more and more freely, until suddenly we emerged with a clean, sweet, fresh sound, into the open sea.

"'Thank God!' I said aloud, and drew in the boat-hook, and made my way aft again to where Captain Gannington now sat once more at the tiller. I saw him looking anxiously up at the sky, and across to where the lights of our vessel burned, and again he would seem to listen intently; so that I found myself listening also.

"'What's that, Captain?' I said sharply; for it seemed to me that I heard a sound far astern, something between a queer whine and a low whistling. 'What's that?'

"'It's wind, Doctor,' he said, in a low voice. 'I wish to God we were aboard.'

"Then, to the men: 'Pull! Put y'r backs into it, or ye'll never put y'r teeth through good bread again!'

"The men obeyed nobly, and we reached the vessel safely, and had the boat safely stowed, before the storm came, which it did in a furious white smother out of the West. I could see it for some minutes beforehand, tearing the sea, in the gloom, into a wall of phosphorescent foam; and as it came nearer, that peculiar whining, piping sound, grew louder and louder, until it was like a vast steam whistle, rushing towards us across the sea.

"And when it did come, we got it very heavy indeed; so that the morning showed us nothing but a welter of white seas; and that grim derelict was many a score of miles away in the smother, lost as utterly as our hearts could wish to lose her.

"When I came to examine the Second Mate's feet, I found them in a very extraordinary condition. The soles of them had the appearance of having been partly digested. I know of no other word that so exactly describes their condition; and the agony the man suffered, must have been dreadful.

"NOW," CONCLUDED THE DOCTOR, "that is what I call a case in point. If we could know exactly what that old vessel had originally been loaded with, and the juxtaposition of the various articles of her cargo, plus the heat and time she had endured, plus one or two other only guessable quantities, we should have solved the chemistry of the Life-Force, gentlemen. Not necessarily the *origin*, mind you; but, at least, we should have taken a big step on the way. I've often regretted that gale, you know—in a way, that is, in a way! It was a most amazing discovery; but, at the time, I had nothing but thankfulness to be rid of it.... A most amazing chance. I often think of the way the monster woke out of its torpor.... And that scum.... The dead pigs caught in it.... I fancy that was a grim kind of net, gentlemen.... It caught many things.... It...."

The old Doctor sighed and nodded.

"If I could have had her bill of lading," he said, his eyes full of regret. "If— It might have told me something to help. But, anyway...." He began to fill his pipe again.... "I suppose," he ended, looking round at us gravely, "I s'pose we humans are an ungrateful lot of beggars, at the best! ... But ... but what a chance! What a chance—eh?"

"The Mystery of the Derelict," first appeared in the 1907 edition of The Story-Teller.

Before Lovecraft there was William Hope Hodgson! The British author's science-based horrors, as opposed to the supernatural ones typical in the fiction of his day—as well as references in his Carnacki stories to ancient manuscripts and invading entities—anticipated, and doubtless inspired, the later works of H. P. Lovecraft.

Hodgson spent several years at sea, starting out as a cabin boy, at age 13, and eventually earning his mate's certificate; and his shipboard life and experiences on the open sea greatly impacted the writer's fiction. Many of Hodgson's stories and novels feature derelict ships, sargasso-type seas, and strange aquatic creatures.

STORY ILLUSTRATION: *JONNY QUEST*, "THE MYSTERY OF THE LIZARD MEN" (HANNA-BARBERA / WARNER BROS)

GHOST SHIP

by James Dorr

THE SEA HAD BOILED THE PAST DAY AT NOON. Just the surface, of course, and far enough distant from our island's shores that it posed no danger, but we could see the plume even past sun's setting, blocking the light of stars.

Even the stars seem large, in the south where we live. As if they, too, were reddening and growing so that each new summer's heat dwarfs prior years' memories. Such was our island land, blistering and baking yet moistened by ocean winds. Thus moderated, and clouded much of the year.

Where, I should say, we liv*ed*.

Where we had cities, and farms, and orchards. Where we took commerce in, exporting, in our turn, fruits and exotic fish. Yes, we were fishers too. Where we had great ports, at rivers' inlets, much as on your mainland. Even *this* far to north.

I feel the cool here, you know, almost to such point as to cause me discomfort—I who am from the far south. Yet who have no home now, save it be this vessel.

And where *it* may be from—

HE PAUSED THEN, a moment, this lone narrator aboard the "ghost ship" as they came to call it, the three on the fishing smack late to return to their own port that morning. They hove to when he had called, not to allow boarding, for he did not wish that. Simply to listen to this figure in wild rags, a *chador* of sorts as if sewn out of sail cloth, a rude hat perched on his head, dark as if stained with grime. All oddly hazy, the ship, the masts, the sails, as if surrounded by the dawn's ocean mist, rising to meet the sun.

The sun itself was still, mercifully, down, but already showing a glow to the east, to match that of a setting moon to the west of them. To north, their own home port.

In silence they waited, until he went on:

I GET AHEAD OF MYSELF. In fact, I do not know where this ship I sail upon has its origin. It was to south of *us* where we first spotted it, drifting in on the wind of the sun's last light, before darkness came to shift winds from land to the sea. You men are sailors—you know of that which I speak.

As I say, it arrived, no man aboard it— no answerer to our hail—fouling itself on the bar protecting our cove from the open sea. Thus in our harbor, yet standing off from our wharves. As I say, silent to our harbor guards' challenge.

I, myself, had spent that day in my lover's bed—that of Darellen who I was to marry. Arrangements had been made.

So happily I, Losheal, bid her farewell at last, leaving for my duty, that of a pole-boater taxiing men and light cargoes from ship to shore. And women, too, of course, all who might need access to and from vessels too deep-drafted even for our longest piers to reach.

Those in our anchorage.

And so I was preparing my oars, my mast-poles and bottom-poles, my small boat's single sail, arranging cushions lest ladies *should* wish to board, snacks for their nourishment, all the things needed for a normal evening's work—noting, of course, as I did the strange vessel now bumping and bobbing as if to escape our port. Held by the jetty's grip until such time as the tide should rise higher, perhaps in the morning. And yet, here it was now, its crew perhaps needing help. Its captain, who knew where?

Silent, its silhouette not fully focused, strangely, as if still half-lost in a dark, unseen mist. As if a ship of the dead—so say some legends. Though here we were realists, as all seamen must be. Believers in what we saw, what we might touch solidly with our own hands, smell with our nostrils. What things we might hear with our own ears, not just be told.

So I was asked by the harbormaster: "Losheal," he said, "you are late enough coming. You dote too much on your love—yes, we know all of that. We know your mistress, too. Yet here lies your job, to go to that vessel and find who it has aboard. Or failing in that, to make a line fast to its bow and tow it in to shore.

"We in turn, while you do this, will fetch doctors, in case they might be required. To hand-by-hand themselves on your line to its deck, testing for sickness before others board her.

"Helping those who need help."

"Yes," I answered.

I did as he ordered me, pushing my skiff from shore, raising my mast-pole and setting its single sail. Using my bottom-pole to reach deeper water, then sailing, then rowing, my way to the waiting hulk.

"Ahoy!" I shouted. There was no answer. I heard with my ears at best a small humming, perhaps as of motion of water against the hull. I smelled a slight rancid smell as I drew nearer, as if of entering a building long disused.

I hailed it again, then cast a line above the ship's bowsprit, catching it on a stay. Letting it loop through, then tying it back to my own small craft's sternpost.

I used a winch aboard my boat to help kedge it free, and so rowed it that way to shore, casting more lines ahead to the pier and those who waited there, helping me pull that way, until the vessel was close enough for boarding. Not by me, mind you, but the

harbormaster, followed by doctors as he had promised. While I in my turn cut my own boat loose to take back to its mooring.

I called for Darellen—she lived not too far from the shore. "Darellen," I told her when she came downstairs, "this is a new thing. A thing we must both see. Put on a day-*chador* in case we are out till dawn, if it should take that long for port-officials to find out this ship's secrets. Put on your day-mask and hat, too, for privacy, lest others spy on *us*"—she giggled at that—"though, yes, you are right, we ourselves have no secrets."

She kissed me to hush me, but then found her day-mask. "Perhaps I shall carry it. That, and my sunhat, though it seems more dark now than I had expected. Is not the moon shining?"

"It's not fully risen yet," I said, kissing her back. I, shirtless myself, in ducks and boots only, for technically I was still on duty. The better, of course, for Darellen to nuzzle her face in my chest as I whirled her around, to face back to the ocean, it, as she said, quite dark even though it had not been that long since the sun had set.

Arm in arm, we wound our way back toward the dockside where we heard the voices of those on the ship's deck:

"No signs of living men."

"But, look! A skeleton—that *is* a man's bones, yes?"

"Yes, and look here, too!"

Then—we could see better ourselves, I think, than those aboard the ship, or even the others who'd gathered close by to find out what was happening—we who, still at some distance, could see the entire scene. We saw what seemed a *moving* of sails and masts, that insubstantialness I had before noted—that unfocused mist-seeming—now shifting, now falling. Covering decks and rails.

We heard men *screaming*!

And then there was more motion, those on the dock running. Those on shore panicking. Everyone pushing, shoving, more screaming—trying to flee. As the dark shifting grew larger, spilling out on the quay as if a carpet. But living. Moving.

Covering, too, those who ran the slowest.

"Darellen," I shouted—the screaming was that loud now! Drowning out normal speech! "Darellen, dearest, we must run ourselves. We must flee to the hills of the northern shore. Do you not have a relative who has a farm there?"

"An uncle, yes," she said. "But it is so far. I would grow tired too quickly."

I understood her point—our island was that large, not just some small city, but a whole country. And if others, fleeing as well, choked the roads—

I had an idea. "Let us hurry this way, then," I said, pointing toward the far section of shore where my pole-taxi was still moored. Far enough from the ship that we might make it safely, especially since *whatever* that darkness was, that rustling, moving mass, pursued the fleeing *away* from where we would go.

She nodded, whispering: "Yes!" Hand in hand, thus, we ran, I behind, she before. Scrambling. Dodging. Down the hill to my boat, she jumping in while I pushed it out from behind. Then sculling, poling, out through the breakwater and to open ocean.

And so we were then safe, at least for the moment. I set the boat's sail and tied down its tiller—it was late enough that the winds were now steady. I took Darellen into my arms and held her while she cried.

"What is it?" she asked once.

"I don't know," I answered.

We sailed that way half the night, anchoring offshore when the eastern sky lightened. My boat, by law, carried emergency rations—that as well as those foodstuffs and delicate liqueurs *I* had packed aboard—which she inventoried while I took the sail down, spreading it over the boom as a kind of tent, so to protect us from the day-sun's blistering rays. Putting off eating, we slept that way through the light, each in each other's arms.

When dusk came, finally, we resumed our journey, eating a little then. And so we went

on for several nights more, the best part of a week, until finding the streamlet that led to her uncle's farm.

We anchored below the cliffs.

Climbing the angled path up to the manorhouse. Finding—*more heaps of bones!*

Darellen shrieked as I half-pushed her, half-carried her back down to the shore, to the safety of our small boat. Pursued by darkness, but not of shadows or ghosts or magic. I say we were realists. We saw now what chased us:

A ship's load of insects. Of swift, starving cockroaches, brought by necessity to become carnivores—first having devoured the ship's rats, of course—drawn from that vessel's hold most likely by the heat from the sea's boiling. A heat which on deck would be hard enough to withstand, but at least up above one would be cooled by breezes. While, trapped in the bilge below—

I had an image of insects erupting to cover the decks, the masts, cabins, the flapping sails. Eating whatever they found in their path.

The ship's crew, its captain....

Again we anchored offshore when the sun rose, Darellen and I making love beneath our sail. Realizing, you see, that it might be the last time.

Then, once more, an idea came to me.

"Darellen," I said, "it is clear there is no escape. Not on land anyway—the roaches appear to have overrun everything, moving faster on shore than we can sail—and our boat is too small to sail over the ocean to find some new refuge. We would perish in storms, or else in the sea's boiling. Just like in *that* ship's hold, we would not be far enough away from it to not be cooked in its heat—just as if in a pot, simmering on a stove."

She nodded. "Yes," she sobbed.

I kissed her softly. "But there is one place where the roaches may *not* be."

"Yes?" She looked up at me.

"*On the ship itself,*" I told her. "The one place where they've devoured everything they could find—where there would be no reason for them to stay. You saw how fast they left when, finally, they understood that there was food for them on the shore. How swiftly they spread away."

"But then for us," she said, "what would we eat or drink? That is, the two of us—I am assuming we could sail the ship ourselves?"

"Enough to get it free of the harbor, when the tide and wind are right. Then, with the trade winds, eventually we would cross other ships' paths, and so could be rescued. And, as for provisions, ships carry many stores, some of which even the roaches may have found distasteful to them. It happens with ships' rats as well," I assured her. "There is *always* something—"

She nodded. She kissed me again and, not all that long after, we made love aboard the ship itself, in the high stern cabin which had been its captain's. We cleaned up the cockroaches' mess, as best we could—searching mainly for stragglers, you understand, but the ship was free of anything that moved as I had predicted. We found tanks of water that had not been broached, and tins, and provisions of dried stuffs they had not touched.

And so, that next night, I cut our lines from the shore, sharing, together, one last look at the city that had been our home. Silent now, as if it were a city of ghosts, which in some ways it was. We had not dared, though, to walk through its streets, even to rescue our own belongings—we were, as I say, realists. *Atheists*, some might claim. We knew that, somewhere, some roaches might still be *there*, with all the nooks and crannies that cities have. We would not take *that* chance.

And yet, I believe now that there *is* a fate-star—a *z'etoile*, as the philosophers call it—that guides the souls of us all. And, with that, an *irony*.

We worked our way around the jetty when the wind and tide coincided and, so, to deep water. We left my small boat behind.

What we forgot, though, is that insects lay eggs. What *they* left behind them, almost microscopic and so we had missed them in our cleaning effort, sweltering, incubating in that ship's hold. Coming to life in the heat of a boiling sea not that first day, nor the second or third, but on the *fifth* day out, as Darellen and I lay in shade in our cabin, its great windows open to catch the following wind.

She screamed just once as a sheet of dark, squirming *forms* cascaded in on us, inundating the deck, the bed. Falling down on us from walls and ceiling.

Carving the flesh from her bones in minutes.

And not even roaches as I could see now that they were upon us. At least not entirely, but something more dreadful. I could see now they had *tentacles* that rippled among their jointed legs. Sprouting between them. Augmenting mouth-parts too. As if, exposed to the sea's vapors so long, they had been mutated to things yet more monstrous.

Or perhaps mated with things themselves from the sea.

Yet, as for me—you see perhaps, now, why I accept *z'etoile*. One's fate, in concept. *For, just as with those of the ship's stores they left alone, something about* me *was distasteful to them.*

And so, now, *I* understand what my fate is to be, to continue sailing, perhaps forever. When my rations ran short the first time, the wind shifted its course again, bringing a clean rain that puddled on the deck, and refilled the ship's casks whether I willed it or not. When one is thirsty, one *will* drink, whatever is offered one.

So it was with food, too, when from time to time my random course takes me into great shoals of fish. As if guided by some force. These practically leap onto the deck themselves, while below at these times, as I gaze from the bow into the ocean's depths, I see what seem to me shadowy forms. Forms with tentacles and jointed legs, much like the "roaches" that share this ship with me—but far, far vaster....

THEY DID NOT BELIEVE HIM—especially not that last!—the three that listened, Bambizin,

Vobul, and the quiet, brooding boy who the others called *Le Petit Poisson*. Such hard luck tales were far too common these days. But the wind had shifted, and in the north, too, the sun's rise could spell danger for those caught out beneath it without protection. So they called "Farewell!" and tacked toward their own home port, a fishing town on their continent's south shore, as a contrary breeze filled the great doomed ship's sails, pulling it back into the fog that had swirled higher with the day's first heat, to east and south out to sea.

They, too, were realists—fisher folk are. They know too much of the ways of the ocean, and those things found on it. They know when to ask, and when not to ask questions. And when not to tell *others* of the things they have seen.

Who would believe *them*?

And so Vobul just shrugged when Bambizin noted how strange the ship looked in that last, brief instant, when it as well as the man aboard it seemed pressed in its *own* fog. A swirling, crawling dark. A thing not quite focused, but shifting. Moving.

And how, in the midst of it, the sound they now heard was of a man weeping.

"Ghost Ship" first appeared in Techno-Goth Cthulhu *(Red Skies Press, 2013)*.

Indiana author James Dorr's most recent book is a novel-in-stories from Elder Signs Press, Tombs: A Chronicle of Latter-Day Times of Earth. *Working mostly in dark fantasy/horror with some forays into science fiction and mystery, his* The Tears of Isis *was a 2013 Bram Stoker Award® finalist for Superior Achievement in a Fiction Collection, while other books include* Strange Mistresses: Tales of Wonder and Romance, Darker Loves: Tales of Mystery and Regret, *and his all-poetry* Vamps (A Retrospective). *He has also been a technical writer, an editor on a regional magazine, a full-time non-fiction freelancer, and a semi-professional musician, and currently harbors a Goth cat named Triana. An Active Member of SFWA and HWA, Dorr invites readers to visit his blog at jamesdorrwriter.wordpress.com*

THE WYVERN

BY JASON J. McCUISTON

CAPTAIN NOAH OGGS TRIED TO IGNORE THE EXCRUCIATING PAIN IN HIS LEGS AS HE STARED OUT THE FORWARD WINDSCREEN AT THE CLEAR BLUE SKY. They had run out of pain killers last night, but were still a full day from Salt Lake City and home. If not for Old Nate's herbal tea, Noah knew the pain would be completely unbearable. He gnawed the end of his pipe and rubbed his thighs so hard his fingers turned white. He hoped Smith had set the bones well enough that he wouldn't be crippled for life. "Report, Mr. Hargreaves."

Benjamin Hargreaves did not turn to face him, just kept a steady hand on the big brass-trimmed oak wheel, watching the endless horizon. Doubtless, the first mate was tiring of the frequent and identical reports, but Noah needed to feel like he was still doing something.

"Cruising at 8,000 feet at a speed of just under 50 miles per hour, Captain. Still on course for home. No problems in sight." Hargreaves's smooth, articulate tone did not betray his exasperation, but Noah imagined he could see the younger man rolling his eyes.

"Engineering?" Noah half-turned his head and snapped the order around the stem of his unlit pipe.

"Same as five minutes ago, Captain." Carla Gomez made no attempt to hide her consternation at the constant demand for reports. "Same as five minutes before that. We're in perfect flying trim. Good on batteries, good on helium, good on everything except our captain. Why don't you go get some rest?"

"You just worry about keeping the *Cibola* in the air, Carla, and let Smith worry about my well-being." Jasper Smith, former medic in the Royal Air Fleet, had been noticeably absent since informing Noah of the lack of pain killers late last night. Noah rubbed his thighs and wondered if he would soon be looking for a new medic for his crew. Smith's problem with pills had been the reason for his dismissal from His Majesty's service.

"What are you going to do with Reese, Captain?" Hargreaves still did not turn. "You realize it was an accident, right?"

Noah frowned and almost bit through the stem of his pipe. Bill Reese was currently locked up in the airship's tiny brig. The aging deckhand's negligence while exploring the ruins of one of the Lost Angels islands had been the reason Noah was now confined to his command chair in agony. Due to the unexpected injury, they had been forced to cut the salvage mission short and were now returning home without enough plunder to cover the cost of the expedition. "I don't know. Probably pay him and cut him loose."

"He's a good man with loads of experience, Captain. He'll be hard to replace." Hargreaves turned this time, to give Noah a knowing, pleading half-smile. The good-looking first mate was always trying to make his wishes Noah's commands.

Noah frowned, knowing better than Hargreaves how good a crewman Reese was. But Reese's actions on this trip had been inexcusable. Since Noah was the one suffering the painful consequences of those actions, he was not going to waffle. Not this time.

The black shadow erupted across the windscreen before he could continue the argument. "Full stop!" An immense storm cloud had somehow jumped into existence not two miles ahead of the airship. The writhing, roiling, bank bristled with multihued lightning and growled with low thunder. It stretched across the sky like the black wings of the Angel of Death.

The temperature on the bridge dropped several degrees.

"What the hell...!" Hargreaves turned the wheel to starboard to guide the ship away from the oncoming storm while Carla worked levers at the engineering panel, shutting off steam to the engines. "Wherever that thing came from, it's still coming on, Captain. Our best bet is to try and run around it, and fast."

Noah rubbed his thighs and gnawed on the pipe. Even at top speed he knew there was no way to get around that massive front. "Climb," he said. They were nearly at the ship's maximum altitude already, but if they could push the limits they might be able to get above the freakish thing.

"You're kidding, right?"

"Dammit, Carla, I said climb."

The engines roared back to full power and Noah felt the deck shudder through his chair. Hargreaves turned the wheel to port and pulled it back. The *Cibola* climbed and the black cloud seemed to grow taller, trying to catch the small airship.

"All hands on deck," Noah shouted into the command tube beside his chair. "Somebody let Reese out of his cage! Smith, get your ass up here!"

"*Madre Dios*. We are not going to make it," Carla whispered.

A fork of green lightning lashed out. The ship rocked, tossing Noah from his chair. A peal of thunder crashed around them like the end of the world, punctuating the pain sawing through his legs. Everything was white and on fire, then suddenly black....

NOAH OPENED HIS EYES.

The sky was perfectly blue, not a shred of cloud remained. He smelled a hint of smoke, noticed the engines were silent. He also noticed the excruciating pain in his legs. "What happened?" he asked the ring of faces standing over him. Carla, Hargreaves, Smith, Old Nate, Reese, and the two youngsters: Jaquan, and Karan Tanaka.

"Lightning strike," Carla said. "Port engine's gone. Could've been worse."

"Where's the storm? How long was I out?"

"Must have been a *wildstorm*," Hargreaves said. "Though I've never heard of one this far away from the frontier. You were out less than ten minutes, the storm's been gone over five."

"Like I said, could've been worse."

"You've had quite a spill, Captain." Smith, the pale, skinny medic pushed his thick glasses up his long nose. "You should let me give you a sedative, and spend the rest of the trip in your quarters."

Noah waved him off. He could see there was something else on the crew's faces, something that looked like fear. "What is it?"

Hargreaves stepped back and gestured at the windscreen. "There's that." Noah pushed himself painfully up in his command chair and followed the first mate's gaze. "We've tried to hail her, but there's no answer."

Filling the forward view was a monstrous grey dirigible, its long gondola pocked with gun-ports, studded with bomb racks, and its dorsal edge surmounted by a row of machine-gun turrets—a war blimp like nothing he'd seen before. It looked ancient in design, but brand new by its royal markings and the sleekness of its airbag. It just hung there in the open sky like it had always been there and would remain in that spot for eternity. Noah's stomach knotted up, but he thought it might be from the bone-grinding pain in his legs.

"It's the *Wyvern*," Reese whispered from the corner of the crowded bridge. The old deckhand was paler than the junkie medic and looked in more physical distress than Noah. "It's the *Wyvern*, come back from hunting the Hodag!" Reese crossed himself and started mumbling a prayer in the depths of his brushy beard.

"What's the *Wyvern*?" Karan asked. She

was new to the ways of airmen. They'd caught her as a stowaway coming back from Fresno four months ago, and she'd been indentured ever since.

"It's a myth, a ghost story to scare newbs like you." Noah knew the tales about the *Wyvern*, every airman in the Pacific City States did. He almost stopped Old Nate from telling the tale, but decided it would give him time to come up with a plan.

"Sometime about 300 years ago," the old cook and quartermaster began. "After unifying the city states under his family's peaceful rule and establishing the Rowland Dynasty, Prince Walter declared that he would take the Royal Air Fleet's flagship into the uncharted Wyld. He meant to hunt down the Hodag, the Leviathan that had destroyed the Old World three centuries before.

"For months his carrier pigeons returned to the royal fortress in Saint George with reports of the ship's incredible adventures. They told of glowing rivers of magic flowing through indescribable landscapes and the towering ruins of ancient cities haunted by mystically-crazed savages and unliving monsters. There were accounts of fantastical beasts and impossibly beautiful vistas, of unimaginable terrors experienced in the face of the unpredictable *wildstorms*. These hurled untamed magical forces into the atmosphere, reshaping matter and energy in defiance of all understanding."

Old Nate's voice dropped to a sinister timbre as he concluded, "The last pigeon brought a horrific suicide note following the crew's disastrous sighting of the Leviathan. The royal family and the fleet promptly destroyed the note in hopes of sparing Walter's legacy. Of course, that only caused the legend to grow ever more evil in the ensuing generations."

"And that's the *Wyvern*?" Jaquan asked, his dark eyes wide as he pointed at the mysterious war blimp.

Noah looked at the faces of his crew and could see the effect the tale and Reese's behavior were having, and not just on the youngsters. Jaquan, the brawny kid Noah thought

of as a son was scared but tried not to show it. Not in front of the flirty young woman beside him, who was mustering her own bravado as best she could.

"That's not the *Wyvern*," Noah said. "What that is, is a prime piece of unclaimed salvage. Royal or not. If there's no living crew aboard, then she's for the taking. There may be parts that can repair our engines, and they might have painkillers in their sickbay. Anything else onboard is fair game, too."

"You mean to board her?" Reese was horrified.

"Mr. Hargreaves, please put Reese back in his cage as it appears he will be of no further use to us this voyage. The rest of you prepare to go aboard. Side-arms, tools, and carriers. I'll remain on the bridge and coordinate with the coms and my binoculars.

"Mr. Hargreaves, you take Smith and Tanaka and search the medical bay and the weapons locker. Carla, you take Old Nate and Jaquan and find engineering and the galley. Once you're back with necessities, we'll make another trip for the goodies."

"Captain," Hargreaves said. "If I may? We don't need to board her. We could launch a grapple line and tow her to Vegas. Even with one engine, we could make it by nightfall. We'd make enough selling her there to pay for repairs, medicine, supplies, and fuel. You could rest in a real hospital."

"I like that idea," Karan said. Noah was not surprised. He knew about his first-mate's fling with his young servant, just like he knew about her plan to use Hargreaves to eventually supplant him as captain. In fact, if he hadn't been so preoccupied with keeping abreast of their little intrigue, he might have noticed Smith's relapse and Reese's drinking.

"Guess what, kids: my ship, my rules. You might have contacts in Vegas, Mr. Hargreaves, but I don't. And I know that if we hauled that thing in, we'd be lucky to get thirty percent of her value from those cowboys. And that's *if* we didn't wind up going to prison for looting royal property. We go aboard and take what we need, what's worth scrounging, then we leave her in the middle of the desert sky with no one the wiser. Now get moving."

As the crew filed out, Noah caught Jaquan's arm and held him back. When they were alone, he said, "Boy, don't make me regret taking you on instead of turning you over to the magistrate for stealing our supplies." He never had in the past three years. "You keep your eyes and ears sharp, and you look after Old Nate and Carla. They both got families, big ones, and Old Nate's about to be a granddaddy."

Jaquan smiled and patted Noah on the shoulder. "And I thought you split me and Karan up so we wouldn't get 'lost' over there for a couple hours."

Noah laughed, though he wanted to tell the boy not to trust that girl. "Couple hours, hah! More like a couple minutes, then you'd be useless for a couple days. You just keep your head on a swivel and do what Carla tells you. Now hand me my gun belt."

TEN MINUTES LATER Noah sat alone on the bridge. His pipe had broken in his fall, so he caught himself chewing on the neck strap of the heavy binoculars. With the engines down, the *Cibola* was strangely silent. He could hear the wind rustling over the canvas airbag above and whistling through the metallic outer decks of the gondola. The ship creaked and groaned in a familiar way. He heard his crew tramp down to the boarding deck, heard the thump of the grapple cannon fire.

He raised the binoculars and saw the line disappear into the deep shadow beneath the war blimp's long, sleek body. It was midday, so the sun glistened on the top of the dirigible while casting its belly into darkness. In short order, Mr. Hargreaves had the relay lines secured. The heavily clothed crew began to hook safety harnesses to the pulley systems. These would allow them to glide across the fifty-foot gulf 8,000 feet above the Mojave.

Just as he dropped the binoculars to his lap, Noah thought he saw movement on the other ship. He jerked the lenses back to his face but saw nothing. He lifted the handset from the chair arm. "Coms check."

There was a second's delay before Hargreaves's voice crackled through the wired device. "Number One is good." Quickly, the other crew members rattled off their call signs through the handsets they carried on their belts. Each set was connected to a wire, which was then bundled with all the other wires and jacked into a spool of cable hooked directly into the bridge coms. Jaquan would carry the spool over to the other ship, then mount it at a central location so the individual lines would feed slack as needed as they moved through the ship.

Noah raised the binoculars again and rubbed his aching legs. He swept the darkened gondola of the other ship but saw nothing. Hargreaves led his crew, one by one, across the lines and onto the derelict. Soon the call came back: "All aboard, Captain. We're splitting up now. My team is heading fore, team two is heading aft."

"Be safe," Noah said before setting the handset down. He felt a knot in his gut and a cold chill on his skin. He rubbed his face and frowned. "I'm just letting all Reese's superstitions get to me."

A bloodcurdling scream ripped through the com.

Noah snatched the handset out of the air before it fell to the floor. "Report! Report! Report!"

"Number One reporting. Nothing yet, Captain." Hargreaves sounded surprised, confused.

"Carla reporting. Same here. Why you so jumpy, Captain?"

"Anybody hear feedback on their coms?"

"Negative." No one had.

"Carry on." Noah dropped the handset in his lap and raised the binoculars again. He fingered the dial to maximum magnification, painstakingly pored over every inch of the mammoth dirigible. She was a great blimp, not an actual rigid airship like the *Cibola*, though she did have an armored exoskeleton of winged, interlocking mesh surrounding her long airbag. An aluminum walkway, spaced with machine-gun turrets, ran along her dorsal line connecting nose to tail. Her darkened gondola was at least ten times the size of the *Cibola's*, and probably loaded with heavy cannon and all manner of artillery shells. The absolute embodiment of Death from Above.

A ray of sunlight slid around the tail's shadow and fell across a sigil painted on the rear of the gondola. It was a great black dragon-thing, blade-like wings menacingly splayed. Cold sweat broke out over Noah's entire body. The knot in his gut dissolved into ice water.

"It can't be...."

Noah picked up the coms handset. He flicked the thumb switch. Nothing happened. He flicked it over and over.

Nothing.

He dropped the useless device and raised the binoculars. He caught sight of Hargreaves, Tanaka, and Smith moving past a row of portholes on the uppermost deck. He gave a tight sigh of relief.

Noah swung the optics toward the stern in hopes of catching sight of Carla's team. He stopped amidships.

He saw people. Maybe a dozen of them. At least he thought they were people. They were moving in the ship's shadows, but remained dark even when they passed a porthole bathed in reflected light.

Noah closed his eyes tight, then tried to strain them into the binoculars for a clearer view. The shadows continued to move, but that's all they were. Shadows. But cast by whom?

"We've reached engineering, Captain." Carla's voice was cool and confident as ever. "No sign of life so far, but everything looks in working order. In fact, though the tech on this thing is ancient, it looks like it rolled out of the factory this morning."

Noah snatched up the handset and flicked the thumb switch. "Carla! Keep on the lookout. I don't think you're alone over there!"

"Captain," Hargreaves's voice cut in. "We're

in the medical bay. We've found no evidence of crew, but this place is immaculate. Even the glass alcohol and peroxide containers are full, intact, and unstained."

"Mr. Hargreaves, can you hear me?"

There was no reply. Noah dropped the handset and raised the binoculars. This time, there was no mistake. He saw figures moving past the portholes, closing on the forward deck. Where his first mate's team was.

"Oh my God." Noah focused the binoculars on the moving figures. He saw them disappear into an interior chamber.

Karan Tanaka's scream cut through the sky separating the two aircraft. Noah heard it clearly though it did not come over the coms.

The coms crackled. "Captain! The crew—" Hargreaves's panicked voice was cut short by gunfire. Five quick pops, then silence. The shadow figures emerged back into the corridor and turned to head aft.

"No, no, no, no...." Tears welled up in his eyes. Noah swatted them away and tried to think. He was trapped in his chair on the bridge with no coms. Someone or something was hunting down his crew over there. On the ship he'd ordered them to board. He'd already lost three people, and now he was about to lose three more. The three who meant the most to him.

He tried to stand but the pain that shot through his legs took his breath and dropped him into the chair like a haymaker. He gasped for air and clung to the binoculars and the useless handset as if they were talismans against evil.

"Reese!" Noah flopped out of the chair and dragged himself across the stamped-metal floor. If he could get to the brig, he could send Reese over to the *Wyvern* to bring Jaquan, Carla, and Nate back. The shadow people had four long decks to traverse. He had two short ones.

Crawling through the hatch from the bridge into the outer corridor, he smacked one thigh so hard he was sure that he knocked the knitting bones loose. He screamed, bit his tongue and tasted blood, but dragged himself on through. He was shaking and weak by the time he reached the stairs leading down to the main deck.

Gritting his teeth against the urge to vomit, Noah pushed himself over the edge and bumped his way painfully down the steps. He was bleeding from his brow and mouth, and had added a dozen new bruises to his broken legs, but he pushed all that out. The only thing that mattered now was saving his crew, his family.

"Reese," he said. He had meant it to be a shout. He tried again, louder this time, as he pushed himself further down the corridor. "Reese!"

"Captain?" The old deckhand's bearded face appeared behind the narrow door's barred window.

"Coms are down. You've got to get over there and get Carla and her team back right now. Hargreaves, Tanaka, and Smith are already dead. You've got to go now." The words tumbled out of him as he dragged himself against the wall, fumbled his keys out of his pocket, and wrestled with the secured hatch.

He flung the door open to find Reese curled against the back of the tiny cell. "I ain't goin' over there, Captain! That's the cursed ship! The ship of the damned!"

Noah's fear and pain exploded into rage. "I'll show you the damned, Reese!" He pulled his revolver and leveled it at the shaking man. "Get your ass up and moving, and get over there and save your crew's lives. I'd be able to do it myself if it wasn't for you!"

"I can't, Captain! I won't!"

"You will!"

"No—"

The thunderous report startled him. Noah had pulled the trigger without thinking—without meaning to. He blinked. Reese's brains and beard were scattered all over the tiny, smoke filled cell.

Noah dropped the gun and backed away from the hatch, shaking and his ears ringing. He couldn't believe he had done it. He was truly alone now, and it was up to him. Broken legs

or not. He took a deep breath and tried to force the murder out of his mind. He crawled toward the bow, where the relay lines were secured and the safety harnesses were stored. Legs would be useless dangling from the ropes, at any rate. Maybe he could get close enough to the ship to shout a warning.

It seemed like it took forever to reach the front of the ship and climb out onto the frigid deck. Noah fought horrific images of his crew being torn limb from limb by the shadow people every aching inch of the way. When he finally reached the bow, however, he saw the happiest sight he could have imagined.

Carla, Jaquan, and Old Nate were slowly pulling themselves back across the relay lines from the *Wyvern*.

Shivering against the cold, Noah pushed himself up against the bulkhead and relaxed. He wiped blood and tears from his face and wished he had his pipe for a smoke. Once his crew were back aboard, they'd cut the lines, fire up the one good engine and limp back to Salt Lake City and try to put this nightmare behind them.

He saw the shadows on the ropes.

"Carla! Jaquan! Nate!" He screamed but his ragged voice was torn away by the high winds. He could only watch as the unnatural dark things slithered along the lines behind his unknowing crew. They moved in quick, jerky motions, not like human beings at all. Noah thought of the coiling serpent painted on the ghost ship's gondola.

The first shadow reached Old Nate. In an instant, Noah remembered meeting the brawny cook when he was a boy, apprenticing to his father. They had practically grown up together like brothers. Nate's scream was higher and louder than Noah would have expected. The big man convulsed, shaking the tethers and relays, then went limp. He hung like a piece of laundry on a line as the shadows crawled over his body.

Old Nate's scream had warned Jaquan and Carla, however, and they frantically increased their speed, both shouting in panic.

The shadows moved faster.

Noah wept, unable to speak as tears froze on his cheeks. He tried to look away but could not as the shadows caught Jaquan. The boy fought against the things, screaming and cursing, but his fists had no effect, while ribbons of blood erupted on his dark skin and his clothing was torn to shreds. Noah's adopted runaway burst in an explosion of blood. A red cloud in a blue sky.

Noah threw himself onto the deck, a cannonball stuck in his throat. His cut and torn hands stretched out toward the dead boy. Stinging tears blinded him, so he did not see Carla's death. He heard it, however. A long, high, wailing scream of rage, terror, and sorrow. It was the scream of a widowed mother knowing she had just orphaned her three children.

Sobbing and shaking, Noah dragged himself back to the supply chest where the safety harnesses were stored. He wiped crunchy tears and snot from his face and saw the shadows closing on the deck. He fumbled inside the chest with ice-cold hands and snatched a parachute.

Noah only had time to get his arms in and the chest strap buckled before the first shadow crawled over the guardrail. Noah looked up into the thing's face and saw the memory of a man. A nightmare memory to be sure, but the revenant that towered over him had once lived and breathed, had loved and hated, had known triumph and loss. Yet all that had ever been human had been torn away and replaced with evil by the wild magic which had reshaped the world. All this Noah saw in the burning green orbs of hellfire that stared out of its empty eye sockets.

Noah rolled off the deck and into the firmament.

He wrestled with the leg straps of the parachute as he tumbled in freefall. The great tan orb of the Earth rushed up at him one moment, the cigar-shaped aircraft outlined against the blue sky fell away the next. His fingers were numb and unresponsive. He only had a matter of seconds to secure the parachute before he was past the point of no return.

Noah buckled the strap on his left leg and decided that was enough. He snatched at the ripcord. He screamed as he was jerked skyward by the deploying chute. The single strap cut into his groin and both of his broken legs felt like they snapped in two again.

The pain subsided to a steady throb and Noah became aware of the wider world. He looked up, past the white edge of the parachute. The two airships hovered high above. He blinked as the sun slid past them. In that instant, the *Cibola* burst into flames. It was already breaking into pieces of smoke-trailing debris by the time the thunderous report reached him. Tendrils of black and white smoke and fire hung in the sky.

The *Wyvern* remained where she was, unharmed by the explosion as if she were just an image projected onto this world, and not a horrifying thing of reality.

A huge black cloud suddenly appeared in the clear blue sky. It enveloped the great warship like protective wings. In a moment, the cloud and the *Wyvern* were gone, leaving only the falling wreckage of Noah's ship as evidence that it had ever been.

He looked down and saw the unforgiving Mojave climbing up to claim him. He knew the story would soon die with him, and that Reese's murder would be avenged. All of his murders would be.

After all, Noah had been the one to send his crew to their deaths on that cursed ship.

👽 👽 👽

"The Wyvern" first appeared in Dark Luminous Wings *(Pole to Pole Publishing, 2017).*

Jason J. McCuiston was born in the wilds of southeast Tennessee, where he was raised on a carnivorous diet of old monster movies, westerns, comic books, horror magazines, sci-fi and fantasy novels, and, of course, Dungeons & Dragons. He attended the finest state school that would have him with the intention of becoming a comic-book artist. Following his matriculation and a whirlwind tour of spectacularly underpaid and uninspired career paths, he finally realized that he was meant to be a professional storyteller. (CONTINUED NEXT PAGE)

(CONTINUED) *Jason has been a semi-finalist in the Writers of the Future contest, and has studied under the tutelage of best-selling author Philip Athans. His stories of fantasy, horror, and science fiction have appeared in numerous anthologies, periodicals, websites, and podcasts. More tales, including his debut novel* Project Notebook, *are forthcoming.*

He lives in South Carolina, USA with his college-professor wife (making him a Doctor's Companion) and their two four-legged children. He can be found on the internet at facebook.com/ShadowCrusade. And he occasionally tweets about his dogs, his stories, his likes, and his gripes @JasonJMcCuiston

THE WRECK
By Alfred I. Tooke

A hundred and fifty fathoms deep it rests on the ocean floor,

With a gaping hole in its crumpled bow that serves as an open door

To a cavern dim where a skeleton grim keeps guard in a gilded suite

Whose polished floor shall throb no more to the rhythm of dancing feet;

For Death swept out of a starlit night, to mock at Life's futile stand,

And drag the arrogant liner down in the clutch of its icy hand,

And souls were stripped of their false pretense, and shown as they really were;

And many a braggart raved and screamed, or whined like a cringing cur;

While many a so-called weakling rose that night to a new estate,

And shrugged his shoulders and wore a smile as he bowed to the will of Fate.

And there, in the cavern, the dead man's bones guard treasure forever lost,

That he tried to save from the grasping wave as the gangway of Death he crossed.

A hundred and fifty fathoms deep he rests on the ocean floor,

In a barnacled coffin of steel that cost a million dollars or more,

And his bones are hid by an inky squid that spawns in the gilded suite

Whose polished floor shall throb no more to the rhythm of dancing feet.

Photo: Lophelia II 2009: Deepwater Coral Expedition: Reefs, Rigs and Wrecks (NOAA Library)

"The Wreck" first appeared in the September 1938 issue of Weird Tales.

*During the 1930s, writer Alfred I Tooke published about a dozen weird poems and a handful of fantastic stories in "the Unique Magazine"—*Weird Tales. *Tooke also penned numerous thrillers for several other pulps of the day, including Street & Smith's* Detective Story *Magazine; The Phantom Detective; Super-Detective Story, The Underworld Magazine, Texas Rangers, and* Cowboy Stories.

CAPTAIN LANE NODDED...

GYRO-CONTROL! *REVERSE SHIP'S DIRECTION 180°!*

THIS IS GYRO-CONTROL, NOW REVERSING SHIP'S DIRECTION!

HE STUDIED HIS WATCH, CHECKING THE BLIP ON THE RADAR SCREEN AS IT LOOMED LARGER AND LARGER...

POWER PLANT, GET READY TO BLAST TO A *STOP* WHEN I *GIVE THE WORD!* TWENTY SECONDS... TEN... FIVE..FOUR...THREE.. TWO..ONE... *NOW!*

THE SHIP SHUDDERED! DEEP WITHIN ITS ALLOY-LINED BOWELS, THE AWAKENED ATOMIC ENGINES ROARED...

HOLD IT...HOLD IT... *NOW... CUT POWER!*

POWER OFF!!

THE SHIP HUNG IN SILENCE IN THE VAST GULF OF SPACE! CAPTAIN LANE SNAPPED ON THE VIEW-SCREEN...

NO SIGN OF *DAMAGE* ON HER, EH, CAPTAIN?

NO! SHE'S AN *OLD* MODEL, BUT SHE LOOKS *SOUND!*

GRAYSON THUMBED THROUGH 'JAYNE'S ROCKET VEHICLES OF THE UNIVERSE,' BIBLE OF ALL ASTRONAUTS!

SIR, THAT'S THE Y-5, A CARGO CARRIER BUILT ABOUT THIRTY YEARS AGO... DECLARED OBSOLETE AT LEAST TWENTY YEARS AGO...

THAT MEANS SHE'S BEEN *FLOATING* OUT HERE FOR OVER *TWENTY YEARS!* LET'S TAKE A LOOK!

THE LIEUTENANT AND THE CAPTAIN, DRESSED IN THEIR SPACE-SUITS, STEPPED INTO THE AIR-LOCK OF THEIR SHIP...

WHY DO YOU GO SEARCHING THROUGH EVERY DERELICT WE FIND, CAPTAIN? THEY'RE USUALLY *PRETTY GRISLY SIGHTS!*

PERSONAL REASONS, GRAYSON! MAYBE SOMEDAY I'LL TELL YOU! *OPEN 'ER UP!*

THE OUTER AIR-LOCK DOOR SWUNG OPEN, REVEALING THE DISTANT PIN-POINT STARS AND THE GHOSTLY SHAPE OF THE DERELICT CARGO SHIP FLOATING BESIDE THEIR PATROL CRUISER! THE MEN PUSHED INTO SPACE...

GOT YOUR *TOOL KIT*, GRAYSON?

GOT IT HERE, SIR!

THE FORCE OF THEIR PUSH-OFF CARRIED THEIR WEIGHTLESS BODIES ACROSS THE ABYSS THAT SEPARATED THE TWO SHIPS...

THE OUTER AIR-LOCK DOOR IS *SEALED!* GRAYSON! WE'LL HAVE TO BURN IT OPEN!

YES, SIR!

THE OXY-ALUMINUM TORCH BLAZED BRIGHTLY, LIKE A TINY STAR, AS GRAYSON CUT AWAY THE AIR-LOCK DOOR FROM ITS RECESSED HINGES...

THERE WE ARE, SIR!

GOOD!

THE CAPTAIN STEPPED INTO THE DERELICT SHIP... GRAYSON CLOSE BEHIND...

GOOD LORD, SIR! HOW MANY BODIES ARE THERE? THE Y-5 WAS A *TWO MAN* CARRIER!

LOOKS LIKE THIS SHIP HAD *PASSENGERS!* SEE IF THERE'S A LOG, GRAY-SON!

GRAYSON BEGAN TO RUMMAGE THROUGH THE ROCKET SHIP'S CONTROL ROOM, LEAVING THE CAPTAIN TO EXAMINE THE BODIES!

HERE IT IS, CAPTAIN! THINK IT WILL TELL US HOW THEY *DIED?*

I HOPE SO! *READ* IT TO ME, LIEUTENANT!

GRAYSON OPENED THE LOG...

"FLIGHT NO. 138... JAN 14TH: LEFT BOSTON PORT WITH CARGO OF MACHINE TOOLS AND..."

SKIP THAT! WHEN DID THEY PICK UP THESE PASSENGERS?

3

LIEUTENANT GRAYSON THUMBED THROUGH THE Y-5'S LOG...

LET'S SEE! "FEB 8TH: ARRIVED AND DELIVERED CARGO"..NOTHING HERE!' "FEB 12TH: STARTED HOME"...NO, WAIT.' HERE'S SOMETHING, CAPTAIN! "FEB 19TH: BAD LUCK TODAY!"

" WANDERING ASTEROID STRUCK SHIP AT 0900, SMASHING OUTER HULL PLATES IN THE FORWARD SECTION... "

GOOD LORD! WHAT WAS THAT, DON?

SOUNDED LIKE WE RAN INTO SOMETHING, PETE! LET'S TAKE A LOOK!

"ATTEMPT TO WELD BREAK FAILED! WILL HAVE TO MAKE EMERGENCY LANDING! LOSING CABIN PRESSURE RAPIDLY..."

GIVE IT UP, PETE! LET'S CHECK OUR LOCATION AND HEAD FOR THE NEAREST PLANET!

GUESS YOU'RE RIGHT, DON!

"FEBRUARY 25TH: MADE EMERGENCY LANDING ON AN UNCHARTED PLANET IN SOLAR SYSTEM IN C-1170! PROCEEDED WITH REPAIRS..."

"UPON COMPLETING REPAIRS, WE WERE APPROACHED BY CREATURES OF THE PLANET!"

WHAT THE...?

HUMAN BEINGS!

IT WOULD BE WISE, GENTLEMEN, IF YOU OFFERED NO RESISTANCE!

OFFER NO RESISTANCE? WHY SHOULD WE?

YOU MEAN YOU DON'T KNOW WHERE YOU ARE?

CONTINUED AFTER NEXT PAGE.

202

"Derelict Rocket," illustrated by Bob Powell, first appeared in the July-August 1961 issue of *Black Magic* (Crestwood Publishing Company).

The story is **a swipe of "Derelict Ship,"** by Al Feldstein and Bill Gaines, with art by Bernie Krigstein, published in *Weird Fantasy #22* (November 1953) by the legendary EC Comics.

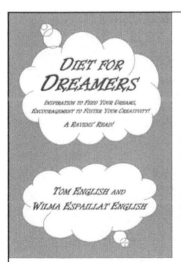